MATT HILTON

The Lawless Kind

HODDER

First published in Great Britain in 2014 by Hodder & Stoughton
An Hachette UK company

This paperback edition first published in 2014

1

A CIP catalogue record for this title is available from the British Library

ISBN 978 1 444 72878 1

Typeset in Plantin Light by Hewer Text UK Ltd, Edinburgh
Printed and bound by Clays Ltd, St Ives plc

Hodder & Stoughton policy is to use papers that are natural,
renewable and recyclable products and made from wood grown in
sustainable forests. The logging and manufacturing processes
are expected to conform to the environmental regulations
of the country of origin.

Hodder & Stoughton Ltd
338 Euston Road
London NW1 3BH

www.hodder.co.uk

Dedicated to my brothers, Davey, John, Jim and Raymond

'The world breaks everyone, and afterward, some are strong at the broken places.'

– Ernest Hemingway

I

The strength of human resilience can be shocking.

Take the bruiser running at me with his gun raised.

I'd already placed two nine-millimetre rounds in his chest and one high in his forehead and still he kept coming. He was dead, of course. He just hadn't realised it yet. He only managed another two steps before his legs went from under him. Even so his finger was caressing the trigger of his MP5 and bullets blistered the air around me. Would have been a poor end to a good day if a corpse had managed to finish me off. As it was there was no guidance to his shots and they all went way over my head: I was in more danger from the falling corpse than the bullets. I met him with a sweep of my left forearm and sent him on his way, even as I targeted the next man to come out of hiding. I placed a single round between the second man's teeth as he shook a machete and shouted a challenge. He went down on his back, surrounded by a billow of desert grit.

'Heads up, Hunter!'

My friend, Jared 'Rink' Rington's shout turned me and the instincts honed through countless hours of point-shooting meant I had placed two more bullets in the third man to rush at me before I even saw him clearly.

'Three o'clock.' Rink again.

Twisting to my right, I rattled off three shots in quick succession, knocking down another machete-wielding man, and then the slide locked back on my SIG Sauer P226. I didn't have to inspect the gun to tell that it was empty. I thumbed the magazine release and allowed the empty mag to fall clear, even as I slapped in a full clip and released the slide. All of this while racing towards the arroyo from where the first living-dead man had emerged. From behind my right shoulder Rink's Mossberg assault shotgun laid down a thunderous accompaniment. Somewhere to my far left our other buddy, Harvey Lucas, halted any attempt by our enemies to flank us. We were covered on the right by a high cliff of sandstone, ribboned with countless striations of colour. We were making ground faster than I'd anticipated, thanks to our opponents' lack of discipline. If they'd had the sense to stay put, instead of charging us like kamikazes, they would've been able to halt our progress. Not that I was complaining.

I slowed on my approach to the lip of the gulley, checking that gunmen weren't hidden beyond the line of sagebrush at its edge. Clear of any resistance, I carried on, and then knelt to offer cover while Rink joined me.

'You see the tunnel mouth?' I indicated an abandoned mineshaft at the end of a natural 'V' formed by the tapering arroyo. 'It's just as Walter said.'

Rink grunted at the mention of Walter Hayes Conrad's name. He still hadn't forgiven our old Arrowsake handler for using us for his own ends while fighting off a white supremacist plot to irradiate the Statue of Liberty. Walter was still using us now, but to be fair, we were also using him. In my book, that made us even.

Rink hadn't been happy when the elderly CIA agent approached us with a view to eradicating this particular pit of snakes, but his sense of honour won out when Walter showed us photographs of the latest shipment of workers to be smuggled over the border. There had been twenty-seven of them, all young Mexican girls and pregnant women who'd paid dearly to be transported into the USA in search of better lives. The gang had abandoned them to a terrible fate, sealed within the steel tomb of the container of a gas truck. By the time the truck with its horrendous cargo was discovered, it was estimated that three weeks had gone by. The bodies were in such a state of decomposition that you couldn't tell where one ended and another began. Apparently the driver had taken to his heels when he thought that the Border Patrol were on to him. When no such thing had come to pass, none of the gang deemed it necessary to go back and release those trapped inside the sweltering confines of the converted gas container. Why bother when they'd already been paid up front? They had promised to carry their passengers over the border and they'd done just that: no guarantee had been given that they'd be alive when arriving in the US. Those bastards would probably lament the loss of their truck more than the lives they'd so callously disregarded.

So Rink had joined me, as had Harvey, when Walter had pointed the finger at the human traffickers responsible. They were known as coyotes, or *polleros*, but to me they were just shit. Some people claim there is a grey area between the coyotes that take a high fee to sneak illegal immigrants into the USA, and those that traffic people to the sex trade and various sweatshops, but I see them all as part of the same problem. This wasn't the first time a truckful of people had been left to die. If it were up to me, it would be the last.

'So this is one of their drops?' Rink eyed the mine with distaste. 'It's an odd place to bring their cargo.'

Normally coyotes would deliver to a drop-house in Phoenix or elsewhere rather than out here in the desert, but this was not your run-of-the-mill operation. These guys were controlled by one of the Mexican drug cartels, and most of those that they smuggled across the border ended up sold into slavery.

The mine was a holding area until their 'product' was classified and moved on to other destinations throughout the States.

'Odd or not, we're closing it down.'

'Just watch out for collateral damage,' Rink warned.

Intel from Walter promised that the mine was currently free of innocent migrants, but Rink was a worrier. Or perhaps he was more level-headed than me.

Giving him a nod, I slipped down the side of the embankment and into the arroyo. The space had been cleared of shrubbery and boulders, making the gulley a rat-run for trucks, and also an exposed place from which to approach the mine. I hugged the wall as I neared the entrance, while Rink and Harvey offered cover from above. Going slow and easy, I listened for signs of life. I could hear only one voice, and it sounded like a one-sided conversation. He was speaking Spanish but I caught enough to tell he was frantically calling up assistance from his cartel buddies. Whether they answered his plea or not wasn't the issue: the cavalry would arrive too late. I slipped into the mouth of the mine, the stink of sweat and urine invading my senses. Many poor souls had been held within these stuffy confines, and I could make out small cells lining the back end of the tunnel. I concentrated on the man hunched down behind an oil drum. The glow from his iPhone gave his features a blue cast. His eyes rolled white in their sockets as he stood up and reached an empty palm my way.

'Don't shoot, don't shoot,' he said in accented English. 'I'm unarmed.'

'So were the girls you raped, you piece of crap,' I snapped at him.

I'd recognised his face, even stretched with fear as it was. Another photograph Walter had shown me was of this man, posing beneath the 'rape tree' where he'd proudly hung the underwear of his latest thirteen-year-old victim. I wanted to shoot him in the face.

'Put down the phone.'

He obeyed, thumbing off the button at arm's length, then making a show of placing it on the oil drum.

'There,' he said. 'I did as you said. Now you must arrest me.'

'Must I? For you to be released by the corrupt Border Patrol officials that you've been bribing?'

'You are a *Federale*, no? You must obey the law.'

I shook my head. 'I'm Joe Hunter, and the law doesn't come into what I *must do* to you.'

The bastard understood where this was heading, and I was glad when he reached behind him to pull out the revolver he'd stuck in his belt. As much as I wished to kill him, I hadn't wanted to do it in cold blood. He snapped the revolver up even as he dropped into a crouch. A curse split his lips a fraction of a second before my bullet did. He fell backwards, and the jolt caused an unconscious pull on the trigger. His gun flashed, but the round was lost deep in the ceiling above him. Gunshot residue would be on his hand, which made things easier when it came to cleaning up this mess.

I walked further into the mineshaft and found where it dead-ended. There were no other coyotes alive. There were no innocents either, to my relief. It was important that nobody had witnessed what had occurred here. As far as anyone would know, the human traffickers had died under the guns of a rival gang. Our weapons weren't on any law enforcement database, and we'd been careful while loading to wear gloves and ensure that every working part of our guns was thoroughly wiped down – even the mag I'd allowed to drop in the desert above. Our gloves, clothing and boots would be destroyed later, and evidence incriminating a rival gang dropped at the scene by Walter's men waiting in the wings.

When returning to the exit I glanced once at the dead coyote. Fucking hyena, more like. This man was the worst kind of scum, but he was only one of many. The only consolation was that he at least would not prey on any other young girl.

'Satisfied?' Rink asked.

'I've barely started.'

My big friend was leaning against the doorway, his shotgun by his side. He looked weary, but that was deceptive. Rink is part Japanese and has mastered the art of philosophical resignation, often wearing the emotion like a shroud.

'You can't kill all the monsters, brother,' he said, an often-cited quote. He reckons that I've a St George complex, one that drives me to seek out and slay the dragons of the world. It wasn't a bad analogy.

'I can keep trying,' I countered.

A clatter of loose rocks announced Harvey's arrival, a rifle canted over his shoulder. Dust had greyed his jet skin, and the aviator shades forming dark sockets in his visage gave him a death's-head look. His wide smile spoiled the image.

'I took it that the fighting was over with when the bullets stopped flying,' he said.

I nodded. 'We're clear.'

'Yeah. Thanks for the heads-up, guys.' From his shirt pocket he pulled out a small electronic device, on which he sent a signal to Walter's nearby clean-up crew.

We moved out into the arroyo to wait for them.

They arrived on foot, three men I didn't know, and didn't care to. They shoved another man before them, a skinny Mexican with one eye white with cataracts. He was another coyote, but not from this gang. Terror shone in his face, and drool hung from his flaccid lips.

As I released the catch to drop my mag, Rink sighed and turned away. I wasn't happy with what was coming, but I told myself that the coyote was responsible for murder, rape and God knew what else. I jacked the slide of my gun, checking there were no stray shells inside, before walking to meet the CIA agents and their prisoner.

'I ain't doing it,' I told Walter's men.

One of them, a severe man who reminded me of the Grim Reaper, offered a wolfish smile. 'I'm happy to do it for you. Give the scumbag your gun.'

The coyote stared up into my face, a prayer behind his one good eye. Unluckily for him, I'm not the religious type.

'Here.' I shoved the SIG towards him. Maybe he thought he was going to get a chance after all. But when he turned to the agent, he knew otherwise.

'Please,' he cried out, 'I won't tell anyone . . .'

The CIA agent shot him in the head.

Before the coyote had finished twitching in the sand, the grim-faced man held out his hand and I passed him the mag. He crouched down and reinserted it in the SIG. Then he manipulated the slide and fed the coyote's dead finger through the trigger guard. He paused once to smile up at me before tugging back on the finger and discharging a round in the dust. Gunshot residue was now on the dead man's hand. For all intents and purposes, he was the slayer of at least five members of the rival gang.

'This is bullshit,' Rink whispered harshly.

He was right. But it was a necessary evil.

'We'll need all your weapons,' Grim Reaper said.

'Stick them in your ass,' Rink replied, tossing the Mossberg down and stomping away. Harvey twisted his mouth wryly. Then he deposited his rifle and followed in our buddy's wake.

'Your friends seem to find this work distasteful,' the agent said.

'No, mate,' I said. 'They find *you* distasteful.'

Before he could form a reply, I pushed by him after Rink and Harvey. We had a debriefing to attend, and afterwards I was going to place a few choice words in Walter's ear. But my anger dissipated as soon as Walter pulled me to one side and told me of his small personal problem.

2

'What's Rink so pissed about? I thought he was going to spit on my boots before he left.'

'You really have to ask, Walt?'

'You guys have just killed a dozen men, what's the big deal about one more?'

'The others had a fighting chance. That last man was executed, Walt. None of us bought into that.'

'We had to make things look like a gang war, son. We had to point the finger at a rival outfit. Any other time you would have capped that guy yourself . . .'

'Not like that.'

'He didn't die in vain,' Walter said, holding my gaze. 'His death keeps you boys out of the frame, keeps you out of prison.'

'And you,' I reminded him.

'That's why I'm not complaining.' Walter sighed, and lowered his frame into a creaking chair. We were in the rear of a large van, converted to a mobile command unit. His was the only chair, placed before a bank of computer screens and other electronic equipment. I stood looking down at him.

'Back in the day none of you would've complained.'

'Back then we were different men.'

'No, son, you were always headstrong and wilful, and didn't always see the bigger picture.'

'That's because we were never shown it.'

It took me a moment to realise that Walter was laughing. He

shook his head. 'Despite what the politicians say we're losing the battle against organised crime. Take these coyotes: we arrest one, another ten spring up in their place. Back when they were just some guys sneaking a few immigrants across the desert, it didn't make much difference. But since the cartels took over, where many of these immigrants are either enrolled as drug mules, or sold into the sex trade or held for ransom, things have changed. We can't stop them, Joe. All we can hope to do is slow them down.'

'What about this talk about a North American Alliance? When Mexico, the States and Canada become a common market like the EU, and they all open their borders, controlling something like this will be nigh-on impossible.'

'It's almost impossible now,' he admitted. 'But we do what we have to do. Slow the gangs down.'

'So this wasn't about avenging the lives of all those women in the truck?'

He shrugged.

'That's what it meant to us.'

'Good. You hold that thought. I have no such emotional crutch.'

'Why can't I find any pity for you, Walt?'

'I'm not looking for pity, just a modicum of understanding. I was tasked with igniting a turf war between the two major coyote gangs working this area. The plan is to cause discord and confusion: while they're fighting each other they're too busy to transport the next shipment of narcotics and illegals into America.'

'If they're too busy fighting each other, then maybe they'll forget about another truck full of innocent people they've left to die of thirst.'

'Let's hope that isn't the case.'

'Like you care, Walt?'

'I care. But there's something I care more about . . .'

He fell into silence. This was a man who had ordered the deaths of hundreds – perhaps thousands – during his time with Arrowsake, and in the years since as a sub-division director of Black Ops with the Agency. He wasn't prone to showing regret, but it was etched on his face now. I waited for him to explain.

Walter was looking old. He'd always been a robust man, whose choice of dress reminded me of one of those TV evangelists. He favoured powder-blue or cream suits, complete with waistcoat and pointy-toed boots. A ruff of grey hair over his ears was thinning even as the baldness of his pate spread. His pallor indicated a man who spent long days under artificial lighting, behind an unmarked door in the bowels of CIA HQ at Langley. But of late some of the muscle beneath his skin had become flaccid, his jowls and eyebrows drooped, and the grey of his hair was yellowing in places. He gave up smoking his beloved cigars some time ago, but I was starting to think he'd left things a little late.

'You OK, Walt?'

He ran a hand over his face as he surfaced from his reverie.

'I'm OK, Joe. My concern is for someone else.'

Relief surged through me. For a second I'd feared he'd been about to admit to being terminally ill. I didn't always see eye to eye with Walter, and had on occasion seriously considered cutting all ties with him, but I still loved the old bastard. He'd been more of a father to me than Bob Telfer, who'd married my mother after my real dad died.

'I'm a secretive man, Joe,' he said.

'Tell me about it.'

'There are things about me even you don't know.'

'If this is about you wearing women's underwear, I'm not sure I want to hear.'

His smile was strained.

'I've never been married, but I'm no monk. Did you ever suspect that I was a father?'

'I've wondered.'

'I have a daughter, Joe. She will be forty-six years old at her next birthday.'

'Wow.' I was at a loss for anything more erudite.

'Sadly she knows nothing about me.' He waved down my frown. 'I agreed with her mother that my identity should remain a secret, to ensure our daughter's protection. I've watched her from afar, assisted financially in her upbringing where and when I could. I'd have loved to have been closer, but I couldn't come clean about her. My enemies would have used her against me.'

I nodded solemnly. When I was married to Diane I had similar fears for her, and for the children we once hoped for. As it was we divorced and Diane was no longer threatened by my occupation. I could see why Walter, still immersed in the shady world of counter-terrorism, would guard such a secret so astutely.

'Her name is Annie,' he continued.

'Something has happened to her?' I ventured.

'No, not to Annie, but to her daughter: my granddaughter, Kirstie.'

Tears welled in his eyes, and again I drew the wrong conclusion. 'Her identity has been discovered by an enemy?'

'No.'

'Then what?'

'Someone has snatched the child.'

'Someone has kidnapped your granddaughter?'

He looked at me strangely. 'I guess I didn't make that last bit clear enough. No, not Kirstie, *her* child. My great-grandson, Benjamin.'

'Aren't the FBI usually the right people for this kind of job?' I was surprised I hadn't heard anything about such a story. But then again I could have missed it: television wasn't something I bothered with as a rule, preferring a quiet room and a paperback novel during downtime.

'Ordinarily? Yes, the FBI would be involved if it were a straight kidnapping, but not here. Seeing as the kidnapper is the boy's father, it's seen more as a child custody issue. Kirstie has tried that route, but there are inherent problems, including that the boy has been taken out of the country. In the eyes of the law both parents have equal claim on the boy.'

'Aren't there rules about transporting minors across borders?'

'There are, but the boy has dual citizenship. He was born in the US but he also has citizenship in his father's country.'

'Hang on,' I said, staring south. 'That's the real reason you dragged us here, isn't it? The father is Mexican, right?'

'You're not as stupid as you look.' His weak attempt at humour didn't merit a response. He carried on, hardly missing a beat. 'If this were simply a domestic dispute, then I'd have no reason to get involved, but . . .'

'He's into something, right?'

'It's awkward,' he said. 'The reason I needed to speak with you in private.'

'Walt.' I knew him too well to continue dancing in circles. He was so entrenched in the secretive world of espionage that he simply couldn't help layering everything he said with large dollops of disinformation. 'Just cut to the fucking chase, will you?'

'I'm about to. It's only . . . well, I'm not sure how you're going to take the news.'

'Try me.'

But still he wasn't ready.

'You know why I'm sharing this with you, son?'

'Yeah,' I said. 'Because you can wrap me round your little finger.'

'That's not entirely true.' He smirked. 'It's because I know I can trust you. I can't take this problem to my colleagues in the Agency. Not all of my enemies are from foreign countries. I need someone whose loyalty is to me, not to furthering his career. If I show any interest in Benjamin's disappearance then questions will be raised. His identity and relationship to me will not only place him and Kirstie in danger, it will also bring trouble to Annie's door. I've worked too hard to keep them safe to allow their identities to be discovered now. I won't be around to protect them forever, Joe. That's why I need someone who'll keep our relationship out of the picture.'

'I get you, but that's not what this is really about.'

'No, it's about the identity of the father,' he confessed. 'If it became public that he was the son of one of Mexico's largest drug cartel bosses then it would effectively hog-tie my mission to destroy them. More than that, Kirstie's involvement with a major criminal would throw real suspicion on my motives.'

It would certainly raise questions concerning corruption, causing a scandal of epic proportions for both Walter and the CIA. If he became embroiled in a witch-hunt then people would start digging into aspects of his life that should never see the light of day. No wonder he wanted to keep a lid on it. It might also bring those of us who'd been Walter's assets under the magnifying glass too.

But I didn't care about that.

What most concerned me was his real objective.

'Tell me, Walt. What's most important to you? Recovering the boy, or hurting the father?'

There was no hint of irony when he said, 'Aren't they both the same thing?'

3

'I can't believe you're allowing the devious bastard to yank our chains again, brother.'

Rink wasn't one to mince words; he could see where my impetuous nature was leading and would rein me in before I jumped into a problem with both size tens. However, on this occasion, I'd sworn I wouldn't reveal Walter's relationship to Kirstie to anyone, and that included my best friend. I was unhappy that Walter had sworn me to silence: normally we shared everything. Though maybe it didn't really matter, because Rink was astute enough to figure things out, and Walter hadn't forbidden me from confirming the truth.

'I've agreed to the job, Rink, and can't back out now. I was hoping that you and Harve would help me out as usual.'

'You know we will, Hunter, but after what just happened . . .'

'Yeah,' I agreed. 'Executing that man in cold blood was a low thing to do, but this job is different.'

'Really? Hasn't Walter just demanded that Kirstie's husband be hurt? You know what he means by that.'

'All we have to do is extricate a kidnapped child. We won't be forced into working with any of Walt's spook squad again if that's what you're bothered about.'

'Somehow I doubt that,' Rink huffed.

'In fact, Walter's specific instructions are to have no interaction with the CIA.'

'Suits me, but what are the odds?'

'Let's not worry about that; we've a kid to rescue, before the war we've just ignited here endangers his life.'

'I'm not happy, brother.'

'To be honest, neither am I. But we're being well paid. You have to admit, the business could do with a cash infusion.'

Rink owned a PI firm based in Tampa, Florida. Due to the current economic downturn, prospective clients preferred to hold on to their cash rather than learn the truth about a wandering spouse or whatever other personal problem they had. The firm had been struggling – no less for the couple of pro bono cases we'd worked in the past few months – and it was in desperate need of a financial boost. Things had grown so bad that Rink had been forced to reduce the hours of his two investigators, Jim McTeer and Raul Velasquez, to the bare minimum. Both Rink and I had private incomes from pensions and savings stashed away after we retired from Arrowsake, but they wouldn't last forever. He'd been good enough to offer me employment when I arrived in the US, and had been out of pocket ever since: I didn't want to watch his business go under. I also hoped to see McTeer and Velasquez earning a wage they deserved and not having to rely on part-time mall security work.

'The cash would be welcome, but not at the expense of our goddamn souls,' he muttered.

I'd always railed at the notion of becoming a contract killer, and that was more or less what Walter was asking of me. The only way I could reconcile myself to the idea was to concentrate on the fact we'd be rescuing a little boy, and if anyone tried to stop us . . .

'I promise you, Rink, things are different this time. Walt isn't using us . . . well, not in the way he has in the past.'

'He's treating us like we're his personal attack dogs, as usual.'

'I prefer to think of us as rescuers.'

'Let's see about that,' he grunted.

That was as good a blessing as I was going to receive, but it was enough. I knew that Harvey Lucas – an even more cautious man than Rink – would join us too. He didn't share our history with Walter, and knew only part of how our old boss had used us over the years. He'd be up for working with us again through loyalty.

'So,' Rink said. 'You gonna spill?'

'Walter's going to brief us as soon as he's done coordinating the clean-up here,' I said. I preferred any lies told to my friends not to come from my lips. One of Walter's favourite phrases was 'plausible denial': maybe he would simply leave out some key details. That would rest easier with me.

Harvey had been absent for the past five minutes or so, having gone off to clean some of the battle dust from his face. He was fastidious that way. But when he came back lugging a Netbook I realised he'd been using the time for more than vanity.

'The wonders of the Internet,' he said, opening the Netbook and placing it on a ledge of rock. 'Even out here in the wilderness you can keep up with the latest news.'

He did some magic with the computer and brought up YouTube, specifically a segment of news lifted directly from CNN. 'Just thought it might be good to see who it is we're up against.'

The news footage was a couple of years old and showed a middle-aged man pushing his way past reporters as he left a courthouse in Hermosillo, Mexico. Jorge Carrillo Molina had been acquitted on murder charges when the case against him collapsed amid allegations that police officers involved in his case were corrupt. He was dressed like a movie star, handsome and healthy, his full head of black hair slicked with oil,

but he looked like a piece of shit to me. My opinion came
from the sneer he cast over the murder victim's family, and
the way he mouthed a silent promise to them. A few seconds
later Harvey brought up a second video file that showed the
aftermath of a house fire, and the three charred bodies being
carted away on gurneys. The victims were named as the father,
mother and younger brother of the murdered man Molina
had previously been investigated over.

Jorge Carrillo Molina was Kirstie's ex, and suddenly I'd
no qualms about putting a couple of rounds in the slimy
bastard's face.

4

I arranged to meet Kirstie Long at a hotel within sight of the Desert Diamond Casino, as well as of the airplanes landing and taking off at the nearby Tucson International Airport. I arrived early. It was an old habit from my military days, when it was always important to get the lie of the land prior to a meeting: you never knew when you'd have to abort in a hurry and it was best to have an escape route in mind. Not that I feared I'd be running from Kirstie, but she'd made some dangerous enemies since falling out with Jorge Molina. You could never be too careful when dealing with their likes.

Compared with the Mexican drug cartels, the coyote gangs were small fry. Since the collapse of the Colombian cartels, the Mexicans had stepped up their game, and now eclipsed their predecessors in power, influence and brutality. They had grown so systematised, each organisation running to almost military exactness, that they now troubled the Mexican government with fears of a *coup d'état*. As many as fourteen hundred police officers, soldiers, politicians, journalists and civilians had recently been murdered by the cartels, and they threatened many more with a similar fate. They had around one hundred thousand footsoldiers, and, unlike most criminal gangs, these men were highly trained and determined killers. An eighth of their number were ex-soldiers or cops who'd deserted to the other side, taking with them military-grade weaponry and tactics.

I killed time eating stuffed tacos and drinking coffee.

When Kirstie's flight was due, I made my way to the airport and recce'd the arrivals lounge for anyone suspicious, but no one got my hackles up. I settled in and waited for Kirstie to disembark. Passengers began appearing, lugging bags, hurried and sweating despite the A/C. I'd seen a photograph of Walter's granddaughter, but even so I barely recognised Kirstie when she appeared, carting a suitcase, carry-on bag and purse. I should have offered to help, done the gentlemanly thing, but I was busy checking out those waiting at the exit, ensuring no one was over-alert to her presence. The problem was, Kirstie was so pretty that she attracted more than one lingering glance, and even a barbed squint of jealousy from one woman. When I was done surveilling, I took more than a lingering glance myself.

I'd pictured Kirstie as a feminine version of Walter, expecting her to be short, even a little dumpy, but she was tall and slim, her wavy auburn hair bouncing on her shoulders as she strode towards the exit. Her lips were pinched, but with determination rather than ill temper. High, chiselled cheekbones framed large eyes in which I recognised her grandfather's grey colouring. But that was where the likeness ended, and I had to assume that she'd inherited her willowy build and good looks from her grandmother's side of the family.

Outside she made directly for the line of taxicabs.

I continued my observations and waited until her cab pulled away before jogging across to the parking lot where I'd left my rental. Knowing where she was heading, I fell in a couple of hundred yards behind her cab, checking the vehicles that followed on to the highway. Minutes later she directed her driver to stop in front of the hotel and I pulled in at the side of the road to watch. She tipped the driver, and was greeted by a bellhop who took charge of her suitcase. Once Kirstie was inside the hotel, and I was happy that she hadn't picked up a tail, I parked my rental in the lot and went inside too. Kirstie was standing by the check-in desk, leaning on the counter while she went through the routine with the receptionist. I drifted closer, catching a waft of expensive perfume pushed my way by a ceiling fan. It was tangy with a touch of citrus, and I liked it. I moved a couple of steps nearer. The receptionist glanced at me; I offered a smile. She looked away, and I allowed them to continue the procedure. Killing time, I again checked no new arrivals were taking interest in Kirstie. There were none.

When they were done, the receptionist handed Kirstie a key card and directed her through the lobby to a bank of elevators to take to reach her room on the second floor. I moved to intercept her, and a momentary flicker of anxiety skipped across her features. Made me wonder how aware Kirstie was of the dangerous situation she'd entered into.

'I'm Joe Hunter,' I said to waylay any fear. 'You were told to expect me?'

She glanced at the reception desk, but the clerk was taking no notice of us. Kirstie gave a faint smile, then leaned a little closer, seeming to enjoy the cloak-and-dagger situation. 'You were at the airport,' she said. 'Why didn't you introduce your-self then?'

I was surprised that she'd noticed me in the arrivals lounge, but chose not to let it show. 'It wasn't the right time or place.'

'You were watching for someone following me? You can relax; no one but you has raised my suspicions since arriving in Tucson.'

Kirstie worked in public relations, and had more than one bestselling mystery author and a couple of mid-list sportsmen on her client list. It didn't seem a career predisposed to spot-ting a covert tail, but thinking about it, I realised that she'd be forever on the lookout for crazy fans dogging her clients. It was probably in her job description to dissuade or redirect anyone intent on monopolising her clients' valuable time at public events. On the other hand she hadn't spotted the craziest man of all when she'd allowed Molina to get close to her.

'It was good that you didn't let on when you spotted me,' I said, 'because some of the people at Molina's beck and call may not be what you expect.'

'I'm not in the habit of approaching dangerous-looking individuals. Well . . . not always.' Again she gave me the fleeting smile, this time one intended to tease. 'Anyway, I probably know better than you do the type at Jorge's beck and call.' She pronounced the man's name with a G – calling him George – and not with the Hispanic H as I'd been doing.

I conceded the second point, and began to walk towards the bank of elevators. But I had to wonder why I struck her as looking dangerous. I suppose she would have expected certain skills from the man going into Mexico to retrieve her son. Kirstie strode to keep up with me, her heels clacking on the hardwood floor. She was still lugging her carry-on bag and purse, but she didn't look the type who expected help, so I didn't offer. In her line of work, she'd have to be the liberated type.

'Let's go upstairs,' I said as I punched the call button on the elevator panel.

'That's a phrase that has come back to haunt me,' she muttered.

Letting it pass, I said, 'You won't be staying in your room, just in case any of Jorge's people have managed to get by us.'

'You really think that Jorge is watching me?'

'You're currently engaged in a lawsuit to win custody of your son . . . Hell, yeah. He'll be watching your every move.'

'He's indifferent to me, Joe. He's too busy watching his rivals to pay me any mind.'

'It's thinking like that could get us both killed.'

The doors opened, and I waited, checking that there was nobody inside the lift. I'd positioned us to the left of the open doors, and if there were somebody inside they'd have to lean out to spot us. Luckily no face – or gun – poked out. I allowed Kirstie to enter first then, after a cursory inspection of the lobby behind us, I followed. As the doors closed I hit the 'basement' button.

'I thought you said we were going upstairs.'

'I did.'

Kirstie gave me a bemused look. In the close confines of the lift her perfume was stronger, but no less pleasant. But I caught a different tang, one of fear. For all her self-assuredness, Kirstie was uncomfortable in my presence. Or perhaps it was because I'd reminded her just how dangerous her ex-beau was.

'So where are we going?'

'Out of here.'

'We're leaving the hotel?'

'It doesn't take someone with Jorge Molina's connections to trace you here.'

'But I've had my luggage taken up to my room.'

'Yeah. That was a good idea. If anyone checks they'll think you're still booked in.' Now it was my turn to offer a teasing smile.

'But my things . . .'

'We can get you new stuff. Anyway–' I checked out her formal blouse and skirt – 'you'll need something more casual than this stuff you're wearing.'

'I have casual clothing in my suitcase.'

'It'll have to stay there. Sorry, Kirstie, but we have to leave without anyone noticing.'

The elevator doors swept open on to a corridor heavy with

the aroma of chlorine, and though we were separated from the indoor swimming pool by a set of closed doors the air was cloying with humidity. From further along the corridor came the sound of runners pounding the treadmills in the health club. A muscular man stood in the hall just outside the lift, but he was expected. Kirstie eyed Rink's looming figure.

'And you thought I looked dangerous.' I smiled. 'How are things looking, Rink?'

'Good to go,' my friend replied. He was wearing an ear bud, which he tapped. 'Coming out now, Harve. ETA twenty seconds.'

Harvey must have given the all-clear at his end, because Rink merely inclined his head for us to follow.

Kirstie held back.

'Kirstie,' I said. 'If you want your son back, you've got to trust us, OK?'

'I want him back more than anything,' she said, as if my words were an insult. 'I'll do whatever it takes. If it means trusting my life to strangers, then I'll do that too.'

Holding her stare for a moment I watched the heat of anger slide away. In its place was a new look. One of desperation. Meeting me for the first time, Kirstie had projected the professional image of a woman determined to rise above the trials she was up against, but under the bravado she was simply a mother terrified for her child's welfare. The flinty look went out of her gaze as tears began to well. I squeezed her arm reassuringly. 'So, come on. I'll introduce you to the others later.'

Rink led the way past the health club and into a corridor marked Fire Exit. Doors at the end were armed with a day alarm, but Rink had already jimmied it so that it wouldn't sound. He pushed the door open a sliver as he cocked his head to listen for instruction from Harvey. He gave us a nod, and pushed outside.

Before Kirstie went through the exit I pulled out a baseball cap and jammed it on her hair. Then I shucked off my jacket and hung it around her shoulders. 'Pull up the collar and keep your head down,' I instructed as I placed one arm round her back and ushered her towards the van Harvey had reversed close by. Rink opened the doors and helped Kirstie step inside the cargo area; between us she was hustled out of sight within seconds. Bench seats ran down both sides of the interior and I guided her to the one on the right. I moved to sit opposite as Rink closed the doors and went to join Harvey in the front. Before we'd settled in, Harvey hit the gas and drove us away from the hotel.

'That was a bit extreme,' Kirstie said from beneath the peak of the cap.

'But necessary,' I concluded. 'You can look up now if you wish.'

Kirstie did so, peering at me in a different way than before. Perhaps the ease with which we'd just snatched her gave her hope that we'd be able to do the same for her boy. I didn't think things would be as easy as that.

5

The mid-afternoon sun was casting razor blades of light off the windows of the hotel as we approached. Unlike the one near the airport, this was a family-owned place, off the beaten track and less likely to be on the radar of anyone seeking Kirstie's current whereabouts. The hotel was a small, original dwelling in the adobe style, but lodge accommodation had been erected on the undulating desert grounds behind it. The hotel looked dusty and sun-parched but an effort had been made at sprucing up the grounds, with roads lined by stone-edging painted white, and neat beds of sturdy desert flowers and shrubs. It was situated approximately ten miles to the south-west of Tucson, but still remote enough that you could imagine you were in the middle of nowhere.

Under bogus details Harvey had arranged accommodation in one of the two-bedroom lodges, and had paid upfront for a couple of nights should we need them. He had collected the keys earlier, so there was no need to check in at the main house. Harvey drove the van past the adobe house to the rearmost lodge. Rink opened the back doors and that was when the searing glint of sun hit me. I scrambled out of the van and put my back to the house, shielding my eyes as Kirstie tentatively followed.

'Where are we?'

'Somewhere we can relax and go over plans for getting your boy back,' I said.

'Will Conrad be joining us?'

I was caught out by her reference to Walter. I hadn't checked if Kirstie actually knew that he was her grandfather: from the formal use of his surname, I guessed not.

'No. He won't be coming.'

'Oh? I had the impression that he was going to oversee everything.'

I patted my shirt pocket, indicating my cell phone. 'I'll be in touch with him if need be. Don't worry–' I inclined my chin towards where my friends were approaching the lodge – 'we can handle this without him.'

'Conrad's a bit strange, isn't he?' Kirstie said as she hitched up her bags.

'Very strange.'

'You said I should trust you, Joe, but I know nothing about you. I don't know much about Conrad either. And yet here I am.' She paused to squint at the sand-blown landscape. Then towards the lodge where Harvey was busy unlocking the door. 'What have I gotten myself into?'

I could have asked myself the same question. It wasn't the first time that we had accepted the job of liberating a child from a dangerous situation. On the last occasion circumstances were not all that we had been led to believe; we'd ended up in a cat-and-mouse pursuit with a particularly dangerous individual. The same would likely happen again. Jorge Molina would not allow us just to run off with his boy, and with the resources at his disposal, our trip back from Mexico would not be a comfortable one. Walter had intimated that it would be best for all involved if Molina did not survive our invasion of his home. Perhaps he was right, but the notion of becoming a hired killer never did rest easy with me. Terminations on behalf of Queen and Country were a different matter and I loathed the idea that we were being pressed into becoming assassins again as much as Rink did. The more I thought about it, the more I wondered what was most important to Walter: that his great-grandson was liberated or that Molina was put in his grave. The latter wasn't something I was prepared to raise with Kirstie.

'Let's get inside out of the heat,' I said, while throwing shut the van doors. 'I'll make the introductions with Rink and Harvey and then we'll get down to business, eh?'

'The sooner the better. I want Benjamin back where he belongs.'

This time I didn't ask, just took her tote bag from her. She paused, then fell into step without comment. Her heels weren't exactly suitable for the terrain, and I hoped she'd had the presence of mind to put a pair of sneakers in her bag.

Cool air washed over us as we entered the lodge. Housekeeping had been by and turned on the A/C. A large fan whirred noisily in the centre of the room, the breeze it kicked up tugging at the drapes over the windows. The way people do when entering an unfamiliar space, Rink and Harvey were busy checking out the other rooms and closet spaces.

'Got a coffee-maker back here,' Harvey announced from the kitchen. Music to my ears.

Harvey came back into the living area and stuck out a hand. As ever his fingernails were well manicured, mother-of-pearl nails glinting in the spill of light from outside.

'You must be wondering what kind of company you've fallen into, Kirstie? Well, let me be the first to reassure you . . . as ugly as Hunter and Rink are, they're not bad guys.' He grinned, showing teeth. 'I'm Harvey Lucas, the brains of the outfit.'

Kirstie accepted his hand but released it quickly with an equally brief glance at me.

'Intelligence ain't all it's cracked up to be,' Rink said, coming forward. 'Not when there's not an ounce of common sense to direct it.'

'Rink,' Harvey chided. 'Don't confuse common sense with being plain common. We can all see the corn husk sticking out your ear.'

'Yep. I'm a country boy and proud.' Rink offered his hand. 'I'm Jared Rington, but you can call me Rink, OK?'

Kirstie shook the proffered hand, her slim fingers lost in Rink's huge mitt.

'Now we all know each other, let's get down to figuring out our next move.' I moved across the room to place Kirstie's bag next to a rustic-looking settee. Most of the furniture in the room looked handmade, albeit by a decent craftsman. The settee was basically a wooden frame, upholstered with thick throw cushions, but it was inviting and no doubt comfortable, and more desirable than the wooden benches we'd sat on during the journey here. I offered Kirstie a place on it.

She looked expectantly at the three of us. We were standing over her, and I felt the closeness of my buddies encroaching on the space, so I nodded each of them to sit. I chose a seat across a coffee table from Kirstie. Harvey sat next to her, a cushion's distance between them, while Rink propped himself against a cabinet, folding his arms over his chest. Though Kirstie hadn't looked intimidated, she visibly relaxed. Without being prompted she reached for her carry-on bag and pulled from it a stack of papers in a clear Ziploc envelope.

'I wasn't sure if you'd need these, but brought them anyway. They're the steps I've already taken to get my boy back.'

'Rather than go through documents, I think it'd help if you just told us in layman's terms,' I said.

Kirstie nodded.

'The problem is that neither Jorge nor I have sole custody of Benjamin, so the usual routes of getting him home have been mired in red tape and bureaucracy. Normally when a child is kidnapped, he must be registered as missing with law enforcement on the National Crime Information Centre system. Where there's a felony charge against the abductor, law enforcement agencies are usually happy to help, often issuing a warrant of arrest for the abductor. When a kidnapped child is taken across state lines or even to another country the FBI will get involved and they too will issue an arrest warrant, even an international one if need be. They will usually arrest the abductors and extradite them back to the US, and bring home the child as a matter of course. However, it's different between Jorge and me, because Jorge has the same parental rights to custody as I have, so I was unable to secure a warrant.'

Kirstie fished inside the envelope and pulled out a glossy snapshot of her son. He was a cherubic toddler with tousled black locks. His light-grey eyes, inherited from his mother, were in contrast to his tanned complexion and dark hair. His paternity wasn't in doubt.

'How old's the boy now?'

'This is an old photo, the last I took before Jorge kidnapped him.' Kirstie's voice hitched at the final syllable. She struggled to get a grip on her emotions. 'He had just turned three then, but now he's almost five. I haven't seen him for over eighteen months . . . Christ! It feels like a lifetime.'

'It's taken eighteen months trying the legal route?' I shook my head at how a child's welfare could be so mired down in bureaucracy. 'Shame we weren't brought in sooner.'

'I've tried other avenues. There are associations, charitable foundations that will help in cases such as mine.'

'Yeah, I've heard a bit about them,' Rink cut in. 'Seen something on TV about some guys who went to South Korea and grabbed a kid for his mom.'

'They can be helpful, but obviously being in the public eye

the better-known associations must work very closely with local law enforcement agencies. One group did offer to help, but on hearing that Benjamin had been taken to Mexico they told me that corruption is so rife in the police force that they counselled against seeking assistance from the Mexican authorities. They warned me that the police would tip off Jorge, or worse, throw us in prison as kidnappers. They offered me legal assistance, support and advice, but they were fearful of repercussions if they acted against Jorge. They learned early on that he is allegedly a highly ranked cartel boss.'

'Allegedly?'

Kirstie shrugged. 'It's no secret that the Mexican cartels don't take infringements against them lightly. Hell, these are the same people who hung a young boy and girl from an underpass during rush hour, slitting them open from throat to groin and allowing their guts to hang out for all to see. Why? Because the two kids had badmouthed them on their blogs, for God's sake!'

'So this foundation was afraid to assist you is what you're saying, for fear something similar would happen to them?'

'They didn't say as much, but, yes, that's what I believe. They were frightened.'

I didn't have to look at Rink or Harvey to guess what they were thinking. To understand the violence the Mexican cartels inflicted on innocent people would salve their consciences, and make them more enthusiastic for the job.

'The charity encouraged me to file for emergency custody, and receive certification from the Secretary of State, to put the onus on the Mexican government to help, but that was a non-starter.' Kirstie laughed without humour. 'The Mexican government are running scared of the cartels half the time, or in their back pockets. I didn't waste my time, I sought help elsewhere.'

'From Conrad?'

'Not directly. I went to my grandmother. She dotes on Benjamin and misses him as much as I do. She offered to find someone who was willing to help outside of the usual channels. I didn't hold out much hope – it's been a long, long time since she was with the CIA.'

I made a grunt of surprise, but when I thought about it, it was pretty obvious that Walter's lover was from the Agency. He had known no other life since he was in his early twenties.

'So your grandma put you in touch with old Walter, eh?' Rink said.

'Walter? Is that his name? He has only ever referred to himself as Conrad. I assumed that was his first name.'

I scowled at Rink, but he only offered a smile that twisted one corner of his mouth. Then I decided, what the hell? 'His name is Walter Hayes Conrad. So he wasn't exactly lying to you.'

'Just being economical with the truth,' Rink put in.

Kirstie frowned. She had no idea about Rink's distrust of our former Arrowsake handler, and voicing his opinion here and now wouldn't help. I think he got that, because he lowered his head and pinched down on a further retort. Kirstie shook her hair off her shoulders. She picked up Benjamin's photo, and stared at it for a second or two. I was worried that she would see a connection between Walter and those identical eyes peering back from the toddler's face. But she didn't seem to. Tears were welling. 'Conrad, uh, Walter, or whatever he's called, promised that he would help me get my son home. And yet, even he was tentative when he realised who Benjamin's father was. Are you sure that you'll be able to rescue him?'

It wasn't the time to tell her that Walter had been hiding a secret and that his reticence was for fear of revealing it, perhaps placing all four generations of his family in a worse predicament.

'He's a complicated man,' I reassured her. 'He was probably just thinking about the right people for the job. Don't worry, Kirstie, we'll do everything in our power to get Benjamin back.'

'You've done similar work before?'

'Yeah, you could say we've had experience of dealing with dangerous people.'

She studied each of our battle-scarred faces in turn. 'I suspect you've seen nothing like the kind of animals Jorge could set loose on you.'

6

The wall-mounted air-conditioning unit roared along on its lowest temperature setting, periodically dripping condensation on the floor. Lying on the bed with a sheet pulled up to her throat, Kirstie Long watched the moisture build, tremble in place then make the drop to the carpet. The regularity was almost metronomic, hypnotic in its way. She began to count the drips and was well into triple figures before she realised what she was doing and made a conscious effort to stop. Within half a minute she was counting again. Counting was something she did as an unconscious stress-reliever, and she often wondered if she had a mild case of OCD. The dripping of the A/C unit was only one of many things she'd counted in the past few hours. She'd tapped the tip of her tongue on each of her teeth, making continuous circuits of her mouth. She had counted the small geometric patterns in the carpet. She had also counted the slats on the window shades, calculating if she'd be able to break her way through them before Hunter or the others entered the room.

It was wrong to think of the three men as her guards, because she was not a prisoner. Not in the usual sense. But if she was not allowed to leave this house, then what else could she be? She had asked to go back to her original hotel for her belongings, and been refused. She had insisted but her harsh words were rebuffed as easily as her pleading. All the men would say was that it was for her own safety. Perhaps her warning that Jorge had some of the nastiest killers at his disposal had not helped her cause: it put the men more on edge. After some further discussion, Kirstie had left them to their planning and availed herself of the shower in the en suite bathroom. Washed, and her hair dried by a sputtering dryer that was little more than a flexible tube hanging from the wall, she had climbed into the bed. Not because she was tired, but to force herself to relax. She was impatient to get started, to bring home her son, and if she didn't lie down she might claw her way through those window slats and run all the way to Mexico.

She wished now that she'd kept her mouth shut about Jorge's resources, but she'd told Hunter and the others how he'd been hiring mercenary fighters, and had built himself a small personal army culled from branches of various Special Forces groups. His reason for doing so was that there was much infighting between the major cartels, all of them jostling for predominance and control of the narcotics and human trafficking routes into the US. Kirstie knew what task he'd put his army to when she tried to grab Benjamin. Conrad struck her as someone with similar assets at his beck and call, and she didn't think Hunter or his pals were any less capable than Jorge's men, but they would be wholly outnumbered and in unfamiliar terrain. She'd contemplated contacting Conrad and requesting further assistance: more men and a support network, but evidently the three men here were all that she was getting.

She thought about the old man and how he'd presented two faces to her. One was cold and hard, the other surprisingly tender. When discussing the detail of snatching back Benjamin, he'd been as cold and soulless as a snake. Yet, afterwards, when he'd done with the planning, he looked as if he wished to embrace her and his eyes had twinkled with unshed tears.

Kirstie had recoiled, not so much from fear as from recognition. She knew those eyes. They were her mother's eyes and those of her own child. They were the eyes she saw staring back at her from the bathroom mirror each morning.

Could it be true?

Was that old man – the soulless CIA man – her grandfather?

When she'd grown old enough to wonder about her heritage, Kirstie had asked her parents about her grandfather. Her mom, Annie, explained that her own mother had always refused to name her father. Embittered by the secrecy surrounding her birth, Annie had stifled any desire to discover his identity, and encouraged Kirstie to do the same. Yet Kirstie had always wondered who the mystery man was. In her teens, she'd attempted her own sleuthing, but her attempts had failed. It was through her search for her grandfather that the investigative journalism bug had bitten her in college, and that was what had led her to her chosen career. Through her work as a fledgling journo she'd made acquaintances of various celebrities, some of whom she'd helped with promo ideas. From there it was a natural step to her current vocation. She had met Jorge Molina through one of her clients at a celebrity dinner, falling for the handsome smooth-talker over margaritas in the bar afterwards. They'd enjoyed a whirlwind romance; one where she'd been carried along on the crest of excitement afforded her by his wealth and associations with many powerful individuals. She'd fallen pregnant by him in the third month of their relationship, was married in the next, and that was when everything had gone downhill. Jorge had shown his real face, something that she had grown to fear more and more as the date of Benjamin's birth approached. As soon as the boy was born, Jorge had dissociated himself from Kirstie, and the next three years had been stifling as she'd been made a prisoner in their home. Rather than a lover, or mother to his child, Jorge had used her as little more than a nanny to raise Benjamin until he was old enough to be cut loose. He took the boy to his homeland, with threats should she follow. It would be ironic if the loss of one family member should lead to the discovery of another. If she had not met Jorge then there'd have been no need for her grandfather to come to her rescue.

Jesus, she thought, if I'd have known finding him was as easy as this I'd have attracted the attention of a sadistic monster long ago.

It was a black joke.

But how could she laugh when Benjamin was still in the clutches of her evil ex-husband? Not for one second did she believe that his father physically threatened Benjamin – Jorge's heir was important to him – yet Jorge inhabited a world where dangerous enemies might target his son at any moment. Worse, she feared that Benjamin would be raised to emulate his father . . . something she had no wish to contemplate. As soon as Jorge had returned to Mexico Kirstie had initiated proceedings for the return of her child. Jorge had countered with a plan of his own. One night two thugs had grabbed her off the street and forced her at gunpoint towards a waiting vehicle. They had taken her to her apartment on the outskirts of Washington DC – the home she'd shared with Jorge and Benjamin – and told her to say goodbye to everything she held dear. Then they'd surprised her by introducing a third man to the mix, this one a lawyer working on Jorge's behalf. Under duress Kirstie had been forced to sign the divorce papers served upon her, and also a backdated pre-nuptial agreement endorsed there and then by the lawyer, giving up all claim to any share of Jorge's estate in Mexico. She'd gladly signed the papers; she had no interest in anything but her child. She had been handed the deeds to the apartment, with a warning that

should the men have to visit her again her next place of resi-
dence would be a casket.

Kirstie wasn't a coward; no mother fighting for her child is.
But the warning had rung loud and clear, and she'd waited
months before summoning up the courage to resume lawful
proceedings to retrieve her son. However, as history had
shown, none of her efforts had born fruit. She had practically
given up hope until her grandmother had put her in contact
with Walter Conrad. Her grandfather?

She'd wondered where he'd been all of her life, but more
than that she now wondered where the hell he'd been for the
past two days. It was over forty-eight hours since Walter had
told her that for Benjamin's sake she must trust him and those
that she was about to meet. That was a big ask, when the man
was so secretive about his motives. And, by virtue of association, so were Hunter and his friends. But then, to recover her
son, she'd sign a deal with the devil.

The A/C unit was struggling to maintain the low temperature. It had begun to roar. She threw off the sheet and stood.
She was fully dressed, wearing the same blouse, but had
exchanged her skirt and heels for cargo pants and sneakers
from her carry-on bag. She glanced up at the labouring unit,
but only to time her step under it to avoid one of those icy drips
getting under her collar. She waited for the drip, then quickly
exited into the short hall alongside the en suite bathroom and
approached the exit door. She placed an ear to the wood.

Voices were mingled in conversation, and she could make
out more than the three she'd become used to hearing. She
thought there were at least five or six men in the room next
door. Because there were no sounds of anger or recrimination, the newcomers must have been expected.

Kirstie raised a palm to open the door before second
thoughts caused her hand to drop. The murmur of muted

conversation had stopped. Kirstie listened hard and caught the soft pad of approaching footsteps. She moved back, and stood with her hands fisted at her sides as someone rapped on the door.

'Who is it?'

The handle turned and Kirstie opened her mouth to challenge the intrusion into her space, but the recrimination fell short. Hunter stared back at her and something about the intensity of his gaze stopped the words in her throat. Colours seemed to shift in the depths of his eyes, blue, green and brown, as he tilted his head to study her. She felt him analyse and catalogue everything about her within a split second.

'We need to talk,' he said, appraising her. 'I'm glad to see you've dressed more appropriately.'

She had an equally analytical eye and took in Hunter's appearance in a rapid sweep from head to toe. He wasn't exactly remarkable to look at, being slightly less than six feet tall and probably in his late thirties or early forties. He had a basic barbershop hairstyle, light brown flecked with grey at the temples, shaved close at the sides and back, a little longer on top. Under a battered brown leather jacket and black shirt, black jeans and boots, she could tell that his body was hard, but unlike those of the muscular sportsmen she was familiar with. But when her gaze returned to his eyes, she sensed something unusual about him that set off a flutter in her belly. She recognised the gaze of a remorseless warrior, but wasn't that exactly what she required? Hunter extended an open hand.

'We're leaving sooner than we thought,' he said.

His wrist was thick, and on the tanned skin of his hand she could make out tiny white scars that hinted at others on his body. Such a hand had likely killed and was capable of inflicting further death.

'Who are you?' she asked.

'You already know that. Trust me, Kirstie, I'm here to help you.'

She didn't move.

'Let me rephrase my question: what are you?'

'Someone prepared to help. Do you need to know more than that?'

'And the old man?'

'I think it's better that he tell you himself.'

'Walter Conrad,' she said, pouting at the name. A childhood memory came to her. She'd been visiting with her grandmother and had snuck up to the bedroom and eavesdropped on a telephone call. She didn't understand what the conversation was about, but she recalled how her grandmother had signed off. 'I love you, Walter.' Kirstie had forgotten that conversation, but now it came crashing down on her in a moment of epiphany.

'Is he really . . . ?' She couldn't finish the sentence.

'Like I said, it's best that he tells you everything.' Hunter held out his hand again. This time the image of a killer's hands had disappeared and she saw the strength as something else entirely. She allowed him to lead her from the bedroom.

The room they entered was still clean and neat, but it now smelled of coffee, and the fan struggled against the heat of so many bodies. Back in her bedroom she hadn't dialled up the A/C because she was hot, but to move around the stale and cloying air. Here the men who'd made the room their temporary home hadn't thought to do so, but had sweated through their plans while downing strong coffee and deli sandwiches. Kirstie registered the smells, but did not dwell on them; she was too busy examining the men gathered round her.

'Where's Walter?'

'He won't be joining us,' Hunter said. 'In the meantime I thought it best that you get to know our friends here, seeing as you're going to be spending some time together.'

The newcomers were a middle-aged Latino with gel in his slicked-back hair, wearing a loose shirt over chinos and sneakers, and a slightly older, grey-haired guy in a sports jacket and slacks, who had ex-cop stamped all over him.

'Raul Velasquez and Jim McTeer, they'll be looking after you while the rest of us fetch Benjamin.'

Kirstie was still holding Hunter's hand. Gently she extricated herself. 'What do you mean, "looking after me"? I'm going with you.'

'Don't worry, you'll be coming to Mexico with us. Once we have Benjamin out of Jorge's hands we'll need you to take care of him. But you can't be in on the actual snatch. You'll be at a safe staging area with these guys. If all goes to plan, and we get the boy back, then it's important that he's with his mother. Otherwise there's no way we can bring him across the border without raising suspicion.'

'You're assuming that Benjamin will be at Jorge's house. If so, I obviously can't be involved, but that might not be the case. If he was elsewhere, say a public place, then it makes sense for me to be there. It would be easier for me to get to him than you guys.'

'Kirstie,' Hunter's eyes were cold chips of ice. 'If Jorge's men are as capable as you say, then you won't get within a hundred yards of Benjamin. He'll be heavily protected, I'm guessing, with operatives watching out for him at all times. They might not even bother warning you this time, but just shoot you dead at the first opportunity.'

'What's to stop them doing the same to any of you?'

'We'll be shooting back,' Hunter said.

7

As we barrelled towards the Mexican border, Kirstie travelled with me and Rink in the rental car I'd collected from the airport, while Harvey, Velasquez and McTeer followed close behind in the van. Now that we were on our way, Kirstie had fallen silent, and in the rear-view mirror I occasionally caught her chewing her lips or tapping her tongue on her teeth as she frowned out of the window.

In hindsight, perhaps I should have chosen my words with more care. Kirstie was fearful enough of her child's welfare without my suggesting there'd be a firefight over him. But I was never one for offering false hope, and it was best that she understood the implications of trying to snatch a child from under the watchful eyes of footsoldiers primed against the unusual. They were waging constant war with neighbouring cartels, all of them jostling for the largest slice of pie, and it stood to reason they'd be on the lookout for anything out of the ordinary. Recently one gang had slaughtered thirty-plus members of a rival outfit, gunning them down during a daring raid on their headquarters, the story making the international news due to its brutality and efficiency, so I didn't doubt that we were facing dangerous and capable enemies who were likely to launch a counter-attack.

After I'd said my piece, Kirstie had looked shocked, and had agreed to remain at the staging post we'd set up on our arrival in Jorge Molina's hometown of Hermosillo. That made me feel a little better about the arrangement. If I'd had my way, Kirstie wouldn't be coming into Mexico at all, but Harvey, and then Rink, had argued that we needed her to look after Benjamin. None of us could care for a small child – not while possibly fighting all the way back to the US. At least Kirstie was no shrinking violet, no damsel in distress requiring saving by one of us. She was tough, I could tell, and determined, and also trained in the use of small arms. Apparently her grandmother had instructed both Annie and Kirstie in firearms, a skill that Kirstie had kept up since being manhandled off the street by Jorge's henchmen. The grandmother had perhaps foreseen a day when it would be necessary for her family to take up weapons, but she could never have guessed it would be under these circumstances.

I checked in the rear-view again. Kirstie had hidden her auburn hair under the cap I'd given her at the airport hotel, and had her chin tilted down so that the peak concealed part of her face. Her gaze was hidden in shadow, but it was as if she sensed my scrutiny and looked up. I caught a flash of pale grey, before one eyelid flickered in a wink. My response was to wink back, and Kirstie nodded at my weak attempt at offering support.

'You OK back there?'

'As well as anybody could be under these circumstances.'

'You should eat something,' I said. We had dined on coffee and sandwiches but Kirstie had had no appetite while going through our final plans. 'Grab something from the cooler back there.'

'I'm not sure my stomach would take food just now.'

'Nervous?'

'No, anxious.'

Beside me in the passenger seat, Rink stirred from a light slumber. Despite snoring gently, he'd been aware of our brief conversation. 'It pays to eat and drink when you can: you never know when you'll next have the opportunity.'

'Do you want something?' Kirstie flipped open the lid of the cooler box we'd prepared.

'Yeah, toss me some mineral water and one of those taco wraps, will ya?'

'What about you, Joe?'

I shook my head. 'I'll get something once we swap drivers.'

'Yeah. Best you don't distract him.' Rink accepted a bottle of water and his food, while glancing around at the scenery. It was featureless desert on one side, with only a few stray spindly bushes dotting the hilly horizon, while on the other there was a narrow strip of tilled land that was surprisingly green. 'Good to see you've managed to drive this far without killing us all,' Rink said. 'I'll take over soon, before the traffic grows any heavier.'

Rink often pokes fun at my motoring abilities, even though I'm skilled in tactical and defensive driving. He doesn't trust me to remain on the right side of the road. Usually I counter by telling him the left side *is* the right side back where I come from, but Kirstie wasn't familiar with our usual banter. I let his jibe go.

'Just finish your food and go back to sleep,' I told him. 'You too, Kirstie. Try to have a nap because we can't be sure when you'll get any decent sleep.'

'I couldn't sleep if I tried. I've too many things going through my mind.'

A sign at the side of the highway indicated that we were nearing the tiny town of Rio Rico, but the approach to the town was sheathed in heat haze rising from the asphalt, so I couldn't make out any signs of life. We were only a few miles off the border town of Nogales where we'd chosen to cross into Mexico. Assuming that Jorge Molina's influence stretched that far north, it was possibly the first place that his watchers would be stationed. It could also prove the first point where we crossed paths with those I was certain were keeping tabs on Kirstie. Just because we hadn't spotted a tail at Tucson didn't mean there was none there. There was every likelihood that they'd called ahead and arranged a welcoming committee for us the minute we crossed from North Grand Avenue – the southernmost tip of I-19 – to Adolfo Lopez Mateos Highway on the Mexican side.

'Even if you can't, pretend that you're sleeping,' I said. 'We don't want anyone getting a good look at your face as we cross the border.'

'Won't we have to be checked by the border patrol?'

'Don't worry. It's easy getting out of the country. Not quite as simple getting back in. I'll do the talking; you just keep your head down, OK? And it's probably best you stay like that until we're on the Mex Fifteen south of town and can be sure we're not being followed.'

We passed an old mission church with an arched façade and walled garden standing lonely on parched earth. There were a number of cars parked on the lot outside, but no tourists or pilgrims in evidence. The church was reminiscent of the Alamo, but then my opinion was coloured by the old John Wayne movie because I'd never seen the original building. Pushing through Rio Rico I found houses and a few retail premises on widely spread lots, so perhaps my earlier description of it as a town was a tad grandiose. Then we were past the houses at the southern outskirt and surrounded once again by desert. Next stop Nogales. I checked for our friends in the panel van and made it out as a dull smudge in the heat haze behind. As we approached the border crossing, Harvey would fall back and place more distance between the two vehicles so that we were not pegged as travelling companions. If we picked up a tail, then it would be good to have back-up behind them.

We had valid – though under bogus details –WHTI–compliant travel documents and passport cards with us and, also in preparation for traversing the border, Walter had smoothed our passage by supplying documents for the van produced under the trilateral Security and Prosperity Partnership that existed between the US, Canada and Mexico. Under the documents the van was registered as a vehicle from a trusted traveller/trader company and therefore should go through the checkpoint without too much fuss. I hoped that was the case, because the van was now carrying all our weapons in hidden compartments. I felt naked without the familiar weight of my SIG down the back of my jeans.

Nogales loomed ahead of us, a sizeable urban sprawl. There were a couple of border crossings at the heart of the city, but we'd chosen to continue on the main highway and cross from Arizona into Sonora by the busiest route. Vehicles would queue on both sides, making the border officials more hurried as they fought to cut the waiting times and meet the targets set by the SPP agreement. It was our hope that we could pass through without raising any suspicion. Not that we expected trouble entering Mexico, but you never could tell.

Entering Nogales proper it was apparent that things were cosier this side of the tall fences that split the city, and it was hard to imagine the slum-like neighbourhoods on the southern side when passing familiar commercial chain stores and food outlets along the main strip. But I wouldn't have to imagine for long, because pretty soon we'd pass through the checkpoints into one of the poorest areas of North America. On the southside lived families struggling under the burden of unemployment and poverty, in shantytowns that pressed almost to the chain link fences. Day by day, people on that side of the marker must look north and pray for the day that they tasted the sweet fruit of the American Dream. No wonder so many immigrants threw themselves at the mercy of the coyote gangs to smuggle them to a new and better life.

Rink reclined in the passenger seat, relaxed and loose, his hooded eyes hidden behind a pair of shades. Any casual observer would think he was asleep, but he was alert and on the lookout for hidden watchers. I checked on Kirstie and found her gaze in the mirror once again.

'Now would be a good time to get your head down,' I said.

'We're not at the border yet,' she replied.

'Near enough that someone might see you. Just do as I ask, OK?'

Kirstie pulled her cap brim lower, tucked her chin into her shoulder and crossed her arms over her chest. From the rapidity of her exhalations her anxiety levels were rising.

'Just stay cool. If anyone does ask you any questions, play dumb. Let me answer for you.'

'Now you sound like my ex-husband,' she muttered.

'I'm asking nicely.'

'Fair point.' Her lip curled into a smile.

There was something about Kirstie that I was beginning to like, beyond the fact she was damn good-looking and had captivating grey eyes. I made myself pull my attention away from the mirror and concentrate on the road ahead. We were entering a built-up area, where signage indicated directions to the border checkpoints. Beside me Rink exhaled, and I wondered if he was again going to offer to drive.

'Don't worry, I've got it.'

'It isn't your driving I'm worried about, brother. Check out the near corner of the building on your right.'

A CCTV camera was mounted on a pole secured to the building and was definitely tracking our progress along the street. Could have been an arbitrary incident, some bored camera operator deciding to check us out, but in my business you can't ignore even random occurrences.

'Could be nothing.' Rink clucked his tongue. 'Then again, it could be something to worry about. Who knows we're heading this way?'

He didn't have to elucidate. He was referring to Walter. But I didn't think our old handler had anything to do with the surveillance of our progress this side of the border. Why would he do that when all he had to do was to ring me on my cell phone for an update? There was no indication who the camera belonged to; perhaps it was shared by various agencies.

'Maybe they twigged on to us because of your ugly mug,' I said, making light of the situation.

'Or they think you're a drunk driver,' Rink countered.

'Could Jorge have enough influence to control officials on this side of the border?' Kirstie's question sobered me somewhat.

'I don't doubt it, but I don't think that's what this is about. Keep an eye out for other cameras, Rink. If they stay on us, it means we might have something to worry about.'

By now we were under the camera, forced to proceed slower as traffic built up in preparation for entering the lanes to the border crossing, still about a half-mile ahead. Checking in my wing mirror, I saw the camera swing to follow our progress.

'Another on the left tracking to find us,' Rink announced.

'Shit. I don't like this one bit.'

'What if someone's realised what we're up to and they're going to stop us entering Mexico?' Kirstie's voice was a few octaves higher than usual.

'Then we find another way in.'

'How could they be on to us?'

'Did you mention it to anyone, because I'm positive none of us did.'

'Only my grandmother knows. Walter Conrad, too, but I can't see either of them giving the game away.'

'So maybe we're worrying about nothing. Maybe they're on the lookout for a similar rental car and picked on us,' Rink said.

'We'll find out soon enough,' I said, pushing the car on and joining the now-static queue waiting to pass through the checkpoint. More than ever I felt the missing SIG as a hollow point at my lower spine. 'OK, now's the time to pretend you're sleeping, Kirstie.'

She tucked down again, following the charade even to the point of snoring softly. I checked out the camera on the left and saw that it was indeed focused on us. From its vantage it would get a clear shot of my face, but Kirstie and Rink would be hidden. I forced myself to relax and ignore the scrutiny.

Ahead of us the traffic began a slow crawl and I could see where they passed through lanes not unlike those at regular toll roads, the difference here being that a structure stretched above them one side of the highway to the other, with observation windows lining it; smoked glass made it impossible to tell if anyone watched from inside. It was more like driving into an underpass than most border crossings I'd ever been through. Nearing it, I noticed the steady flow of pedestrians making their way in and out of the country via turnstiles and walkways behind tall metal railings. Hundreds of Mexicans – possibly thousands – worked on the Arizona side of Nogales and must traverse the same route on a daily basis. It would be just another mundane facet of their day and something that they performed by routine. I watched for anyone who did not move at the same pace as the others, but no one stirred my suspicion. Checking my rear-view, there was no sign of the van or our friends. Probably that was a good thing considering we still held the attention of the observation camera. I rolled on, approaching the gate, with a dust-sheathed bus spewing diesel fumes from its exhaust alongside the car. Traffic cones directed me into a bottleneck, but there was no option but to press forward. Cars were stalled ahead and behind now, and if anything should kick off we'd be stuck. Still, I didn't fear ambush here at the crossing; not where armed Border Patrol officers were stationed, so again I forced myself to relax.

When it came to it, a bored-looking uniformed woman, who barely glanced at the documents I flashed, flagged us through the crossing. It was good that our concerns had been unwarranted, but almost too easy. Then we were in that short strip of no man's land and facing the Mexican side. Whereas the US port of entry had the look of most other utilitarian governmental buildings, the Mexicans had erected two large interconnecting arches that reminded me of a seagull's wings in flight. It was beautiful in its own way. It was also anomalous when compared to the backdrop of the older structures around it, painted in pastel colours, and a complete contradiction to the hovels in near sight on the crests of hills to the east. Again we passed beneath the seagull's wings with no trouble. I immediately began checking for cameras swinging our way, but it appeared we were no longer under scrutiny. The road opened before us and I gave the rental gas, moving away quickly should anyone decide to take a second look. I couldn't say why I was worried – apart from the relative ease with which we'd entered the domain of our soon to be enemy – but I had developed that itchy feeling on the back of my neck that we were in someone's sights. Usually when the old spider sense strikes, it's something I pay close attention to. Yet, there and then I was relieved to be moving, heading for the prearranged meeting place we'd set up with Harvey. The only thing that would ease the feeling was having my gun back where it belonged.

8

We followed Mex 15 south, and pulled into the parking lot of a freight company beyond the outskirts of Nogales. The dusty lot was lined with empty cargo containers, but its fleet of trucks must have been out on the roads. Parking out of sight of the office buildings, we waited until the panel van drew alongside and approached as Harvey alighted from it. Across an unpaved road was the entrance to a water park that also offered paintball ranges on a chunk of fallow land beyond the pools and water slides. Business didn't appear great today and if we were noticed, an untrained observer would think the weapons we began to unload to the trunk of the car were paintball guns. I checked the action of my SIG before slapping in a magazine, and inserting the gun in its usual carrying position. Already I felt much better.

'You know the route you have to take for Hermosillo, right?' Harvey asked.

I tapped my head. 'Up here, buddy.'

'We can take the lead if you like, but I'm guessing that you'd prefer us to cover your ass?'

'Yeah. Did you catch any attention back at the checkpoint?'

'None.'

I told him about the CCTV cameras filming our progress across the border.

'Chance?' he offered, but I could tell his take on that was the same as mine.

'If someone is on to us, you can bet it's not good news. I'd prefer it if you guys held back here and let us get a head start; see if anyone is following our trail.'

'I'll let Velasquez and McTeer know.'

'OK, we'll get back on the road.' I checked my wristwatch and it was later than I'd assumed. We planned to be at Hermosillo by daybreak, in order to launch surveillance on Molina's compound. With an idea of his day-to-day activities, we might find an early opportunity to snatch Benjamin from under his nose. This time tomorrow, I fancied we would have a plan in place, but not if we dawdled.

'Gimme the keys, brother.' Rink held out a hand.

I didn't mind handing over driving duties, so I tossed them to him. Kirstie eyed me.

'You want me to climb up front and give you the back seat?'

'Nah, there's room for the two of us,' I said.

Rink and Harvey shared none-too-subtle smiles. Kirstie glared at them, but softened a touch as her cool grey gaze swept me top to toe. With a shrug, she climbed back in the car, hoisted the cooler box over the front headrest and placed it on the passenger seat. 'I hope you don't snore like your buddy.'

'You ain't heard nothing yet, girl,' Rink said. 'Think buzz-saw crossed with a rutting yak: that's Joe's snoring for you.'

'Ignore him. I don't snore.'

Rink and Harvey shared a look of disbelief.

'We'll see. Just be warned. I might not be responsible for how hard my elbow hits you if you do.'

'Fair enough,' I said with a grin. I gave my friends a stern look. 'Arseholes.'

Rink clapped Harvey on the shoulder in parting, offered McTeer and Velasquez a lazy salute and we set off, a long journey ahead of us. 'Wake me after four hours, Rink, and I'll spell you.'

'You got it,' he promised.

Yet it wasn't my friend who woke me hours later, but the anguished cry that broke from a woman's throat.

9

*A man was silhouetted against the full moon; his figure featureless
and flat, two-dimensional. He held a knife down by his right thigh,
the only thing about him that caught reflection. He aimed the knife
at Kirstie's throat.*

*She was running again, her feet sinking deep in loose sand that
threatened to hold her in its embrace. The baby she held tightly to her
chest further hindered her flight. The child was terribly silent and for
a moment Kirstie experienced sickness rising in her throat: what if
she had crushed the life out of the baby in her desperate attempt at
keeping him safe? She wanted to check that the boy was breathing,
but to do that she would have to halt, and the shadow man would
catch her. She ran, uttering moans and curses at the clinging sand.*

*Ahead of her loomed two massive boulders. Unlike the spectral
blue of the moonlit sands, these boulders were the red of copper, or
dried blood. A narrow gap offered flight between the towering
columns and she rushed towards them. In her peripheral vision the
shadows flickered as her stalker gained on her. If she could make it
through that narrow gap surely the shadow man would not pursue
her, because on that side assistance was waiting. There was black-
ness between the boulders, yet weirdly she could see through it, all
the way to the beckoning figure at the far end. She did not know
who her saviour was, couldn't make out his face, but his beckoning
arm was enough to tell her he was her lifeline. A ragged cry tore
from her throat and she ran on, her feet slipping and sliding now
in mud that had no place in this terrain.*

She tripped and fell.

To save the baby she twisted, and went down on one side, sliding in the deepening quagmire. She floundered to get up and in her haste the swaddled child flew from her grasp. Kirstie bit down on her bottom lip, straining to reach the child. Unable to grab the trailing blanket, she went to her hands and knees and scrambled forward, the mud now baked-hard clay as she toiled up an incline towards the sanctuary of the boulders. Almost as if the baby was attached to a line and the distant figure between the boulders reeled it in, the blanket continued to slide away from her grasp. She lunged and grabbed it, pulling the bundle tight to her chest.

Distantly a voice called to her.

The figure continued to urge her forward. In the swirling shadows she could make out eyes, at once blue, green and brown as though the colours shifted like the desert sand. She recognised those eyes, and she felt the burgeoning of hope.

She stumbled on, and now the rocks rose up on both sides. Yet the gap between them was too narrow, and so black she feared she'd been struck blind by fear.

But that didn't last.

Eyelids flickered open in the dark wedge where light failed to exist. The irises were the same pale grey as her own and those of the baby in her arms, a family trait. Kirstie stepped backwards; more afraid of this than anything that had gone before. The blanket was moving now against her body, and she looked down, hoping to find her baby boy squirming in her grasp. The baby was as inert as the desert around her. Naked, it was cold and hard to the touch. She stared at a porcelain face, the painted features cracked and crumbling to dust.

No, no, no . . .

The eyes in the darkness moved towards her, and the shadows formed and solidified around the knife it held. She opened her arms and the porcelain doll fell and shattered at her feet, as she invited in the blade that plunged towards her. Her cry of terror was not that she was about to die, but that she had failed her boy.

She continued to scream as her son, Benjamin, grown to manhood under his father's tutelage, rammed the blade deep into her throat, again and again.

10

Reaction made me reach for the gun in my waistband, but after a few seconds of mild panic I pushed back the fog of sleep and realised that Kirstie had merely cried out in her dreams. I noted the sweat pasting her auburn hair to her face, the rapid flicker of her eyelids as she continued to endure some horrendous nightmare. It was a second or so before I realised she was slumped across my lap, my left arm draped protectively over her.

'I didn't want to disturb you,' Rink said from the driving position, 'seeing as you were both so comfortable.'

'Jesus, Rink . . .' I slowly extricated my arm.

'Both of you sleeping like babies. Well, you were until something seemed to upset the lady.'

Whether it was our subdued conversation or some final dramatic act in her dream, Kirstie snapped awake. She was looking at my knees, and it was as if she wondered where the hell her nightmare had taken her now. She shot bolt upright and stared at me from the opposite corner of the car.

'Oh my God! I'm so sorry!'

'Hey, no problem,' I reassured her. 'If it's any consolation, I didn't even know you'd fallen asleep on me until a few seconds ago.'

Kirstie glanced accusingly at Rink, but my buddy merely grinned. Her scrutiny went back to me, and in particular my thighs. A dark patch stained the denim near my right knee.

'Oh, God! I drooled all over you.' She batted at the side of her face, embarrassed all to hell, as she sought to wipe away any incriminating evidence.

'That's a novelty for Hunter . . . women drooling over him.'

'Glad you find it funny, Rink,' I grumbled.

'Now you know what it's like to be me.' He broke into a loud crack of laughter.

The joke helped bring any further embarrassment to a stop, for both of us. I shook my head in mock disbelief. 'You'll get used to Rink soon enough, Kirstie. He has this inflated impression of his looks. When I look at him I see a bulldog chewing a wasp, but some women seem to find the rough-and-ready look attractive.'

'Don't confuse "rough-and-ready" with "rugged",' Rink said, still laughing.

'Or "rugged" with "conceited"?'

'No harm in believing in yourself, brother,' he countered.

To Kirstie I said, 'That's why he never wears a hat. He can't find one big enough for his head.'

The banter was serving its purpose. It alleviated Kirstie's embarrassment, but also pushed away the lingering memory of her dream. She tucked back her hair and reached for the cap that had fallen on the floor between my feet. As she leaned close I experienced a mild flutter of electricity that rode my body all the way to my throat, and my senses were filled with her closeness and the scent of her perfume. It was an intimate moment. Kirstie was staring at me, and I looked enquiringly.

'You OK?'

'You were in my dream.'

'I was?'

'Yes. But not like that.' She gently shoved Rink's shoulder with the heel of her palm. 'I was being chased.'

'By me?'

'No . . . someone else . . .' She didn't expound, but I noted a flicker of horror dart across her features again. 'But you were there. You were leading me to safety, but, well, I didn't make it.'

'Want to tell me who was chasing you?'

'I . . . I don't remember.'

Kirstie was lying, that was obvious, but I wasn't about to press her. My attention was drawn by Rink's soft hiss. I looked past him to lights in the road ahead. They were red lights, strobing off and on, interspersed by a blazing white that cut harshly into my retina. Someone stepped away from a car, waving a flashlight up and down, then directly on the front of our car. The torch bleached the windscreen; trail dust and dead bugs fogging the glass.

'Fucking inept cops,' Rink growled. 'You'd think they'd know better than blinding a goddamn driver. What does he want to do . . . run me off the goddamn road?'

Yeah, I thought, even an inept cop should be more careful than that.

I checked the position of my gun, ensuring that the tail of my shirt concealed it.

11

Having dozed for who knew how long, I had no clue where we were, other than it was somewhere remote. Still dark, with a patchwork of stars amid low cumulus clouds, the horizon was a meandering wave of hills and valleys, where only a few pinpoints of light showed habitation. On the opposite side sheer cliffs pushed for the heavens, broken fingers of stone interspersed by large and forbidding bulwarks. There were certainly no streetlights to illuminate the car sporting the gumball lights. Our headlights were countered by the strobing red and white, making the figure moving towards us appear to stutter in his stride with each flickering beam.

'What the hell is this all about?' Rink swayed uneasily as he applied pressure to the brake pedal.

'Whatever it is, I don't like it.' I pressed a button on my cell phone, sending a prearranged signal to Harvey a few miles back.

Kirstie looked fraught.

'Don't worry, just keep your head down like before and let me do the talking. Here . . . pull your cap down.' I eased the peak round so that it covered much of her face, even as she settled into the corner as if deep in slumber. The cop would have to lean down on my side to see Kirstie, and I'd do my best to block his view.

The flashlight beam stroked the windscreen, sending daggers of light inside.

'Asshole,' Rink said. 'He's deliberately trying to blind us.'

'Playing the big man, trying to intimidate us,' I muttered.

I ignored the approaching figure, peering into the deep shadows between the buttresses of rock nearby. Nothing.

'Son of a bitch!' Rink transferred his foot to the gas and pushed the car forward.

Immediately I snapped to battle mode, grabbed Kirstie and shoved her down into the space in the well behind Rink's seat. In the next instant I slipped out my SIG and racked the slide. Then I snatched a look to see what the fuss was all about.

The figure approaching us *was* deliberately blinding us, to conceal the shotgun he held braced to his shoulder with his opposite hand. As Rink pushed the car towards him, he had to move out of the way, drop the torch in order to get full control of the gun. He was wearing a uniform, I noted, but this was no random police stop. He fired the shotgun, and flame jetted through the air currents a full foot in length from the muzzle. Thankfully he was off balance and his shot ill-aimed. The lead pellets struck the top right of the windscreen, starring it, but the angle and velocity of the car helped redirect the shot up and away.

Rink yanked down on the wheel, aiming the car sideways at the cop, who had to leap for his life. He went down on his knees, but then twisted quickly and fired off another wild shot. Hitting the window button, I swung my SIG to cover him but was loath to shoot him. Despite firing on us, he was still a cop and out of bounds where my codes of practice were concerned. In the dark I caught only brief details of his uniform, but it appeared official – though I wasn't familiar with the local police dress code. Then again, his approach – not to mention his choice of weaponry, which I now recognised as a sawn-off pump-action shotgun – wasn't regular police tactics.

We tore away from him as Rink trod on the gas.

The cop fired another load of shot after us, and the dull concussion echoed through the car as the pellets struck the trunk. I checked Kirstie was unhurt. Her face was a pale oval, her eyes large and startled, but there was no hint of pain. Up close a sawn-off is a devastating weapon, but not much use against a car moving at speed.

Then we were flashing past his parked car, and there was nothing that marked it as an official police vehicle. It was a bottle-green pick-up truck, the wheel arches corroded. The rack of lights on top looked jerry-rigged, fed by a cable running through the open driver's window, probably to the cigarette lighter inside.

'That was no cop,' Rink said.

'What the hell was he then?'

'Carjacker? Robber? Beats me.'

'Probably not alone in that case.'

My words proved prophetic. A hundred yards ahead of us another pick-up truck burst from hiding in a ravine that cut like a knife slash through the cliffs. The headlights were dead, but only until the truck hit the highway and swung towards us. Then they flicked to high beam.

'Bastard!' Rink cried as the harsh light invaded our car.

Quickly checking behind, I saw the first man running for his vehicle, even as a third truck burst from concealment in our wake and accelerated after us.

'We should've expected something like this,' Rink growled. 'Especially after what happened at the border.'

Even though the cameras at the checkpoint had observed us, it didn't follow that an ambush should have been laid for us here. I trusted that Harvey or one of the others would have spotted an obvious tail, so there was no way anyone could have known where we were heading. This had to be random: robbers lying in wait for the unwary. Yet something about the scenario troubled me more than the prospect of fighting off armed thieves.

Rink ducked just as the windscreen exploded as a bullet struck the upper left corner. Chunks and slivers of glass rained over me, and out of instinct I squeezed my lids tight to avoid injury. When I looked again, the truck in our path was weaving side to side, attempting to block all lanes of the road. What did the driver think we were going to do? Stop?

Rink forced more speed from our rental, and I leaned past him.

'Ears,' I said in warning, a split second before my SIG cracked noisily. Rink didn't flinch but already he must have been half-deafened by the nearby blast. He gritted his teeth and powered directly at the truck, even as I continued to fire through the shattered windshield. Below me I could hear Kirstie's faint yelps with each empty shell that bounced across her shoulders. I watched where my bullets struck the other vehicle and tightened my grouping. Moments before I'd been reluctant to shoot; thinking the first figure was a cop. Now the rules had changed. I placed six rounds through the low corner of the windscreen exactly where a driver would be hiding behind the steering wheel. This time the truck shot across the shoulder at the side of the road and impacted with the cliff. The hood crumpled, the rear end thrown skyward, and a man was ejected from the bed, flailing in the air before he too struck the unforgiving rocks and moved no more. I doubted the driver had survived my bullets, and the likelihood was that any passengers would have been squashed when the cab was compressed to a quarter of its original dimensions.

Two vehicles were still pursuing us, and likely a number of armed and determined enemies, but now the road ahead was clear, and no way could they catch us. Not that I was ready to cheer just yet. I'm a firm believer in Murphy's Law, and if anything could go wrong it probably would. There are too many variables to rely on luck remaining on your side. A tyre could blow out, the engine could seize, or another third-party element could enter the fray, and slow us enough for our pursuers to catch up.

Or Rink could hit a one-eighty skid so that we again faced our enemies, which was precisely what he did.

Ordinarily the tactic would be madness, but I wasn't complaining. The only way we could be certain of escape from these determined attackers was to neutralise them and we couldn't do that while running away. With a screech of rubber on blacktop, the car shot towards the two oncoming vehicles. I hit the release on the magazine and it fell in the spare front seat, rattling across the cooler box. Then as Rink accelerated I slapped a fresh mag in place and readied the SIG for action. The first truck's gumball lights punched shards of conflicting hues across the cliffs that were now on our right. The third vehicle in their pack had overtaken the first, and was heading for us; illuminated by flashing lights were two men on the back who were holding long guns. One of them fired but the round was lost in the desert somewhere; then the second man opened up, which was more troubling. He was armed with a machine-gun and was rattling bullets at us on semi-auto. They walloped the front grill like a roll of thunder. The car shuddered with the impact, but kept moving.

Rink concentrated on driving. He had a gun in a shoulder rig, but to go for it now would compromise his control of the car. It was my SIG against a rifle and an MP5: not good odds.

'Give me a weapon,' Kirstie shouted. 'I can help.'

'You can help by keeping your head down,' I shouted over the continuous roll of my gun as I rapidly squeezed the trigger. Within seconds the slide locked back and I hit the mag release and slapped in a fresh one.

I had starred the windscreen of the oncoming truck, but hadn't got the driver this time. The men on the back fired at us, and I could hear their war cries over the roaring of engines and rattle of gunfire. Bullets shattered one of our headlights and tore chunks in the hood. Rink ducked and dived, avoiding bits of heated metal thrown through the open window.

'Drop that motherfucker with the machine-gun or we're dead!'

'That's what I'm trying to do!'

I leaned fully over the passenger seat so I had a clear view through the windshield, and loosed a close grouping of three rounds at the machine-gunner. Whether I hit him or not, I wasn't sure, but he disappeared, ducking down behind the safety of the cab.

Then we were swerving around the truck and I caught the pale flashes of passing faces both inside and on the rear of the truck. Four men in total, plus the bogus cop. Our odds weren't looking much better than before. We had to change things in our favour.

Rink pushed the car forward, steam now billowing out from under the buckled hood. I craned round, watching the truck driver perform a decent one-eighty turn. The gunners were up again and firing. It would take time to catch up with us, unless the damage to the engine of our car stalled it within seconds. Something under the hood was making a regular knocking noise, but then that could have been the bullets hitting the road beneath our wheels.

Kirstie struggled to move, but was jammed by my knees. She was reaching for her purse, and I had an idea she wasn't looking for her lipstick. 'Leave it alone, Kirstie. It's more important you keep out of the way than join in the fight.'

She struggled free, snapping at me, 'No one is going to stop me saving Benjamin!'

'A bullet in your goddamn skull will,' I snapped back, and I shoved her down, just as we came in range of the bogus cop. He was driving much slower, wary that we might try to ram him, and had poked the muzzle of the shotgun out of his window. Flame erupted from the barrel and lead peppered the rental. Something incredibly hot burned a furrow across my scalp and I knew that I'd been hit. Thankfully it was a glancing blow and the shot didn't embed itself in my cranium. Still, it was as if I'd taken a punch to my forehead and white sparks flashed through my mind. Blood began pouring across my features. I questioned the validity of the man's bloodline, cursing viciously as I batted blood from my eyes. Immediately I squared the muzzle of the SIG on the spot behind the shotgun and fired. My shots were wild and designed to halt a second blast from the shotgun. The driver hit the brakes, swerving on to the hard shoulder, then on to the soft sand: unfortunately he didn't collide with the cliffs the way his first buddies had.

In our engine something shrieked, and more steam hissed banshee-like from under the hood. The car bucked as it began to lose power. Then it bucked again and the engine went silent.

'Shit,' I said against the new hush.

The other truck was barrelling up behind us; on the back the gunmen rose up and the machine-gun and rifle spat fire.

12

The cliffs were our best hope of refuge, but at that moment we were rolling on tyres alone, and though Rink angled off the road we only made it a few yards before the front sank in the loose sand. Rink piled out of the door, pulling his gun from his shoulder rig, while I grabbed hold of Kirstie and yanked her up.

'OK, get your gun. Things have changed now.'

Kirstie snatched her purse, and I was already ducking out of the door. Our saving grace was that we still had the car side on to the approaching gunmen, but that advantage would last seconds only. I helped Kirstie out, then pushed her down behind the wheel, to offer some protection: the car's body wouldn't halt a round, and Rink had already claimed the spot behind the engine.

I took a quick look over the trunk, saw the truck had slowed and the men on the back were searching for targets. Beyond them, the bogus cop had abandoned his vehicle and was jogging towards the fight. But that was all I got of the scene; I snatched my head down as bullets caromed from the roof of the car, spinning wildly away among the nearby cliffs. A second later, Rink returned fire across the hood, and his bullets banged loudly as they struck the truck. Brakes screeched.

Kirstie was scrabbling through her belongings and came up holding the gun she'd chosen from the stash we'd brought with us. It was a Glock 19, a good fit for her hand. I watched her slip the clip out, check her load and then slap it back in place, before racking the slide. She knew her guns. But it was one thing shooting paper targets, quite another a living thing. Particularly when the living target was shooting back. 'Your safety's the most important thing, Kirstie. Only use your gun if you've no other option.'

Rink glanced our way.

'We're sitting ducks here. We gotta make it between those boulders back there. Go now. I'll cover you.'

I didn't wait. Propelling Kirstie before me, I headed for a fissure between the rocks. Bullets smacked the back end of the car, but already we were out of their line of fire and safe but for ricochets. By the time our attackers found a bead on us, I'd already pressed Kirstie down behind some boulders at the mouth of the narrow canyon.

'You OK?'

'I'm fine. But you . . . oh, my God! Your face looks horrible!'

'Now you're beginning to sound like Rink.' She didn't get the joke. I wiped the trickling blood off my features. 'It's nothing. Scalp wounds bleed like crazy, but I'm fine.'

To prove my point I bobbed up and fired half-a-dozen rounds at the truck and the men now crouching behind it. I didn't get a hit on one of our attackers, but that wasn't my purpose. Rink sprinted over and joined us while they kept their heads down.

'Fuckers are too determined for thieves,' he said, as he found a place from where he could return fire.

'They have to be my ex-husband's people,' Kirstie said.

I shook my head. Something about the scenario was troubling me. I didn't think these men had anything to do with Molina, or Benjamin, because there was no way they could've known where to launch an ambush on us. Besides, Molina would have sent more capable killers than these. There was something else happening here, but I agreed with Rink that they were too committed to be mere opportunistic thieves. They'd already lost more than they could ever achieve from continuing the attack. Perhaps they were so angered by the deaths of their friends in the first truck that the fight had grown personal.

More bullets chattered against the fissure walls, and the time for worrying about motive was over. What did it matter? They were attempting to kill us, and knowing the reason for that didn't amount to zero weighed against the need to stay alive.

Leaning out past the rocks, I checked their positions. The four men were down behind their truck, bobbing up and down like whack-a-moles on a funfair while they took pot shots at our position. I ignored them in favour of checking where the fake cop had gone. The son of a bitch had laid the trap, but now that things were becoming unhinged, he was heading back for his abandoned vehicle. He turned briefly and the moonlight flooded his features, giving me a first look at his face.

Two things struck me.

He was no Mexican.

And I recognised him.

A bullet cut a chunk from near my shoulder, and I ducked down. By the time I looked again, the fake cop had clambered inside his truck, and his face could no longer be seen. He reversed on to the road and took off in the opposite direction. His friends fell silent, wondering where the hell he was going, but their confusion only lasted a few seconds. The sound of another engine had joined the fray, and I was relieved to hear that our back-up was almost upon us. To help Harvey and the others gain a safe position where they could offer protection to our flank, both Rink and I began firing at the truck. Curses rang out loudly, all in Spanish.

The machine-gunner made another attempt at finishing us off, and we had to stay down until he'd expended the thirty-plus rounds in his magazine. But as his gun fell quiet, we took more pinpointed shots at them. His wild shooting had served a two-fold purpose: yes, he was trying to kill us, but it was also to cover his buddies as they got back inside the truck. Three of them had squeezed inside the cab, while the one with the machine-gun was in the process of climbing on the back. Rink shot him, a bullet through his left thigh. It hit only a second before mine took a sizeable portion of his skull. He performed a slow-motion tumble off the back of the truck like the bad guy in a Western movie swan-diving off a saloon roof.

Those inside the truck had had enough, especially now that they were outnumbered. They took off at speed, leaving their dead gunner lying on the asphalt in a widening pool of gore. His MP5 must have fallen on the bed of the truck as he'd toppled off. We studied him from our concealed position.

'I winged him so we'd have a live prisoner,' Rink said.

'Tell the truth. It was just poor shooting.'

Rink snorted out a laugh.

'Would've been good to find out what the fuck that was all about.'

'Maybe,' I concurred. 'But he was still capable of shooting, so I prefer him this way.'

It would have been handy to have a live prisoner. There was something decidedly odd about the attack, and answers from an injured man would've been welcome. However, what was done was done and not worth moaning over.

'Maybe we'll find something interesting on his body.'

'Go for it,' Rink said. 'You shot him, made all that mess, feel free to be the one to check through his clothing.'

'Since when were you so squeamish?'

'Since that CIA asshole executed that guy back at the mine,'

Rink said, his voice barely more than a whisper. 'You OK, Kirstie?'

She was shocked, not by what she'd just lived through as much as what she'd overheard. A question was building, but she couldn't yet find the words.

Stepping in quickly, I took her by an elbow, just as Harvey brought the panel van to a halt behind our abandoned rental.

'Come help me unload the car. We're going to have to travel on from here in the van.'

'Was Rink talking about Conrad? Did *he* execute someone?'

I chose words that weren't exactly a lie. 'Walter doesn't do any wet work. He's a sub-division director, who works out of an office at Langley.'

'Who also gives the orders,' she whispered. 'Which makes him as culpable as the one holding the gun.'

Any argument would have rung false, so I was glad when Harvey, McTeer and Velasquez all scrambled from the van for an update. I left Rink and Kirstie to bring them up to speed while I approached the dead man on the road. Most of the top of his skull was gone, but there was enough left of his face for me to recognise a local. He was swarthy, round-faced, pock-marked across both cheeks, and he had a large star tattooed on his neck. Gang tag, I assumed. His clothing was casual, mainly blue denim but for a cotton T-shirt and stained sneakers. Blood was all over him, and – not because I was repelled by its sight but because he could've been carrying a disease I'd no intention of catching – I used the barrel of my gun to push back his jacket to check the inside pockets for ID. There was none to find, but I did discover a billfold in his hip pocket. Inside it was a couple of grubby twenty-peso bills – which didn't amount to much – alongside a short stack of brand new US fifty-dollar notes that looked as if they'd come fresh from the bank. Ten in all. Five hundred bucks. The guy had sold his life cheaply.

The presence of the cash gave me a number of important clues. He wasn't a regular thief, reliant on taking our belongings to earn his living. Someone had paid him to take part in this ambush. I bet that similar sums of money had burned up with the bodies of those trapped in the crashed truck, now sending billowing flames up the front of the cliffs. For such a low sum, the person in charge had struggled to find competent killers, and had simply rounded up local gang boys willing to do the job. It told me that the ambush had been organised to catch us, yet was rushed and mishandled by the one in charge. The guy dressed in the police uniform was most likely responsible for the attack, and therefore our enemy.

'James Lee Marshall,' I whispered to myself. 'How the fuck did you end up here?'

13

'You know that punk with the shotgun?' Rink asked.

We were back on the road, streaking towards Hermosillo with the dawn breaking over the fields behind us. After cleansing our rental car of all identifiers, we'd torched it. The dead machine-gunner had been added to the pyre, seated in the driving position to confuse any investigation of the scene. When we got the chance I'd drop the rental company a call and tell them that the car had been stolen while parked outside a bar in Tucson – let them jump to conclusions of their own. Now, while Harvey, McTeer and Velasquez cluttered the front seats, the rest of us were in the back of the panel van, bruising our backsides on the wooden benches. I'd just told Rink and Kirstie about recognising the bogus cop.

'I only got a brief look at his face, but I'm pretty sure it was him.'

Back when I was still with the Parachute Regiment, the airborne infantry element of the British Army, I'd fought alongside an exceptional soldier named James Lee Marshall. I was a headstrong teenager, looking for a role model, and Marshall had been an inspiration and my best friend. He joined up before me, and had served with both 2 and 3 Para, gaining the experience to pass selection to 1 Para, the Special Forces Support Group. I was about eight months behind him on my career path, and by the time I was selected for a tour with SFSG, Marshall was already a legend among the lads. Our paths crossed occasionally, but following my promotion to sergeant, and leading my own unit, we were deployed to different theatres and our contact grew minimal. After I was recruited to Arrowsake I lost touch with him completely and gained a new best friend in Rink. I later learned that Marshall had lost the sight in one eye to an IED while working transport security following Desert Storm and had been medically discharged. I'd rarely thought about him over the intervening years, and had assumed that he'd been absorbed back into Civvy Street, had perhaps married and raised children. I hadn't expected him to turn up here in Mexico as some criminal's hired gun.

Then again, there but for the grace of God go I.

I've often pondered my choices over the years, and know how close I was to becoming something similar while hiring myself out as a problem-solver back in the UK. Even as I was bringing vigilante justice to the gangsters and hoodlums of my hometown of Manchester I consoled myself that I was only hurting bad people. I was righting the wrongs that the police were unable to touch. But I know that it's a subjective thing, and my code of honour would remain questionable to fainter hearts. Yet I stand by my decisions. I helped people who were unable to help themselves, taking the fight to those who would hurt them, and yes, sometimes my methods were unorthodox. But I'd never taken a criminal's money to hurt a woman desperately seeking to be reunited with her abducted child. That was the big difference between Marshall and me, it seemed, and he'd lost the right to be considered my friend. Now I could only think of him as an enemy.

I told them what I knew of his fighting prowess.

'That was a long time ago,' Rink said, unimpressed. 'He didn't come across as all that special. Way I saw it, he fucked up big style.'

'He underestimated us is what he did. I'm pretty certain he

didn't know who – or what – he was up against, and miscalculated the number of gunmen he needed to finish us. Think about it: most drivers, unprepared and taken in by the lights and the police uniform, would've been sitting ducks. He'd have taken them out as they sat wondering why the police had stopped them. It's why he chose a sawn-off. One shot would have ripped through the interior of the car and probably got everyone inside with one blast. It was pure luck that you spotted the gun and realised what he had in mind.'

'Lucky, yeah,' Rink agreed. 'I suppose if he hadn't been juggling that flashlight as I hit the gas, things might've turned out differently.'

Kirstie was watching us from below the peak of her cap. Her jaw was set in thought.

'How'd he know where to lay his ambush?' she asked.

'I've been thinking about that,' I said.

'And?'

'If he's involved with the people who were monitoring us at the border, I guess they could've plotted our route across country from there. That's supposing they know where it is we're going, and why.'

'And if he isn't? There was nothing random about that ambush. I haven't your experience, but it's clear to me they were waiting to ambush and murder *us*.'

'Let's hope that he isn't on Molina's payroll or snatching Benjamin's going to be impossible,' Rink said.

'He has to be working for Jorge . . . who else could it be?'

I had another idea. 'Give me your purse, Kirstie.'

'My purse? Why?'

But she handed over her handbag and I emptied the contents on the floor of the van. 'Anything among that stuff you don't recognise?'

Kirstie shook her head. There were the usual items you'd

expect a woman to carry. I concentrated on the bag, checking zipper compartments, running my fingers along the stitched seams. I found nothing unusual.

'Your carry-on bag next,' I said, handing over her purse so that she could shovel her belongings back inside. She snatched up a couple of tampons that she palmed out of sight with sleight of hand.

'What exactly are you looking for?'

'Your bag, please?'

She put two and two together. 'You think that someone slipped a tracking device inside it?'

'It'd be one way of knowing which route we took, and plotting where to ambush us along the way.'

'But who'd have the opportunity? You've been with me since I got off the airplane in Tucson.' She hit me with a challenging stare, almost as if I was the one under suspicion.

'Let's not jump to any conclusions until we know for sure there is a bug, eh?'

My examination of her bag was more thorough this time, because her carry-on was more likely to have been compromised than her purse. On the flight, she would have slung it in an overhead compartment, and there'd have been an opportunity to slip a bug inside it. It would explain why I hadn't spotted the watchers I'd expected when shadowing Kirstie at the airport and beyond: why chance being seen when they could monitor her movements from afar? It was all sound logic, except there was no device. I checked her cell phone, but found nothing unusual about it, and even Molina wouldn't have the necessary contacts to infiltrate her cell network provider to continually track her position.

I handed back the phone.

'What now?' Kirstie asked, her mouth curling into a smile. 'A full body search?'

'No need for that.' I got a look from Rink that said: 'Spoil-sport'. 'You might want to check your pockets and collar, just in case someone slipped a bug on to them when your clothes were still in your carry-on bag.'

'What exactly am I looking for?'

'It'll be small, probably with a wire aerial attached. I think you'll know if you find anything out of place.'

Kirstie ran her hands through her trouser pockets, then she leaned forward for me to check her blouse collar. Everything came up clean.

'So there isn't a bug?' Rink said.

'Not one that I can find.' Giving Kirstie my own cheeky smile, I said, 'Maybe you should check your smalls next opportunity you have.'

She rolled her eyes, but her exasperation was an act. 'I showered and changed back at the motel. I'm pretty sure I'd have spotted trailing wires coming out of my underwear.'

'When you two are finished flirting, maybe you'll start thinking a little straighter.'

I was about to deny the flirting, but, actually . . .

'I think we've established that you're not bugged, Kirstie,' Rink said, 'but there's something we haven't considered.'

'The rental car?' It was obvious when I thought about it.

I'd left it parked at the airport hotel while we took Kirstie in the van to our hotel in the sticks. Only once she was safely in the lodge and we'd made our plans had I gone back to fetch it. If anyone following Kirstie witnessed our actions when bundling her in the van, they could quite easily have attached a transmitter to the car they'd seen me arrive in. We had been certain we weren't under surveillance, but what other answer was there? The reckless attack by Marshall and his cronies made me think our enemies amateurs. Now I had to reconsider. I banged on the panel separating us from the cab. 'Stop the van first chance you get, Harve.'

'What's wrong?' The separating wall muffled Harvey's voice.
'Hopefully nothing.'

Within a few seconds the van decelerated and angled off
the road. The tyres rumbled over rougher ground, the bumps
and jerks shaking our bones through the bench seats. The van
swayed as it came to a halt. I opened the back doors. 'If anyone
wants to stretch their legs, now's a good time.'

I got out, followed by Kirstie and Rink. Without me having
to ask, Velasquez appeared on the right, followed a moment
later by McTeer, taking up positions where they could view
the road from both approaches. Sometimes I forgot how valuable they were as colleagues, but this time I was glad they were
along. Harvey opened his door and stepped out. I don't know
how he did it, but he always looked pristine, as though a
personal style expert had just dressed him. In comparison, I
felt like a mess, what with the dried blood on my shirt from
my earlier head wound, and my clothes being rumpled and
stained. Made me wonder if Harve had a grooming kit in his
laptop bag, because he was even freshly shaved, and, as he
approached, I got a waft of expensive cologne.

'How sure can you be that the van wasn't compromised?'
I asked.

Harvey gave it some thought. 'There was a time when we
were all inside the motel just after Velasquez and Mac arrived
when someone could have got to it,' he admitted. 'Why, what
are you worried about?'

'Tracking devices.'

'To put a bug on the van, they'd have to have known where
we were in the first place. You think someone followed us back
to the motel?'

I wasn't thinking that way, but it wasn't yet time to voice my
concerns.

Rink was making his way round the van, crouching and

feeling along the sills and wheel arches, the easiest places for someone to attach a magnetic device. To spare Harvey's neat clothing, I went down on my back and checked the undercarriage. I didn't expect to find anything and didn't. Rink had finished his check with similar results.

'The van was locked the whole time we were inside,' Harvey pointed out, 'and they couldn't have got under the hood without triggering the alarm. I don't think they got to the van.'

I stood staring up at the sky. The sun was coming up behind me, making the sky overhead a pot-pourri of pastel shades while the western horizon was wreathed in purple haze. The contrail from a jet liner had broken apart, making a dotted line through the heavens. The highway was deserted, bordered on either side by tilled fields, with distant buildings marking small farmsteads. A few goats grazed on scrubby grass; nothing else moved that I could see. But that didn't mean they weren't there. I'd had similar misgivings when Kirstie had first arrived in Arizona: that someone was watching her beyond my ability to spot them. I caught a look of realisation from Rink. He stalked over, nodding me out of earshot of Kirstie. 'The van was supplied by Walter. You think the old bastard has been monitoring our movements?'

'He doesn't need to,' I reminded him. 'Walt knows where we're going and what we intend doing when we get there. He can call us any time for an update. Plus, why would he organise an ambush and try to have us killed? If he had, he wouldn't have sent one soldier and a bunch of local gangbangers.'

'I suppose you're right. But we have to consider something else.' He stabbed a finger at the van. 'That van *is* from a CIA pool.'

'You think the Agency got wind of Walter's private mission, and sanctioned the hit on us by Marshall?'

'Just a suggestion.'

'But why would they want us to fail?'

'Who knows what operations they're involved in concerning the various cartels. Perhaps they don't want us blundering into the middle of an op they've got going concerning Molina.'

'Bit extreme having us killed, isn't it? They could quite easily have followed legal protocols and had us arrested by the genuine police.'

'Walter's not the only one with enemies inside the Agency,' Rink said. 'There are certain individuals who would prefer to see us dead. Maybe they saw this as the ideal opportunity to kill us and strike a blow against Walt.'

Pondering those words we joined the others by the van. I waved everyone together, while Rink took over sentry duty from Velasquez and McTeer.

'There's a possibility that the van has a tracker inside somewhere, but without tearing it to pieces we'll never find it. The thing is, we can't abandon it. Not yet. We still need to get to Hermosillo fast. From here we're going to have to be alert at all times, because you can bet your arse there'll be another attempt on our lives. If you need the toilet, I suggest you go now, because we're not stopping again until we reach Hermosillo.'

Kirstie checked out the flat land, where the tallest obstacle nearby was a boulder the size of a basketball poking from the gritty earth. 'I think I can wait.' She climbed inside the back of the van, allowing the men privacy to go through with the necessities.

Taking my own advice, I took a leak on the shoulder of the road. Back in the van, Kirstie was holding her Glock in her lap. I didn't comment, or ask her to put it away. If further attack were imminent, we'd need all the firepower we had.

14

Hermosillo was a huge city, but then it is the capital of Sonora State. It was spread throughout a natural basin, dotted with large rock formations – one of them known locally as The Bell standing proud over the city, adorned by twin telecommunication towers that blinked with aircraft warning lights in the early-morning haze. To look at the city's location with a different eye, I could imagine that this was once an inland sea, and the rock formations islands that spotted its surface. But then what did I know of prehistoric Mexico? The city was a mixture of high culture and extreme poverty. On the one hand there was the neo-Gothic Cathedral of the Assumption, the neoclassical Government Palace, and the grand façades of the Museum of Sonora, and on the other, tenement buildings and humble adobe structures both decrepit and overcrowded. The place was known as the Sun City, but I wondered how often its poorer denizens actually lifted their heads from abject poverty to view the brilliance above them. I made a silent bet that Jorge Molina lived in opulence while making his living from the subjugation of those poorer souls. There he would find the customers for his drugs, the girls for export to the sex trade, and the footsoldiers of his private army. I hated him passionately.

That I was growing to admire his ex-wife so much may have been a factor.

Following the incident earlier, those of a faint-hearted

disposition would have succumbed to anxiety, even hysteria. But Kirstie had grown more resolute. Maybe she had inherited some of the grit from her grandparents, who could not have survived as long in their positions with the CIA without having staunch hearts. Or perhaps I was underestimating the love of a mother for her child.

The van was parked on a shoulder of dirt high on one of the ancient islands, so that we could observe the city before driving in later. If indeed the van's position was being monitored, no one had tried a second assault on us during the drive here. On the outskirts of the city it was unlikely we'd be troubled too much so we'd taken the opportunity to stretch our legs, and consume some of the food and drink we'd fetched. Having eaten a sandwich and gulped down a bottle of water, Kirstie had retreated inside the van, as much to escape the burgeoning heat as from fear of discovery.

Having had my fill of the view of Hermosillo, I climbed back inside to find Kirstie sitting on the bench seat she'd occupied since losing our car. Her Glock was pushed into her waistband, at the back, mirroring my usual carrying position. She was staring into space, her mouth slightly open, the tip of her tongue dancing from one tooth to the next. I took it that she was not in the mood for company. I was about to back out of the van when she looked directly at me and smiled. It would have been rude to leave.

'This is it, Joe,' she said. 'The point of no return, eh?'

I came to sit next to her.

'Yeah. This is where things begin to get dangerous,' I said with no hint of irony.

Her chuckle was strained, but she shifted, squaring her shoulders, subconsciously showing that she was ready for any challenge. Her shoulder touched mine, but she didn't move away. Neither did I. In the close confines of the van her perfume was heavier, a musky edge to it, and my eyelids closed as I savoured it. I exhaled, and Kirstie perhaps mistook the sigh for concern.

'Do you think everything will be OK?'

Her face was inches from mine.

'We must have faith.'

'In God?'

'In whatever gives you strength,' I corrected.

'You're talking about the abilities of you and your friends.'

Pinching my lips, I nodded slowly.

'You're pretty sure of yourself. I don't mean that as an insult, Joe.'

'I didn't take it as one. Maybe I can come across as rather conceited, but unless you're certain of your abilities you shouldn't be in this kind of business.'

'I wish I was as confident.'

'Of us?'

'Of myself,' she corrected.

'You're doing just fine.' I patted her knee, then quickly withdrew my hand for fear she'd misconstrue the gesture.

'Am I? Maybe it doesn't show but I'm terrified. Not for myself. I'm terrified for Benjamin and what he might become if we fail to rescue him from Jorge.'

'That's only natural.'

'Are you ever afraid?'

'In situations like this? All the time.' I hung my head, wondering if I'd just admitted a truth I shouldn't have. Kirstie required a fearless champion, not someone who admitted to weakness. 'But fear is good. Fearlessness can make you reckless, whereas a healthy regard for your life keeps you alert. Soldiers learn to embrace their fear, to control it, and use it to take the war back to their enemies with more determination.'

'That's rather philosophical,' she said. 'How do you do that when you can barely think straight, your stomach's in a knot and you can't stop your hands from shaking?'

If a soldier had asked that question there'd have been one answer: suck it up. But these circumstances demanded a different approach. 'You think of your kid, and you do it for him.'

Her eyes glossed with tears. 'That's what I'm trying to do . . . but it doesn't seem to be working.'

'I think that when it comes to the crunch you'll surprise yourself, Kirstie.'

'I hope you're right, Joe.' She placed a hand on my forearm, her fingers gripping tightly. 'But right now I really need the reassurance. Will you do something for me?'

'Yeah, of course, what is it?'

'Will you please hold me?'

'Sure.'

I opened my arms and Kirstie moved into their embrace, pressing her face into my chest so that the cap fell off and her hair spread over my shoulder. She held on tightly, her shivering detectable wherever she was pressed to my body. There was nothing sexual about the embrace, just one human being seeking solace in the closeness of another. A moment later the sobbing began, and I adjusted my arms to hold her tighter, to help her through the moment of heartache. My left hand fell on her hair and I smoothed it over her ear and brow, even as I told her that everything would turn out just fine. We remained that way for perhaps some minutes before her weeping subsided and she stopped shaking. Slowly, as if unsure of herself, she lifted her face. I felt her breath on my lips and it was my turn to shiver. The tips of her fingers traced the wound on my scalp, before trailing down my cheek to my jaw. I exhaled a pent-up breath, and she opened her mouth as if to accept it. To ease its passage I leaned in and our lips brushed. I felt an electric spark jump between us, and gave in to the inevitable attraction. I've loved women before – my ex-wife Diane, Kate Piers, Imogen Ballard – but it was a long time since I'd kissed anyone the way I surrendered to Kirstie's mouth.

Hell if I know where that kiss would have led if Rink hadn't chosen that moment to bang on the side of the van.

'Time to roll,' he called loudly before coming round to the open doors.

By the time he appeared, I was on the opposite bench, scratching my head as though checking out my wound, while Kirstie had pulled the cap back on. Rink said nothing, but he knew. He spared our blushes for as long as it took for Kirstie to feign sleep once more, then he dug me in the ribs with an elbow and showed me his best shit-eating grin. I grinned back like a besotted teenager.

15

'Getting in is going to be difficult. Getting out could be impossible.'

Raul Velasquez sat down at the café table I'd commandeered in a market square in an old part of the city. I'd ordered him a Coronita, just the one light beer, because we needed our full wits about us. A wedge of lime had been jammed in the neck, and Velasquez used the fleshy part of his thumb to press it further into the liquid. He took a long draught of the cold beer as I considered his words. My own beer was about half finished, but I didn't touch it for now. From the doorway of the restaurant an elderly man was being over-attentive, and each time I reached for the bottle he took a step forward, anticipating another sale.

'Numbers?' I asked.

'Best guess is around a dozen. Not all of them are footsoldiers, some of them are staff. And that doesn't include Molina or his father. Unfortunately I didn't get a look at either of them.'

'Supposing that they have six house staff, that leaves at least eight guns to contend with.'

'Perhaps more. I was only able to count those I saw, but there could have been others inside. One of the house staff has to be considered a bogey as well. He's a chauffeur, but most of those guys double as bodyguards.'

'Did you see the kid?'

Velasquez shook his head.

I reached for my beer. 'We need to go back.'

Velasquez had been the obvious choice to run first surveillance on Molina's home. He could pass as a local in a way that none of the rest of us could. An ex-cop and practising PI, he had experience of conducting surveillance, but that was with a law enforcement eye and not military. He'd said that it would be difficult getting inside the walled complex, impossible to get back out again, but he was talking from a cop's perspective. Rink and I and, to a lesser extent, Harvey, came with a different skill set, and had experience of infiltrating and escaping enemy strongholds.

Taking up his beer, Velasquez quaffed the contents in one long swig. I took some dollars from my pocket, waving for the waiter. He looked disappointed that we weren't going to add a second round, or better still a full meal, but remained professionally polite; smiling and thanking me for the tip I loaded on top.

We headed out of the market square, passing stalls selling everything from fruit and vegetables to pirated copies of the latest Hollywood movies and pop hits. Here in this older quarter of the city the houses had a colonial style, with balustrades at the upper floors, arched doorways, and plaster façades. Each building was painted a different colour from the pastel palette, with the occasional vibrant canary yellow, magenta or rust red. A few were even a dull grey, never having seen the application of paint, the plaster webbed by cracks, and the odd bare patch under which the original brick showed through. But they were more interesting to me for their shabbiness.

Around us the street was teeming with activity, mainly locals making the most of the market, but there were plenty of white faces in the crowd too. Tourists were more common now in Mexico and often strayed further than the beachside resorts and pyramids. It helped me blend in, but it also gave equal opportunity to the likes of Marshall, or other mercenaries. As we walked I engaged in counter-surveillance techniques, but saw nothing that caused worry. Velasquez was also looking, but from his easy chatter I took it that he hadn't spotted a tail either.

There were police officers on the sidewalks, toting side-arms. Some of them looked like fresh-faced kids, but others were tough veterans. I noticed that their uniforms weren't the same as the one Marshall had dressed in for the ambush. He'd underestimated his enemy: always a bad thing. But I shouldn't underestimate him either. He would have expected the charade to last as long as it took to blast the occupants of the car with his shotgun, and after that it wouldn't have mattered if we'd seen through his deception.

'Were Molina's guards on high alert?' I asked.

'They were disciplined, if that's what you mean, but no, I wouldn't say they were on edge.'

'So Marshall isn't working for him, then. He'd have reported his failure to stop us out in the desert; Molina would have strengthened his defences.'

'Looks that way to me,' Velasquez said.

'Which begs the question: Who the fuck *is* Marshall working for?'

'Maybe we're missing the obvious. What if the ambush was just what it first looked like: robbers? There's nothing to say your old buddy isn't working for the gang that attacked us.'

I thought about the stack of brand-new US dollars in the machine-gunner's possession, and begged to differ. Plus, Marshall had led those punks, he wasn't just another hired thug brought in to bolster their number.

We turned into another street, this one lined with restau-rants, gift shops and street traders with their wares spread on blankets and tarpaulins on the ground. There were even more people than in the market. Kids darted through the throng of tourists. Some of them were pestering the rich Yankees for change, while others were more furtive about the way they earned their cash. I'd have walked with one hand on my wallet, but I was more concerned about the gun in my waistband. I noticed that Velasquez crossed his arms over his chest, holding tight to the gun hidden under his left armpit. There were fewer police in evidence here, unless they were undercover. I kept a discreet eye on the kids, because if anybody could spot a plain-clothed cop it would be them.

We reached the far end of the street without incident, moving into an open square, at the centre of which stood a fountain. There was a statue of a Mexican general astride a horse, but he wasn't an historical figure I recognised. Tourists were posing in front of the statue while their friends snapped photographs. I disregarded them as I scoped the rest of the square. The crowds were less dense here, but there were dozens of people sitting at tables outside the cafés that lined the square's perimeter. Later, I guessed, the punters here would sample stronger delights than the coffee and soft drinks they nursed now. Many were reading newspapers, or fiddling with cell phones and e-book readers, but many others were content to people-watch. It made things more difficult to spot surveillance. But not impossible. I caught the eye of a man who was paying more attention to me than I warranted. Practised as I was in counter-surveillance, I allowed my gaze to wander away, kept my face immobile, as if I hadn't noticed the scrutiny. But I was the proverbial duck on a pond, outwardly calm but paddling furiously beneath the surface. The sudden rush of adrenalin wasn't simply because I'd spotted a watcher, but because, as with Marshall, I recognised the man's face.

'Velasquez.' I said his name softly to elicit a natural response, and he turned his head to me with less than mild curiosity. To the observer we would look like two friends in conversation.

'We've a shadow. White guy, early forties, wearing denims and a grey shirt, at nine o'clock.'

Velasquez was experienced enough to avoid looking for the man.

'Cop?' he asked, as we continued nonchalantly across the square. 'Or one of Molina's men?'

'Neither,' I said. 'He's another guy from my army days.'

'He recognise you?'

'Without a doubt.' In the split second that our gazes had stuck, I noted the involuntary widening of the man's eyelids. He was as surprised to see me as I was him.

'You think he's working for that Marshall dude?'

'Without a doubt.'

Ian McAdam was another para with whom I'd served, but I had never seen eye to eye with him. Last time I'd met the surly northerner we'd parted on unfriendly terms, primarily due to the fact that the imprints of his two front teeth were embedded in my forehead after I nutted him.

If you find a gold coin on your path, it's human nature to scan the ground for more. The same with bent pennies, and I began checking for other faces from my past. My memory wasn't jogged, but I saw another watcher furtively steal into the doorway of a gift shop as we approached. This man I didn't know, but I knew what he was. Even as he concealed himself behind a curtain of hanging shawls on display, I saw him touch the hidden microphone and whisper an urgent message. I took it that McAdam was filling him in on who and what I was.

I purposely kept my face turned away, not to hide my features, but to see the man's reflection in the window of a shop opposite. As we moved past he craned out to get a better look, perhaps checking for signs of weapons.

'What do you want to do about this?' Velasquez whispered.

'We can't forget why we're here. This is about saving a little boy. But while we're under surveillance by other potential enemies that makes our task more difficult.'

'That's what I'm thinking. You think it's time we lose these jokers?'

'No. I think it's time we find out what the fuck they're doing here.'

'You want to front them?'

'You good with that?'

'I'm good.'

'Be careful. McAdam's an ex para, so he'll be no slouch. I don't know anything about the other one but we have to assume he's got skills as well.'

'Could be others,' Velasquez pointed out. He didn't appear perturbed by the odds, but Velasquez had been a narcotics cop in the meanest districts of Miami and Tampa, so facing down a few tough guys was nothing to fret about.

'There'll definitely be others.' We couldn't make the mistake of going in overconfident. 'But we only need one of them . . .'

I outlined my plan as we walked from the square and into a narrower street, watching all available reflective surfaces – a shop window here, the chrome fender on a car there – to make sure our tails were still in place. Then at a crossroads, Velasquez went left and I went right. I was happy a few seconds later to note that only one of the men had followed me, happier still when I paused to peer in a gift-shop window and caught sight of my pursuer stumbling to a halt and then attempting to conceal himself in a doorway. McAdam never had been the shy and retiring type. He was a loudmouth, the kind who walks swinging his shoulders and with a get-the-fuck-out-of-my-face attitude. They weren't traits conducive to good undercover work. He was struggling to keep a low profile, and why he never guessed that I'd made him surprised me. I wondered how he'd managed to stay alive all these years.

16

Walking with determination, as if I had a destination in mind, ensured that McAdam tripped over himself in his haste to follow. Because he hadn't yet crept up and tried to sink a blade in my liver, his instructions must have been to watch me, find out where I was going, and report back to whomever was in charge. That would be Marshall, because McAdam had always been sycophantic around him. Supposing that Marshall was hiring himself out as a merc these days, it was fair to conclude that he'd bring along a few of his old cronies for the ride.

Having no prior idea of the layout of the city, I was looking for somewhere out of sight of the throng of civilians before fronting McAdam. He might not be willing to answer my questions, and the sort of encouragement I had in mind didn't need witnesses. I was in a narrow street now, away from the tourist area, and the cafés here didn't sell designer coffee. Locals sat inside small openings that reminded me of lock-up garages – complete with roller shutter doors – around small wooden tables on which stood bottles of unbranded tequila and whisky. As I walked past they watched me indifferently with hooded eyes. There were few people out in the street, and I bet myself that McAdam was having a difficult time now that he couldn't lose himself in the crowds. I made things easier for him by facing forward and walking without a care.

A doorway on my left presented the opportunity I was looking for. As if this was the place I'd been intent on reaching

I entered it, then slowed as I walked down a narrow alleyway, giving McAdam an opportunity to view me from the alley mouth. Underfoot the cobbles were greasy and stained with spillage from trashcans. Fresh air didn't enter this place that often, and the atmosphere was stuffy and foul. I rounded a bend, but placed my shoulders to the wall, listening. There was a faint mumble, as if McAdam was reporting his location to his buddies over a comms link like the other man had worn. His step was furtive as he followed me down the alley: not so self-confident now.

I hurried down the next section, passing blank walls of once-white adobe, stained yellow with neglect. More trashcans and a larger plastic Dumpster overflowed with refuse. At the far end was a doorway, the wood cracked and flaking with dry rot. Reaching it seconds later, I pulled the door open. It resisted me, made a loud creak, then stuck where the warped wood caught on the cobblestones. That served my purpose. I left the door open, but retraced my steps and ducked in behind the Dumpster. I felt for my gun, loosening the grip of my waistband, but not yet pulling it out. Then I waited, breathing slow and easy.

There was a moment when I thought McAdam had chickened out, unhappy to pursue me further into the warren of alleys. But then I understood that he was simply being prudent. He had to have heard the creaking of the gate, assumed that I had gone through it, but was sensible enough to check before bolting round the corner. There was the pad of feet on cobbles. McAdam was breathing heavily, panting as he spoke into his comms mike. I couldn't make sense of the words, but I got the drift from the string of expletives that followed. He began to pick up pace.

The last thing I wanted was for him to make it through the gate; a quick glance outside had shown that it led directly on to a street, where we could be spotted. Voices filtered into my hiding place, directly through the wall against which I crouched. It sounded like another of those drinking dens judging by the ribald voices raised in argument. I didn't want a group of drunks spilling into the street to watch what was about to happen. I timed each approaching step, preparing for action.

Immediately McAdam loomed in front of me I came out of my crouch, coming up silently in his wake as he hurried for the gate. If my objective was to kill him, I could have done so, without fuss, probably without him even realising I was there, but that wasn't my purpose. I flat-armed him with both palms against his left shoulder. Thrown off balance, he had only one place to go: into the juncture between the open door and the wall to which it was hinged. He hit hard, rebounding amid a shower of flaky adobe knocked loose from the wall. I threaded my hand inside his exposed left elbow, hooking his forearm in the bend of my arm, and used the locking of his shoulder to propel him round and out of the gap between door and wall. Stunned by the collision with the wall, he offered no resistance as I bore down on his locked arm and threw him at the cobbles. He went face down, arms and legs splayed, like a starfish out of water. With one eye on him, and happy that he hadn't been toting a weapon, I quickly thrust shut the door to block any inquisitive passers-by.

By the time I moved back to him, McAdam had got his arms under himself and was pushing to his knees. Shoving a heel against his backside, I pushed him deeper into the alley, only then slipping out my SIG. He was relatively unhurt, but his ego had been dealt a heavy blow. He snarled and cursed as he swung over to reposition his feet. I snatched the earpiece and mike set, gave him another nudge of my boot, this time in the chest, and he went down on his backside, blinking up at the gun I held. Give him his due: he didn't try to bluff his way out of the situation.

'You going to shoot me, Joe?' he said in a whining Glaswegian tone.

'Only if you don't tell me why the fuck you're following me.'

'That's good of you. But what if I haven't got anything to say about that?'

I shrugged, aiming my SIG at his crotch. 'Then I'll shoot you for old times' sake.'

'You're still holding a boner over *that*? Fuck, mate, that's old news. Shit, I haven't even thought about Mel Green in twenty years. You seen her? I bet she's fat and grey with half-a-dozen bastard kids running round her feet.'

Actually Melanie Green had died of a heroin overdose less than two years after we'd fought over her. We were both nineteen years old at the time, young and stupid, and smitten by the perma-tanned dolly bird who served in the NAAFI bar. She'd been giving both of us the come-on and we'd fallen for her wiles. Drunk on watered-down lager we'd gone at each other, and afterwards McAdam was missing two front teeth, I'd a double indentation in my forehead, and Mel had gone off with another smooth-talking Scots lad called Graham Smith. She'd been the epitome of the camp tart and had earned the nickname of Naafi Mel, but this time the acronym stood for 'No Ambition and Fuck-all Interest'. Yeah, she was a tramp, but she didn't deserve the way she ended up. I decided to keep her sad fate to myself.

I said, 'I see you never got your teeth fixed.'

He poked his tongue through the gap. 'You think I'd hold a grudge because you knocked my teeth out? Shit, Hunter, are you forgetting the times you had my back in Belfast? Or I had yours?'

'That's what's bothering me, McAdam. Why are you my enemy now?'

He squirmed to a better position, so that he could hold out his open palms. 'Who said we were enemies? Do you see a weapon?'

'Don't play me for an idiot. You were following me on your buddy Marshall's orders. Don't deny it.'

'Marshall was your friend, too.'

'Only until he tried to blast me with a sawn-off shotgun. See . . . stuff like that makes me question the validity of old friendships.'

'In Marshall's defence, he didn't know it was you until things got out of hand.'

'So he did recognise me then?'

McAdam grimaced like a tourist with too much salt round the rim of his tequila glass.

'If he did, he didn't make an effort to call off the attack,' I went on. 'Kind of suggests he didn't give a fuck for our old friendship.'

'What would you have done in his shoes?'

'I wouldn't take a job where an innocent woman was caught in the crossfire.'

'Oh, yeah, I forgot. You always were the holier-than-thou type, weren't you? Don't talk shit, Joe. You've killed women before.'

Sadly it was true. When taking the war to terrorist strongholds it was an unfortunate fact that women – and occasionally children – caught a bullet or piece of shrapnel. I wasn't proud of the fact, but I'd never willingly have sighted either in my crosshairs. There were evil women, as murderous as men, dangerous with weapons and their wiles, but since I left the military I'd never come across one that I had to kill. Jimena Antonia Grajales a year or so back was a blemish on my tally card, but it was her pet hit man, Luke Rickard, who saw her off.

'You're admitting that it's the woman Marshall's after?'

'You're putting words in my mouth.'

'Would you prefer a bullet?'

'C'mon, Joe, we both know you aren't going to shoot me in cold blood.'

'Want to bet?' I aimed directly at his face. His mouth slid open, offering me the gap between his teeth as a target. 'If Marshall isn't after the woman, why attack us? Why have us followed now?'

McAdam showed me his palms again. 'You know I can't tell you that, Joe. There's a code us guys work by, and you *never* give up your sponsor.'

'That depends on the motivation.'

I didn't shoot him, just kicked him again, but it was enough to put him on his back. He blinked up at me, realising that the good ol' days were well and truly behind us.

'Now,' I said, aiming my gun at his gut, 'start talking or so help me . . .'

'Fuck you, Hunter. I'm telling you nothing.' McAdam scrambled to stand up, and I allowed him to get halfway before pressing the muzzle to his forehead. 'Fuckin' shoot me then,' he snapped. '*Just fucking do it!* If I tell you anything I can expect much worse than a clean bullet in the skull.'

I'd learned some of the atrocities the cartels employed to punish people – disembowelment, beheading, immolation, limbs hacked off and the victim left on a railway track, where you would hope to bleed to death before the next train came through – so it didn't surprise me that McAdam would have a fear of his masters, yet something troubled me about that scenario. Basically, I believed him when he said that this had nothing to do with Kirstie Long, but if Marshall and McAdam weren't working for Molina then whom?

The question took me back to our suspicions about

tracking devices and who could have placed them on our vehicles. At last I'd figured it out.

'Get up, arsehole.' I withdrew my gun, took a couple of paces back.

'Why, you going to make me run so you can shoot me in the back?'

He had made it to his feet, turning his left side to face me, trying to hide the movement of his right hand at his side.

'Maybe they're your tactics, McAdam, not mine. Now take your hand away from your weapon or you'll be sorry.'

He lifted both hands again, completing a pirouette so that his shirt hitched up to show he didn't have a concealed gun in his belt. 'I told you I was unarmed.'

'Yeah,' I lowered my SIG. 'But I told you I was going to shoot you . . . so we were both lying.'

The pinching of his eyelids told me he was absorbing my words, and coming to the wrong conclusion. He thought I was softening, that old friendships outweighed new enmity. It showed how different we were. He snapped down his right arm, and from his sleeve jumped a gleaming blade, a spring-assisted Gerber knife. In the next instant he lunged, the knife spearing at my throat.

His sneak attack would have been successful had I not noticed the rig attached to his forearm when I'd first knocked him down. The fact that he tried to rip out my throat vindicated what I did next. As I reared back, taking my throat away from the blade, I snapped a kick into his testicles that brought him to his knees, emitting a deep low moan from the depths of his guts. His arms lost the will to stab as they folded instinctively to cover his injury. I allowed gravity to pull down my foot, and this rocked my upper body forward, adding weight to the barrel of my SIG that chopped into his mastoid like an axe. McAdam went down, out cold.

I stood over him for a few seconds, wondering if allowing him to live was a mistake I'd later regret. But my mind flitted back to those times when we'd fought as comrades, and how, after I'd been shot by an IRA sniper, it was McAdam who'd laid down covering fire, then risked his arse to drag me clear of a second attempt on my life. I owed him one. But now he'd received payback.

I crouched over him, careful of the blade in his outstretched hand, and slapped him awake. He moaned, his lids flickering, then he opened his mouth to say something, but all that came out was a hacking cough that sprayed bile over his shirtfront.

'We're even, McAdam. You saved my life once, now I just saved yours. You can go back to Marshall and whichever fuckwit he's working for, and tell him how hard a fight you had with me before I escaped. That bruise on your neck and the swelling in your balls should be enough to convince them. But hear me . . . come at me again, and nothing will save you.'

17

'Good to see you alive and well, Hunter. How'd you get on with your old buddy?'

'McAdam was always a big mouth, but he didn't have much to say this time,' I said.

Over his cell phone, Velasquez had directed me a few blocks across town from where I'd left McAdam nursing his wounds and contemplating his future. Velasquez hadn't come to blows with his tail, having lost the man as we'd agreed, before seeking a common meeting point from where we could continue our original walk towards Jorge Molina's home.

I told him what had happened in the stinking alleyway, but left out my assumption about who was actually behind Marshall and McAdam. If I was correct then now was not the time or the place to confuse the issue. We were here to liberate a child from his abductor; everything else could wait.

'I've spoken to Rink,' Velasquez said. 'He offered to come on over and help bang a few heads together but I told him you had it under control.'

'Bet that pleased him?'

'Harvey and Mac have practically stripped the panel van back to the chassis, but they haven't found a tracking device. They think the van's still good for when we get out of here.'

'Good.' Actually it would have been better if they had found a bug, one that could be destroyed; because it meant the one in situ was too cleverly hidden. That confirmed my suspicions about who was directing Marshall and his men. 'Did Rink source another vehicle yet?'

'Yeah, he was able to purchase a car with cash, no questions asked.'

'Great, we'll need two vehicles. I trust the car isn't an old junker?'

'Don't worry; Rink knows his stuff when it comes to cars.' Rink had a weakness for flashy models, and usually tooled around the streets of Tampa in a Porsche or something equally classy.

The streets were filled with shoppers and the lunch-hour crowds sitting at pavement cafés indulging in cold drinks and snacks. It was a scene similar to the one where we'd picked up on McAdam and the other tail, but nothing untoward was triggering my radar this time. We had to be careful, because within another block we'd be in sight of Jorge Molina's home turf. We walked on, talking through our plans for infiltrating Molina's house by this afternoon.

'Take a look and see if you think it's achievable.' Velasquez gave a subtle nod of his head, and I glanced where he indicated.

Jorge Molina's house was in a walled compound on the south-facing side of one of the rock islands that rose above Hermosillo. It stood where Spanish Colonial-style buildings faced each other across a wide plaza. Once horses and carriages would have made the ride up the incline, important residents of Hermosillo attending functions in the big house at the head of the street. Now the plaza was a pedestrian zone, the only vehicles in evidence a utility truck parked at the lowest end where workers were digging up a section to get at duct pipes, and, nearer to the top of the hill, a motorised road sweeper cleaning the gutters with its whirling brushes. I wondered if Molina – or more correctly his father – had influenced the local council to control public access to the house, making it more difficult for enemy vehicles to approach undetected.

'OK, I see it, but this isn't the way we'll be going in,' I said.

'Just wanted you to get an idea of the scale of the place. I did my recce from further up on the hillside where you can see down into the grounds.'

At the foot of the plaza a number of pedestrians moved along the cross street on which we stood. It was almost as if there was an invisible barrier that forbade them from marching up the hill, and I guessed that the locals knew the approach to Casa Molina was out of bounds. If we tried to get much closer a guard would be dispatched from the gatehouse to dissuade us. Even from where we stood, like two guys in innocent conversation, I could make out a turreted structure to the left of the ornate gates. The turret looked to be a couple of hundred years old, but had been recently modified to include a broad, smoked-glass window behind which I could make out the silhouette of a man peering down the plaza. That the guard would have easy access to a weapon was a no-brainer. Covering my scrutiny with a less than subtle tilt of my head, I searched beyond the gate and high walls to where a large house stood astride the foot of the hillside. It was a rambling hacienda-style building, added to over the years so that it now boasted three wings as well as the original central structure. The roofs were a collection of flat terraces and pitched clay tile. Two figures patrolled the terrace, their attention on the grounds at the back. Velasquez had estimated that there were around a dozen people inside: it looked to me as if it could comfortably accommodate a hundred or more.

Earlier I'd put down Velasquez's trepidation to the fact that he was looking at the plan from a police officer's perspective, and I'd brushed off his concerns. Molina's house wouldn't pose a problem for Rink and me in the normal sense; we'd infiltrated heavily guarded terrorist compounds on more occasions than I could recall. But this time I had to consider a major factor. Then we'd been on seek and destroy missions; this time it was about securing and protecting a child's life. Fighting our way out past determined guards and an enraged father might indeed prove nigh-on impossible. I thought about Kirstie. If her boy was killed in the firefight, it would destroy her. But only after she'd clawed out my heart with her fingernails.

I have a natural ability that I've taken care to train to a point where I can mentally snapshoot a scene, which I can later recall in minute detail. Not that I have a photographic memory, something that only features in spy novels and sci-fi movies. I have to make a conscious decision to remember a place or face, and so I trailed my gaze over the scene now, noting every feature of the house and grounds, mentally painting a picture in my head. Satisfied, I nudged Velasquez and we walked away, heading for adjoining streets that would take us up towards the heights behind the house. Up there we'd have to be careful, because unless Molina was a total idiot, he'd know that his home was vulnerable to surveillance from above, and would have extra watchers in place to guard his back.

Actually, it appeared that his defensive ring also extended to these adjoining streets, because as we ambled upwards, circumventing the grounds, we passed at least three guys we pegged as Molina's footsoldiers. They weren't dressed or armed like guerrilla fighters, but their body language gave them away. Velasquez had said that the guards looked alert to him – if not alerted – but he'd only checked out those men inside the property. These ones, the pavement artists, were as jumpy as fleas as they scanned the faces of pedestrians or those in vehicles. Perhaps it was because Velasquez looked like an ageing homeboy that we were spared their scrutiny. Having lived in sunny Florida for the best part of two years, my sun-darkened face unshaven, my hair under a ball cap, and my clothing a little scuffed up, I resembled a passing local myself. If any of them got a look at the colour of my eyes, they'd make me for a Yankee – an odd irony – so I kept my gaze averted as we plodded upward.

We made it to the heights above the compound, finding a gap between two houses that offered a view downhill from where we could see the layout of Molina's house and the wall around it. I counted three men patrolling the rooftops, one of whom occasionally scanned the hillside with a handheld scope. We didn't fear discovery, but there was only a short window of opportunity before one of the outer ring of guards began questioning our presence. If they were worth their salt. I did my memory-snapshot trick again, and just as we were about to move off, something important caught my attention.

A car had entered the compound via the front gates. It came round the side of the house and parked in a wide space at the back where Molina's small fleet stood ready to trans-port him wherever he desired. Two men got out. I could have done with a loan of the rooftop guard's spy scope, but I could see enough to recognise one of the men. This time it wasn't a face from my para days, but a more recent encounter than that. Some of the answers to the questions I'd been asking began to fall in place.

The tall white man, dressed in a black suit and white shirt, grinned a rictus smile as Jorge Molina came out to greet him. They shook hands before Molina waved him inside, out of the beating sun. The second man followed them unbid-den; simply muscle along for the ride. Then they were inside and out of sight.

'This complicates things.'

'Say what?'

'What looked difficult before has just gone up a notch or two,' I said cryptically.

Velasquez was used to my odd English ways, and didn't question me further. 'That's why I like working with you, Hunter: never a dull moment. Sure beats patrolling a fucking shopping mall.'

On the way back to rendezvous with the others, I formulated a get-in plan, but still didn't have a clue how we'd make it out safely with a squalling child in our arms. Not now that our supposed allies had turned up to warn Molina we were in town.

18

'You sure you know what you're doing, brother?'

Crouching on the hillside above Molina's house, I looked across at Rink who was practically invisible against the night sky. It was six hours since I had perused the site with Velasquez, and darkness had fallen abruptly. A low-lying bank of clouds shrouded the moon. All I could discern of Rink were the whites of his eyes, and a faint scar on his chin given him two years earlier by a madman's knife. His teeth weren't visible because he was hitting me with a concerned frown, his lips downturned in that great sad-faced fish way he has.

'It's a bit late to back out now.'

'I'm not talking about the plan,' he said. 'I'm talking about Kirstie.'

'I don't know what you're getting at.'

'I'm talking about the canoodling you were doing earlier.'

'Canoodling? Now there's a word I've never heard you use before.'

'It's your goddamn Brit slang rubbing off on me. You know what I mean.'

'That wasn't canoodling. She was upset and I gave her a little reassurance.'

'By sticking your tongue down her throat?'

'It wasn't like that.'

'Would've been if I hadn't had the good sense to bang on the van and bring you to your senses.'

'Jesus, Rink, what's the problem? You keep telling me to get myself a good woman. I thought you'd be happy for me.'

'I didn't tell you to jump into bed with Walter's grand-daughter.'

So that was what he was concerned about. Hell, he was allowing his enmity towards Walter to colour his view of Kirstie. That wasn't like him.

'It's almost incest for Christ's sake,' he growled.

If we hadn't been poised to enter an enemy stronghold, possibly on a suicide mission, I might have taken him to task for that comment. All right, I did look on Walter Conrad as some-thing of a father figure, but it wasn't as if we shared blood.

Rink's never backward in berating me. He sees it as his duty to keep me on the straight and narrow, and will often rein me in if he thinks I'm overstepping the mark. Christ, maybe that made Rink a surrogate mother. I thought about suggesting as much but he might take it the wrong way.

'Lay off, will you, Rink. It was a kiss and cuddle, nothing more. Jump into bed . . . hell!'

'OK, OK, I exaggerated, but you know what I mean, brother. We both know how impulsive you are. You'll let your feelings for Kirstie affect the outcome of this mission. I know it. You know it.'

'Can't afford to, Rink. This is about the boy. Benjamin. And if you're finished doing your agony aunt bit, let's go get him.'

'Lead on.'

I was happy to be moving, especially when it shut Rink up from here on in – at least on the subject of my love life. Now he was my brother-in-arms, just the way I liked it.

We were both dressed for purpose in black trousers and shirts, black boots, and our faces blackened with greasepaint. We moved down the hillside, a pair of ninja warriors assault-ing the shogun's pagoda. Earlier I'd noted a tight angle in the wall where the compound had followed the contours of the cliff, and saw it as our best opportunity to enter the grounds undetected. There were CCTV cameras mounted on the walls, but where the wall made a tight wedge there was a blind spot. We could drop into the grounds between the cameras, then make our way across the parking lot to the rear door where Molina and his guests had entered the house.

Further up the hillside were clusters of houses, but lower down the cliff face was bare of habitation. The terrain was formed of jagged boulders interspersed by narrow gullies, and we were able to follow the course of one of those without fear of meeting a civilian. Anyone lurking among the rocks would prove unfriendly, so we moved with intent. We were heading into the compound with a shoot-to-kill mentality.

We didn't surprise any watchers in the gullies.

Approaching the wall, I paused about fifteen yards out as Rink ran directly to it, planted his back to the rough adobe and cupped his hands. As soon as he was set, I jogged forward and stepped into his hands and he boosted me up on to the parapet. I flattened, checking that I was in the dead arc between the scope of the cameras, and that none of the guards had noted my presence. There was no call to arms, so I hooked my knees round the top of the wall, riding it like a stunt horse while I reached down and linked forearms with Rink. He swung up with ease and spread his bodyweight along the top, facing me. After a quick check around, he swung off the other side and I helped lower him to avoid too much noise when his boots hit gravel. I then swung off the wall, into the stirrup of his hands and then to the ground. We both went to a crouch as we pulled out our weapons and searched the compound for movement. One man was moving along the terrace roof with a flashlight in one hand and a cigarette in the other. He wasn't shining his torch in our direction, a good sign.

Earlier, Harvey had worked his wizardry on his laptop, finding old blueprints of Molina's place on a site about historic houses of Hermosillo – long before the Molina family took control of it. The charts only showed floor plans of the original structure, so there were rooms in the three newer wings that we had no idea about. However, the door to which we headed was located in the original building, so we had a basic idea of what was inside. The first thing we expected to find was a guard or two.

Crossing the parking lot, we passed the cars, including the one in which Molina's surprise visitor had arrived. Rink crouched by the back left corner, jabbing his KA-BAR knife through the tyre. Then he repeated the process on the front. While he was engaged with this task, I was busy disabling Molina's fleet. Best-case scenario was if we could put all of Molina's cars out of commission, but there would be other vehicles at the front, or maybe parked out of sight in the large garage I could now see butting close to the right back corner of the compound. The first part of our escape plan was on foot, and the last thing we needed was to be run down by a vehicle full of gunmen.

But that was for the future. First we had to spirit the boy out of his father's clutches without alerting the household. Constrained by laws, there was no way we could have contemplated our actions. To sneak the boy out it was inevitable that some of the people inside would not live to see the dawn. But, recalling the crimes these men were responsible for, I'd no qualms about dropping a few of the sadistic butchers. In my mind's eye I caught a fleeting image of the two kids who had been disembowelled and hung from a bridge. The vision firmed my resolve.

Using hand-speak, Rink indicated that he was going to enter the house first. I nodded, then covered him as he approached the door. Rink's a big man, but he moves with the grace of a hunting cat. I watched him, conscious of any movement in my peripheral vision. Subtle movement is easier spotted in the periphery than searched for head-on. I caught a tiny object arching past to my right: the extinguished stub of the rooftop guard's cigarette. I couldn't see him on the roof, but there was a faint glow of his flashlight sweeping towards the wall where we'd entered. We were already under his line of vision, so I checked for soldiers on the ground. There was a low mumble of conversation from somewhere round the corner to our left. I moved quickly to join Rink by the door, placing my back to the jamb while I covered the space behind us.

Rink held up his left hand, three fingers extended, and began a countdown, lowering each digit in turn. As his hand formed a fist, he leaned into the door and used the same hand to twist the handle. Rink nudged open the door as I turned to cover his entrance. As soon as he was in and in a covering position, I followed, going to one knee and bringing up my SIG. We were in a broad vestibule, hardwood parquet flooring underfoot. The walls were tall, with embossed picture rails high towards the ceiling. No paintings hung from the rails. The space looked utilitarian: the tradesman's entrance. Doors to the right indicated storage rooms. They were scuffed near the bottom, possibly where cleaning trolleys were wheeled in and out without much care for the paintwork. There was a whiff of bleach in the air. Rink closed the outer door, then moved down the passage, staying close to the left wall so he could see each of the doors clearly; no one was about to surprise him by bursting from hiding in any of those rooms. Reaching the far end, he halted, alert to anyone approaching while I came more slowly. I checked each door along the way. My assumption had been correct – the cleaning staff used those rooms for storage.

Rink was facing another door. A heavy one, controlled by a sturdy spring mechanism at the top and solid enough to double as a barrier against fire. On the far side I guessed we'd enter the house proper, and from what I could recall of the blueprints there was another passageway running left to right beyond it. Originally the sitting and dining rooms took up much of the space towards the front of the house, but these could have been relocated once the three extra wings were added. It was doubtful that the rooms here had been adapted to accommodate a young child, but you never could tell.

Rink listened closely, before teasing the door open inwards, towards us. He slipped through the gap, checking both ways. He had his left hand down by his thigh and I watched the instructions he signalled with his fingers: all clear, move right. I advanced out into the hall, turning to the right and sweeping the space with my gun. The area was clear of guards or household staff. Good in a way, bad in another. I expected more resistance. Now that the man responsible for sending Marshall, McAdam and the others after us was here, Molina must be on high alert. Had we walked into a trap?

Our plan to snatch Benjamin was rushed and a successful result depended on its apparent bravado. Ideally, we could have done with more assets, more equipment, and a better get-out plan – a helicopter to fly us all back over the border would have been ideal – but we must make do. Because we were concerned that Molina might be aware of our presence in the country, we'd decided on getting in and out again before he'd made full preparations to deter us. It took a lot of guts, and not a little stupidity, to hope we could sneak into his house without encountering his gunmen, but luckily I'd plenty of both. If this was a trap, we'd just have to spring it.

With everyone's agreement, including Kirstie's, we'd decided on the best approach to getting Benjamin away from Jorge Molina unharmed. Trying to snatch the kid while he was outside the walls of Molina's home would surely mean a gunfight, whereas by invading the enemy nest we stood a chance of spiriting him away without exposing him to gunfire. But would that idea hold up if Molina had been informed we were coming? Had he pulled all of his guards round him and his boy? I really hoped not.

From a distant room there was the murmur of conversation, dulled by the intervening walls. I couldn't make out words, but the voices helped smooth over any concern that we were walking into a trap. Surely the talkers wouldn't advertise their position like that . . . unless they were bait? No, I didn't think that was the case. Perhaps McAdam had reported back to his employer and they'd assumed that we had been frightened off by their surveillance. Or my old para mates had a different agenda than any of us had realised. When I'd mentioned 'the woman' to McAdam he hadn't admitted any knowledge of Kirstie Long, so there was always the chance they'd no idea why we were here in Mexico.

Then why attack us in the desert? Why follow us in Hermosillo?

To hell with the 'whys'.

I moved on, checking doors as I progressed. Rink was mirroring my actions along the opposite spur of the hall. I came to another closed door, this one at the end of the passage and blocking my way. I leaned close, listening. When no sound came back to alarm me, I pushed open the door and found myself in another short passage at a right angle to the first. This was a later addition to the house, and led to the last of the three wings. If looked at from the front of the house, the wing was furthest to the left. The mumble of conversation was more muted now, meaning that I'd already passed their position. I could hear a TV playing somewhere above me. Unless Jorge Molina had a love of Disney cartoons, the television was playing in a child's bedroom.

I caught Rink's attention, pointing above me. Rink nodded and headed to my position. Without waiting for him, I entered the second passage and saw that it ended at the foot of some stairs. As soon as Rink was in place to cover my back I went up, treading softly to the outside edges of the stairs to minimise the noise.

The stairwell kinked back on itself halfway up, and I made sure to stay close to the outermost wall, so I'd have a clearer view as I went round. My SIG was snug against my right breast – many people lead the way with their gun, only to have it knocked from their hand before they see their assailant and I wasn't going to make that mistake. My caution was unwarranted because the stairwell was empty. I gave Rink the OK sign. As I went up the remaining flight he moved up to the halfway point, covering the lower ground as he came.

The staircase met another landing. A room was directly opposite, the door partly open to reveal a playroom. Toys were discarded where a bored kid had dropped them. There was another room adjacent to it and from under its closed door flickered the blue/black shadows cast by a TV. Donald Duck was berating someone. I smiled back at Rink. He frowned, puzzled as to what had tickled me. I pointed down the hall to another closed door. Jorge Molina didn't strike me as the fatherly type: Benjamin would have a nanny, and that room was likely hers. Rink moved to cover the door while also watching the stairs.

It was still early in the evening; a nanny wouldn't have gone to bed yet and the last thing we wanted was for her to discover us. Neither of us was prepared to hurt a civilian, least of all a woman trying to defend a child against abduction. I hoped she wasn't inside Benjamin's room with him.

I inched open the door.

The only voice to make a fuss was Donald Duck's.

The room was too big for a single child lying in a cot-style bed against the far wall. It appeared to have been adapted for a kid, but was too clinical to offer stimulation to a growing and fertile mind. There was only the bed, a sideboard on which the TV played, and a small wardrobe. More like a cell than a goddamn bedroom, I thought. Benjamin was stretched out on his bed in that abandoned way that small children have, his arms flung above his head, legs akimbo. He was wearing blue and red pyjamas, a Spiderman outfit without the facemask. In repose the kid didn't look anything like his mother, but had the dark hair and complexion of his father. He whistled gently as he slept.

I searched for something to swaddle him in, then decided on taking the boy from his bed, blanket and all. To do so, I had to put away my gun.

Now came the difficult part.

If Benjamin woke with a black-garbed stranger looming over him, face blackened and looking like a bogeyman fresh from under the bed, he would scream the place down. Yet he looked out of it. A quick glance towards the cabinet on which the TV stood confirmed a suspicion. There was a medicine bottle, a local brand that looked like the syrup you feed kids when they're teething or need help sleeping. Jorge didn't want his meeting interrupted by a needy toddler and had ensured Benjamin would sleep the night through. Though I didn't approve of his parenting skills, he'd done me a favour. I picked up Benjamin, pulling the bedding round him, and held him to my chest. The boy murmured, his eyelids flickering, lips smacking faintly, but he didn't waken. There was a teddy bear in the cot, but my hands were full, so we had to leave it behind. I turned quickly and exited the room.

Rink led the way down the stairs, while I adjusted Benjamin's weight to hold him in my left arm. We'd made it in, grabbed the boy, but we were a long way from safe. I took out my SIG but was careful to keep it well out of the way of the kid. The corridor at the bottom remained empty. We hurried to the next hall and Rink went ahead. My nerves were on edge, my breathing loud in my ears. I fairly ran up the last corridor that took us back towards the cleaning rooms and the exit door.

We'd almost made it to the large, scuffed fire door when a figure emerged from an adjoining door to our right, obviously with no expectation of running into a couple of invaders. It took a moment for his brain to register what he was looking at and a second or so more to shout a warning. By that time it was too late.

Rink launched himself through the air, his right arm cocked at the elbow. Marginally above the tall guard's height, Rink drove his fist forward. He was still clutching the stock of his handgun, but it was his knuckles that went directly into the bridge of the guard's nose. The sound was like someone driving a stake into the ground with a mallet, and the force smashed the guard down. Rink's momentum took him on top of the man's body, and he straddled him, taking him quietly to the floor. He knelt on the man's chest, hand poised to deliver another crushing blow, but the guard was out of it, his face a ruined mess. He hadn't had chance to let out a cry, but anyone within hearing distance must have been alerted to the concussive smack he took to the face.

I sprang past Rink to the fire exit and hit it open with my shoulders, just as a voice was raised in query from deeper in the house. Rink jerked his chin to tell me to get going. This wasn't part of the bargain: no one was staying behind.

'Come on,' I whispered harshly.

'I'll slow them down.'

'I need you with me. I can't fight my way past the other guards while carrying a kid.'

That must have made sense because Rink lunged after me as I spun into the short corridor and raced for the exit.

A number of voices – some Spanish, some English – rang out, and the chase was on.

19

While it was only the two of us inside the grounds, we hadn't come without back-up. Kirstie was safe at the base we'd set up in a motel on the east side of Hermosillo, watched over by Harvey Lucas, but Velasquez and McTeer were in position to aid us in our escape. The only problem being, they were still at the far end of the plaza beyond the front gates, waiting in the van they'd parked alongside the vehicles of the utility repair crew digging up the road. Hiding in plain sight was always better than trying to be furtive, and the gate guard had spotted nothing suspicious in one van among others.

We hustled towards the front gate, shouts ringing out as Molina sent his men in pursuit. No one had fired on us yet, but the guards on the rooftops were swinging their flashlights to get a bead on us. I was thankful for Benjamin's presence in my arms because I could hear Molina yelling at his people not to shoot. In the confusion I doubted that the message would be relayed to all.

'Keep moving brother, I'll cover you,' Rink hollered from behind my shoulder.

I kept moving.

There was a rustle as Rink dropped to one knee, then came the repeated snap of his handgun. I cringed with every shot because as well as keeping the pursuers off my back, Rink was inviting return fire.

Our back-up team must have heard the shots, because there was the sudden roar of an engine from beyond the gates.

Powering on, I hugged the child against my chest, concealing him from those behind, but also using my body as a barrier.

The guard came out of the gatehouse.

He was holding a firearm.

The only good in the scenario was that he was caught in a flux of indecision. Someone must have called him to bar my path, but without placing Benjamin in harm's way. Jorge Molina was proving a more caring father than I'd thought. The guard brought up his pistol, shouting in Spanish, but he didn't fire. I had no such constraints. As I ran, I held my SIG before me and rattled off bullets as rapidly as I could squeeze the trigger. Running and shooting is poor form. It's highly unlikely you'll hit a target with the gun jostling with each step. But that was fine by me. I didn't intend to kill the guard, only to show him that he'd best get the fuck out of my way. He seemed the sensible type. He took a staggering run from my path and threw himself down on the floor. I fired another round, saw it strike sparks five feet or so from his head, and he dropped his gun, both hands over his head, yelling surrender. Maybe it would have been better if I'd forced him to open the gate, but there was no time for regret. I charged at the barrier, then swerved towards the gatehouse just as the familiar panel van reversed at speed into the gate. The gate was designed more for intimidation than to be a secure barrier, and it was forced open, the bolts buckling and then giving with a metallic shriek. The right-hand gate sprung wide while the other hung limp on its hinges. The back doors of the van were dented, the paintwork scratched, but the mechanism hadn't been damaged. Velasquez threw open the doors, standing on the cargo bed with his arms out to receive Benjamin.

'Get him inside.' I thrust the boy into Velasquez's hands. As he twisted round, racing for the far end of the compartment, he hauled up a steel sheet, and placed it between Benjamin and harm's way. Velasquez propped his gun hand over the steel to offer cover. Already I was searching for Rink.

My big friend was retreating slowly, targeting those rushing him from the direction of the house. Two men were already on the floor, groaning in agony. More than half a dozen others were strung out in the grounds, and because he wasn't holding their boss's child, Rink was fair game. Only because they were panic-shooting was Rink still alive. That wouldn't last long. I released my depleted clip and slapped in a fresh one, racking a round into the chamber. Taking a few steps away from the van to divert fire from Benjamin, I laid down covering fire while Rink worked his way backwards. A clatter to my right alerted me to the guard who'd recently given up the fight. He'd decided he was back in it, and had picked up his gun; now that I no longer held a human shield he wasn't put off shooting at me. Idiot should have kept his head down. I shot him through the throat.

McTeer threw the van into drive, pulling away from the buckled gates. Velasquez shouted at us to get inside.

'Go!' I shouted. 'Get the boy out of here!'

'We can all get out now,' Velasquez yelled. Little Benjamin wasn't so doped up and began howling.

'No. We have to slow any pursuit. Do what we agreed, guys. Get the fuck going. Take Benjamin back to Kirstie.'

I moved deeper into the compound, targeting those trying to kill Rink. I was happy to hear the roar of the panel van's engine as McTeer took it at speed down the plaza, the doors slamming shut and blocking Benjamin from harm.

Molina's men were seeking cover behind anything that could halt a round. Some were on their bellies on the ground, others concealed behind raised stone flower beds. We were out in the open, and it was a good job that none of the combatants had rifles or we'd be dropped in seconds. Their guns – like ours – didn't have great accuracy over a distance, but we were better skilled.

'Rink, to me, buddy.'

He jerked his head to confirm he'd heard, but he was still kneeling, firing at those nearest him. To stand now would be suicide. I jogged away, zigzagging to avoid being brought down. Up on the roof one of the guards played his flashlight beam over me, and I began drawing fire.

While I ran, skidded to a halt and then backtracked, Rink came up to his feet and began to backpedal, still shooting. I heard him grunt and knew he'd taken a hit.

More people spilled from the front of the house. Had we come here with the express purpose of assassinating Jorge Molina then here was my opportunity. I could see his thick head of hair as he ran down the front steps, shouting orders. But that wasn't my purpose – despite Walter's none-too-subtle instruction – so I didn't fire on him. He was too far away to ensure a hit, and others with guns in their hands warranted my attention. His face was rigid with anger. I spied another face in the open doorway. The light shining from inside cast the man in silhouette, but I recognised his bony countenance and the skull-like shape it made. I fired a round at him. It struck the wall to his right, but it was enough to make the bastard dive back inside.

Engines began growling, and a vehicle nosed round the side of the house, until its softened tyres buckled and split and the rims settled to the ground. The driver threw open the door, using it as a shield as he drew down on us. Rink fired a grouping of three shots at the door and the man was forced to take cover inside, shouting in a mixture of agony and rage.

Just then another car rounded the corner. It too came on flat tyres, but the driver was taking it cautiously, flanked by two more guards who were crouching behind the car and using it as a shield.

'Time to move, Rink,' I shouted.

This time he was able to run back to the gate, covering me while I also moved towards the guardhouse. Gunfire forced me inside while Rink charged out and on to the open plaza. He swerved right, placing the gatepost between him and the rolling attack. More of those who'd been taking cover were emboldened by the actions of their mates and came out of hiding, moving across the compound in a skirmish line. Bullets began tearing the guardhouse to pieces, cutting through the open door and striking the office space inside. I had to take cover, as much from the ricochets as anything else.

'Get the fuck outta there, before they corner you!'

Rink's shout motivated me.

No way could I go back out of the door on this side, and it was the only open exit.

So I took the other option.

I turned my gun on the thick sheet of smoked glass that had been added to adapt the turret into a modern gatehouse.

My rounds punched the glass, but only served to star the thickened pane. I required something with more mass to even hope to make it through. A chair and desk were situated below the window, neither of which would be any good to me: the chair was too light, the desk too heavy. A filing cabinet to the right of the entrance door was a more viable battering ram. Shoving away my SIG I hauled it up, grunting at the weight, before tipping it so the sharp angle of a bottom corner was lined up with the window. I heaved the cabinet, almost tearing the tendons from my shoulders with the effort. The cabinet struck the window, bursting free a chunk of glass the size of my head, then fell on to the desk with a huge bang. It was accompanied by the renewed wallops of bullets striking the inside of the room. Some of the rounds cutting inside the office helped weaken the window, but it remained a substantial barrier.

Not that I was about to give up. Returning to the door, I fired at those advancing on my position from behind the cover of the slowly moving car. Then I turned my gun on the driver, firing through the windscreen. The slide on my SIG locked open. Grabbing for the final cartridge of ammunition in my belt, my hand fell on empty space. Son of a bitch, during my run with Benjamin the clip must have worked loose and fallen out there in the darkness. If I didn't find a way out of the guardhouse in the next few seconds I was finished.

I ran back to the cabinet, hauling it up and swinging it again at the place where the window was already broken, knocking loose another large shard. To my dismay I saw now that a plastic film had been added to the outside of the pane. It was going to be the devil's own job breaking through. To remind me how precarious my position was, a fresh volley of rounds cut the air beside my shoulder, the bullets bouncing crazily around the room. A chunk of red-hot metal scored a line across my left forearm.

In the next few seconds Molina's men would be on me. My first thought was whether I could take the fight to them; perhaps snatch a gun from one before the others brought me down. My second thought: I hoped that my sacrifice had earned Velasquez and McTeer enough time to get Benjamin well out of the way.

A sudden crash against the window brought me round. Rink's figure had jagged edges, but that was only an effect caused by the shattered prism of glass. He kicked again, driving forward with his heel. The weakened glass was resisting my efforts from within, but pressure from the other side helped tip the balance. Rink – who I've seen snapping baseball bats with kicks during demonstrations of his karate skills – slammed the glass a second time. The lower half of the glass buckled inwards. There wasn't room for me to get out without ripping myself to shreds, but it was enough for Rink to toss me a spare magazine of ammo.

I snatched it up and replaced the empty one in my gun.

The timing was just right, because the car was almost upon me, the driver angling it to block me inside the room. I fired almost point-blank and got him in the chest this time. Using the car as a barricade, the others dropped out of sight, but only for a few seconds. Then they were up again and bullets tore through my sanctuary. I caught another ricochet, this time losing a strip of skin from my right thigh. Hurt like a bastard, but I couldn't let it stop me. I returned fire, forcing the attackers down. Rink had given up on the window, returning to a position where he could fire at an angle from behind the far gatepost. His crossfire gave me the opportunity to go for broke and I took it.

I ran the few short steps up to the desk, then hurled myself over it. Covering my skull with my elbows, I pounded into the weakened glass. There was no cinematic explosion; the film held the glass together in a gummy embrace, cocooning me. But the window was irrevocably damaged now, and my hurtling bodyweight was enough to rip it from its frame. I tumbled outside, the shards of glass enveloping me, a thousand prickles as they jabbed through my clothing. Thankfully my momentum helped me roll free of the vicious blanket, and I came out of the roll splattering droplets of blood. I dreaded checking the damage, but had to. If I'd severed an artery, then that was it. A quick run of my hands over myself told me I'd picked up dozens of tiny punctures and scratches, but the most significant cuts remained those made by the ricochets on my arm and thigh. The blood trickled from me, but at least it wasn't pumping out.

Rink was hurtling towards me.

'Get the fuck outta here!' He didn't even stop to scream in my face.

Then we were charging down the plaza.

We were clear of the compound, but it was a long way back to the US border.

20

'Is it them?'

Kirstie jumped up from a wooden stool next to the breakfast counter. She'd heard the thrum of an engine filtering in through the door followed by the soft squeak of brakes as a vehicle pulled to a halt outside the motel room. The wait had been agonising, made all the more interminable by her anxiety that the van might never return. For hours now she'd been on edge, counting every repeated pattern she could find – from the designs in the curtains to the carpets, the bedding, even the tiles on the ceiling – but it had failed to occupy her thoughts. She'd been too concerned about the fate of her boy. She had been separated from Benjamin for so long, nothing mattered but getting him back. Yet another concern worried at her like a toothless old dog on a bone. If, no, when – she must be optimistic – she was reunited with Benjamin, what if he did not recognise his own mother? The trepidation slowed her enough for Harvey Lucas to intercept her dash to the door.

'Let me check first, OK?' Harvey went to the window and poked open a gap in the blinds. Down by his side he held a Glock, primed for action should the arrivals be unwelcome.

Kirstie watched the man's features smooth out, his shoulders relaxing as he exhaled.

'It's them.'

'Do they have Benjamin?'

'I can't tell. I can only see Mac in the front seat. Whoa, hold up, Kirstie!' Harvey grabbed her to stop her from throwing open the door. 'Give me a few seconds to check everything's all right.'

Kirstie stood in the centre of the motel room, her hands twisting together. It was probably best that she'd left her handgun in her purse otherwise she'd have been firing rounds into the floor. Harvey returned to his spyhole and peered out once again, watching as McTeer slipped out of the van and headed round the back. Kirstie wasn't conscious of tapping her tongue on her teeth. She started forward again.

'No. You must stay out of sight.' Harvey cracked the door open.

'I need to know . . .'

'A few seconds.'

There was a rush of footsteps, and then Harvey admitted Velasquez, carrying a blanket bundle in his arms, followed seconds later by McTeer, who came in backwards, watching outside. Kirstie's attention was focused on the bundle in Velasquez's arms. A cry broke from her, part relief, part tortured howl as she lunged for the unresponsive child swaddled in the blanket.

Velasquez relinquished his hold as Kirstie pulled Benjamin into her embrace and tugged free the blanket that covered his face. She feared Benjamin had suffocated and her terror didn't abate when the boy's face was revealed. His eyes were shut, his mouth hanging open. 'Oh, God! What's wrong with my baby?'

'Relax,' Velasquez soothed. 'The boy's fine. He's just a little drowsy, that's all.'

'What did you do to him?' Kirstie's voice was full of accusation.

'Wasn't anything we did. You can blame his daddy for that.

I think he's had some sort of medication to make him sleep. He hardly woke all the way back.'

Kirstie wasn't listening. Benjamin had stirred, his lips smacking together, his eyelids cracking open a sliver. His pupils were out of focus but very much alive. There were dried tears on his plump cheeks, testament to his short periods of wakefulness. Kirstie couldn't hold back her own tears, weeping with no shame or self-consciousness before the trio of men. She began kissing Benjamin, her lips feeling the warmth of his skin, the faint tickle of his breath. She wanted to squeeze him so tightly her body would absorb his. The men were in conversation around her, Harvey stalking back and forth between her and the door. The pounding of her heartbeat muted their voices. Yet something impinged, and for the first time she thought of someone other than her child. She tuned into their voices.

'We should go back,' McTeer was saying.

'No. Our instructions were to secure Kirstie and the boy and then get out of here.' Harvey didn't appear convinced by his own argument.

'We could go back,' McTeer insisted. 'Velasquez and me. We could take the van now that the kid's out of harm's way.'

'We need the van to move on from here,' Harvey said. 'Hunter would have it no other way.'

'We had to use the van to ram the gates,' Velasquez said. 'Molina's guys have seen it, so it's probably best we dump it now and find some other form of transportation for Kirstie and Benjamin. I vote that we go back, make sure the guys got out alive, and then torch the fucking thing. Harvey, you could arrange another vehicle in minutes if you wanted to.'

'I could, but Hunter would have my balls in a sling if I did. You knew what the mission was before we came in, guys: it's about getting Kirstie and Benjamin safely across the border.'

Still hugging Benjamin, Kirstie peered at the Hispanic man and his rugged-faced companion, McTeer. She knew she should thank them for bringing her boy back to her, but those weren't the words that slipped from her mouth. 'You left Joe behind?'

'Not out of choice.' McTeer scowled at the ground, as if by meeting her gaze he'd invite further scorn. 'Rink was trapped inside the compound and Hunter went back to help him. Nothing we could say or do would have stopped him. If you know Hunter and Rink, you know they're attached at the hip. Hunter made us leave, and it's probably best for the boy that we did. Fuckin' gunfight was going crazy by then.'

Kirstie blinked in astonishment. Not at McTeer's explanation, but at how hard his words hit her. Hell, she barely knew either man, and though she'd shared an intimate moment with Hunter, well, that shouldn't mean much. It was just a moment of weakness where perhaps she'd have sought comfort in anyone's arms. Nonetheless, the thought that she'd never lay eyes on Hunter again twisted a sharp blade through her heart. 'He . . . uh, they'll be OK though, won't they?'

'They're tough *hombres*,' Velasquez didn't meet her eye. 'If anyone can find a way out of a hornet's nest it's those two. Still, I'd prefer it if we went back to check.'

'You're not the only one, but we had our orders, and if we don't do as we were asked, then Hunter and Rink staying behind would've been for nothing.' Harvey was the only one thinking with his head over his heart. He stared at his friends, unflinching.

Velasquez shoved a palm through his dark hair. It glistened with sweat. 'OK. So we follow the plan.' He turned to Kirstie. 'You ready to go?'

Kirstie checked on Benjamin. His eyelids flickered again, his grey irises rolling side to side in sleep. 'I've everything I need right here,' she said. 'I'm so relieved to have my baby back. Thank you ... Thank you all,' she said, meeting each man's gaze in turn.

'Thank us when we've got you both home,' Harvey said. Then, to his colleagues: 'Grab all the stuff you can carry guys, we're out of here in two minutes. We can only hope that Joe and Rink made it out alive. We won't know until they fail to meet us at the next rendezvous.'

21

'This way,' Rink called, taking a left bend at speed.

I was charging along behind him, scattering shards of glass in my wake as the vigorous exercise shed them from my clothing. Pounding round the same corner, I barely escaped a bullet that clipped stone chips from the front of the building.

'Shit, they're determined fuckers,' I muttered to Rink.

'And indiscriminate about where they're shooting . . .'

He had that correct. All the way down the plaza we'd evaded a storm of bullets as Molina's men pursued us. We were fortunate that we hadn't been torn to ribbons, and only the fact that the men were running as they fired had saved our arses. This early in the evening, most of the daytime sightseers had gone back to their hotels, preparing to return later when the bars were in full swing. Revellers were few, as was traffic on the main routes. Probably a good thing because if the crowds were as tightly packed as earlier then there would have been numbers of casualties from the bullets whipping through the air after us.

Now that we had a building blocking the view of our pursuers there should have been a cessation of gunfire, but it didn't slacken. Men furious at our escape still rattled off rounds from pistols and machine-guns alike. I considered going back to the corner, dropping a few of the scumbags with pinpointed shots, but didn't. I kept on running as hard as I could.

This had never been part of the plan.

We had hoped to spirit Benjamin out of the way

undetected. The guys in the van would drop us back at our car, parked midway up the hillside behind Molina's compound. Now we had a long run uphill with a swarm of maddened hunters after us. Time for Plan B. The problem was, there wasn't a Plan B as such. How can you plan for the unknown? It was all about making decisions on the run now.

A hundred yards or so further along I dropped to one knee as Molina's men sprinted round the corner. I allowed three of them to charge from cover before firing, and caught the backmost high in his left shoulder. He slapped a hand to his wound even as he crumpled, letting out a cry that echoed between the buildings of this narrower street. By the time his buddies realised they were under fire they had committed themselves to the chase. I shot each of them, not sure where I hit but clearly in places guaranteed to take them out of the fight. One of them howled, but the other fell silently.

Another gun barked close by. Rink had made his way to the opposite side of the street and crouched behind a parked car. He aimed so that his bullets struck the wall at the corner, in an effort at halting any further pursuit. I got up and continued running, then another hundred yards further along I turned and knelt, covering him as we pepper-potted out of range of their guns. On foot we had a good lead on them, but it was a matter of moments before they'd find a vehicle to continue the chase. We also required transportation but all the vehicles on the street were newer models and no way could we hot-wire them the way we could older cars. At a cross street there was moving traffic. For a second I entertained the idea of hijack, but that wasn't in my nature and I kicked the idea loose. Instead we ran.

To slow the chase further Rink led us into a narrow alley, not unlike the one where earlier I'd confronted McAdam. Vehicles couldn't follow, but Molina's men would have greater knowledge of the layout of the streets than we did and might be able to cut us off. We spurred on, and burst from the alley into another street running parallel to the plaza a few blocks over. The rocky mound loomed above the rooftops, lights from the homes up there egging us upward.

Just as I entertained the notion that we might make it back to our car an SUV came tearing down the slope towards us. Molina – or one of his men – had called in back-up from the watchers who ringed the streets beyond his house. Worse, from some distance came the wail of sirens as police responded to the sounds of gunfire. One thing I was certain of was that the local cops – whether in Molina's pocket or not – wouldn't look on us favourably.

Rink ran right, and I went the other way, jogging up the sidewalks, placing parked vehicles between ourselves and the SUV speeding towards us. In the middle of the road they could simply have run us down, but now we'd taken that option from them, we forced them to have their eyes on separate targets.

A trio of innocent bystanders stood on the sidewalk above me. They looked confused by the roar of the engine and the gun-wielding man running towards them. Panic took hold, and a middle-aged couple clung on to each other, even as their younger friend tried to tug them to safety. Seconds later, a man in the SUV poked his gun out of the window and fired at me, careless of the civilians in the way. The woman shrieked, while her husband rattled off a curse of alarm. Thankfully none of the trio was hit, but that could change any second.

'Get inside, now,' I yelled at them, pointing to a nearby doorway. Receiving only terrified looks, I tried out my meagre Spanish. '*¡Entra ahora!* Get in there. Now! *En ese país. Ahora, ahora!*'

The trio scattered, but not for the door I indicated; they ran up the hill before me. They had no idea that I was the good guy here: to them, blood-splashed and holding a pistol, I must have looked like the one they must escape. With no choice left, I dodged between two parked cars and on to the road, drawing the gunfire away and allowing them to flee. Rink shouted but I couldn't hear his words for the roar of the SUV and the banging of gunshots. Probably he thought me *loco* too.

The SUV was ten yards away, two men inside. The driver was furthest from me, placing the gunman and the most immediate threat on my side. I dropped low to one knee, sighting him, but before I could get off a shot the driver hit the brakes, and the SUV skidded, turning side on. I had to leap backwards to avoid being crushed as the back end swung violently towards me. I went down flat, my head snapping back and striking the road. Inky whorls edged my vision, but I didn't have time to absorb the shock, instead rolling into a space between two parked cars. Pushing up with my left arm, I fired blindly at the SUV, but it was continuing to spin away and all I hit was the rear fender. Pain blazed through my left leg, my knee pulsing in agony. Biting down on the pain, I shuffled back on my buttocks, trying to get the stationary car to my left to act as a barricade.

That was when the driver got the SUV under control. The rear lights flared like a devil's fiendish glare, and I realised what the driver had in mind. The tyres spun as he hit the gas and reversed towards me. Frantically I backed away, my twisted knee shrieking in pain. The SUV slammed the parked cars and I was caught between two crushing shapes that bucked and lurched as the SUV powered them up on to the sidewalk. The back end of the car to my right lifted high in the air, the SUV pressing it up and over, and were it not for the one to my left that jammed hard to the front of a building I'd have been squashed beneath the SUV's tyres. As it was, the tilted car threatened to crush me if the driver of the SUV thought to pull away quickly. I searched for an escape route, and my only chance was to go beneath the back of the car to my left. The problem there was that it had been compressed, concertinaed in on itself. For the second time in a few crazy minutes I was covered in raining glass as the car's rear windscreen exploded. Luckily the glass was in chunks and not razor-sharp like the first lot.

I searched for a shot. Didn't have one.

But I scrambled up, ignoring the burning in my knee as I was filled with the red haze of battle. The driver was still going heavy on the gas, trusting the vehicles to imprison then crush me to a pulp. I fired directly through the back windshield. I heard a corresponding shout of pain, but the curse that followed told me that I'd failed to kill either of the bastards. Bullets began punching through the glass as the gunman inside returned fire, even as the driver threw the gear and pulled away. Forced down again, I was barely missed by the car on my right as it slammed down to earth. More glass and bits of twisted metal clouded my vision, and I felt the rush of displaced air as I collided with the crushed trunk of the other car, my sore knee taking the brunt. Fresh pain shot through me.

I went after the two in the SUV, but Rink was already there. While they'd been intent on turning me into a red smear on the sidewalk, Rink had run up unnoticed. He lifted his gun, and without remorse shot the driver point-blank in the side of his head. The SUV had already been moving across the street, but now it was out of control. At speed it continued towards the buildings on the far side. The gunman, seeing his immediate future, tried to leap from the car, but before he'd got the door even part-way open, the SUV crashed through the façade of a store, wedging itself tightly among the collapsing masonry and wood beams.

'You OK, Hunter?' Rink asked as I limped over the road.

'No . . . I'm fucking pissed!'

I went to the SUV, my SIG raised, murder in my heart.

'*Ayúdame . . . por favor. Ayuda . . .*'

I heard the plaintive cries of the gunman trapped between the frame of the door and a splintered beam. Suspecting a trap, I moved in with my gun centred on his ashen face, inviting him to lift his gun. Then I noticed the blood frothing from between his lips, so dark it looked like oil against the pallor of his features.

'*Ayúdame . . .*' he repeated. Help me.

Suddenly the rage left me. I'd killed men in similar positions, but that was in the heat of battle where their continuation of life might mean a bullet in my spine as I walked away. This man was in no position to fight. He was crushed. I could tell that his ribcage was mush and that the blood bubbling from his lips and nostrils was filling his throat. He was in no shape to do anything but beg. I lowered my SIG.

Struggling for the correct words, I told him his friends were coming and they would help him. '*Tus amigos están por llegar. Ellos te ayudarán. No puedo hacer nada.*'

'*Por favor . . . ?*' he beseeched.

Shaking my head, I walked away. '*No puedo hacer nada,*' I repeated at a whisper: I can do nothing.

He didn't agree, damning me to hell.

'*Usted puede ir al infierno, hijo de puta!*'

'There's gratitude for ya.' Rink smiled grimly. 'Maybe he'd have preferred you to shoot him in the face?'

I wasn't in a joking frame of mind. As a parting insult the gunman had called me a bastard. It was how I felt, too. I had to keep reminding myself that moments before this man had been trying his hardest to murder me, but as we jogged away up the hill I was still picturing the blood bubbling out of his mouth. I very much doubted he'd hang on long enough for his friends to help him.

The pain in my twisted knee was a hindrance, but the

endorphins flooding my system numbed the worst of it. If I was to rest now my leg would stiffen and I'd struggle to get moving again. So I ploughed on, loping behind Rink as he headed for the high ground. A quick check over my shoulder told me that our other pursuers had momentarily lost our trail, but they couldn't be far away. The trio of civilians had disappeared off the street, but there were other faces watching from windows and doorways, drawn to the fight now that the immediate danger was over. Any one of those witnesses might direct the police – or even Molina's men – after us at any time. They couldn't be expected to understand that we were actually the good guys, not after what had just happened.

At the head of the street was a wall. Nothing as substantial as the one surrounding Molina's home a little farther over; this was mud brick and adobe, and beyond it was a pretty garden that would be colourful in daytime, but was now a series of gnarly silhouettes on a sequence of low terraces. Rink bounded over the wall, then used it as a barricade to cover me as I clambered over less gracefully.

'Couple of the bastards down there,' he said, indicating the distant cross street. 'They've spotted their buddies and are heading this way.'

Ignoring them, we moved into the garden, tracing a route through cacti and small shrubs that tugged at our clothing. Rink paused to check the way we'd come, but there was no view downhill. Which meant we were out of sight of our hunters. We found a gate and exited the garden on to a narrow road that wound a trail up to where we'd left our car. Maybe we'd get away without further bloodshed.

No sooner had that wishful thought struck than headlights blazed behind us and another SUV came streaking after us.

'Yup, they're determined fuckers,' Rink said, echoing my words from earlier.

22

This SUV was travel-stained. Dried mud pasted the wheel arches and trail-dust smeared the windows. The wiper blades had cut wide swathes through the grime on the windshield. I doubted that the vehicle was one used by Molina's men around his plush home, which meant its occupants weren't his hired hands. Not his usual crew at any rate. These had been brought in and it didn't take too much imagination to guess who they were.

'Fucking Marshall,' I spat.

'What are they doing just sitting there?' Rink asked.

When the SUV had first come roaring round the bend a similar attack to the one down the hill appeared to be underway. Yet, as Rink and I fanned out, finding concealment behind a low wall and a tree bole respectively, the brakes had screeched and the SUV came to a halt, rocking on its chassis. Because of the glare of its lights – on high beam – and the dirt on the windshield, nothing could be made out of those within.

'Maybe he's having second thoughts.'

'More like he's waiting for reinforcements. He's probably heard about what happened to those other punks and doesn't fancy a similar outcome.'

'Makes sense.'

'Or he could be a coward,' Rink said scornfully. 'He ran away the last time we met. You sure he's the hard bastard you say he is?'

'Back in the day I knew nobody tougher,' I said. 'But who knows how much he's changed over the years?'

'Back in the day, I bet he wouldn't have worked for a scum-bag like Jorge Molina.'

I hadn't mentioned my suspicions regarding whom Marshall was assisting. I hadn't been sure – still wasn't to be honest – but the presence of Molina's guest had given me a good idea. Rink didn't trust Walter Conrad as it was, and the inclusion of this man in the picture wouldn't help.

'Whatever his game is, we can't afford to sit here like this.'

'So let's go and kill the fucker,' Rink urged.

'Not yet, I want to see how he plays things first.'

'You want to give the asshole a chance?'

'To explain himself,' I said.

'Hunter, that frog-gigger tried to kill us out in the desert. Now you want to go speak to him like he's an old buddy?'

'When he ambushed us, I don't think he knew who he was up against. I think it's when he saw my face, realised who he was attacking, that he chose to back off.'

'He ran away because he saw our back-up team arriving and knew he was outgunned. Same thing he's doing now.'

'We don't know that. Could be half a dozen gunmen in that rig.'

'And you want to walk over and find out?'

Without answering, I stood up slowly. No way was I relinquishing my gun, but I held it ostentatiously away from my body.

'Shit!' Rink didn't do more than spit out the curse, before he leaned out round the bole of the tree to offer cover should things turn out differently than I hoped.

'I'm just going to speak to him, then we're out of here.' I stepped over the low wall and began walking towards the SUV, trying not to limp. The car's headlights caused me to squint as I approached to within twenty yards. I could sense their scrutiny but still couldn't make out who was inside, or how many of them. In hindsight walking out there without a get-out plan was bordering on lunacy, but I trusted Marshall not to gun me down in cold blood. The lights were lowered, and I was now able to see two figures in the front seats. If there were others in the back I couldn't tell. I halted in the centre of the road, my SIG pointed away from the car.

The tableau held for what felt like a lifetime. From a distance came the strains of an emergency siren. The local cops had joined the hunt and it wouldn't be long before a squad car came our way.

'Marshall,' I called out. 'Let's not fuck about any longer. If you're going to try to kill me, bring it on. If not, let's speak.'

'Tell the Jap to lower his gun,' replied a gruff voice I hadn't heard for the best part of two decades.

'Don't worry, my friend isn't going to shoot unless you try something dodgy.'

The passenger door opened and out climbed a tall figure, also holding a pistol down by his side. It wasn't James Lee Marshall, but his lickspittle buddy, McAdam. With slow deliberation he lifted his gun and aimed it loosely my way. His shoulders and neck were tight with restrained anger.

'What's good for the goose and all that shit,' said Marshall easing out the driver's side. 'Your boy shoots me, McAdam shoots you, Hunter.'

'Fair enough. Hopefully neither of us needs to get shot, eh?'

'Mind you, after the beating you gave McAdam earlier, I wouldn't blame him if he put a round in your gut.'

Aiming my warning at his friend, I said, 'Just remember my parting words, McAdam, before you try anything stupid.'

Trying to sound tough in front of his leader, McAdam laughed at my bravado. The sound was strained because he knew what would happen if he tried to get the drop on me. Chances were he'd hit me, but it'd only be a split second before Rink took his face off.

'I'm not afraid of you, arsehole. Never was.' Trying to regain face, McAdam grinned manically, showing a glistening gap between his front teeth. His whining Glaswegian tone didn't do much to convince me.

'Sounds like your balls are still aching,' I said.

'Fuck you, Hunter.'

'It'd take a bigger man than you.'

Marshall shook his head as he came forward. 'Christ, it sounds like the good old days listening to you two. Never did see eye to eye, did you?'

'Never had that problem with you, Marshall.'

'Yeah. How the world turns, eh?'

Fearlessly he'd approached to within ten feet of my position, angling his body so that he could see Rink and the gun that was aimed at his head. The beams from the SUVs head-lamps struck his right eye, and it shone glassily, like a Christmas bauble. He'd turned side on so that I wasn't on his blindside.

'It looks as if life's treated you OK.' Indeed, apart from the obvious glass eye, and a scar that cut a razor slash across his cheekbone, Marshall looked remarkably fit for a man who'd made violence his lifelong habit. He stood over six feet, a tad taller than me, and was broad-shouldered and long-limbed. His sweat-dampened shirt clung to a chest almost as well developed as Rink's. It was only the scattering of grey at his temples, and the thinning of the hair on top that spoke of the two decades since last I'd laid eyes on him.

'Can't say the same for you, Joe. When we came round that corner back there and caught you in the headlights, I had to take a second look. Shit, man, have you been bathing in a slaughterhouse?'

I had pretty much forgotten how bad I looked. There was blood all over me from the dozens of cuts received during the earlier gunfights. My clothes were frayed and torn in a couple of places, dust and blood adhered to the material as sticky mud, and dark sweat stains showed under my armpits. Yeah, I had to admit: I looked like shit. 'Trust me, my wounds are superficial.'

'You always were one lucky son of a bitch. Could have done with you when my convoy was hit, and I ended up with this.' He touched a fingertip to his blinded orb. 'You'd have probably caught the fucking rocket in your hands and lobbed it back at the ragheads.'

'Heard you were hit by an IED.'

'RPG,' he corrected. 'But you know how people like to use the buzzwords, right?'

See-sawing my head, I said, 'Shame it had to happen. You must have been pissed at the army when you were medically discharged. Is that why you're now happy to work for an arsehole like Jorge Molina? A dig at your old employers?'

He smiled, glancing down at the road. 'I'm not working for any wetback Mexican drug dealer. But I think you already guessed that.'

I didn't confirm that I'd guessed who his employer was. Let him confirm things for me.

'So why try and stop us out in the desert?'

'We were misinformed about your intentions.'

'Misinformed how?'

'After what you and your crew did to that coyote gang back in Arizona, it was believed you were heading out here to sow further dissent among the competing cartels. We were sent in to ensure you weren't successful.'

'You were told we were coming to Hermosillo to assassinate Molina?'

He didn't have to answer. His smile said it all. It also confirmed that they were working for the man I'd seen in Molina's company, because how else would he know about our fight with the coyotes? 'When you had the opportunity to rub out Molina you didn't take it. That tells me that killing that bean-eater was never your intention.'

'We're not interested in him.'

'I know that now. You came to steal his son.'

'We're here to liberate a US citizen. Molina kidnapped the boy.'

'Whatever,' he said.

'So that's why we aren't trading bullets now? You know that we aren't here to kill your mark, so there's no beef between us?'

Marshall shrugged. 'No sense in fighting you when the job's been done.'

A quick glance at McAdam told me that he was still pissed at me for beating the shit out of him in the alley, but he didn't look as if revenge was on his mind.

'Good to know,' I said. I trusted Marshall's word, just not far enough to offer him my hand in friendship. 'We go our separate ways then?'

'For now.'

'That doesn't sound too promising.'

'Right now I've followed instruction to the letter. Can't guarantee those instructions won't change.'

'Shame if they do,' I said. 'I'd hate to have to kill you.'

'Same here, mate. But we're both professionals, Joe. You do what you have to.'

'I don't even want to kill you, McAdam,' I said, directing my words at the Scotsman, 'but I meant what I said earlier. If either of you come at me again you'd best come shooting.'

'We're on the same page then. No hard feelings?' Marshall

held me with his one good eye, and up close like this I noticed that it jiggled slightly, compensating for the lack of binocular vision.

'That remains to be seen, doesn't it? You don't have to accept any new instructions.'

'Make me an offer I can't refuse,' Marshall said, his lip twitching. 'Exceed what we're being paid and I'll walk away, taking all my lads with me.'

Snorting, I shook my head. Marshall grunted out a laugh. He'd never been expecting a deal. He was reminding me that this was all about the money. Fuck the right or wrong of it. Fuck old friendships.

'Here are a few words of advice for you, lads. Your employer summarily executed the last person that worked for him when his services were no longer required. You think you can trust him to pay you, or is he planning a similar severance scheme for you when this is over?'

'I'll make sure I keep my good eye on the prick,' Marshall said. Then he nodded towards Rink. 'You and your pal best get going – sounds like those wetbacks are on their way.'

I pinched my bottom lip between my teeth, releasing it with a sigh. 'I hope it's another twenty years 'til I see you again, Marshall.'

'Me too.'

Suddenly he lifted his gun. I didn't flinch because he'd aimed it back at his SUV. He fired five shots, placing three in the front grill, two in the centre of the windshield. 'There,' he said, a cloud of cordite hanging in the air. 'Looks like we were ambushed. Saves us answering any awkward questions about why we didn't run you down. Now, get going. They arrive before you're out of sight and I'm going to have to start shooting at you. I don't trust your pal over there to miss if he shoots back.'

'Trust me. He wouldn't.'

He smiled again, a twinkle reflecting off his glass eye.

'See you, Joe.'

'Hope not,' I said, and turned away.

23

Jorge Molina's benevolent mask had slipped, revealing the sadistic creature that Howell Regis always suspected lurked behind the thousand-dollar haircut and Botox. The fact that Molina's was a base character was no revelation; in fact, Regis had counted on Molina's brutish nature when first he'd groomed and then recruited the man to his scheme.

Having strangers invade his home and abduct his son wasn't what had caused Molina's rage so much as his soldiers' inability to deliver the heads of those men to him. He was currently in one of the large meeting rooms screaming threats, punctuating his point with a punch or slap. Fearful of what lengths Molina would go to next his troops were rushing off in search of the interlopers, considering disappearing should they fail to bring back the heads of Joe Hunter and his friends.

After spotting and identifying Hunter and Rink out near the front gates, Regis had slunk back inside the mansion, to wait out the storm and to figure out how he was going to mollify Molina when the asshole turned his attention on him. There was only so long that Regis could keep up the mask of benevolence he wore and if Molina chose to get physical, well, fuck the scheme. In his belt he'd tucked his gun, and he wasn't loath to place a round or two between Molina's teeth if it came to it. There were plenty other egotistical little shits among the cartel bosses to be cajoled and manipulated into line. Still, for the time being it remained in his interest to reassure Molina that this slight hiccup should not throw a wedge between them, or disrupt the plan. Money, resources, and most of all time were an issue for Regis, or more correctly for those directing him.

The Mexican cartels were growing more powerful every day. Some of the smaller factions were still only loosely knit and involved in armed conflict with each other, while jostling for control of the lucrative routes into the US. But some, like the powerful Sinaloa cartel, were run with military precision and might. Molina's outfit was small potatoes in comparison, but he'd affiliated his group with them. His father, Felix Eugenio Molina, remained an influential and respected voice, because he'd convinced the Sinaloa bosses to infiltrate and align themselves with the Mexican federal government and military, with a view to annihilating the rival groups, therefore controlling the multi-billion-dollar drug- and people-trafficking enterprises.

Now, the Sinaloa cartel was made up of so many defecting federal agents and military personnel, that should they dominate the other cartels they would be in position to launch a *coup d'état* against the federal government. If that day came, factions within the CIA wanted their own men at the helm. For years, in secret, Regis and other CIA agents had trained, supplied and sponsored cartel footsoldiers, while also preparing assets the likes of Jorge Molina to take positions of command in the new government.

When stumbling over Walter Hayes Conrad's scheme to send his hitters into Molina's household Regis had feared the worst, and had mobilised his team of hired mercenaries to halt them. Conrad was engaged in a different and opposing plot to destabilise the coyote gangs up north, and it had come as a surprise that the old bastard had placed Molina in his sights: why would he have to send Hunter to snatch Molina's child?

It didn't make any sense to Regis. There was more to it than met the eye, and Regis wished now that he'd overheard more of Conrad's discussion as he'd lurked outside the command module van, eavesdropping after the gunfight at the mine. At the time he'd been more concerned with discovering if his execution of the last of the coyotes had raised any suspicion. Regis hadn't killed the man in cold blood to cover Hunter's part in the slayings, as he'd made out, but to shut the man up before he could blurt out anything more. 'Please . . . I won't tell anyone . . .' the coyote had begun, and Regis was sure that he would have ended with, 'that I'm working for you.'

Happily, neither Conrad nor Hunter had seen the execution as anything other than the cold-blooded actions of a CIA cleaner – something both had experienced in the past – and his involvement in the sponsoring of the coyotes hadn't been uncovered. But he hadn't been as pleased to hear the two men plotting an attack on Molina. If the plan to place their man at the head of the next government were derailed by the injudicious actions of a sub-division director unaware of the plot, it would be a blow to all involved. Regis's own boss, Thomas Caspar, would blame him, and rather than give Regis the go-ahead to groom an alternative asset, he'd hand the task over to another agent better placed. Such an eventuality would spell the death of Regis's career, and he'd be burned with impunity. Indeed, he could expect no less than another CIA cleaner to execute him as coldly as he had the coyote.

Through the walls he could hear that Molina's apoplexy hadn't diminished. Regis's fantasy about shooting the man had never been serious. Kill Molina and he'd never get out of the house alive. Kill Molina and he'd be back to square one. It was important that he manoeuvre the scheme back on track. While Molina was blowing up a storm over his stolen heir he wasn't concentrating on the major issues at hand: snatching the reins of control from his father, and securing his place at the head of the cartel. Felix Eugenio Molina had the ear of Joaquin 'El Chapo' Guzman, leader of the mighty Sinaloa cartel, not to mention Mexico's most-wanted man, and it would not do for his ill health to jeopardise his influence before Jorge was in position to take his father's place. Cancer and Alzheimer's disease were dual time bombs, and Regis had no idea how much time was left on the clock.

He thought he might have a solution to the problem.

If he helped recover the little brat, it would calm Molina and bring him back to the negotiating table with a clearer head and considerable gratitude. What better way to have Jorge in his pocket than have the man indebted to him for bringing back his son?

He took out his cell phone and punched in buttons.

At the other end a man answered curtly.

Regis didn't bother with formalities, he simply went into business mode – after all, that was the language mercenaries understood.

'There's a change in instructions if you're interested in naming a price. Yes, indeed. That is agreeable. Good, then we have a deal?'

Receiving an affirmative, he smiled, his face taking on the death's-head grin that so perturbed those who saw it.

'Bring back the child,' he said. 'Oh, one more thing, Marshall. I will pay double – call it a bonus – if you also bring back the heads of Kirstie Long and Joe Hunter. Their delivery is the only way to appease Señor Molina.'

24

Ten miles north of Hermosillo wasn't far enough from Jorge Molina's house to feel safe, but it was where we'd earlier agreed to rendezvous. After our run-in with Marshall, Rink had led me back to our car, while I checked the route behind us in case we'd picked up a tail. All seemed clear and Rink drove us away from the hillside, avoiding the main routes, until we discovered a highway out of the city, leaving behind both the police and Molina's soldiers. It took the best part of two hours from blasting our way out of the compound until we arrived at the meeting place: a parking lot at the rear of a derelict diner that was a dilapidated, graffiti-scored eyesore on the roadside.

Harvey was first out of the panel van when we pulled in alongside it. He seemed his usual cool self, but couldn't hold the mixed emotions in check. He was both relieved to see us alive and worried for what was still to come.

'Jesus Christ, guys, don't do that to me again.' He came forward to grab each of us in a manly hug. 'I was worried you hadn't made it out.'

Slapping him on his shoulders, I said: 'We made it. It was a close call, though.'

'I can see that.' He appraised my dishevelled state, taking in the blood, dirt and slivers of glass. I looked like crap but at least I wasn't full of bullet holes. 'The guys wanted to go back for you but I told them we had to keep to the plan . . .'

'That's exactly what you should've done,' I reassured him. 'Wasn't an easy decision.'

Velasquez and McTeer joined us, and hands were shaken and shoulders slapped. The guys had done as asked and all had ended well.

'OK,' Rink said, 'now we have to get moving again. We need Kirstie and Benjamin in the car with you guys; me and Joe will take the van.'

If the panel van was being tracked it was time to dump it. The car Rink had purchased was large enough for the three men, woman and child, plus the few pieces of clothing, supplies and equipment they required. We could now replace the van with something less obvious. Time was an issue, but there was something I wished to do first.

'Just give me a minute with Kirstie.' I caught a brief glance from Rink, but he knew I wasn't planning on 'canoodling' with Kirstie again, I only wished to check on her and the boy. He nodded at the others to give me some space. They walked away a short distance, while Rink related what had happened after the gates were rammed and they took off. Old soldiers love to tell and hear war stories.

Feeling some trepidation, and with no idea why, I opened the back doors of the van and looked inside. Kirstie was lying down on a bed of jackets, her small son held in the protective circle of her arms. She was murmuring to him, but as the doors swung wide she blinked up at me. Her face was a pale oval in the dimness, but her grey eyes – sparkling with tears of relief – shone. I climbed inside and went towards her, sinking to my knees despite the prickle of glass against my skin, and peered down at the boy.

'How is he?'

'He's fine. Sleeping naturally now.' Kirstie used her finger-tips to brush a stray dark curl off Benjamin's forehead. How often had she repeated the gesture since taking Benjamin in her arms? Many times, I guessed.

I raked through my pockets and came out with the bottle I'd grabbed from the nightstand in Benjamin's bedroom. 'Either Jorge or someone else was feeding him this.'

Kirstie's features relaxed as she eyed the bottle. It was as I'd assumed: the formula was nothing more sinister than a paracetamol suspension, a syrup used to treat pain and fever in small children and infants. This was further confirmed when Kirstie drew down Benjamin's bottom lip to show where his gums appeared red and swollen.

'He woke up as we were driving here. I . . . I'm not sure that he remembers me. It's been so long, Joe. How do we ever get those years back? How do I become his mother again?'

'Love.' My answer stated the obvious, but what more was there to say? 'He'll get to know you soon enough, Kirstie. Once you're home the bond will grow again. Trust me.'

'Do you have children?'

I shook my head. I'd never been as lucky.

'You were married, though, weren't you? Harvey said you and your wife split up.'

'We did. I was married to Diane for fourteen years. Sadly, things didn't work out as we'd planned.'

'She didn't love you?'

'Quite the opposite. She loved me too much to stick around and watch me self-destruct. She couldn't take the violence that constantly surrounded me. She didn't want to end up a widow.'

'Do you miss her?'

'With all of my heart. There isn't a day goes by when I don't think about her. Sometimes it's just for a second or two: I'll see a face in a crowd that reminds me of her, or someone says something that brings her face to mind.'

'Is there any chance that . . .'

'We'd get back together? No. Diane has a new husband. She's happier with the arrangement than I am, to be honest.'

'But you've moved on, right?'

'Yeah. Took me a while. I found someone else, but then I lost her too.' I had no desire to go over the past. It hurt too much.

'Kate Piers,' Kirstie said. 'Harvey told me about how she was killed.'

'Harvey seems to have told you quite a lot.'

'Don't blame him; I wanted to learn more about you. He also told me that you and Imogen were together for a while. Imogen was Kate's sister, right?'

'Sounds a little sordid when you say it like that,' I said, tempering my words with a smile.

'No . . . not at all. I've heard how you got together, but, Joe, you must see it was a relationship destined never to last?'

'Yeah, that's clear to me now.'

'My marriage to Jorge was always going to fail. The trouble was I was too blind to see that. I was young, stupid, dazzled by love. Perhaps I was dazzled by his wealth and status as well. Jesus, how shallow does that make me?'

'We're all wise in hindsight.'

'We are.' Then she asked the question she'd been building up to. 'Do you regret kissing me, now that you've had time to think about it?'

'No. You needed comforting, I comforted you: where's the harm in that?'

'That's all it was? Mutual comfort?'

Scrubbing a hand through my hair – slivers of glass and blood clots notwithstanding – I looked down at her and her sleeping boy. 'No. OK, I wanted to kiss you. Have done since I first saw you at the airport.'

Kirstie looked down, as though to check on Benjamin, but she couldn't conceal the tiny smile that tugged at the corner of her mouth. 'Would you kiss me again if I asked?'

Hell, yeah, but this was neither the time nor the place. We needed to get moving. 'Maybe if you ask me another time? When we haven't half the gunmen in Mexico chasing us.'

'Rink doesn't approve of me, does he?'

Her question came out of left field. How had she been party to a conversation that even Harvey couldn't have told her about? But then I got it: she'd been picking up on Rink's attitude all the way here.

'Trust me, Kirstie. Rink doesn't disapprove of you. Hell, he'd die for you. It's something else that's troubling him about your—'

I caught myself before blurting out the secret of Walter and her lineage.

Kirstie proved she was no fool though.

'Rink thinks it's inappropriate for you to have a relationship with Walter Conrad's granddaughter. It's OK; you don't have to confirm anything. I'm no longer the naïve young woman that fell into bed with a drug-dealing murderer. Walter Conrad is my grandfather. It's as plain to see as that Benjamin is my son.'

It was pointless denying the truth, so I didn't. Neither did I confirm anything, so my pledge to Walter was safe. Instead, I explained about my connection to Walter. When I'd been with Arrowsake, he'd been my stateside handler, but more than that he'd become a friend first, then something much more important. My real dad died when I was a child, and my mother's second husband, a cold, humourless man who barely tolerated my presence in the house, raised me. I grew up without the love of a father to guide me, and had turned to the Army for somewhere to feel like I belonged. But it wasn't until a few years later, when I was recruited to the specialist counter-terrorism squad, that I'd found the surrogate father I'd been seeking. Walter Conrad was a scheming, twisted manipulator, but despite that I loved him. And I knew that he loved me too. I understood now that I was the surrogate child he'd been seeking to replace his own that he could neither touch nor hold. Also it was plain why he'd sworn me to silence about Kirstie and Annie's bloodline. His fears that they would be targeted by his enemies had been borne out, and that was before they even knew that Kirstie and Benjamin were his kinfolk. To what ends would his opponents in the CIA go should they ever learn the truth?

'It's not like we're blood relatives or anything,' Kirstie said, teasing me with a flutter of lashes. 'At worst we'd be kissing cousins.'

'Let's talk about that another time,' I said, resting my hand on her shoulder. When Imogen and I fell into each other's arms it had been through survivor guilt syndrome on both our parts. A relationship based on such raw emotion could never amount to much other than sex; there was plenty of passion but little love. Right now, Kirstie was caught in a stressful, confusing situation and I didn't want her to regret throwing herself at me once this was over with. 'We have to move you and Benjamin to the car, and get you on your way again.'

'OK.' Even in the dimness the blush flooding her features was evident. She stood, holding Benjamin close to her chest, and I steered them to the open doors. Benjamin was stirring.

'Are you my mamma?' The little lad's voice was sweetened by his drowsy state.

Tears beaded on Kirstie's cheeks.

'Yes, I'm your mommy . . . and I love you very much, Benjamin.'

'I'm not Benjamin any more,' he said, pouting his bottom lip. 'I'm Benny. That's what my papa calls me.'

'No sweetie, you're *my* Benjamin.' Kirstie used a finger to tease that forelock again, and the boy squirmed against her touch.

'I'm Benny,' he said, trying to twist out of her grasp. 'I don't want to be your *Benjamin*.'

Then the boy was howling, and inside the van it was like an emergency siren going off. Rink and McTeer appeared at the open doors, but I waved them away, signalling I had everything under control. Kirstie was distraught, and I took her into a hug, holding them both until the medication sent the boy back to a shallow doze.

'Oh, God!' Kirstie was disconsolate, the tears on her face now rivers. 'This is my worst nightmare. That bastard Jorge has already begun to change him. God damn him! Benny Molina . . . it even sounds like the name of a mobster!'

I touched her face, tracing the tears with a fingertip. 'He's just confused, Kirstie. Once he's been with you a few days he'll begin to see things more clearly. He isn't Benny Molina. He's Benjamin Long. And if I have anything to do with it, that's the way he'll stay.'

25

The van burned brightly, belching oily smoke into the night sky, but from the distant highway it would look like yet another bonfire off in the gullies, where farmers often set fire to garbage, or to brush scoured from their fields. I doubted that anyone would come to investigate the flames, and even if they did, it would be unlikely to be any of those men working on behalf of Jorge Molina.

It was an hour since we'd waved off the packed car, and Rink had taken care to go across country to a remote spot nearer to a different highway. Had we been tracked via device or satellite, it would look as if we aimed to leave Mexico via a more north-westerly route than the actual one we'd chosen. As it was we'd decided on showing our faces nearby, more or less staking ourselves out like bait to draw any hunters away from the others, but not while we were still on foot with no hope of escape from more mobile enemies. Neither of us was comfortable with the idea of boosting a car, but it was a case of needs must.

When I was a boy of fifteen, I knew a lad called Simmy. I don't even recall his actual name; he came into my small circle of acquaintances as a friend of a friend, and I only ever knew him by his nickname. Back then kids were defined by their musical tastes and you banded together with like-minded individuals. Often you didn't care much for some of those in your group, but they became your pals nonetheless. At the time there was a resurgence in mod and skinhead culture, and I was in among it simply because I preferred the older styles of music to the New Romantic stuff that was all the rage. Simmy was a hardened skin; he had the suede head, the black Harrington jacket, skinny jeans and braces, and ox-blood Doc Marten boots. He also sported a self-inflicted tattoo across the knuckles of his right hand. ACAB, it said. I recall falling out with him when he revealed what the acronym stood for: All Cops Are Bastards. In his bigoted opinion, anyone in a police uniform was the enemy.

We had to ensure that we didn't make the same mistake now.

The Mexican police are often on the receiving end of a bad reputation as being corrupt, uncompromising and violent. It was unfair, because there were more selfless people who only wished to uphold law and order and raise the quality of life for their families and neighbours, than there were the greedy pigs who took bribes from criminals. The officers responding to the shootout at Molina's home might well be those that were in his pocket, but now that we were out of their immediate jurisdiction any police we met needed to be thought of in the former category: good guys doing a difficult job. No way must we engage the police in battle until their actions dictated otherwise. The only problem was that by stealing a car we were inviting trouble from the local peacekeepers.

We jogged out of the gullies and across a parched field, keeping a low profile as we passed a small adobe farm. The crop had been harvested, and only the stems of plants jutted from the earth. I'd no idea what the crop was, but it was tough going underfoot. We made it back on to a dirt trail, deeply rutted by tracks formed by the massive tyres of a tractor. As we progressed it began to rain. Ordinarily that would have brought a curse from me, but I hadn't yet had the opportunity to clean up, so it was a blessing in disguise. The blood and dirt began to wash out of my hair, and from my face. As I followed Rink down the trail, I teased some of the longer shards of glass from my clothing, dropping them on the earth.

We stayed off the highway, keeping to fields and untilled ground. At a previously dry wash, now trickling with muddy rainwater, we were forced up on to the road, but as soon as we were past the obstruction Rink led us inland again. Another adobe farm was outlined as a series of squat geometrical silhouettes against the gently undulating horizon. A single light burned above the door of the main house, but none beyond its windows. The family there had most likely retired, preparing for an early start and hard day of labour the following morning. This family didn't look to be as poor as at the first farm we'd avoided, but that didn't make me feel any better about stealing their vehicle. Even so, our needs were greater than theirs: lives depended on us taking their car.

The car was an older model Dodge pick-up that sported a hard plastic shell on the back. A few agricultural tools and a pile of empty sacks lay on the cargo bed, nothing of real importance to the running of the farm. It opened to Rink's touch and no alarm began to yelp. The keys were even hanging from the ignition barrel. Still, he didn't turn the engine over. The last thing we wanted was for the farmer or his family to come to investigate; neither of us had any desire to hurt anyone. Rink released the steering lock, and also the handbrake, then together we pushed, free-wheeling it down the slight hillside to a point a couple of hundred yards away from the house where any noise would be drowned by the drumming rain. When we had gone far enough for there to be little fear of confrontation, I scrambled inside and Rink turned the key. The engine coughed, whirred, then caught, and blue smoke erupted into the heavens. He took it easy down the rutted trail until we found the highway.

'Gonna have to find a gas station soon,' Rink said, noting that we were practically riding on fumes. Perhaps the farmer hadn't bothered to secure the pick-up because he knew a thief wouldn't get far with their ill-gotten gains. Adding validity to this thought, Rink said, 'Can't get more than fifty miles an hour out of the old girl, but maybe that's not such a bad thing.'

'We'll swap it for something with a bit more *oomph* further down the road,' I said.

'Unless Molina's punks catch up with us first. We couldn't outrun them in this old heap.'

'Don't tempt fate,' I said. 'If the van was being tracked, they're probably on the way to its final signal. Soon as they find the van's been burned out they'll figure that we're in another car. Won't take them long to check that farm back there and discover what we're driving.'

'I hope the bastards don't punish the farmer, thinking he was in cahoots with us.'

I hadn't considered that. Made me sick to think that the innocent farmer, a victim of theft, might soon become a victim of violence too.

I dug out my cell phone and, after checking it had a signal, hit a hot key. Usually when contacting Walter I would use secure relays to bounce the call off various satellites, but didn't bother this time. This phone was a throwaway, as was its twin that Walter held; they couldn't be traced to us. Walter picked up after the first ring. I had to jam the phone tight to my ear to hear him over the rattle of rain on the cab roof.

'Joe? How are Kirstie and Benjamin?'

'You must have been expecting my call?'

'I've been on goddamn pins since last you called. Tell me, are they with you?'

'Not exactly . . .'

'What? I'm receiving reports about a gun battle at Molina's house: don't tell me you failed to get the boy away.'

'Relax. Kirstie and Benjamin are with Harvey and the others. Me and Rink are playing backstop, trying to slow down the pursuit.'

'I'd feel much better if you were with them, son.'

'Harvey and the guys are good. They'll see that your folks are safe.'

'I'm not doubting their abilities . . . it's just, well, I know that you and Rink are better.'

As is often the way with Walter, his words were double-edged. In one breath he was complimenting us, while also criticising my decision to send Kirstie and Benjamin ahead with the others. I didn't bother replying, just went straight to the issue at hand. 'There's a problem, Walt. That arsehole that was at the mine in Arizona with you; the one that executed the coyote?'

'Howell Regis?'

'If he's the skull-faced bastard that pulled the trigger, then, yes.'

'Wait on! You're telling me that Regis is out there in Hermosillo?'

'Unless he's got an identical twin.'

'What the *hell* is *he* doing there?'

'I was hoping you could throw some light on that,' I said. 'We seem to have stumbled into a bigger plan for Jorge Molina than simply abducting his son. Regis is all buddy-buddy with him, a welcome visitor in Molina's home from what I witnessed. Here's the bigger problem, Walt: Regis – or someone he's working for – has been on to us from the beginning. We were under surveillance as we crossed the border, and a few hours later a kill team was sent to stop us. The team is made up of mercenaries, a couple of whom I know from back in the day. After we got the boy out of harm's way we bumped into those guys again. It seems our intentions were misconstrued. They thought that we were there on wet work, Molina the target. Someone back at your end thinks you sent us to kill their pet cartel boss, and they aren't happy. And they aren't going to allow a second attempt either, so watch your ass. Maybe they'll figure that you're the key to stopping us and try to harm you.'

'Don't worry about me. Concentrate on getting Kirstie and Ben home ... I can look after myself.' Walter fell into an uncomfortable silence. Likely he was mulling over who was guiding Howell Regis and what he had to do about it. Knowing Walter he was more concerned about protecting his position than his skin.

'Just make sure that your protection detail is on full alert, Walt, OK?'

'Yeah, yeah, will do. Listen, I've some investigating to do at this end. You concentrate on bringing my folk home and I'll let you know what I find.'

'You were worried that your relationship to Kirstie would be discovered ... I've a feeling that's inevitable.'

'Not if I can help it.'

Walter hung up, and I was left wondering at the sudden steel in his voice. Walter had mellowed over the past two decades, had grown weary with the violence and murder that constantly surrounded him, yet, as he rung off, his parting words were those of a ruthless and resilient field operative.

Rink had given me privacy while he concentrated on driving the rattling pick-up, guiding it through the deluge. But he'd heard every word and was ruminating over them. His question wasn't what I expected. 'Do you ever regret signing up with Arrowsake?'

'Yes. When I look back at what it was, I wish I'd never been part of it. But then I also think about what it has given me and I'm grateful.'

'Granted. If we hadn't been with Arrowsake, we'd never have met. I've a good friend in you, Hunter, a brother. But when I think about everything that we've lost, I wonder if it was worth it.'

'Thanks,' I said.

'Aah, I'm not talking about you. I'm talking about family, stability, *peace and quiet*. All the things other people take for granted.'

He was right, of course. The brief we had, with all the fancy titles and political correctness removed, amounted to us being little more than guided missiles. The faceless men at the top of the Arrowsake command structure relayed instructions down the line, through the likes of Walter, and we acted without question. We were idealistic, we were patriotic, and looking back, we were misguided. We were assassins. That's all there'd been to it when everything else was stripped away: killers. Such men didn't deserve family, stability or peace. I had fooled myself into thinking that my marriage to Diane could weather my career, and when I retired we'd have all of those things. It had been a halcyon dream and, like most dreams, it evaporated in the cold light of reality. Rink had known a stream of women, but he hadn't settled down, had no children. It wasn't that he didn't desire a wife and kids, he was too afraid that his old associations would bring harm to them. If either of us had fully realised what we were signing up for then, we'd have run away screaming in denial. So yes, like Rink, I regretted ever joining Arrowsake, the secretive UN coalition counter-terrorism unit. We were supposed to negate terrorist threats by taking pre-emptive war to those who would target UN countries. Thinking about it now, we were more terrifying than most potential aggressors.

Rink wasn't really directing the question at me, though. I guessed he was thinking about Walter, and wondering if the old man regretted the life and career choices he'd made. Did he rue the day he and his lover brought life into their dark world? We feared for our loved ones – both living and dreamed-of – but was Walter any different? Had he a darker take on the meaning of family ties? By their blood relationship Annie, Kirstie and Benjamin could become targets of men whose agendas might not match Walter's. Was Walter's biggest regret that his family was his weakness? His Achilles heel? I pretty much doubted it; I'd heard the tough edge to his words. That wasn't the voice of a man who regretted having kids. It was the voice of someone determined to make whoever threatened them sorry.

'One thing I don't regret,' I added.

'What's that?'

'Arrowsake gave us the skills to help others. If we hadn't signed up, who would Kirstie have called on to help bring home her son?'

Rink shook his head, rumbling out laughter that added a deep undertone to the drumming rainfall. Briefly he turned from the road ahead to hold me under his gaze.

'Hunter,' he said.

'What?'

'You always find a way to make something shitty sound attractive and noble.'

'It's the only way I manage to sleep at night.'

26

Howell Regis listened intently to his cell phone over the chatter of the other men in the room. He tried to filter out the noise, concentrating instead on the British voice on the other end of the line. Sometimes he struggled to understand what James Lee Marshall was telling him; the man made no allowance for his thick northern English accent.

'To clarify, you've found the panel van?'

'Aye. I already told you that,' Marshall said.

'Sorry. I can barely hear you for all the hollering going on here.'

'Tell the fuckin' bean-eaters to shut the fuck up then.'

'I'm sure that would go down well with my host.'

'Fuck him, too. He can dress himself up in fancy clothes, but he's still a fuckin' drug-dealing wetback arsehole. He should be showing *us* respect, not the other way round.'

'Lest you forget, Marshall, it's important to the CIA that Jorge Molina is treated with courtesy and deference, in order that he stays on-side when he ascends to take his father's place at the head of the cartel. Telling him to "shut the fuck up" wouldn't meet those criteria any way you try to fancy it up.'

'OK, so open your ears and pay attention. I can hardly hear myself speak for the fucking downpour and don't want to have to keep repeating myself.'

'Can I also remind you to show courtesy and deference to me. Who's paying your wage cheque, Marshall?'

'Fuck deference, you prick. You need me more than I need you. Now listen up: the van's been torched, and the tracking device you planted inside it is offline. Now, the way I'm seeing it is that only two men left the scene. It's pissing down here, but I can still see that only one vehicle drove in, didn't leave, and two men left on foot. I'm guessing that Hunter is one of those two, and probably his big Jap mate, judging by the size of the footprints.'

'What about the others and Molina's boy?'

'They'll be in another vehicle, taking a different route to the border. If it was me, I'd have done exactly what Hunter has: laid a false trail.'

'How far are you behind Hunter?'

'The van hasn't been burning very long; I think he's still nearby. His first priority will be to find alternative transport. McAdam and three of my men have gone on ahead. They're rousting every family between here and the highway out of their beds, making them check if their vehicles are all accounted for. We'll know soon enough what they're driving. Then you can relay that info to all of Molina's footsoldiers between Hermosillo and the border. With eyes on each major road junction they'll be spotted soon enough.'

'I want you to concentrate on finding the boy.'

'Yeah, but there's a problem with that, isn't there? Unless we get incredibly lucky and one of Molina's bean-eaters happens to spot them, we can forget about finding the brat. But if I can catch Hunter, I'll make him tell us where they plan to rendezvous, and I'll get the boy back then. You asked for the heads of Joe Hunter *and* Kirstie Long; well, this is the only way I can guarantee both.'

A sudden burst of activity caught Regis's attention. Jorge Molina was pushing his way through the group of his lieutenants, heading for Regis, his face set with determination.

'Give me a second or two here, Marshall, will you?'

'Yeah, just don't be too fucking long. I'm getting soaked standing out here.'

Molina strode directly to Regis and stood so close, a waft of warm air, a heady mix of expensive cologne and sweat, surrounded him. Molina's teeth were clamped together, his lips lifted in a snarl. The only thing that belied the image was the feral light of excitement in his gaze.

'Is that your hired killer on the phone?' Molina's voice carried no hint of his Hispanic heritage. Not surprisingly, as he'd been raised and schooled in the USA. Before Regis could confirm he was speaking to Marshall, Molina plucked the phone out of his hand. 'Listen to me,' he snapped, without preamble. 'I have a man on the road at Oasis Carbo. He has just spotted this "Hunter" at a gas station ten miles north of your position. I suggest you get your men there now.'

There was a threat to Molina's final sentence, one that Regis hoped Marshall would not rise to. When there was no change to Molina's face, Regis relaxed.

'They are travelling north on Carretera Quince – Route Fifteen – towards Santa Ana in an old Dodge pick-up. Green with a white hard plastic shell on the back.' Molina relayed the registration number from memory; having absorbed the details, Regis assumed, during the brief telephone call he'd received minutes before. 'I will send men to assist your team, as well as warn those in Santa Ana, Magdalena and Nogales to set up rolling roadblocks. Stop this "Hunter" and you will be well rewarded. Fail, and you will wish you never came to my backyard.'

Molina flipped the phone at Regis and he caught it out of the air.

'That,' Molina told him, 'is how to motivate your people, Regis.'

Regis nodded, smiling graciously at Molina's wisdom, before turning his back and pressing the phone to his ear. 'Marshall?'

'Shut the fuck up, Regis. I've a job to do.'

Regis was left with the dead buzz of white noise as Marshall set off in pursuit. Not for a second did Regis think Marshall's alacrity was due to the cartel boss's threat; it was more from his desire to capture Hunter. It was almost as if Marshall had something to prove.

27

'Well, I'd say that Molina's men are on the way, now, brother.'

Rink was at the steering wheel of the old Dodge while I rode shotgun. Actually, the phrase was a misnomer, because all I had to hand was my SIG. A check of my available ammunition told me that I'd one full clip and just three spare rounds left over from earlier. Rink wasn't much better off with only half a clip in his gun. Usually we used the same ammunition so that the rounds could be shared between us, but his gun was chambered for .357 while my slightly larger stock was of nine-millimetre Parabellum. Still, Rink was adaptable, and didn't require bullets to defend himself.

'Yeah, job done. I only hope we didn't make it too obvious that we were trying to be seen.'

'Does it make a difference? Let them come, I'm ready for them now.'

'No. I meant that they'd figure we were trying to draw them away from the others. There aren't that many direct routes from Hermosillo back to the border. Maybe they'll send most of their guns to cut off those roads instead of chasing us.'

'I got that. But I think after what happened at his house, Molina has to try to catch us; otherwise he's going to lose face with other cartel bosses. He'll be determined to make an example of us, to prove he's got the steel balls to hold his own against them. He'll send everything he's got after us, and concentrate on getting his son back later. Way he sees things, if he kills us there'll be no one left to stop him from taking Benjamin back from Kirstie whenever he likes.'

'I guess we have to factor in Marshall and his goon squad.' It was regrettable that it had come to this, but the lure of money could make enemies of the best of friends. Marshall hadn't been a friend the way Rink and Harvey were to me now, but he had been someone I'd have risked my life for when we fought side by side. He'd been a good soldier back then, a tough and resourceful bastard, and even missing an eye and twenty years older, he was no doubt still equally tough and resourceful. Pity he had grown to be more of a bastard. Back on that hillside the only reason he hadn't drawn on us was because there was nothing in it for him. Why fight, and possibly die, for no reward? But I was wise enough to believe he was after us now. Howell Regis – the Grim Reaper – would have made him an offer he couldn't refuse.

When I was with 1 Para there was a lot of competition among the lads. Who could run the furthest? Who could carry the heaviest weight for longest? Who was the fittest? Who was the best shot on the range? All banter, and an integral part of the job to ensure you continuously pushed to be the best of the best. One question that often came up: who was the hardest in the regiment? There was a time when James Lee Marshall held that title hands down.

Then a brash youngster called Joe Hunter entered the running, and the lads were of a split opinion. If I hadn't been flown to other theatres of war then, sooner or later, Marshall and I would have been pressed into proving the issue. I was on the way up; people would assume that I'd something to prove by beating him. But the opposite was true. He was the old champion and it was for him to protect his position as alpha male.

When I was chosen over him to represent 1 Para as their delegate to Arrowsake, it must have hurt. Sounds egotistical, but they were only looking for the very best of the best, and they'd found Marshall wanting. Wonder if the rejection had stuck with him all these years? I hadn't thought about Marshall in the best part of two decades, yet the moment I'd recognised his face in the glare of lights on the highway, something had stirred in me. It was the emotion that old boxers must feel when they proclaim they could have been a contender for the title belt. I admit to telling myself that I could take him. Part of me was even looking forward to him showing up again.

'Let them come.' Rink was obviously of a similar opinion.

He'd been acting out of character since back at the abandoned mine. His misgivings were all to do with his mistrust of Walter, as we'd already established, but now we were in the thick of things his mindset had adapted to the problem at hand. His blood was up, and he was ready for the challenge. Now that enemy combatants were pursuing us, he was in the zone where it was the two of us against the world. Nothing mattered to him now but defeating all comers. Faced with the number of enemies we must have, there was no one I'd rather have at my side than Rink; after all, he had been the very best that the US Army Rangers could field to Arrowsake. But, I had to remind myself, this wasn't about us two versus an army of bad guys; this was about safely returning a woman and child home. We couldn't fight this war on our terms. Where we both preferred to take the battle to Marshall, Regis and Molina, we were forced to play fox to their hounds. We had to run, lead them astray, split their forces, and then – where it was unavoidable – mount a defence.

Back at the gas station at Oasis Carbo, next to a fleapit stretch of rundown houses and derelict businesses, we'd spotted a guy taking far too much interest in us to be coincidence. He was in his mid-twenties, but his sunken, cadaverous features spoke of a tough life and meagre nourishment, and

made him look two decades older. He was sitting in a rusted
Impala that looked as old and infirm as he did, and had
hunched down behind the wheel as we'd drawn up at the gas
pumps next to him. His eyes had grown saucer-wide when
he'd spotted us in the cab of the Dodge and it wasn't out of
jealousy of our ride. Without pumping gasoline, he pulled
away but completed a U-turn a couple of hundred yards
further along the highway, where he sat watching us fill our
tank. Apparently he wasn't as poor as he first appeared, as he
had enough money to furnish himself with a cell phone.

Fearing he might be desperate enough to please his boss
by attempting a hit on us, I readied my SIG as we drove
towards him. Yet, if he had a gun, he wasn't stupid enough to
draw it. Either that or his cell phone bill meant he couldn't
also afford ammunition. I was glad not to have to kill him:
the poor sap was probably forced into working for Molina in
the vain hope of paying off some highly inflated debt. Allowing him to complete his job, we passed him by, and out of the
corner of my eye I watched him hunker down so that only
his eyes and tufts of unkempt black hair jutted above the
window frame. After we were well past, he completed another
U-turn and followed us far enough to be able to relate which
direction we followed on the highway, then he pulled into the
side of the road.

'By the way that guy just pulled over he was ordered to back
off,' I said. 'My bet is that Molina or Regis are coordinating an
attack further along the way and didn't want him to alert us.'

'Yup, that's the way I'd play things, I was him,' Rink said.
When he's preparing for combat, his southern drawl grows
more pronounced.

When I'm facing battle I tend to grow monosyllabic, and
nothing was about to change now. We had no idea where,
when or how Molina's men would come at us, so there was

little point in debating it. We sank into silence for the next ten minutes or so. Once I caught a glance from Rink. He was smiling: probably because he noticed that the blood had drained from my features. I could feel the tell-tale coldness at the tip of my nose that said I'd adopted my killing face. Usually it perturbs Rink, but now he appeared to have recognised an old friend. His features didn't look any less stern. He held his chin so rigid that the scar below his bottom lip nigh on glowed in the faint wash of light from the dashboard.

A signpost indicated that we were ten miles from the town of Benjamin Hill. The town's name was ironic, seeing as we were planning on protecting a child of the same name. I searched the evening horizon for sight of hills, but the valley was wide here and all the landscape appeared to be of the same featureless formula as the sky. The earlier rain had stopped but the clouds still hung low, obscuring moon and stars alike. The only pinpricks of light were from one homestead way off to our right and the wan yellow lights of a train heading towards Hermosillo on our far left.

Actually that wasn't the entire truth. When I checked the side mirror I caught the twinkle of headlights on high beam a couple miles behind us. I must have grunted or something because Rink said, 'I saw them.'

'Maybe you'd best put your foot down.'

'I've already got the pedal to the metal. This is as fast as we get from this old gal.'

Checking the mirrors once more, I could tell that the lights were growing in size and brightness. 'They're coming at some rate. It's a safe bet that it's Molina's lot.'

'Well it sure ain't Wile E. Coyote chasing Road Runner,' Rink laughed. 'Not unless Acme does a line of high-performance vehicles these days.'

'We can't outrun them. Likely they've seen our tail lights

already, so not much hope of hiding from them either. Leaves only one option.'

'Yup . . . we meet and greet the frog-giggers.' Rink touched the butt of his gun, unsnapping the safety strap off his holster with a practised flick.

I began looking out for somewhere we could wait, a place that offered more cover than the undulating desert floor around us. Within a half-mile I saw a track running alongside the highway, leading across the desert to a cluster of agricultural sheds behind which towered electric pylons. 'Can you make it over there?'

Rink made only a cursory inspection of the shoulder of land separating highway from farm track, then veered to the right. The Dodge handled the transition from asphalt to loose soil to hard-packed dirt with little complaint, and we were travelling parallel to our original route. Then the trail swung east and up a shallow incline towards the sheds. Turning so I could peer beneath the plastic shell on the back of the pick-up I saw that the speeding vehicle had covered half the distance between us now. It would be apparent to those inside that we had changed course. 'We've only a couple minutes before they get here.'

'Long enough,' Rink reassured me.

The Dodge bounced over the rough terrain as Rink went off-road, cutting across a wedge of ground that doubled as an unofficial garbage dump. A barbed-wire fence marked the southern boundary of the agricultural site, but Rink merely ran right over the top of it and into a yard that fronted the buildings. There was no house evident, only sheds in which were parked various wagons, tractors and machines I didn't recognise. The sheds were in differing levels of disrepair, some solid and sturdy, others almost rusted through. I took it the place was a shared compound where farmers stored their larger machinery. Chains and padlocks were strung across the entrances of the buildings. They would do little to hamper determined thieves, but judging by the decrepit nature of most of the vehicles it was unlikely a determined thief would bother with them.

Bringing the Dodge to a halt alongside a large tin structure that leaned precariously to one side, Rink baled out and I was only a second or two behind him. Rink made his way round the back of the pick-up and leaned inside, while I checked on the progress of the speeding vehicle. True to form, it too had bumped over the shoulder and on to the farm track: definitely some of Molina's crew. Way back along the highway was a second set of lights, maybe more than one.

When I looked back, Rink had disappeared as silently as a dissipating spectre. For such a big man he could move with the stealth of a cat. I went for shelter inside the nearest off-kilter shed. As the approaching car bounced up the rutted road its headlights caught me in their glare, before I ducked into the deeper well of shadow inside the shed. As I retreated, the car swung my way. No way could they see me now, so I ran for the back of the shed where a fainter oblong of night marked an open hatch. I went out of it, and ran along the back wall, then kept low as I traversed a narrow strip of land sown with broken glass and indeterminate metal objects: it was apparent that the site was built on reclaimed landfill. Then I entered the next building along and raced for the front, having to swerve round a combine harvester that didn't look as if it had seen much use in the past couple of decades. The air was full of dust motes and an overriding smell of rust, but I clamped down on the urge to cough. Making it to the front door, I placed myself behind a thick upright support beam. It would offer little protection if any of the men in the car came packing a high-powered rifle, but was better than the thin tin sheets to each side of it.

Remaining in the shadows, I sneaked a peek outside, just as the car – an SUV I recognised from earlier in the evening – powered through the yard and screeched to a dust-kicking halt. Doors sprang open on both sides and disgorged the passengers – three in total. In the next moment, the driver threw the vehicle into reverse and backed wildly away. Out of my line of sight I heard the SUV halt and the driver's door come open. He was trying to set up a second arc of fire to pen me inside the sheds. Sadly for him, I wasn't in the one they all assumed.

The three who'd decamped from the vehicle had strung out in a skirmish line, but from the glances they cast at each other, none was too eager to be first to enter the shed I'd recently fled from. They moved from foot to foot, aiming their guns like they were juggling hot rocks. Each was equipped with a handgun, I was happy to note, but I couldn't see the driver so he might have been more heavily armed.

One of the three shouted a challenge, telling me in heavily accented English to come out. He didn't sound Mexican though, more Eastern European: one of Marshall's team of mercenaries. I neglected to reply. The men were nervous. They weren't keen on the fact that they'd been ordered into a full frontal assault on the shed, leaving them open targets to counter-fire, but glances past my position said they were more afraid of retribution levied by their boss than being cut down by me. The driver must have given a wordless command, because the three suddenly steeled themselves and began blind-shooting at the shed. Their bullets clanged off the machinery inside.

'Hey you . . . inside the shed. This is your last chance. Come out or we'll be forced to come inside and kill you.' It was the Eastern European who'd shouted the challenge. Did he actually expect a reply?

I watched as they moved forward to flank the open doorway: two on one side, one on the other. They were now obscured from view by the angle of the shed wall, but I guessed that a man on each side would triangulate their line of fire while the other entered the shed low. It would be a few seconds before they realised there was no return fire, and a few more after that before they figured that I was either dead from their first volley, hiding deeper inside, or that I'd fled the building and they were wasting their time in there. By the time they computed all that and formulated a new plan the best part of twenty seconds would have passed. It was enough time for me to sneak up behind them and cut them down as they came outside. I couldn't do that with the driver covering their retreat, though. I had to get him before he got me.

I searched for an exit that offered a way to surprise the driver. Midway along a loose tin sheet allowed me to slip into a narrow space that was chock-full of oil drums and less identifiable trash. I began squeezing my way to the front. Despite my efforts to move with the stealth that Rink exhibits, the empty drums foiled me, and one of them made a hollow thrum as my knee knocked against it. I ducked, and not a second too soon. From the front the narrow space was lit by machine-gun fire.

The drums had given away my position, yet they redeemed themselves by saving my skin. The bullets cut through the first few, but the metal barrier slowed them enough that they didn't make it all the way to where I crouched. As the shooter reassessed his firing position, I bobbed up and fired at him. Didn't hit him though. He sprang to the corner of the shed, and began hollering to his friends. I recognised the voice and its Scottish burr. Ian McAdam, the bastard.

McAdam leaned round the corner and fired again. The piece of shit had got his hands on an M-4 Carbine, an assault rifle.

But I was waiting for him to make such a move, and calmly fired, in total disregard of the bullets tearing my surroundings to shreds. McAdam cursed, a new note of pain making his voice more whiny than usual. He ducked out of the way again.

Immediately I went forward, because he'd expect me to go the other way, and doubtless he was directing his buddies to cut me off. I dodged and swerved round the drums, then raced out of the gap between the sheds and into the open. I dived for the floor as McAdam let loose a hail of death. Only my surprise move saved me, because he was unprepared for my appearance and his shots were wild and off-target. I fired back at him and while he was engaged in scrambling for his life, I did likewise. One of the others, having given up on the assault of the first shed, fired his pistol, and the earth next to my right knee lifted in a mini-explosion of dirt. Swearing loudly I commando-rolled away and found shelter behind their SUV. A glance downhill told me that my position was growing more precarious by the second. The headlights I'd noted earlier had grown to a procession of vehicles streaking towards the battle; it would be minutes before they arrived. Fuck it, I told myself, concentrate on the immediate problem. Rushing to the front of the SUV, I propped my SIG over the hood and shot at the man who'd come close to killing me. He fell, telling me that I'd scored a hit, but not enough to finish him. He backed up, butt-shuffling away even as he returned fire. Checking for McAdam, I assumed the Scotsman had taken refuge inside the building where I'd hidden moments before.

The two other men weren't immediately apparent.

But that scenario only lasted a few seconds. One of them was in the narrow space filled with oil drums. He shot at me, using the angle of the alley to line up his shots. His bullets struck glass and metal on the SUV but thankfully didn't find flesh. I shot back at him, making a mental note of how many rounds I'd used. Too many had been wasted for me to have any hope of taking on the number of reinforcements coming. I required more ammo, more guns.

McAdam leaned out of the building and let loose with the M-4.

The SUV danced on its chassis as the rounds punched through it. I ran, zigzagging to avoid making an easy target. Unbelievably none of the bullets ripping through the air hit. It was that or I was dead and it was my spirit that continued the run. As I went to my knees and felt the shock go all the way to the top of my head I was sure that I still inhabited my corporeal body. Graceless, I went down on my front, before rolling side over side, bullets churning the ground where I'd been seconds earlier. Then I positioned myself to shoot at the gunman approaching from my right. It was the third of the assault party, the man with the Eastern European accent. He swore and I made him as Estonian. I'd fought his like before, listened to their guttural obscenities. I hit him in the throat and cut off his next curse. He went down, dead from a severed spine, and his gun was knocked from his fingers. Unfortunately it was well out of my reach. To go for it would make me a sitting duck for McAdam and the injured man, who'd managed to back all the way to the doorway of the first shed I'd entered. The last gunman was still in Oil Drum Alley, but from the collision of knees against metal he was ploughing forward to join his friends.

Bullets cut towards me from two directions and I was forced to move, running for the field of garbage Rink had brought us across. He'd squashed the barbed-wire fence under the tyres of the Dodge, but it had sprung back up – albeit less level than before – and blocked my passage. Rather, it tried to. I went through it, mindless of the barbs that clutched and tore at my already tattered clothes. I was sorely scored, but when weighed against a few bullets in the spine, I'd gladly take the minor abrasions, though, I stupidly thought, I might require a tetanus jab at some point. Lockjaw was the least of my fucking problems.

Beyond the wire fence was a shallow ditch, and I went into it belly first. The sides offered only meagre protection; they wouldn't halt the bullets, but they offered concealment as I crawled away. As it was, my opponents were wary of my strategy and began shooting at various points along the ditch, hoping to pin me down while one of them could move in and finish me for good. Immediately I jerked up, fired two rounds and the slide locked back on my SIG. Swearing under my breath, I searched for the mag that held the few spare bullets I had on me. Dropping the depleted magazine, I slapped in the new one, fully understanding that I'd barely enough bullets left to kill the three here, let alone the number who must now be approaching in the convoy of vehicles. Yet I refused to be fatalistic, and reversed my crawl, worming my way back towards the original position where I'd come through the fence. McAdam and the seated man continued to fire at where they perceived my crawl to have taken me. I knew without looking that the last of my opponents would be moving in, now that he was clear of the alley, to shoot me from behind. I sat up quickly, eyes scanning, and saw the man less than ten feet away, already past my current position. He caught my movement in his peripheral vision, but before he could fully turn I shot him in the side, then as the impact twisted him, placed another round in his open mouth.

That left two enemies.

Only one bullet, though.

The odds of killing both men with one shot were beginning to look decidedly against me.

28

McAdam's assault rifle chattered and eruptions of dirt danced overhead. I flattened down in the ditch. Huge spurts of dust, pebbles and plant life hosed my prone body, but to my relief none of his bullets hit.

Then there was a cessation of the noise and fury.

'You can't get out of this alive, Joe,' McAdam taunted me. 'You may as well give up and come out of the ditch or it'll end up being your grave. Come out and I promise I'll do you nice and clean. I'll even see that you get a decent burial.'

'You're all heart, McAdam,' I called back. 'Actually, that's not true. You're full of shit; no room in there for a heart.'

'If I come over there, I'll have to gun you down. But that won't be the end of it. You'll be taken back, your body paraded by Jorge Molina for all the cartel bosses to see.'

Probably hung from an underpass and disembowelled, I thought.

'So come on over, McAdam. See which one of us is left lying in a ditch.'

He must have switched to semi-auto, because there followed three shots so closely grouped that the triple rattle blended into one hit on a snare drum. Earth danced at the rim of the ditch, forcing me to squeeze my lids shut to protect my eyesight. Not for a second did I believe that McAdam was coming for me.

'Come out, Joe. For old times' sake I'll be good to you.

Clean shot to the back of the head. You won't even see it coming.' His voice remained distant. But the sound of approaching engines was growing louder. Also, I heard a shuffle of movement further to my left. While McAdam tried to distract me, the other man was sneaking in to finish me off. He was lame from my earlier bullet, dragging a leg as he moved in on my hiding place.

I glanced at my SIG. One round. One shot. One kill. I had to go for it, and have faith that McAdam didn't put a bullet through my skull during the brief time I was in his sights.

'What are you getting out of this, McAdam? Hope they're paying you well for turning on your old mate?'

'I'd do this for nothing,' he called back. 'We were never mates, I always thought you were a tosser.'

'Funnily enough, I thought the same about you.'

While I was still calling out, I sat up, gun held in both hands for stability. I zoned in on the sound of shuffling and saw the silhouette of the injured man as he prowled towards the lip of the ditch a good twenty yards away. In the dark, in a bad position for shooting, it was going to be a tricky shot, but I had to take it while McAdam was still absorbing my words and considering his response. I almost pulled the trigger, but didn't.

There was no need.

Rink – who'd been absent from the fight for good reason – suddenly came off the floor like a prowling tiger going for the kill. Even I had no idea where he'd got to in the darkness, and the men trying to kill me had temporarily forgotten about him. The injured man tried to turn his gun on the unexpected attack, but he was too late. Rink drove the garden fork he'd taken from the Dodge into the man's gut with such force that he was lifted off his feet. The sharp tines speared through his innards and spine and protruded from his back. Rink was no slasher-movie killer; he didn't go for the grandiose by lifting the man on the end of the fork, he simply thrust downward, taking the man to the ground, and then released the handle so he could grab the dropped handgun. He placed a bullet in the man's head, putting him out of his misery. Rink is like that: a thoughtful killer.

There was no room for philosophising, and I didn't think of his merciful act at the time. Then and there I still had McAdam, and an M-4 Carbine, to worry about. I twisted quickly, sighting on the ex-para. More correctly I sighted from memory of where his voice had last come from. He was very close to the SUV now, and it was partly between him and me, offering him some protection. He had turned, staring in a moment of horror at what had just happened to his friend, but he had the machine-gun shouldered, and he was a moment away from spraying Rink with bullets. I fired first.

My bullet missed him, but it struck the corner of the SUV with a bang and a spray of sparks. It made him flinch, and his barrel went high as he pulled the trigger, hopefully higher than Rink was tall. McAdam swore, bringing the gun round on me. I swarmed out of the ditch, keeping low. Now the SUV that offered him protection gave me some cover too. McAdam had to move in order to aim round the back of the big vehicle to get a bead on me.

He fired, and my only recourse was to go belly down on the earth again. My sore leg screamed with pain, but I had to keep moving, and I went across the ground on my hands and knees as McAdam's bullets first sought me then arched away to tear Rink to bits.

The dull roar of the M-4 was punctuated by three rapid cracks.

The machine-gun fell silent.

Glancing through the dust that swirled in my vision, I saw

Rink advancing, holding the gun ready in case he had to put McAdam out of his misery too.

I rose up, beckoning Rink. If McAdam was still alive then it was my duty to do the merciful thing.

Except McAdam was as dead as dead could be.

Rink's shots had found heart, throat and skull, amazing shooting at any time, let alone while under fire from a machine-gun: amazing or incredibly lucky. I knew which Rink would choose if asked – for such a centred guy he could also be a bit of a tongue-in-cheek braggart when it came to his prowess. Now wasn't the time for bragging though. Under difficult circumstances we'd come through, but things were about to get much worse.

The foremost vehicle of the convoy was now ploughing its way across the landfill site, while two others continued up the track to cut off our escape route, the three of them all trying to trap us with our backs to the open desert. Shoving away my SIG, I lifted the M-4 from McAdam's dead fingers and shot at the nearest car. The bullets churned their way up the front grille and found the windscreen. Men's shouts of alarm rang wildly from within, competing with the smack of bullets through metal. Doors flew open and those inside leaped out, seeking a safer place than the confines of the car where the ricochets were as dangerous as a well-placed bullet. I fired another spray of bullets and then the mag was empty. A quick check of McAdam's prone body didn't hint at a spare magazine. But I didn't throw away the gun, I ran for his abandoned SUV, just as Rink also charged for it.

If there was extra ammunition I didn't see it, so I threw the gun in the back while I hit the button to start the engine. Rink climbed in, choosing the back seat where he could manoeuvre and offer covering fire.

'That was an impressive move with the garden fork,' I told him.

'That guy didn't dig it so much. Didn't have the guts for gardening, eh?'

I groaned at his awful puns.

'I was thinking of conserving ammunition,' he said more seriously. 'While you were scuttling around like a rodent, I was collecting the spares from the guys you killed.' He dropped a couple of clips on the passenger seat to prove his point. 'Those bullets should fit your SIG. If not . . . here.' He passed over the Glock he'd taken from the man he speared. Then he was rummaging in the back, and I heard the slap of a magazine going in the M-4, and the bolt released. 'Army Ranger weapon,' he said, 'wonder how the fuck it got into cartel hands?'

'It's probably not the only American weapon making its way across the border. Makes me wonder about Regis's part in this. I'd bet my life it's why the CIA is kissing Molina's arse. They deal with him, put him in a position of power at the head of the cartels, and he's a ready-made multi-million-dollar weapons buyer.'

'If you don't get moving you'll probably cash in on that bet.'

Just as Rink's warning came, so did the bullets. The men who'd decamped from the vehicle had found places to hide, and were now intent on bringing the fight back to us. The other two cars were bouncing into the yard, guys leaning from the open windows with guns, like a bunch of rednecks shooting mailboxes. I hit the gas. Rink smashed the back windshield with a short burst of rounds, then as I wheel-spun away he loosed his next volley at the approaching cars.

'Grab on to something, Rink, things are about to get a little rough.'

With bullets stitching patterns in the air around the SUV I drove not for the road, but for a space between two of the sheds, hoping this one wasn't chock-full of oil drums. The SUV lost both wing mirrors to the narrow walls, but that was all, and it blasted out back and through a barbed-wire fence with little hitch. The SUV was a warhorse in comparison with the Dodge, and it bounded across a strip of hard-beaten earth and on to the untouched ground of the desert. Here the desert floor was formed of a series of ruts, the soil blown into small drifts by the wind, then baked hard as clay by the sun. We bounced and jigged, but the SUV kept going straight and we shot between the electricity pylons. Taking the vehicle to fifty miles an hour was like riding a bucking bronco, but we were clear for now of our pursuers' guns. They hadn't followed us into the alley, but were most probably seeking other routes round the cluster of sheds. We'd won some respite, and the gap was broadening. I wondered how far from their enemies Kirstie and the others had made it by now.

29

'Keep the little one quiet, don't look up and we should be fine.'

It wasn't the first time she'd heard those words, and she supposed it wouldn't be the last before this journey was over. Then again, Harvey's instructions didn't do much to calm Kirstie's racing heart. They were heading for the border crossing at Agua Prieta/Douglas, a four-and-a-half-hour drive of more than two hundred and thirty miles through the Sonoran Mountains. Right now they were around the midway mark, approaching a small town called Moctezuma on Carretera Federal 14, seeking Mexico 17, which would take them north towards the USA. Their journey had been uneventful, and Kirstie had concentrated on comforting Benjamin. Now he was beginning to stir. Perhaps he could sense his mother's anxiety as she noted the black and white Policia Federal cruiser passing them by. At first the police car had continued, accelerating away, but a few hundred yards ahead the brakes had been applied. Kirstie was positive that the cops inside were checking them out in their mirrors. The fact that all they would see in the dark was the glare of headlights didn't register in her mind. But then the lights on top of the car were switched on, and the cop car slowed, forcing them to a halt as well.

'Just play it cool, people,' McTeer said from the front passenger seat. 'Let's not forget that these are supposed to be the good guys, yeah?'

'Depends on your perspective.' Velasquez was sitting alongside Kirstie in the back of the car. 'Some of these guys are worse than the scum they're supposed to protect their people from.'

'We can't jump to conclusions,' Harvey warned, as he slowed down to pull in behind the cruiser, 'but neither can we be suckered just because they look official.'

'Half the fucking cartel footsoldiers are municipal or federal cops that've jumped ship. I've still friends and family here, they tell me tales all the time about the methods some of these assholes employ.' Velasquez adjusted his posture so that his gun was concealed beneath his thigh, but still accessible.

'Listen to civilians and they'll have you believe all cops are bad guys,' McTeer said, in support of his past career as a law enforcement officer. Velasquez had also been a cop. 'Keep calm and remember that we have a kid in the back, OK.'

Yes, never forget that, Kirstie wanted to add. She looked at Benjamin and found the boy staring at her quizzically. He wrinkled his nose and closed his eyes. It wasn't a cute look: it was as if he hadn't liked what he'd woken up to. She could feel his chest rising and falling and his breathing was erratic. He'd cut himself off from her because he hated what he'd seen. No, she told herself, she mustn't keep thinking that way. Jorge would have played mind games with the boy, turning him against his mother, but wouldn't instinct win over when it came to her son's affections? He hadn't been with Jorge long enough – or at an age where he was susceptible to brainwashing – for him to learn to hate his mom. She recalled that strange and disturbing dream where an adult Benjamin had chased her, and how he had shown how like his father he'd grown by piercing her with a blade. They were irrational fears born from her stressed subconscious: nothing about the dream had been real. The real threat lay in what they faced now. The two Federales strode towards them, one playing a flashlight over the car. It reminded her of the attack during the initial trek to Hermosillo, and she felt a doomed déjà vu infecting her now.

McTeer wound down the window.

'Evening officers, is there a problem?'

The two cops were close enough that their black uniforms didn't blend so resolutely with the night. Their badges – a seven-pointed star – stood vivid on their chests. So did the weapons on their belts. One of the cops held his hand close to the snap holster, but on hearing McTeer's question, or rather his American accent, relaxed somewhat.

'Are you people heading for the border?' His interest didn't linger long on Kirstie or her son. As per Harvey's instructions, she kept her head down.

'Yes, sir,' McTeer replied politely. 'Returning home after a trip to meet friends in Hermosillo.' He chose to bend the truth, rather than go for an outright lie. The cop didn't seem suspicious of the answer. 'I wasn't speeding was I, sir?'

'No, sir.' Professional courtesy engendered a similar response. 'There's a problem on the highway ahead. You'd best find another route north if possible.'

'What kind of problem?'

'The route's closed ahead. You should turn back.'

'This problem with the road, is it expected to last long?'

'The road could be closed all night. Look, I don't want to frighten you people, but there is an ongoing police operation against gang activity a few miles ahead.' The cop eyed McTeer, while slowly nodding his head. 'It's not something *innocent people* should be party to. You understand?'

Kirstie heard the friendly warning in the policeman's voice, and she glanced up to check she wasn't mistaken. The policeman winked at her. The second cop had backed away, waiting while his partner finished up. His demeanour said that he would rather be somewhere else: possibly a few miles north where the operation was ongoing.

'Appreciate it,' McTeer said.

The cop merely flicked a finger against the side of his head in salute, then walked away. McTeer waited until the cops were back in their cruiser before he turned to bait his pal, Velasquez. 'What was that you were saying about Mexican cops?'

'OK, so some of them are good guys. But that's all down to perspective, as I said. They've heard the reports coming out of Hermosillo, that a group of Yankees have taken the gang boss's son. It was obvious that they knew who we were, and yet they chose to turn a blind eye.'

'He was warning us that there was an ambush ahead: where's the wrong in that?'

'Not exactly what you'd expect from a cop doing his duty, that's all.'

'You'd prefer it if he'd tried to arrest us?' McTeer asked, his voice full of incredulity.

'Just saying it was still a corrupt act.'

'Then thank fuck for corruption,' McTeer said.

'I'm surprised that he didn't have his hand out for a bribe before he walked away,' Velasquez continued.

Harvey sighed. 'I for one would happily pay him. If he hadn't given us the heads up, we'd have driven directly into a trap. As it is, we can find another way through the mountains, without Molina's boys snapping at our heels the entire way.'

'Unless he's setting us up for an ambush somewhere less public than the highway,' Velasquez warned. Kirstie was staring at him with a look of horror. He shrugged. 'Just expressing my concern, lady.'

Kirstie directed her next question at the two men in the

front. 'If we don't follow this highway, which way do we go? And if we don't get to Douglas, as planned, how will Joe and Rink know where to join us?'

'I've still got my cell phone,' Harvey reassured her. 'We'll just make alternative arrangements as necessary.'

'Why not call them now?' Up ahead the Policia Federales cruiser pulled away, sending up a plume of road-grit in its wake as it sped off. The emergency lights had been extinguished, but the cops were in no less of a hurry to head north.

'They're busy.' Harvey was party to his friends' plan to play decoys and draw Molina's bullyboys after them and had no desire to slow them down with unnecessary telephone conversations. 'Best we leave them to it.'

'I'd be happier knowing they're still alive,' Kirstie said.

'I've no argument there, Kirstie. But neither do I want to distract them. Who knows what they're contending with at the moment?'

Velasquez cleared his throat. 'Bet they don't have a friendly neighbourhood cop watching out for them.'

30

When not in my car, my favourite mode of transport is rail travel. I prefer a train over airplanes or coaches, because you can relax, watch the scenery, get up and walk around, stretch your legs when you wish, or visit the buffet car to grab a coffee or sandwich at your leisure. Trains for me are – in general – more comfortable all round. But I had to admit to not enjoying my current ride.

This train was carrying freight. It was a colossal beast, forging its way through the Sonoran Desert, all noise and fury, with very little light to mark its progress. Earlier I'd spotted another train headed south for Hermosillo, loaded down with passengers by the dozen, but this one held only a handful of crewmen, and all of them were up at the front. Fewer people to see us clamber aboard as the train slowed to negotiate the points at Benjamin Hill, where the men working inside the huge engine sheds didn't notice us; fewer people to be endangered when Marshall and the rest of Molina's hired killers caught up with us.

After losing our pursuers, we had dumped McAdam's SUV behind one of the engine sheds at the depot in Benjamin Hill, before getting on to a rear container-car of the freight train. The SUV was out of sight of the highway, but the vehicle would be discovered soon enough, and killers would be dispatched to each station along our route to cut off our escape. However, I didn't expect that they'd be in place as we swept through the long bend towards the station at Santa Ana, the wind battering our bodies, trying its damnedest to rip us from our tenuous hold on the train. Perhaps by the time we arrived at Magdalena, or maybe Imuris, they would be ready for us. They would definitely be waiting at Nogales, where the train would be subject to border control before it was allowed to continue into the USA.

Currently we were travelling adjacent to the highway, the terrain a series of low foothills as we headed in the direction of the Sonoran Mountains, but soon the ridges would grow tall around us, the tracks hemmed in by the road to one side and steep rock faces the other. The train slowed marginally as it took the right-hand bend towards Santa Ana, but didn't have a scheduled stop and continued through the station. Faces of weary travellers were pale blurs on the platforms as we roared by. No one raised a fuss on seeing two guys hanging precariously to handholds on the side of a hopper filled with scrap metal. As I recalled from the maps we'd consulted before parting company with Harvey, Magdalena was a few miles away, and Imuris not far after that. That was where we planned to jump from the train, evade our pursuers and appropriate another vehicle to take us through the mountains on the Magdalena De Kino/Cananea road, where we could finally pick up Mexico 2 to Agua Prieta and meet up with our friends once more.

But then workable plans never were my strong suit.

This was proven when we arrived at Magdalena, the train slowing to not much more than walking pace as it crept towards a level crossing adjacent to an industrial estate.

'I don't like the way this looks,' Rink said as he continued to cling to the side of the freight container. He'd slung the M-4 machine-gun over his shoulder.

He was forward of my position by around ten feet, and had

a clearer line of sight along the side of the train. Lights from the industrial units spilled on to the tracks, allowing for some view, but I doubted that Rink could see all the way ahead to what had caused the train's unscheduled stop. However, he surprised me.

'Looks like there's something on the tracks,' Rink called. 'It's a stalled vehicle or something. There are men with lamps, warning the driver to slow down.'

'I don't like it either,' I said. 'I've a feeling those guys aren't rail workers. Time we got off this train, I think.'

The land was largely undeveloped on the left-hand side of the tracks, a strip of ground dotted with stunted shrubs and dirt trails, before it climbed towards the nearest peaks. On the right, the same side of the train to which we clung, there was a narrower strip of fallow land alongside a broad road-way, this dotted by parked cars. A little ahead of us, between the train and the obstruction on the level crossing, stood a long green and cream building topped by terracotta clay tiles, which I took to be the station that served the commuter trains. Sure enough, a few seconds later I read a sign that said: '*Estación del Ferrocarril Magdalena*', and could see rooms with barred and arched windows, one of which was a ticket office. It appeared closed for business, but on a raised patio that extended from the building as some kind of obser-vation deck, a trio of figures moved. One of them had a flashlight, and was playing its beam along the carriages. In moments the light would find Rink, hanging like a four-legged spider from the edge of the hopper.

Good strategy would be to edge round, using the hopper to shield us as we dropped from the slowly moving train, then we could scurry across the fallow land and avoid the men poised to capture us. But that wasn't a strategy we could follow. We required transportation, and the only vehicles I could see were the cars dotting the roadway behind the station. I turned, holding on to the side of the carriage with one hand as I pulled out the Glock 20 given to me by Rink earlier. The spare ten-millimetre ammo had not been interchangeable with the ammo for my SIG, so I'd shoved that deep in my waistband and elected to keep the Glock handy. I checked the ground for hazards, saw rocks and spiky plants, and thought, 'Fuck it.' Rather a few bruises than hang around and be shot by the men on the observation deck.

'C'mon, Rink,' I called urgently, even as I leaped clear of the train.

Landing in the shallow gulley at the edge of the tracks, my feet sank into soft silt and pebbles. I staggered on my sore knee before righting myself and looked for my friend.

Rink was only seconds behind my decision to leave, but it was a second too late and the beam of a flashlight caught him mid-flight. A shout of warning sounded from the deck. The flashlight-wielder stabbed the beam around, checking where Rink had got to, and for the briefest moment it played over me, then jerked back to keep me illuminated. I sprinted as fast as my injured leg could manage, and I was hard put to avoid the bullets that dogged my path. Rink moved parallel to me, about ten yards nearer to the station.

The angle of the building offered some protection from the gunmen on the deck, but only until we ran out on to the road. From beyond the structure came more shouts, all in Spanish, and the sound of an engine firing to life. A vehicle roared towards us from where moments earlier it had blocked the level crossing. There was also a deep thrum as a second engine revved.

'Rink,' I yelled, 'get back to the train.'

My friend didn't question my insanity.

With the car out of the way, the train crew must have

decided it was much safer for them to leave the area where a gun battle was about to erupt. The engine gave a roar as it was given more power, the wheels squealing in protest as they fought for traction. I ran back the way I'd just come, trusting that the man with the flashlight had gone to the front of the building in order to catch us as we ran for the road. The train was picking up speed, and I wasn't sure that I'd be able to match it in order to scramble aboard.

Rink flashed by, vaulting the last few yards and grabbing at a bracket on the side of one of the large skip-shaped hoppers on the rearmost car. He slammed into the metal wall, but clung to the bracket, then turned and reached out for me. I put my head down, pumping my arms and legs as I charged after him.

'C'mon, goddamnit,' Rink called through gritted teeth as he stretched for me. I pushed the Glock into my waistband, freeing both hands, then leaped the last few feet. Rink grabbed my wrist and I felt his powerful fingers dig painfully into the flesh and sinew. Fuck, it hurt, but nowhere near as bad as it would going under those huge steel wheels. I scrambled for balance, skipping out of the way of one wheel rim that threatened to dismember me. Then I scrambled a bit more, got my feet under me and punched upwards with the force of both knees.

At the same time Rink hauled me up, grunting at the dead weight. Opposing forces worked against us and there was no clean way to pull me onboard. I swung up and hooked a leg over the side of the carriage deck, but the other trailed and almost got caught up in the piston working the wheels. I smelled hot oil and steel as the mechanism clashed close to my flesh. Then Rink was tugging me once more, and I was jerked further on to the car and able to work my other leg up beside the first.

'You on?' Rink demanded.

'Barely.'

'Good. You're on your own now, brother.' Rink released his hold and I almost fell off the train. But I'd managed to grab at the hopper, and jammed my left hand into a slot on its side and hung there for grim death. Rink moved away, placing himself in a shallow niche between two of the large steel containers, bracing himself so that he could draw his weapon once more. He chose his pistol over the machine-gun.

The train was rolling again, picking up speed, passing the station building. I fought to regain balance and made it to my knees, craning round so that I could check what was happening. The car that had recently blocked the tracks was out of sight, probably behind the station house, as those inside searched for us. The men on the deck had their backs to us. That would have been it. We'd have given them the slip if it weren't for more of Molina's henchmen standing near the edge of the tracks. It was the men with lamps who'd originally planned to stop the train. As we thundered past, they spotted us on our precarious perches, and began hollering. Seconds later they were shooting.

Hot metal clanged off the cold steel around me. Showers of obliterated rust rained over my shoulders and scalp, adding to the accumulation of muck I already wore. I wasn't in a good pose to shoot back. But Rink was. Braced in the narrow alcove, he was protected from two sides, while having free rein to return fire. He held his handgun in a two-fisted grip, and he snarled viciously as he picked each shot. One of Molina's gunmen went down hard, and I was certain he was dead. A second man was much noisier as he fell, so likely he would live. A third man ran sideways like an oversized crab, trying to avoid Rink's aim while he fired at us both indiscriminately. He was armed with a MAC-10 machine pistol: the famous 'spray and pray' weapon favoured by criminals involved in drive-by shootings. Thankfully the gun on fully automatic was notoriously inaccurate. As he danced along, the man's shooting was as wild as the look on his face. Rink put two rounds through his lungs and dropped him in the dirt.

By now those on the observation deck had been alerted to our presence by the shooting, and the screaming of the injured man. They turned to join the fight, yelling at those beyond the station, but already we were moving out of their effective range of fire. Some of them took pot shots but they had little chance of hitting us. I was tempted to flip them the middle finger but I was too busy trying to avoid falling off the train.

Rink came along the side of the hopper, balancing on the narrow strip of carriage bed available to us. He shoved his gun away, and offered me a hand. He lifted me easily this time and set me on my feet. I hooked an arm over the top of the hopper, held on grimly.

'They'll be after us again,' I said, like I was the wise Oracle of Delphi.

'No shit, Sherlock,' Rink said. 'But at least we've a head start. That's supposing our buddies up front don't decide to stop the train and run for cover.'

'I'm not sure they'll even suspect we're still on board. I wonder how often they have to run an ambush. Maybe they thought those arseholes tried to stop the train to hijack their cargo, and don't know about us.'

Rink shrugged. 'Whatever, I doubt they'll slow down for anybody else waving lights from the side of the track. Not sure they'll even slow down at Imuris.'

'Then it's going to be a hard landing, because we'll have to jump.'

31

'Twice now your man has failed to catch them. I'm beginning to think that Marshall is allowing his old friend to give him the slip on purpose.'

Jorge Molina gave Howell Regis a look that also included the CIA man in the accusation. They were walking across an open lot, behind them the car they'd recently abandoned, as well as a large tin structure from which the paint peeled in flakes and blisters. Two of Molina's armed bodyguards followed in close formation.

'I can assure you that Marshall knows where his loyalty lies.'

'Yes . . . in cash,' Molina spat.

'That's correct. But we are the people holding the purse strings,' Regis reminded him. 'It was circumstance that allowed Hunter and Rington to escape the first time. Had McAdam held off a few minutes then Marshall and the reinforcements would have arrived in time to corner them. As it was, McAdam was too keen to prove a point and was found lacking. Hunter and his friend were then able to steal McAdam's vehicle and escape. Can I also remind you that Marshall was not in evidence at Magdalena: those were your men, Jorge. Neither incident can be blamed on Marshall. I have faith in the man. He has served me well in the past and will do so again.'

Molina growled out a curse. Regis could not discern the man's words, drowned as they were by the continuous chop of blades scything the night air. He ducked, following Molina under the rotor blades of the helicopter that had recently been towed from the confines of the decrepit shed. Unlike the structure that protected it from the elements – not to mention the prying eyes of tax inspectors or jealous rivals – the red and white helicopter was a sleek and well-maintained craft. Molina's father owned it, but the old man had little use for it these days and Jorge had inherited it.

The spacious Bell 429 could seat up to eight people, so it was roomy enough to allow Molina and Regis to sit opposite each other in the aft cabin, the two bodyguards settling in on the far end of each plush seat. Molina's pilot, a moustachioed man, bald of head, was at the controls, his earphones in place, while his co-pilot checked that everyone was safely inside before closing the doors and seating himself alongside the pilot. The pilot had already had his instructions, yet he still called back to Molina for final confirmation.

'Agua Prieta.' Molina had to yell to be heard over the *whopping* of the rotor. He turned to regard Regis once more. 'I intend to be there when my ex-wife attempts to cross the border. I will be the one to show her the error of thinking she can take something from *me*. I will cut her throat even as I pluck Benny from her arms. Sometimes, Mr Regis, there are things a man must do himself, don't you think?'

'Indeed,' Regis said.

'I will hold you to that thought.' Molina offered a smile that reminded Regis of a caged wolf prowling behind a fence, eyeing the juicy human morsels just out of reach, and planning how best to draw them to its waiting mouth. 'Should Marshall fail to deliver Joe Hunter's head, then I expect you to give me his. We understand each other, no?'

'Marshall won't fail.'

Molina slapped the pilot seat, ordering the man to get going.

As the helicopter rose into the night sky, he nodded once at Regis. 'Let us hope that's the case. Failure demands heavy compensation.'

Regis neglected to answer.

Yet he was thinking hard.

CIA masterplan or not, there was no way he would allow the jumped-up little greaseball to take his head. His gun was primed and ready for the moment that Molina's bloodlust got the better of him. He surreptitiously checked out the body-guards, but neither man was paying attention to the English conversation, though they'd have to be idiots not to pick up on the undertones. Regis knew that the bodyguards were ex-Special Forces, but he was certain that he could draw, shoot them, and get their boss all in under two seconds. The pilots would be no problem. With a gun to the pilot's nape, they'd take him anywhere he demanded.

No. It wouldn't come to that, he decided.

He had been tasked with pandering to Molina's wishes to gain the man's trust and he'd do his utmost to give the man what he desired. If that meant handing him Marshall's head, then so be it. His own head was something else.

Regis worked under the auspices of an Agency divisional director, Thomas Caspar, who was more than equal in rank to Walter Hayes Conrad, and who could, if Regis requested, override Conrad's part in this mission. It was not unknown for different departments of the CIA to work counterpro-ductively on similar problems. You only had to look at Osama Bin Laden, fêted on the one hand, and hunted on the other by separate parties within the same agency. It was obviously the same here, where Caspar saw Molina as a valuable asset, while Conrad – whose brief was to upset the movement of human traffic across borders – saw him as a stumbling block to be removed. Though Regis could not understand why

Conrad had dispatched his pet mercenaries to steal Molina's son. Where was the value in such an operation, except maybe to cause Molina some inconvenience while trying to get Benjamin back?

He could contact Caspar if necessary; have him order Conrad to hand over the child. But he doubted that Molina would be satisfied with such an arrangement. The burning hunger in the man's face had nothing to do with getting his son back; it was all about punishing those who had the temerity to take something from him. Molina would pursue the thieves with equal determination if they had lifted a trinket from his bedside cabinet, or a single peso from his wallet. Molina was – after all – the man who planned to murder his own father, Felix Eugenio Molina, before the old dodderer lost all credibility with the other cartel bosses, and they moved in to take away what should rightfully be bequeathed to him. He could not do something as obvious as chopping off Felix's head, which Regis suspected was Molina's preferred method; instead he had been slowly poisoning him with doctored medication. Now he was intent on finishing off the old man with a massive overdose, and looked forward to dancing at his funeral.

'There is always an alternative to this problem,' said Regis.

'There is no alternative. I want Joe Hunter dead. I want Kirstie-*fucking*-Long dead. I want *everyone* that aids them dead.'

'Why not allow them all safe passage to the US, then take the boy when they least expect it? They will feel safer across the border, and less likely to put up a concerted defence.'

'I relish the fight, Regis. Don't you see that?' Molina glanced at his bodyguards, who turned away. 'I must show my competitors what will happen to them if they ever dare move against me, or what *belongs* to me. There is no fearing a "concerted defence". I will batter every defence down, and I will take their heads, and it will be on this side of the goddamn border.'

Regis held up his palms in surrender. Good luck, he thought. He'd witnessed Joe Hunter and friends in action and suspected that Molina was relishing a fight he might just regret. Molina feared losing face, but actually he should fear losing his head.

32

Back in Depression-era America, men in search of work frequently travelled the tracks, hopping on and off trains, sleeping in stock carts alongside the other hobos making the same journey. I'd watched old black and white movies depicting those travellers, thought how hard life was back then and somewhat admired the lengths to which desperate men would go to find paying work. Our presence on the back of the freight train wasn't for such a noble cause, but Rink and I were equally desperate. The train was the only available mode of transport that could outrun the convoy of vehicles that dogged our trail all the way to Imuris.

In those old movies, the hobos took whatever opportunity they could to leave the moving train, because they could not allow themselves to be found aboard by station guards who'd first beat them, then throw them in jail on vagrancy charges. Usually they were depicted leaping from fast-moving trains into discreetly placed haystacks or rivers to cushion their fall. We didn't expect or receive such luxury. When we jumped it was on to sun-baked soil as resilient as concrete. The impact in both my heels was redirected all the way up to the crown of my head, despite my effort to tuck and roll, and for a few minutes afterwards I worried that I'd lost a full inch in height. Moving was painful, but I concentrated on the faces I conjured in my mind's eye and they helped push me forward. Kirstie and Benjamin were relying on me, and I'd be no help to them lying down and complaining about my myriad hurts. Rink seemed unaffected, but then he had that samurai resolve to fall back on. He could be cringing inside, yet his face was set in Zen-like tranquillity. Mine was twisted in a grimace, as I made my way through the alphabet consigning a curse to each letter, and only struggling when it came to 'Z'.

Imuris was a small town in comparison with Hermosillo, or even Magdalena, and we were fortunate to arrive before Molina's cavalcade of footsoldiers. There were enough of them to have encircled the place and denied us a way in. But time was an issue, they'd be arriving shortly, and best that we were on our way before they did.

We required a reliable vehicle, because the next leg of our journey was through the mountains, some at high elevation, where the least we would need was a working heater. Although hot during the day, it was barely above freezing at night, and I'd not thawed out from my precarious train journey. Most of my aches and pains would be alleviated if I wasn't so chilled. It didn't help that my clothing was ripped, full of tiny glass shards and spotted with dried blood that felt like cardboard against my flesh. All added to the continued misery.

Sometimes Rink can read my mind. Or perhaps I wasn't complaining as silently as I thought.

'First things first, we need to get hold of a coat for you. C'mon over here.' He led the way towards a homestead on the outskirts of town. The house was in darkness, and whoever lived there had exercised caution and locked the place down tight. It was a low, single-storey dwelling with a flat roof from which old TV antennae protruded. Also on the roof were lines holding various items of laundry. The family probably thought that it would take a desperate thief to climb to the roof and steal their meagre clothing: they weren't wrong.

Rink unslung the M-4, placing it on the ground next to the

house wall. I boosted Rink with my cupped palms, and he went over the parapet and on to the rooftop with the agility of a cat. He was only up there a moment before a couple of shirts rained down, followed by a heavy woollen sweater. There was no coat, but beggars can't be choosers. I stripped out of my sweatshirt and rolled it up, then thankfully pulled on one of the shirts. It was thick, a heavy denim. It was also too small for me, so I left the top three buttons undone, as well as those at the cuffs. The sweater was a tad looser and didn't constrict as much. I felt much better, though I did feel guilt over the theft.

Rink came down from the roof in a fluid motion that hardly made any noise. 'Nice to see you in some colours for a change,' he whispered. My appropriated sweater was red and green, with small animal motifs that wouldn't have looked out of place at Christmas. For one who usually dressed as though he'd raided Johnny Cash's wardrobe, the bright colours were anathema, but the immediate warmth consoled me. Rink pulled on the spare shirt, allowing it to hang loose so he could still get at his weapon, but the extra layer offered some warmth. He then hitched the M-4 over his shoulder.

Rink began to move away, seeking the next item on our list, but I paused. Pulling out my wallet, I took out most of the bills and laid them on top of my discarded sweatshirt on the front doorstep. I sat a rock from the garden on top of the stack of dollars. I didn't leave a note: the money would explain my guilt at stealing the clothing. Mexico wasn't full of the lawless kind, the likes of Jorge Molina and his footsoldiers; it was full of decent, hard-working people who couldn't afford to have their belongings stolen from them.

Rink shook his head in bemusement. 'I've known you all these years, and still you surprise me.'

That was Joe Hunter through and through, a conundrum: a

violent man who didn't flinch at killing, yet one who found the act of petty theft abhorrent. The way I squared away my odd sense of morals was that the victims of my violence generally deserved it, those of my thievery didn't. Simple.

Imuris was quiet. It was late – approaching midnight by my reckoning – and most people would be in their beds. There was no sign of nightlife, no bars, no clubs, no parties, but then we were still on the outskirts so that wasn't unusual. There were cars and trucks. Dozens of them. Yet most were either too new or too old to steal. New models meant security was an issue; older vehicles might not be roadworthy for the trip over the mountains.

I followed Rink as he assessed and rejected each vehicle. Then he found a Subaru station wagon parked in the lea of a home that doubled as a general store. The Subaru was wedged between rows of crates and baskets; some of them holding husks of sun-dried fruit and wadded paper. He moved for the car, pulling out his KA-BAR knife in anticipation. I shadowed him, but paused to lift aside a couple of teetering crates that might fall and alert the neighbourhood when we moved the car. Placing the crates out of harm's way, I turned to watch Rink check the door and find it locked. It didn't slow him. He wedged the tip of his KA-BAR between the door window and frame and worked it in so that most of the blade was inside. Then he levered down and the window dropped an inch or so. Rink gripped the blade of his knife between his teeth as he inserted both hands in the gap, rose up on his toes and bore down with all his weight. The window was shoved off the winding mechanism and dropped into the well inside the door. Rink pulled up the manual lock, opened the door, and passed the machine-gun over into the back seat. In the next instant he was inside and had released the brake, while I went to the back and began to push, taking the car silently from under the lean-to and on to the road. I continued to push until we were a hundred or so yards clear, then went round to the passenger side and climbed in. Rink was busy under the dash, having already broken open the ignition barrel, and was paring and rejoining wires. The engine barked to life. We were moving.

Trusting to his natural sense of direction, Rink headed out of town, steering well clear of the railway station, and got us on to a road that headed deeper into the mountains. We'd left the rain behind some miles to the south-west and here the sky was cloudless and the stars brilliant in the gaps between the high mountain peaks. Ours was the only vehicle on the road. It was peaceful for the first time in many hours, and I silently warned myself to remain alert. If I allowed the tranquillity to lull me, the next thing I'd know was waking up, sleep-muddled and at low ebb. Though the temptation was great, I couldn't allow even a nap. Not while danger still threatened at any second.

'I wouldn't mind a strong coffee right about now,' I said.

Rink made smacking noises with his lips. He was as thirsty as I was. Neither of us had drunk or eaten anything since before we left to grab Benjamin. I consoled myself with the knowledge that I'd gone many hours longer than this before, but it didn't help. I began to root through the glove box, hoping to find some water, but there was nothing of the sort. On the back seat was an old blanket that smelled of dogs, the M-4 machine-gun, and that was all. But there were boxes in the cargo compartment in the back. I clambered over and fished through the contents, hoping for succulent fruit, but again was disappointed. It seemed that the packages held only cleaning supplies, and I wasn't ready to drink bleach just yet.

Returning to my place up front, I didn't have to tell Rink the bad news. He didn't comment. What was the use of complaining?

He kept the car moving. A few hours and we'd be at Agua Prieta, then across the border to Douglas where we could drink our fill.

At least that was my hope.

33

Harvey Lucas called a halt, for which Kirstie was grateful. Benjamin had woken up, mewled at his mother, said he needed pee-pees, and then hugged her tightly, sobbing. His weeping was from confusion and fear, a need for consolation and comfort. Kirstie was elated that the boy had chosen to come to her for both.

While McTeer and Velasquez stretched their legs, talking quietly, Harvey stood sentry as Kirstie coaxed Benjamin to urinate at the side of the mountain road. Since the friendly tip-off from the federal policeman, they'd been using tracks and lesser roads that meandered through the hills and Kirstie had no idea where they were now in relation to the border crossing. She decided to ask Harvey, once her boy's needs were seen to. The little lad was having trouble – through embarrassment at being surrounded by unfamiliar people – and Kirstie encouraged him. She glanced once at Harvey's tall frame, but the man had his back to them out of decency, standing stock-still as he surveyed the valley below for lights.

Finally Benjamin managed to get a stream going, and it lasted an inordinately long time. He kept his head averted, his shoulders slumped as Kirstie crouched behind him, holding him by the waist. When he was done he snapped up the waistband of his pyjamas, and Kirstie offered to straighten his clothes but he wriggled out of her grasp, running off the road towards a cluster of rocks. Kirstie stood dumbfounded for a second, before she gave chase. She must have cried out, because suddenly Harvey was racing past her, his long limbs eating up the ground between her and the fleeing boy.

Benjamin fled to the boulders, but there was no way he could climb over them, so he bolted to the left, surprisingly fleet for his age. However, he lost a slipper, and his next few steps were completed with a limp. Harvey scooped the boy up, and held him, while the boy howled like a coyote seeking the full moon. Kirstie recalled that horrible dream where she'd been chasing the boy as she clattered up to Harvey and reached out for her son, feeding his slipper back on.

'Let me go,' Benjamin bleated, and tried to strike at Harvey with his balled fists.

'I'll take him,' Kirstie said.

'I want to go home,' Benjamin continued, his fists drumming on Harvey's chest with as little force as hummingbird wings.

'I'm taking you home, Benjamin. Mommy's taking you home.' Kirstie's voice broke on the final syllable.

'Maybe you should let him settle first,' Harvey said.

'He's my son. I'll take him.'

'I want my daddy,' Benjamin sobbed.

'Benjamin . . . don't you know me? It's me, your momma.'

'I'm Benny. I'm Benny. I'm *Benny*.' The little boy kicked and squirmed. Kirstie moved in close, and Harvey allowed her to take the boy; she swung him round so that they were chest to chest and she held his head to her shoulder. She smoothed down his hair, petted his shoulders. McTeer and Velasquez came up, the loose dirt crunching underfoot.

'Everything OK?' McTeer asked.

'Yes, everything's fine now,' Kirstie said, though it didn't feel that way to her. She hugged Benjamin tightly, smoothing his hair under her palm again, feeling his tears hot against her neck. 'Let's just get back to the car and get going. The sooner we're out of this godforsaken country the better.'

'Couldn't agree with you more,' Harvey said.

It was as if Benjamin had used up all his energy because he was floppy in her arms as Kirstie carried him towards the car. But he wasn't finished yet. 'Why are you doing this to me? Why have you took me from my daddy? You're bad. *You're all bad people. I hate you!*'

The nightmare came back to Kirstie once more, and if ever Benjamin could spear her on a blade, his accusation had just done so. A sob broke from her, one that carried echoes as she slid into the back seat and held tightly to her son. She had never hated her ex-husband as much as she did now.

Harvey slid in beside her while the others switched driving duties, Velasquez now at the wheel. Kirstie could feel Harvey's gaze as the car began a crawl along the mountainside. She looked up. The dome lights had gone out, but she could make out Harvey's angular features, the glint of his eyes. Harvey placed a consoling palm on her forearm.

'He needs time to adjust. Believe me, once we're back home, he'll familiarise himself with you and your surroundings and it'll be like he was never gone.'

Benjamin had succumbed to exhausted sleep, his mouth hanging open, a bubble of saliva softly cracking with each exhalation.

'Did you hear what he said back there?'

'He doesn't hate you, Kirstie. He's a small child. He's confused and doesn't have the necessary words to explain his feelings. He's frightened, mixed up, doesn't know how to describe those emotions except in basic terms. He doesn't hate *you*, he hates what's happening to him. But once things calm down, then he'll show his feelings towards you in other ways. Give him a few days and he'll be saying he loves you.'

She knew that Harvey was speaking the truth, of course. But he hadn't taken her original question the way she'd intended.

'I meant the bit about us being bad people.'

'It's a fine line when you work in this business,' Harvey said.

She felt him shift alongside her. He didn't seem at ease with whatever conclusion he had come to. 'It's no easy thing, killing,' he went on, 'but sometimes you have to satisfy yourself that you do so for the greater good.'

'You don't strike me as a killer,' Kirstie said. Fleetingly she thought of Joe, and how she'd seen in him a man who did have the necessary cold edge to kill a man in combat.

'I've had to be,' Harvey confessed. 'Both as a soldier and since. It's not something I've ever got used to, but it's something I've come to accept.'

'Rink strikes me as being of a similar mind,' Kirstie said.

'Yup. In an ideal world, Rink would have no need for violence. He loves life, sees it as a gift to be cherished. Despite all those goofy one-liners of his, he's a real poet at heart.'

'What about Joe?'

'He's a good man.'

'You sound convinced of that.'

'I am.'

'Yet he is violent, and has no qualms about killing?'

'Only for the greater good,' Harvey said, labouring the point.

Kirstie considered his words. She was attracted to Joe Hunter, as she'd been to Jorge. Was that a fault in her psyche, that she was drawn to dangerous men? Like Hunter, Jorge Molina was violent and – as she'd come to learn – also had no qualms about killing. Where was the difference? There was only one answer: Jorge's 'greater good' was directed to his own benefit, Hunter's to everyone else's. They were opposite sides of the same coin, she decided. After everything had gone so disastrously wrong with her previous relationship was it any surprise that she'd be attracted to a man that was the exact opposite of her ex-husband?

Harvey's breathing had changed, and it took Kirstie a moment to realise that he was laughing.

'You like him, huh?'

Kirstie blushed and smiled, breaking the crust of drying tears on her cheeks. It felt good to push back some of the sadness Benjamin's unsettling words had created.

'Do you think he . . . uh . . . likes me?' she ventured.

'Isn't it obvious?' Harvey asked. 'I mean, yeah, he'd go out on a limb to save any woman's child, but I've never seen him this determined before.' Harvey laid a hand on Kirstie's forearm a second time, squeezing it gently. 'You ready?'

'Can I ask you something first?'

'I thought you already were asking me stuff.'

'It's not about Joe. The man who sent you here to help get Benjamin back . . .'

'Walter?'

'Yes. Walter Conrad. Is he my grandfather?'

Harvey didn't reply. The only light inside the car was the occasional backwash from their headlights as they passed large roadside boulders, so she couldn't make out his face for a clue. Finally he exhaled. 'No one has said as much to me,' Harvey said, 'but I'm not an idiot. I only have to look at you to tell that you're Walter's kin.' Harvey gently touched Benjamin's sleeping head. 'And the little one.'

Kirstie exhaled, a weary sigh of resignation. 'If I were to ask you if Walter Conrad is a good man, what would you say?'

'I'd ask you if you really wanted to hear the answer,' Harvey said.

Kirstie chose not to ask.

34

Like many people, I'd formed misconceptions about Mexico. It wasn't a country I'd visited during my military career, and my wanderings since hadn't brought me this side of the border. My idea of Mexico was that it was an arid land, dominated by sand and grit and cacti, where poor people lived in adobe huts and made their way around by donkey or mule: shame on me for my ignorance.

We were in the high Sonoran mountain range, and here the land was verdant, with tilled terraces bursting with crops. River courses were few, but they had to be there, perhaps hidden by the greenery. The homes that we passed were a mixture of humble dwellings, productive hill farms, and exclusive millionaires' pads. I didn't see a single donkey or mule, but plenty of horsepower in expensive SUVs and saloon cars. The highway was well maintained, and the tyres of our borrowed Subaru station wagon ate up the miles. The rain was now many miles behind us, and the sky was a star-studded fresco. On our left I caught fleeting glimpses of the constellation Ursa Major – the 'Big Dipper', or 'Plough', depending where you came from – standing almost end on end in the northern heavens. To my right was Orion, the stars that formed the belt some of the brightest objects in the sky. Forgetting for a moment that we were only minutes ahead of men intent on killing us, it was easy to soak up the grandeur and beauty of the scene.

Ahead of us twinkled lights of a town. I couldn't recall the name of it from Harvey's map.

'More trouble?' I ventured.

'Best we prepare for anything, brother.' Rink eased up a tad on the throttle as he surveyed the town. It didn't look very large and was set to the right of the highway in the natural wedge of a valley between two hills.

'I'm not sure the road even enters the town,' I said. 'We could keep on going.'

'We need food and water,' Rink reminded me.

'I'm good for a while yet,' I said. Pursuit would be fast and determined, I assumed, and we'd no time for tending to our basic needs.

'Thought you'd be dying for a coffee by now,' Rink said. 'What with your caffeine habit and all.'

To be honest, my head was thumping with withdrawal symptoms, my vision tunnelled, my fingers shaking. But those symptoms could equally have been down to adrenalin dump after our many hours of running and fighting.

'I've got my name on a gallon of espresso when we arrive in Douglas. Keep going, Rink. Unless you need something . . .'

'I'm good,' he said, but he couldn't disguise the rasp of a dry throat.

We bypassed the unknown town, both of us glancing longingly at the lights and the promise of sustenance, and discovered that the road began to climb higher, going into the first of many curves that took us through the range. Within minutes we were at an elevation many hundreds of feet higher. I craned round, checking behind us, but the road was lost to sight by the bends and steep cliffs. A long way back in the valley headlights twinkled momentarily, but then the lie of the land hid them again. No way could I be sure it was the lights of our pursuers but the odds were high.

Rink grunted something unintelligible, and I shifted my gaze to the right to see what caused his mild concern.

'Helicopter,' I said unnecessarily.

A chopper was skimming through the sky, coming at a right angle to us. Had the craft been higher, or had we been still way down on the low part of the road, I wouldn't have been able to discern what the craft was, but here I could make out the wasp-like shape and the configuration of its running lights.

'You think it's them?'

'We'll know soon enough,' Rink said, ducking for a view past my body. 'At least it doesn't look like a gunship.'

'Doesn't mean they haven't any guns onboard,' I cautioned.

Our handguns were largely ineffective against a helicopter while we were driving, so I leaned in the back and grabbed the M-4, preparing it for action. There was no sign of aggression or even interest from those in the chopper yet, so I kept the machine-gun hidden down on my lap.

Rink remained at a steady speed, unalarmed and unhurried. We'd look like local night workers out on an errand.

The helicopter zoomed closer, and now I could make more out of the shape of the craft, even some dim colours – red and white – against the star-flecked heavens. Wasn't a police or military chopper, I was pleased to note, but a commercial type that I recognised from the Bell catalogue. I'd learned more about helicopters since Harvey had acquired one as his ultimate man-toy, though he'd recently used it to bolster his income offering flying tours around his hometown of Little Rock, Arkansas. He'd had me out on a few pleasure flights with him, and not too long ago had also drafted his helicopter in during a rescue attempt when some of our old enemies snatched Rink. I'd been thinking about taking flying lessons, but time hadn't allowed yet.

The chopper suddenly changed its flight path.

'Crap,' Rink muttered under his breath. I adjusted the M-4.

The helicopter banked towards us, then levelled out and began flying parallel to the road, and I sneaked a look to check that a door wasn't being opened to allow the barrel of a rifle to poke out. There was no way to discern faces inside the craft, but I counted a half-dozen figures seated front and back.

'Play it cool,' I said, over the chopping of the blades, 'they're just checking us out. We don't seem to be causing too much of a stir.'

No sooner had the words left my mouth than the chopper drifted over us, then lifted dramatically heavenward and out of sight. I could still hear the *chuck-chuck-chuck* sound of the rotor blades, but it diminished in volume as the helicopter headed over the nearest peak.

'What do you think all that was about?'

'I doubt it had anything to do with Molina. Their lights would have given them a good look at my face when I checked them out, and they didn't seem to recognise me.'

'Or they didn't want you to know that they recognised you.'

'True,' I said. 'Maybe it's best we keep one eye on the road behind us and another one on the sky. I'm going to keep this gun handy.'

And that's exactly what I did for the next twenty minutes or so. The helicopter didn't return, and I put down the close scrutiny of those onboard to nothing more than inquisitiveness. There was no hint that anyone chasing from behind had made any progress. Once I did spot running lights blinking in the sky, but they were a mile high and probably belonged to a commercial airliner. When nothing transpired, I began to relax. It's a fault that should never affect a soldier in the field. Pain, hunger and thirst had helped keep me edgy until now, then the spike in adrenalin on seeing the helicopter heave into sight had perked me up, but now that the danger had passed

that old enemy, fatigue, began to creep in. My mind was growing woolly, my eyelids so heavy I could barely prop them
open. Maybe Rink was feeling the same, because he was a
second too late to react as a large vehicle suddenly lurched
into view to block the carriageway.

His shout of warning, and the sudden deceleration as he hit
the brake, threw me forward in my seat and into wakefulness.
But I was confused, and couldn't make out what we were
seconds from striking. Whatever it was, it was five times the
size of the station wagon, and probably fifty times heavier. I
dropped the M-4 so that I could throw my forearms over my
head. Rink managed to pull the hood away from a head-on
collision, and when we hit it was the right fender and passenger door that took the brunt of the impact. I was thrown
around, my shoulders slamming something solid, then
rebounding to hit something only slightly less concrete. The
second object proved to be the window: glass chunks exploded
all over me for the umpteenth time that night. The glass glit-
tered, but then that could have simply been the flashes inside
my skull. Darkness edged my vision, and the meagre contents
of my stomach flipped into my throat. Blood gushed from
both nostrils, from my face impacting my own arms. Shit, just
when everything seemed to be going so well.

My friend was shouting, exhorting me to do *something*, but
my head was ringing so hard I couldn't determine his meaning. He was pulling at my left arm, shaking me, pulling me
free from the slowly deflating airbag that had saved me from
further injury. Then he had to concentrate on the car, as he
tried to pull away from the massive vehicle blocking the road.
The station wagon began to twist away from the massive wall
of steel and cogs as I pushed and punched at the airbag to
clear my view. Shaking some lucidity into my brain, I recognised huge wheels in a caterpillar track. Suddenly a deeper

roar swallowed the scream of the Subaru's engine. The big vehicle, which a deep part of my psyche recognised as an earth-moving machine – a Caterpillar excavator to be precise – began to pivot after us. Rink yelled again, and in reflex I ducked, just as the attached bucket on the pneumatic arm slammed down on the roof of the car. It hit above the rear seats, compacted the roof downward and more glass exploded. The Subaru was forced down on its chassis and for a second I expected the tyres to blow, or the wheel hubs to collapse off the axles. To my surprise the Subaru survived the first crushing blow. But a second followed, just as Rink was hitting reverse, and this time the colossal power of the machine struck on the bonnet, jamming the engine and the entire front end of the car towards the road surface. The back wheels lifted skyward, then dropped with a solid thud when the bucket was withdrawn for a third try at mashing us.

Our car was dead, and we would follow if I didn't get my arse in gear.

The roof of the car was buckled, and my head had little clearance, making it difficult to bring the M-4 to bear on the driver up in the cab above the tracks. I forgot about the long gun and pulled out the Glock 20 instead. I fired through the now-open windshield, and my bullets struck sparks from the cab but to little effect.

'Out, out, out!'

Rink's command motivated me and I pushed and kicked at the door. It was solidly jammed in its frame, a fold of the buckled roof wedging it firmly in place. Rink's door was also twisted out of shape, but the lock had been broken and the door burst open as he forced a way clear. I went for the next best exit. I got up on my seat, wrestling past the airbag and through the smashed windshield. I earned yet more scratches to my patchwork of earlier cuts and scrapes, but didn't stop to worry about them. I fired again, the Glock snapping in my hand, and this time I hit window glass in the cab. I hadn't stopped the driver, but his reaction caused him to pull on the controls and the bucket plunging down to flatten me against the metal work swept to one side and dug a furrow in the road a few feet away. I'd left the M-4 in the station wagon, and we didn't have the luxury of retrieving it. Recovering from his near miss, the driver swung the excavator towards the car and the nearside track bit into the fender, then rode up on to the hood, crushing the car beneath its thirty-plus tons.

Rink was shooting, but not at the driver. Other men had appeared from the side road, and he engaged them. I had little time to worry about the newcomers. I was inches from being pulverised, so scrambled on to the running shelf alongside the cab. It was like riding a rhinoceros as the huge machine tore a swathe over the station wagon, crushing it to an unrecognisable heap of buckled metal. I caught at a handle protruding from the cab wall, and avoided being thrown to the earth. The cab worked on some sort of lazy Susan set-up, allowing the cab to pivot at angles to the tracks, allowing for more dexterity with the digging arm. The driver hit levers and the cab jerked right, then left, and my boots skidded out from under me. Thankfully my grip held and I wasn't deposited on top of the caterpillar tracks where I'd have been chewed by the interlocking links. By the time I fought to my feet, the driver had gone for a second tactic. He withdrew a gun and began firing madly, sending his bullets through the window and door at me. I felt something score my side, and a flash of agony went through me, but instinct kicked in and I returned fire, using the same reckless method as he. A scream rewarded me, but he wasn't dead. Hearing the man cursing in Spanish, I used the source of his voice as a target for my next round. Then he was silent.

Gunshots still rang out of the darkness, but they were barely a distraction when the dying or dead driver lost control of the levers and the excavator began a rumbling path across the road, spitting out parts of the Subaru as it progressed. The bucket swung one last time, then dipped towards the ground, digging in. The forward momentum of the tracks caused the back edge of the bucket to gouge the road, but then it stuck firmly, and for a moment the huge machine worked furiously against its own power. The front end rode up, lifting on the support of its arm, before hitting the point of no return where the arm could no longer hold it aloft. The pneumatic arm buckled and collapsed, the joints shearing and sending missiles of metal shards all over the place. I was already leaping for my life, as I could see what was coming next.

I hit the road and went down on my belly, rolling on my side as the excavator plunged off the elevated road. It teetered for a few groaning seconds at the lip, before disappearing into the chasm below. Several concussive explosions and the massive rumble of earth and rocks that joined it in avalanche marked its fall. I experienced a moment of fear where the road surface trembled beneath me, and I expected it to break free from the mountainside and tumble into the valley thousands of feet below, taking me with it. But my concern was unfounded. The road held.

Now all I had to worry about was the gunmen who outnumbered Rink and me three to one.

And if that wasn't bad enough, car headlights broke the gloom behind as those we'd avoided at Imuris came to join the fight.

Still it didn't end there. This was a real triple dose of danger.

The fucking helicopter was also back.

35

As secure as the telephones were at Langley, Walter Conrad couldn't risk the opposition having infiltrated the system and placed their own monitoring devices in and around his workplace. His office was regularly swept for bugs and listening devices, but he was paranoid enough to expect that the technicians who carried out the task were the ones who would install them in the first place. They were drones, workers who took orders from those further up in the hierarchy, and could be easily coerced to feed Walter disinformation. There were many in the Company envious of Walter's position who would not hesitate to harm him to gain an elevated status.

On record Walter was a sub-division controller, but most of his peers and superiors understood that he enjoyed a level of protection that far outweighed his official role. Some knew of his background with Arrowsake, without fully understanding the implications, and looked on him with suspicion, with distaste or downright hatred. Walter – without their knowledge – was still attached to Arrowsake, and had the ears of the cabal of powerful individuals at its head. It had long been suspected by conspiracy theorists that for all their implied importance, presidents, prime ministers and premiers did not hold genuine power. They were figureheads, poster boys set in place to reassure the masses that democracy was alive and well. Those faceless men and women who worked in the shadows held the real power. Unlike presidents and prime ministers, they did not serve an elected term; they were constant and transcended all governments, a shadow network that manipulated and moulded world affairs. The conspiracy theorists weren't far off the mark.

What Walter's enemies failed to realise was that he not only enjoyed the protection of the hidden government, he also had access to support the likes of which they could only dream of. For years now Walter had been employing Joe Hunter and Jared Rington to clear up problems that had to be kept off the books. It was through his influence that actions that would normally have sent both men to prison for extended terms had been sanitised, their involvement hidden and the files rubber-stamped Ultra Top Secret by the Secretary of State himself. Hunter and Rington were intrinsically good men doing despicable jobs on behalf of men who cared less about them than about those they condemned to death. But Walter was unlike his bosses. He had never been prone to demonstrations of love, but he held a special place in his heart for both men: to him they were like sons. There were jobs he'd tasked them with which he sorely regretted. He'd lied to them, manipulated them, but he'd always protected them. They were violent men, yet moral. There had been jobs for which they were not suited. On those occasions Walter had employed different assets, as he would employ one of a different mindset now.

Thomas Caspar's agenda in Mexico was threatening Walter's blood kin. Walter had gone to his Arrowsake bosses, confessing to them his relationship with Kirstie Long – and by virtue of it to Annie, and her mother, Miriam Decker, the retired associate deputy director of National Clandestine Services. He knew he was swapping one potential threat to his family for another, yet his priority was dealing with the issue at hand. His admission had been received favourably

– although Walter came away from the meeting with a sour taste in his mouth and the feeling that nothing he'd admitted had come as a surprise to his bosses – and sanction for his plan granted.

Now Walter waited at his secluded fishing retreat in the Adirondacks. His security team was ensconced within the lodge, while Walter had taken a walk down by the river. Ordinarily when sitting on the shelf of rock jutting over the tumultuous water, he'd have with him a fishing pole and bait box. This time he held only two satellite phones, both of which he knew were clean. One phone he'd used to speak to Joe Hunter. The other was linked to a matching phone in the hands of another man. An update from either source was long overdue, and Walter sat nervously waiting for news. In all honesty, Walter wasn't sure which one he wanted to ring first.

36

Rink had found shelter up against the hillside, hiding behind boulders from a recent landslide. He was trading bullets with the group of men who had swarmed from cover when they thought the excavator had done its work. However, now that the huge machine had plunged into the valley they had nothing to hide behind, forcing them to find places of safety along the roadside behind similar boulders.

The only cover available to me was the crushed Subaru. Yet again I was dismally low on ammunition and forced to pull out my SIG to bolster the Glock that would run dry very soon. I crouched behind the twisted hulk of metal that had so recently been roadworthy, wistfully thinking I could still get to the M-4 if only those men weren't shooting at me. The headlights of the reinforcements' vehicles were growing harsh behind me, and they'd be on the scene within seconds. The helicopter hovered overhead, the downwash of its rotors whipping the air, adding to the grit and dust and bullets churning around me. The only upside was that it was making me a more difficult target to the gunmen on the ground.

'Get your ass over here, Hunter,' Rink yelled.

He understood how untenable my position was. Talk about being stuck between a rock and a hard place. That was only the half of it.

'I would, but it will probably get shot off!'

'That's gonna happen soon enough if you don't get the fuck outta there.'

Rink stood up, offering himself as a target. It was an incredibly brave and loyal act, or plain stupidity. Whatever, I wasn't about to waste it. I rushed out of hiding as bullets began punching the hillside around Rink, firing blindly at those crouching in the rocks. Something, a bullet or ricochet, had nicked me earlier, but it was only one of dozens of singular pains I was experiencing, all of them blending to one dull ache that wasn't about to slow me now. I charged in among the boulders between Rink and the others, surprised to find I was still alive. I fired one last round from the Glock and then the slide locked back. I dropped the gun – it was a hindrance now – swapping the SIG to my right hand.

'You still alive, Rink?'

'Is your ass still in one piece?'

'For now.'

The headlights of approaching vehicles had become bouncing beams attached to solid objects. Three cars screeched to a halt, more coming up the hill behind them. The helicopter rode the sky on a parallel to us. Its searchlights lit the hillside with a harsh glare that deepened the shadows behind the rocks in which we hid. The six men on the ground blocked our escape that way.

'We're fucked,' I said.

'Try stating a point, will ya?'

Men were pouring out of the parked vehicles, some taking cover, others moving for the rock face to flank us.

'How many bullets you got, Rink?'

'Not enough to go around,' he said. 'Four, five maybe, I kinda lost count.'

I had three.

'We're fucked,' I said once more.

'Not yet,' Rink said.

He fired three of his short stock of bullets at the helicopter, and sparks flashed where they struck the cockpit. In response to the surprise attack the chopper wobbled as the pilot fought with the controls, then it dipped away, dropping from sight below the roadway. I listened intently for a corresponding crash and explosion, but there was none. The chopper hove into sight again, this time a good four or five hundred yards out, well beyond effective handgun range.

While I was waiting for the helicopter to crash and burn, there was a sudden lull in activity while everyone apparently checked out the re-emergence of the craft in the sky. Rink didn't wait. Following his attack, he'd leaped from hiding and charged nearer those in the rocks. As he hurtled past me, I saw his free hand come out with his KA-BAR and I understood he was going for broke. I jumped up and went after him.

The lull was shattered.

Bullets began scorching the air around me, from front and back. My mind was set in the red zone of battle and I didn't give a fuck for bullets. All that was left to us was to go balls to the wall, and the devil take the hindmost.

Rink was running and dodging between boulders, projectiles missing him by a hair's breadth, but he went on, undeterred. I couldn't see his face, but I guessed it wouldn't be pretty. Not for those that he was coming for. As brutal or tough as those guys were they would be on the back foot when facing something like Jared Rington bulling towards them. I went after him, ducking and diving to different boulders, trying to confuse the shooters, giving them a choice of elusive targets to further confuse and disarray them. I caught another stinging wound, but it was more likely to be a fragment of bullet or rock chip that scored my shoulder because it didn't slow me.

A man rose up directly in front of Rink. My heart was in

my throat, because I thought he had the drop on my friend, but that wasn't so. He'd depleted his bullets and was fumbling to get a spare magazine in his gun, torn between the advancing behemoth that was Rink and the job at hand. Caught between the two tasks, he could concentrate sufficiently on neither. Rink capitalised on the situation by driving his KA-BAR into the juncture of the man's neck and shoulder. It was a killing blow and the man went down without a sound. I continued to sprint for Rink's position, and saw him duck, and come back up with the dropped gun. He slapped the fresh mag in place, and then tossed it back to me. I caught the gun, but shoved it away in my belt for now.

Behind us the shooting had been curtailed. Friends were loath to shoot at us for fear of hitting those beyond us. Either that or they were simply racing after us to corral us again, but I didn't have time to check. Our unspoken plan was basic: storm the enemy position, kill them or force them to flee. It was the only way that we could reach the vehicles they'd arrived in. They hadn't come here in the earthmover, but by fast car, and had utilised the excavator as a more effective roadblock. Their vehicles had to be parked within the service road from which the attack had come. If we could reach a car we still had a chance at escape.

Rink went down.

I wasn't worried.

His sudden movement had been controlled, smooth and without a loss of forward momentum. I imagined him scuttling between the scatter of boulders like a huge lizard on all fours. Giving him an opportunity to gain a good position, I yelled to draw fire at me. Madness, but that was what the situation required. The bullets did come my way and I was forced to duck down among the rocks. Bobbing up, I returned fire, picking my shots. Three rounds, not a single kill. I fed the SIG into my waistband for safekeeping, and took out the gun liberated by Rink moments before. I double-checked that the mag was secure and racked the slide, arming the gun. It was an old Browning, with thirteen bullets in the magazine if memory served correctly. The nine-millimetre rounds would fit my own gun, but there was no time for messing around. Taking a moment to press my back to the rock, I looked back towards where the cars had drawn up in a ragged barricade to block our route back towards Imuris – like we'd ever contemplate going back! Silhouettes moved before the glaring lights, and one of them appeared taller and broader of shoulder than most around him. Marshall was here. I felt no rancour towards my old friend, just then. My mind was in a killing place, and it didn't think ill of any individual: each man out there was an enemy to be killed without favour or discrimination.

Up until now Molina's men had proved less capable than I'd been led to believe, but I guessed they had been run-of-the-mill footsoldiers, recruited from the criminal gangs. Marshall and his mercenary crew were a different kettle of fish. Now that the 'specialists' were on the scene I could expect a tougher fight. The blood pounded in my head at the thrill of the situation. But I couldn't give in to the base sensation that flared through me; this wasn't about sating my need for bloody competition with worthy opponents, but about ensuring a woman and child made it safely home.

It was also about not allowing my friend Rink to get cornered while I took a break to catch my breath. I moved out, staying low as I went forward. Gunshots rang out, but they had slowed in intensity, and I was sure that those crouching among the loose rocks of the landslide had no idea where Rink had got to. A hollow croak punctuated the gunfire, and the shooting lessened. Rink's blade had taken another of them.

There was some shouting. It was in Spanish, the words so

garbled that I couldn't make any sense of them. I took it that those facing us were hollering for assistance from their pals who'd fallen idle while they waited to see how the battle would turn out. In response I heard an English accent yelling, 'Hold your fucking fire, I told you.'

Marshall wasn't commanding me to lay down my gun, but the men with him.

The chopping racket of the helicopter swooping in covered whatever words came next.

I ignored everything, moving for the nearest of Molina's men, pinpointing him by his panicked yells. I made it to the boulder behind which he was sheltering. He had no experience in guerrilla warfare. He was struck by fear and doing very little to assist his cause. Despite his terror, he remained a threat if I allowed him to live. Exhaling quietly, I braced my legs, lowering my centre of balance, then quickly tilted my upper body so that I could see round the boulder. The man had his body pressed to the stone, as he tried to look round the far side. He was unaware of my presence, and died with no clue as to where the bullet had come from. Three of the original six were now dead, and things were beginning to sway in our favour once more. But that was only while Marshall held his own and the rest of Molina's fighters back. I could hear nothing for the battering wind from the rotor downwash, and wondered if there were killers moving among the rocks behind me. It was highly likely, so my best move was to go on.

Two shots rang out.

A man yelled.

There was a single crack of a bullet striking the rock face.

Then a figure broke from cover and ran out into the road.

He went down on his face among the debris from the wrecked Subaru. In the confusion one of his own had brought him down, no doubt thinking I was the fleeing man. Again Marshall roared an order to hold fire.

That left only two men to block our escape route.

A solid *thunk!* of steel through flesh marked the demise of one of them.

Only one man stood between a vehicle and us.

Minutes ago, in an unsavoury manner, I'd stated that we were finished. Now I was beginning to fancy our chances of surviving the ambush. Though others on the scene had other thoughts on the subject, and they were putting them into action.

Bullets began pounding the floor all around me.

Unbeknown to me, while I'd been engaged in the running fight among the boulders, the helicopter had put down, and one man on board had been handed an assault rifle. Now that gunman was leaning out of the open door of the chopper as it hovered over me and was trying his damnedest to finish me off. I had no place to hide from an aerial attack.

My original idea re-formed fully in my mind.

'We're fucked,' I thought as I curled in a ball to avoid the flying bullets and the shower of rock chips cutting through my clothing.

Suddenly the chaos ended.

The helicopter still hovered overhead, the gunman leaning out, but he had held his fire on someone's instruction. I doubted that the command had come out of pity. Molina would rather torture me to death than offer a clean bullet through the skull.

'Hunter? Can you hear me?'

'I hear you, Marshall.'

'Toss your gun away, mate.'

I considered shooting at the helicopter, gambling everything on the off chance I could hit the man with the rifle before he tore me to ribbons.

'You don't stand a chance,' Marshall yelled. 'You're surrounded. Don't let the fuckers shoot you while you cower in the dirt. Throw down your gun, stand up like a man, and show these bean-eaters what kind of men the Paras turn out.'

'Turncoat arseholes like you don't do much for their reputation,' I shouted.

But he had a point. I didn't want to end up torn to pieces without having stood up and faced death.

'I swear, Hunter. You've about three seconds before we start shooting again. I've men surrounding your position; so don't even think about trying to run. That gunner up in the air, he'll get you in seconds. I'm giving you an opportunity to save face before you're torn a new arsehole. Throw away the gun, stand up and walk out here.'

So I did.

I made a show of tossing the gun on to the road, and watched as it slid across the gritty surface until checked by a piece of mangled metal.

'That's a start,' Marshall called. 'Now the other gun. The one with the bullets.'

Bastard had realised I was too quick in giving up my only weapon. The first gun I'd thrown down was my empty SIG.

'Can't blame me for trying,' I said.

'The gun, Hunter. Then show me your hands.'

Reluctantly I also threw the Browning on the road.

'Stand up. Slow and easy like.'

I stood, holding my hands high overhead.

'Now walk out. Stand in the road where I can get a good look at you.'

'You going to shoot me down like a dog, Marshall?' I moved out, placing myself a few yards out on the shoulder of the road. Marshall was a good twenty feet away, moving closer, covering me with the barrel of an AK-47.

'The way you did to McAdam?'

'That was a fair fight. You know it.' I didn't mention that it was actually Rink who'd killed McAdam. The less they thought about Rink the better.

Marshall chewed his bottom lip as he approached. He was caught briefly in the chopper searchlights and his glass eye twinkled like a star in its death throes.

'Is that what you're looking for now?' Marshall said. 'If it was my decision to fight you, then I'd oblige. I wouldn't mind going hand to hand with you; always thought I could take you, Joe.'

'It looks as if we'll never know. What happens now? You hand me over to Molina then walk away counting your blood money?'

'Yeah, that pretty much sums it up, Joe.'

The helicopter had moved away, but only so the pilot could find a place free of wreckage to set down. Ignoring Marshall's gun I watched as Molina stepped down from the open door. He was wearing a steel-grey suit, black shirt, grey tie and buffed shoes. His hair was coiffed and oiled. Looked like he was on his way to a business meeting. Only the machete he gripped said otherwise.

A moment behind him came Howell Regis. He was cradling the machine-gun across his middle, looking mighty pleased with himself for capturing me. Watching them approach, I wasn't sure which of them I wanted to kill first.

Except it appeared I was going to precede them both to the grave. Molina came at me, and with each step the machete rose a few inches higher. It was the end of the road for me, but I wasn't going out without a fight. If I could cause enough confusion, then Rink could slip away. I hoped my friend would find it in his power to avenge me.

I advanced to meet Molina, opening my arms to invite a

wild slash at my neck. Come on, I challenged with my stare, try and take my head. I was so focused on him that I missed Marshall as he lifted the stock of his rifle and slammed it against the back of my skull.

37

The river foamed wildly, a dull roar that had faded to white noise inside Walter's head. He paid the river sounds no heed, and had zoned out from the background noises of windblown trees, birdcalls and splashing of jumping fish. He listened for only one thing: the trill of a phone.

He had two distinct ringtones programmed into the cell phones he held. Both were old-time numbers by Elvis Presley, the first a cover of 'Since I Met You Baby', originally performed by rhythm-and-blues pianist Ivory Joe Hunter, and a bit of an in-joke at the younger Joe's expense. The second was a track from the movie *King Creole*, and aptly titled 'Trouble' considering the identity of the man on the other end of that phone.

Walter waited. The gentle strains of the first track would mean that his granddaughter and her son were safe, the more bluesy intro that she was only partly in the clear, but that Hunter's job would have been made slightly easier.

He continued to wait.

A man called out from up at the fishing lodge, one of Walter's bodyguards checking on him. Without replying, Walter merely waved an arm, indicating the man should go back inside. A second enquiry didn't follow and Walter trusted the man had obeyed.

The swish of water over rocks became a singular buzz that no longer had definition or clarity, and Walter was lulled into a trance-like state as he sat on the damp rocks, his heels locked so he didn't slide from his perch into the river below.

He didn't know how long he'd waited. He was loath to check the time, for counting the seconds would make the wait all the more interminable. He merely sat, a phone in each sweaty palm, urging either to ring by bobbing each cell up and down in turn. Anyone watching him would think he was crazy, but Walter could care less.

When the horn section intro kicked in Walter almost dropped the cell in his hurry to answer.

He offered no preamble; no enquiries concerning the good health of the caller or anything else trivial, but went direct to the point.

'Is it done?'

'It's done.'

Walter breathed out, long and loud.

'Well?'

'You have my gratitude,' Walter said.

'Good enough. But there's also another matter. You owe me, right?'

'Tell me you didn't enjoy the task you were set.'

'I enjoyed it. In fact, it felt real good to get back in the saddle again. But that's beside the point.'

'I'm a man of my word. I'll speak to my superiors on your behalf, have you reinstated.'

'Thanks. Since I was made to look a fool, it has been a little difficult to reassert my position. I've been stuck in goddamn limbo for the best part of a year.'

'You're back now. You've proved your abilities and I'll recommend that you are returned to full field duties with immediate effect, plus recompense for what you've lost through being sidelined.'

Now it was the caller's turn to sigh.

'Who'd have thought that by assisting the very man responsible for ruining my career, justice would be done?'

'Yes.' Walter considered how the caller would take his next words, but chose to say them anyway. 'You owe Joe Hunter.'

'Yeah. I owe him.' No clarification of the statement was offered, but it was loaded enough to send a shiver of unease through Walter.

Walter was almost done talking; he had another call to make. Yet he preferred to know the details that would ensure the man he was about to call would pay attention.

'How did you do it?'

'Garrotte. What else? Would be a shame to waste the opportunity this time. Never did get the chance to take off anyone's head last time I played Vince Everett.'

38

'No, no, no, no . . . this can't be happening now!'

Kirstie Long buried her face against her son's chest, as if by breathing in his scent, feeling the beat of his heart against her cheek, she'd never be forced to let him go again. The very real possibility that he would be taken from her made her cry, but they were cold tears of rage. After everything that they had gone through, what the men assisting her had done on their behalf, she would die before willingly handing Benjamin over to his father. But she could not allow her child to be harmed.

They were at stalemate.

Harvey Lucas, McTeer, Velasquez, all of them were willing to sell their lives to give Kirstie and Benjamin a chance at survival, but should they fight, they would invite a storm of bullets to shred the car, and those bullets would be indiscriminate about whose flesh they tore apart.

The men and women surrounding the car were prepared to dispense death at a heartbeat, but they understood the consequences of harming Jorge Molina's boy. They held their fire, but there was no allowance for Velasquez to steer the car out of the cordon that surrounded them.

Everything had gone reasonably well since Benjamin's impromptu escape and recovery up in the hills, and they'd made progress, both in miles to the border and in Kirstie reassuring the boy that he was safe and loved. Perhaps as fatigue began to set in, as the border crossing came into their sights, they had made the mistake of relaxing their guard and had allowed themselves to drive directly into a trap. Recrimination would have to wait. It was no one's fault that they had been surrounded, or that they had not recognised the ambush for what it was until the vehicle in front had slammed on its brakes, forcing Velasquez to take avoidance tactics, only to be rammed by another vehicle that had lain in wait on a cross street. A utility van had driven into the rear fender of their car, pinning them between the three ambush vehicles and a row of steel bollards set into the edge of the sidewalk.

Harvey was cursing himself for missing the vehicles closing in on them. Had they been out in the empty tracts they'd easily have recognised what was coming, but here in Agua Prieta it was edging towards dawn and already numbers of cars were about, people heading off to work, or making an early start across the border.

'What are we gonna do, Harve?' Unofficially Harvey had taken on the mantle of leader, and McTeer, a man capable of making his own decisions in a pinch, still deferred to his better judgement.

'We have to think of the boy.'

All three adults knew that, but they shared nods of acknowledgement at Harvey's wisdom.

Benjamin, wide-eyed with alarm at the sudden screech of brakes and dull collisions, had other ideas. 'Mommy, I don't want to go home.'

Kirstie wasn't sure if the boy meant her home or the one from which he'd recently been snatched.

'I won't let anyone hurt you, Benjamin,' she promised, holding him closer.

Velasquez had turned off the engine. There was no means of forcing a way out of the crush of vehicles. Instead of holding the wheel, he took out his gun.

McTeer reached across, pushing down his friend's forearm. 'Keep that outta sight, buddy. They see you lift a gun, they might get itchy fingers.'

'They won't shoot,' Harvey said. 'They want the boy alive.'

'They're not getting him,' Kirstie said, raising her head to bare her teeth, a lioness protecting its cub.

Fighters were surrounding the car now, waving guns, challenging the occupants, yelling at them to throw out their weapons.

'There's not much else we can do,' Harvey said, his voice ragged with pain. 'It's the only way we can save him.'

'I'm not giving him back,' Kirstie yelled. Her challenge was as much to her companions as to those outside.

Harvey said, 'If we refuse, we'll all die, Kirstie. Then there won't be another opportunity to get Benjamin back from them.'

'You're saying I should hand him over on the off chance we'll be allowed near him again? They'll take him away and that'll be the end of it.'

'We have more chance alive than dead.'

'They'll kill us the second we hand the boy over,' Velasquez put in. 'I say we put a gun to his head and use him as a hostage while we walk out of here.'

'What?' Kirstie looked ready to rake the eyes from Velasquez's head.

'I don't mean that we'd really threaten him. It'd just be an act,' Velasquez said. 'Until we could get out of here.'

'No! No way. What if they decide to shoot anyway?'

'They're gonna shoot sooner or later,' McTeer said.

'Kirstie. Please. Trust me, OK?'

Kirstie snatched a look at Harvey's pleading face, then at each of the other men. They were pale with despair and she understood that was a rare emotion for them.

'Oh, God . . .' Kirstie lifted her son so she could meet his gaze. 'I won't let anything happen to you, baby.'

Benjamin's bottom lip trembled, but for the first time he looked trustingly at his mother. Kirstie's heart swelled with joy, but not for long.

A sharp crack introduced the next warning from outside. One of Molina's footsoldiers jabbed the muzzle of his gun against the passenger window, close to McTeer's skull. His words were in Spanish, but he was clearly demanding that they come out of the car. As he did so, the car jamming the doors inched away a few feet, allowing a man and woman to move in, both holding handguns. They pointed them threateningly through the windows at Kirstie and Harvey, then the woman pulled open the door.

In English, the woman said, 'Get out, and don't try anything stupid.'

'Go to hell,' Kirstie spat.

The woman contorted her face in a snarl that turned her pretty features ugly. With her free hand she reached in and grabbed Kirstie by the hair. She dragged her from the back seat, and Kirstie still was not ready to give up her son. Benjamin screamed as she attempted to push him back inside into Harvey's arms. However, Harvey was already on his way out, waving his hands, begging for leniency. The woman snatched Benjamin, and Kirstie went for her. The man with the handgun slapped its butt hard against the back of Kirstie's head and she sank to her knees.

'Son of a bitch!' Harvey struck at the man, but he was careful to do so with his open hands, merely pushing the man away. Others of Molina's gang moved in, noisy and threatening. 'Take it easy, goddamnit! There's no need for violence, you've got the boy.'

Velasquez had also slipped from behind the steering wheel.

He made a show of throwing down his pistol. He was the best placed to communicate with the gang in their own language. No one wanted to hear what he had to say though. Two gunmen grabbed his arms while another kicked him hard between his legs. Velasquez slumped down in the grasp of his captors.

McTeer came out of the car bellowing, his deep voice echoing off the buildings that hemmed them in on two sides. Harvey also was engaged in loud debate, but it was getting them nowhere. Others moved on Harvey and McTeer, frisking them for concealed weapons, some of them rough-handed, slapping and punching them into submission.

Within seconds all four of them were kneeling on the road. As the crow flew they were less than a mile from the border crossing, but assistance from the authorities was beyond their grasp. Especially when a couple of their captors, including the woman who now held Benjamin, wore official Border Control uniforms. Kirstie tried to get up, arms reaching for her boy. A young man wearing cargo pants and loose shirt kicked her down again. He placed a revolver to her head, screaming words she couldn't comprehend.

The woman backed away, taunting Kirstie with a slow smile.

Kirstie screamed at her. For a third time she attempted to stand.

Hands clutched her, but this time it was Harvey who held her in place. 'Kirstie, wait . . .'

Someone else was standing just beyond the ring of gunmen. An older man, suited and booted, different from the others, who were all local toughs or crossing guards on the take. He was silver-haired, trim and healthy-looking, privileged, unused to the scutwork the others knew on a day-to-day basis: a local lieutenant in Molina's network? The man was talking on a cell phone, relaying news of their capture and the recovery of Benjamin to the main man. He took his instructions with nods of his head, before switching off the cell phone to allow him to lift both hands in the air to attract attention. He didn't raise his voice; it was apparent that he was calling the shots and all here had been waiting for instructions. Some of those gathered round appeared bloodthirsty, and would have no qualms about slaying them in the street, while others were more wary. Some even wore expressions of regret and pity, but weren't prepared to act or say anything in their defence, such was their fear of speaking out against the cartels.

Kirstie was in no fit state to listen to the man's words, but felt some of the tension go out of Harvey, his grip relaxing marginally. He whispered words that didn't do much to comfort her, or reassure her that they would get Benjamin safely away, but maybe they had just won a momentary reprieve of sorts.

'They're not going to kill us,' he said. 'Not yet anyway.'

39

'Wakey-wakey, rise and shine, Hunter.'

I woke up in agony.

My skull was throbbing from where the stock of Marshall's rifle had knocked me unconscious. My muscles ached everywhere, cramps twisting them into knots. Even my insides were shuddering with waves of pain, brought on by the twin tortures of nausea and hunger. My throat was parched beyond belief, and swallowing the sticky blood in my mouth had me gagging and heaving. It didn't help that I was in a pose designed to promote intense stress on the body. My wrists were bound behind my back, but yanked up in the air by a rope suspended from a metal hook in the ceiling. My naked toes barely touched the floor. My head and neck hung forward, and to look up meant fighting against the opposing forces jabbing through my shoulders, adding to the agony. My clothing had been removed, all but my undershorts, and icy-cold water dripped from my torso. Marshall must have doused me when he'd arrived to rouse me from slumber. If I could have reached with my tongue I'd have licked some of the moisture from my skin, but that would have made me all the more pathetic. My situation was shit, and there was no hope of it getting better soon.

But despite all that I was happy.

Perhaps 'happy' was a poor choice of word.

I was relieved.

I was alive.

Never would I have believed I'd escape from the high mountain pass with my head still attached to my neck, but there I was. Maybe I should have been fearful, because the only reason I could imagine for being spared decapitation was so that my captors could torture me before I died. A swift chop of a machete was possibly too good for me in Jorge Molina's opinion. I envisioned the fates of others that crossed the cartels and expected a far more gruesome end than a clean execution. However, fear wasn't in my remit. Death was a probability in my line of work, not worth fretting over. Life meant a second chance at my enemies. Life was good, and the pain a blessing – as contradictory as that sounds. Enduring the pain gave me something to rage against and build up my motivation to survive.

'Where am I?'

'Hell.' Marshall chuckled.

From my bent-up position I was staring at his chest. Fighting the agony that flared through my contorted shoulders, I craned up to meet his one good eye.

'Quit the amateur dramatics, Marshall. Where am I?'

'You know the rules, Hunter, you don't tell prisoners intelligence they can use later.'

'So let me guess. I'm near the border, right? Probably Agua Prieta.'

Marshall grinned, but offered no clarification. He didn't have to. It made sense that I'd be dragged towards the border, Molina probably hoping that he could perform a double whammy and stop his ex-wife before she was able to flee the country. He wouldn't have transported me across the border itself: too many questions would be asked. He'd probably figured – or Regis or Marshall had – that we'd planned to meet up with the rest of our party once we'd given those pursuing us the slip. The geography didn't allow for many options other than that we were heading for Agua Prieta when I was captured.

'You're lucky to be alive, Hunter. Maybe that won't be the case if you keep on asking questions.'

'I'm an inquisitive kind of guy,' I said.

'You're a fucking idiot. Why don't you open your ears and listen for a change?'

'What're you going to say, Marshall? Probably a few threats, a few jokes at my expense, some taunting, some swearing thrown in for good measure. There's nothing that I want to hear from you.'

'You've a low opinion of me these days, huh?'

'Only since you chose to take money from a murderous pig like Jorge Molina.'

'I don't work for Molina.'

'Regis then. You work for him, and he's kissing Molina's arse.'

Marshall chose not to answer. The faux humour had gone out of him. 'Think whatever you want, Hunter. It doesn't matter. The truth is that you've an hour left to live and about fifty-nine minutes of it are going to be painful for you. So listen up. Time's short.'

'Did Rink make it?'

'Your big Japanese pal? Yeah, he made it. But he's not much good to you stuck way out in the mountains. Forget about him coming to your rescue, he's too busy running for his life from the team Molina sent after him.'

That was quite an admission, seeing as moments before he'd said that information wasn't shared with prisoners. Relief trickled through my tortured frame. Rink had escaped certain death, so giving myself up had not been in vain. I didn't fear that a team of Molina's gunmen was chasing him; they had no idea who – or what – they were up against.

'Tell me, Marshall, why are you here when it means that Molina gets less time to torture me? You pulled some kind of favour so you can beat the shit out of me first?'

'Molina's otherwise engaged. Oh, that's right. You don't know, do you?'

'Know what?'

'Your girlfriend,' Marshall said. 'Or should I say the former Mrs Molina? She was captured barely a mile from freedom. Bit of a shitter, eh? Bet you're pissed that you gave yourself up? What was your idea, Hunter? That while Molina was tormenting you it would give Kirstie a clear run for the border?'

'I didn't give up,' I lied. 'I fully intended taking that machete from Molina and sticking it in his gut. Would've killed him if you hadn't done me a dirty from behind.'

'I saved your life, you ungrateful piece of shit.'

'By knocking me out and having me carted here to this . . . what is this place . . . a goddamn meatpacking plant? You didn't save me, you condemned me to a slow death.'

'I kept to our deal, Hunter. I told you if you came out unarmed I'd save you from Regis's bullets. I did that. Maybe you didn't notice, but when you were gearing up to face Molina, Regis had a bead on you with that cannon. He was about to rip you to shreds; I knocked you down to stop that from happening.'

'Big of you,' I said.

'Maybe more than I could expect from you?'

'Maybe,' I concurred. 'Back in Hermosillo I told you what would happen if you came at me.'

'Our old mate, McAdam, learned that the hard way.'

The stress on my shoulder blades was terrible but no way was I going to show the weakness. I held the position, craning up to meet Marshall's gaze. Since the accident where he'd lost an eye his scars had faded. If it weren't for the glassy stillness of one unwavering pupil it would have been hard to spot the prosthetic. The other eyeball flickered as he studied me.

'McAdam was never a mate,' I said. 'Even after he dragged me off that Belfast street he hated my guts. If it wasn't for the fact questions would have been asked, he'd have happily left me there to be shot again by the sniper. You, though, Marshall, you were different.'

'Trying to sweet-talk me now, eh? A minute ago you looked ready to tear my throat out with your teeth.'

'My opinion hasn't changed. I'm only surprised that the good man I knew back then turned out to be a piece of crap.'

To my surprise Marshall gave a genuine laugh. 'Guess I made some poor life choices between then and now.'

'Were you envious of me?'

'What's to be envious of? It's not me that has ended up on the end of a rope waiting for a psycho-wetback to come and gut him.'

'Selection,' I said. 'When you were turned down by Arrowsake and I got in over you. If it's any consolation, the deal with Arrowsake wasn't what any of us imagined. Arrowsake was poisonous, Marshall, and has tainted everything it touched, including every aspect of my life since. Trust me, I'm the envious one.'

'I don't give a fuck about Arrowsake turning me down. I gained an employer who pays better and doesn't try to fuck you over all the time.'

'You can't trust Regis,' I said.

'I'm not talking about Regis or the CIA.'

'Fucking Molina? You just said you don't work for him.'

'I'm not talking about that psychopath either.'

I waited.

He appeared to be considering what to say next.

In the end I could bear his silence no longer.

'Come on, stop keeping me in suspense. Or is this just another way of torturing me?'

Marshall moved away. I could only follow his progress by swinging at the end of the rope, dancing around on my toes. It almost dislocated my shoulder joints, but I had to keep him before me, watch his every move. Marshall walked to the far wall and leaned against it. He crossed his arms over his chest. Watched me watching him. The room was large, an echoing space with brushed-steel walls, long steel trestle-type tables along both sides, complete with drainage gutters that fed to grates in the tiled floor. A large stainless-steel sink, over which hung a flexible metal coiled hose, dominated the back wall. The coppery scent of blood was pungent, but the stink could have been coming off me. I'd assumed that it was a workspace in a meatpacking plant, but it could simply have been the back room of a butcher's shop. Apt, considering what Molina had in mind.

We held the tableau for some seconds. Water dripped from the faucet, adding tempo to the span of time, each drop the ominous ticking of a countdown to Armageddon. Marshall was deep in thought, his good eye focused on a space somewhere between us, or on some far-distant place. He exhaled slow and long, then studied me and finally shook his head at the pathetic image I must have made. 'I can't help you, Joe. You're fucked.'

'So what happens now? You walk away? Turn your back and forget I'm here? Or are you going to stick around and watch me cut to shreds?'

'Depends, Joe.'

'On what?'

'Whether I'm asked to stand and watch or not.'

'Arsehole.'

'Life's shit,' Marshall sneered, 'and then you die. In your case much sooner than you probably care for. But then again . . . maybe a quick death would be preferable.'

Marshall moved for the exit door.

'Hey,' I called.

He halted but didn't look back at me.

'What about when it comes to an innocent woman? You prepared to stand by and watch that happen too?'

He only picked up his stride again and went to the exit. He placed a hand on the latch, but paused there.

'Why did you come here, Joe?'

I wasn't sure if it was a question or an expression of regret. Either way it was rhetorical. He opened the door and stepped out, leaving me hanging on the end of the damn rope. As soon as he was gone, I folded at the waist, groaning in pain as the spasming muscles in my lower back competed with those in my neck to torture me most. No sooner had I relaxed than something bumped against the door, and the latch was shoved up. The door swung open again, and I expected to see my old mate return to finish the conversation.

But it wasn't him.

It was Jorge Molina, and he was carrying a rope, heavily corded hemp as thick as his wrist that dripped moisture on the tile floor. The rope was stained dark. I got a fresh waft of blood and understood how he'd employed the rope. Now it was my turn to be on its receiving end.

I bared my teeth.

'Bring it on, you murderous bastard,' I challenged him.

Molina ignored my taunt.

He walked past, with me dancing on my toes to keep him in view. He approached the stainless-steel range at the far end of the room and fed the rope into the sink. Then, watching me with a gaze as hard and soulless as a lump of concrete, he took down the hose and aimed the nozzle at the rope. Hitting a lever, he allowed the water to spray all over the woven hemp. He wasn't washing off the blood of its previous victims, but weighting the torture weapon all the more. That or he meant to make the rope more pliable so that it would impact on the maximum area of my body with each swing. Bastard intended hurting me bad.

40

The first stroke of the wet rope came to my abdomen.

I'd never known pain like it.

I've been shot, stabbed, beaten, but nothing came close to the agony induced by such a simple torture implement as that length of soaking hemp. First came the solid cudgel-like blow, followed a moment later by the rasping tear of rough fibres across the skin, compounded by the blast of atomised moisture that cut deep into the dermis. I'd swear the stinging welt rose an inch from my hide even before Molina jerked the rope away for strike number two. He slashed me across both thighs this time, and there was nothing I could do to halt the recoiling of my muscles, the involuntary spasm of my legs that snatched my toes from the floor and left me hanging on the bindings round my wrists. It almost tore my arms from their sockets.

I fought the pain, tried to get my feet under me.

Molina walked behind me and the next blow came blind, yet not unexpected, to my lower spine. There was no way I could alleviate the pain or the tortuous position of my body. I shuddered out a cry that hurt almost as much as the physical torture.

Molina had no pity.

He slashed the rope across my right triceps, and I feared he'd broken my arm. If that was the case, and he'd done a proper job of shattering my humerus, it might have alleviated some of the pain in my shoulders when my arm gained an extra joint and allowed more freedom of movement. Yet my arm wasn't broken, the damage was centred in the tissue of my muscles and skin. I couldn't hold in the cry that followed, yet there was enough rage in me to change it from one of beseeching to one of challenge. Molina snorted at my bravado and played the rope across my buttocks in a way that was repulsive, as suggestive of male rape as if he'd whispered the threat in my ear. The lascivious way in which he allowed the stiff rope to probe at my backside was more insidious than the promise of further beatings. I twisted away from him, trying to face my tormentor.

He grabbed my bindings with his free hand, yanked me back to where I'd started. Craning my head round, I could barely see where he shortened his grip on the wet rope. In the next instant he thrust the rope between my thighs, hauling up on it so that the rope whacked me painfully in the testicles. I thought I'd black out. I would have vomited if my stomach hadn't been so empty.

'I used this on her,' he said.

His voice was unaccented. He sounded like an Ivy Leaguer, and not the Central American gangster he was.

'That's all you could use on her, you limp-dicked piece of crap,' I croaked.

'Did you fuck her?'

'What?'

'You screwed her, right? I'd expect no less from the cheap whore.'

'Does that give you a secret thrill, Molina? Thinking of another man screwing your wife? What's wrong: you can't get it up these days without some sick stimulation?'

Molina jabbed me in the balls again.

'I raped her, Joe Hunter, and I did not need *this*.' He jabbed me for a third time, and if not for the fact my scrotum had shrivelled tight in reflex to the abuse, then major tissue damage would have resulted. 'I used this–' another jab – 'after I'd finished with her, to ensure no other man would go with her again.'

'Bastard.' My curse came nowhere close to what I wanted to call him. But I couldn't think of words strong enough to express my hatred, not when his words had just given me hope. Maybe he was toying with me afresh, but from what he'd just given away, Kirstie was still alive. Violated, perhaps, but still alive.

'Kirstie is the mother of your son,' I reminded him. 'Does that mean nothing to you?'

'No. She was a whore when I met her, was a whore throughout our marriage and things haven't changed since.'

Molina hauled me round, this time using a fist in my hair to manoeuvre me into position. He was in kicking range, but I had neither the strength nor the hope that I could hurt him badly enough to satisfy me.

'What did she promise you, Joe Hunter?' He pronounced my full name as if it was something to be despised. 'Did she offer to fuck you if you came to my house and stole my son? Is that why you chose to become my enemy, Joe Hunter? Do you think the promise of her stinking pussy was worth it?'

'You disgust me,' I growled. 'You think you're some big shot, but you're nothing. You're a foul-mouthed punk, a fucking coward who won't even face his enemies on level ground.'

'I disgust you?' Molina laughed harshly. 'Well isn't that a shame! By the time I'm finished with you, you'll know what genuine disgust feels like. Here, how's this for starters?'

He spat in my face.

I held his gaze while the saliva dribbled down my cheek and dripped from my jaw.

'My friend, the CIA agent, tells me you used to be something,' Molina went on. 'He warned me that you were a dangerous adversary, Joe Hunter. I believe that his impression of you is somewhat overblown. *You* disgust me. *You* are nothing. *You* are an inconsequential piece of meat waiting to be butchered. But I'll still take much delight in cutting you to pieces. Perhaps I'll bring the knife soon, but–' he made a show of eyeing me up and down – 'you still require some tenderising.'

'Like I said: Bring it on.'

'Thank you. I will.'

The wet rope slashed across my chest. Every strand of the rope felt like a single brand that tore at my skin. It was difficult to hold back the tears, but I managed, though my eyeballs stood out with the effort.

'You have insulted me, Joe Hunter. Both your attack on my home, and the stealing of my son, I take very personally. Such acts cannot be tolerated. I am a man with enemies, Joe Hunter, far more powerful than you. Once they learn of your deeds they will appraise my position in the hierarchy and find me wanting. They will believe that they can attack my home, take my son, and maybe try to take everything I own, including my life. You have caused me untold embarrassment and inconvenience, and the only way to put things right is to make a supreme example of you. I will show those who now think me weak that they are *wrong*. This–' his next strike came furiously and almost tore my lips from my face – 'is nothing to what I have in store for you and your friends.'

I hung from my bindings. The pain in my mouth outweighed the rest and was the only thing that held back the creeping unconsciousness that swam through my vision like dirty flood water.

'How did you ever expect to succeed in your stupid plan? Did you think a line on a map would stop me from taking back what is rightfully mine? Had you made it across the border, did you think the pursuit would end there? I'd hunt you and my whore wife to the end of the earth if need be. I would not stop.'

'Please . . .'

'Please what? Spare you?' Molina laughed, and it was a nasty sound.

'Please hit me again,' I corrected him. 'I can't bear to listen to your bullshit any longer. You're so far up your own arse you give suppositories a bad name.'

My words hit him like a slap to the face. He took a step back, blinking slowly, his features darkening with a flush of anger. He allowed some of the rope to slip through his fingers, lengthening the part that trailed from his fist. He was preparing to let loose a flurry of devastating cuts on me. He took a half step forward, and was checked by a bang on the door. He swung to the source of the noise, the cords in his neck straining with unchecked anger. I wasn't sure if he was mad at me or at the untimely intrusion of Howell Regis, who came in unannounced.

'What do you want?' Molina's voice came out high-pitched, like the spoiled brat I believed him to be.

Regis checked me out. He curled his lips back on yellow teeth as he appraised my battered body, not in distaste at the state of me, but at the fact I was still alive.

'I need to speak with you, Jorge.' Regis waited, still disgusted that I was in the here and now. 'It won't wait.'

'I told you I wasn't to be disturbed.' Molina gripped the rope, as if he would lash out at his co-conspirator for having the gall to distract him.

'It's important.' Regis's voice had taken on a wheedling tone. He was fearful, and I wasn't sure it had anything to do with Jorge Molina or the wet rope.

'This is important,' said Molina, shaking the rope in my direction.

Regis jerked his head, indicating that Molina should follow him outside. Apparently whatever he had to say wasn't for my ears. I wondered – no, hoped – that Rink had found his way to Molina's den and was tearing the place apart.

Molina snorted, but he threw down the rope. He looked at me. 'I'll be back.'

'I'll be waiting.'

Both men left the room. The door was heavy and insulated. It didn't fully close behind them though, the catch holding it open a fraction. It didn't offer an avenue of escape, not while I was strung up like a Christmas turkey, but it allowed me to hear the sound of their heels fading down the hall, even if I could make out nothing of the bitter words they shared in low whispers.

The timely reprieve had most likely saved me. Molina's rage was such that he was prepared to beat the innards from me with his torture device. I'd goaded him into the act after all, in the hope that – somehow – he would make a mistake and come too close to avoid the teeth I'd have sunk into his windpipe. Now, I realised, all I'd achieved was to prolong the intense agony, and the lingering death I was assured when Molina returned, calmer of mind.

Earlier I'd hurt everywhere.

That was nothing now.

I'd gone beyond mere pain, transcended a plane of existence where sheer agony dominated everything and there was no respite.

However, as I've noted before, the strength of human resilience can be shocking.

I was so beaten up, my muscles and tendons on fire, my skin crawling as though an electric current surged across it, my brain thumping so madly inside my cranium, that I'd have been forgiven if I gave up and slumped against my bindings. But I didn't do that. No. As soon as my enemies were out of earshot, I immediately craned up, searching for a way out of my predicament.

I could see where the rope had been fed over a ceiling-mounted hook. The hook itself was attached to a bracket that ran the width of the room, wall to wall, and had been fixed to sturdy wall mounts by heavy bolts. Other empty hooks decorated the length of the bracket, and I assumed that animal carcasses had once been lined all along it, worked on by various butchers in the workspace. There was nothing complicated about the set-up. The rope hadn't even been doubled round the hook, it was merely fed over it, and the other end tied to a retaining loop on a wall above one of the stainless-steel worktops. If I could gain some freedom of movement for my arms, I thought I might be able to flip the rope off the hook. I contemplated attempting the impossible and trying to forward-roll at the end of my bindings, taking body and legs through the gap between my elbows. Maybe a circus contortionist could have achieved the move, but not me.

Next I wondered if I could tip forward at the end of the rope, do a mid-air headstand and feed my toes into the narrow gap between the bracket and ceiling, using the strength of my legs to suspend me while I tried to flick the rope from the hook. Yeah, right. Even if such a move were possible, it would mean dropping to the floor with nothing but the top of my head to cushion the blow.

I had to find another way.

My fingers were too numb to work on the knots. Even if I had sensation in my fingertips, the entire weight of my body had hung on those knots and had cinched them tighter than I could ever hope to loosen. I checked out the nearby worktops and calculated my chances of reaching them if I jumped, but that was a non-starter: there was not enough play in the ropes.

I was certain that Molina had used his rope device on my friends, the blood was testament to their beatings, but I doubted he'd done anything to Kirstie yet, despite his sordid bragging to the contrary. That was all so much bullshit to torment me. Even so, I believed that Kirstie's torture was imminent, and perhaps being raped by a length of stiffened rope would be the least of her suffering. While I still breathed there was no way I'd allow it to happen. Even if that meant ripping one of my arms out of its socket, I'd never give up trying to save her. But dismemberment was low on my escape plans. There had to be something to help me, if only I could figure it out.

The only item nearby was the sodden rope Molina had discarded.

I fished for it with a big toe, trying to drag it towards me. I had the ludicrous notion that I could manipulate the thick rope between my feet, bending it and folding it so that I could form a wedge to jam under my soles and give me the extra elevation I required to gain some slack in my bindings. There was as little chance of that plan succeeding as my ideas of aerial acrobatics earlier. The rope was out of reach by about six inches, whichever way I strained and stretched.

Frustrated I threw myself back and forward, hoping that the weight of my body coupled with gravity would be enough to snap the rope or tear the hook from the bracket. It was pointless, and only served to place extra stress on my shoulders. Finally I got my toes under me once more and, bent as far as I could, I heaved in racking gasps of air. I could feel the focus of my rage altering from a need to escape to a sense of futility. In this state I was no good to anyone.

A noise brought my head up.

My contortions had brought me round to face the partly open door. Filtering through the narrow gap came the sound of footsteps in the hall. I could count only one set of feet. Whatever the urgency, Regis hadn't held Molina's attention for long: Molina was returning to finish what he'd started.

I steeled myself, determined that this time I'd take the beating without uttering a sound, make the bastard move closer to taunt me, where I'd then go for broke. If I killed that piece of shit, then maybe I could stand on his corpse and gain the slack I required. Yeah, right! There was about as much hope of that as of me winning the lottery, and I hadn't even bought a ticket.

The door swung inward and a silhouette blocked the light from outside. Too big to be Jorge Molina. My heart pumped hard for a few seconds, and then it was as if a pin had popped a balloon. It wasn't Rink come to rescue me, but James Lee Marshall who'd returned for round two. Something glinted in his right hand, and I recognised it immediately as a Fairbairn-Sykes commando knife, a weapon whose use we'd both been trained in during our Para days, and one I'd grown infinitely familiar with while at Arrowsake. He must be nostalgic about our past and wanted to kill me with a weapon I'd appreciate.

As he moved into the room, he was bathed in the sterile glare from the overhead striplights. The look on his face wasn't one of humour, triumph, or even the stern set of one on a murder mission. It was a look of intense regret. Marshall actually looked sorry to be the one to kill me.

I stared at him as the lid drooped over his good eye. Call me crazy, but I could feel no hatred for him.

'So Molina sent you to do his dirty work?'

'Shut it, Hunter.' He was sickened by what was about to happen, and I felt a bit sorry for my old mate.

'If you're going to do it, do it clean, OK.'

Marshall simply moved round behind me. He didn't want to

look into my face while he slipped the blade in. I contemplated kicking back at him, hoping to score a hit to his bollocks before I went, but knew Marshall wouldn't fall for that trick. It would only piss him off and perhaps force him into wounding me sorely a few times before administering the *coup de grâce*.

Though violent death was something to fight against tooth and nail, it was always on the cards for someone engaged in my lifestyle. I'd accepted that I'd probably end up on the point of a knife or riddled with bullets sooner or later – and how I'd avoided that up to now amazed me as much as it did everyone else who knew me – and as a warrior I'd always planned to go out without regret or recrimination. Yet, I didn't want to die like this, executed like a pig in a slaughterhouse. Not while so many others still depended upon me. Never had I begged for my life to any man, but I was on the cusp. I opened my mouth, hating the pinching in my throat as I attempted to form words.

'I said to shut it,' Marshall said. He grabbed my head in his left palm, forcing me to face away from him, and the dagger drove in towards the small of my back. Immediately I collapsed, the strength to stand failing me, my mind full of exploding stars and a wash of red that turned rapidly to black.

41

Rink stood over the corpse of a man.

It wasn't the first he'd stood astride during this long night.

The team who'd searched for him in the mountain pass had fallen to knife and gun, one of them to a broken neck. Rink had appeared in a blizzard of dust from out of a mound of grit dumped by the bucket of the excavator when Molina's men had first moved it to launch their ambush. From behind he'd grasped the hunter's head between his palms and wrenched it round so he was face to face with his would-be slayer. The man had died wordlessly, probably unaware that he'd even been set upon.

Rink had taken the man's gun, blown away another punk, and then disappeared into the darkness once more.

The two that remained had no idea their friends were corpses and came on, confident that their prey was trapped in the quarry at the head of the pass. Rink allowed both of them to enter the dead end, before he dropped from the rock wall from which he hung to land on the back of the rearmost, his KA-BAR pistoning in and out of both lungs so hard he heard the crunching of ribs. The racket of snapping bone carried even if the man's death cry didn't. The final man turned and fired, but Rink had already moved. The bullets tore the knifed man to shreds before he could die from the blood flooding his lungs. While the final gunman stared in incredulity at his slaughtered friend, Rink knelt calmly in the shadows of the cliffs, and picked his shots that took a chunk of the man's skull and holed his chest cavity.

Before the lights of the last car had been lost to sight, Rink was on the road in a vehicle commandeered from the ambushers. Those he followed had no idea that he could have survived the odds stacked against him, or that he was so close behind. Luck, it seemed, was in Rink's favour when he discovered bottles of spring water, a bag of corn chips and some pistachio nuts in a cooler box. He drove, sating his thirst and hunger, if not his need for revenge. That was something to be savoured for later.

Jorge Molina and Howell Regis had gone on ahead, taking the more direct route over the mountains in the helicopter. Hunter's old pal, James Lee Marshall, had overseen the transportation of their prisoner in the large SUV that led the pack. Not for the first time, Rink considered gaining on the caravan of cars wending their way through the passes, with the intention of launching some kind of rescue. He knew his chances of a successful result were nil, so he held back, waiting patiently for a better chance. Damn your misguided loyalty, Joe, he'd thought at first. What the hell were you thinking? Hunter had given himself up so that Rink could escape. They should have stuck closer together, and they'd have found a way out of the shoot-out. But he soon realised that Hunter's selflessness was for another reason. Hunter knew he'd be captured, probably savagely tortured, but he'd drawn the focus of the search from Rink, allowing him this opportunity to free his friend when the odds of both of them escaping with their lives were higher. Joe probably thought that by giving Molina a target for his fury, he'd be distracted from his pursuit of Kirstie long enough for Harvey and the guys to get her and the child safely over the border. Hunter had been wrong in this: from what Rink had understood from the conversations he'd overheard while lying in hiding, Kirstie and the others had already been captured. Molina and Regis had gone on ahead so that the punks could enjoy quality time with her before Hunter was delivered to them.

The drive to Agua Prieta had taken a few minutes over an hour, and it was the longest, most nerve-racking sixty-three minutes of Rink's eventful life. Each second was a lifetime as he thought about what pain Harvey, McTeer and Velasquez must already be enduring. Thankfully – during the drive at least – Joe wouldn't have to tolerate much suffering, because the blow he'd taken from the rifle stock would put him to sleep all the way back. Rink's hope was that he could release his buddy before he was delivered to Molina, but it was a hope dashed, because the SUV was driven directly into a warehouse building on the outskirt of Agua Prieta and a roller shutter closed behind it. The other vehicles in the rolling column had parked, some of the men going in, others remaining in the yard, standing guard or toking on cigarettes they passed around in celebration of a good night's work.

The warehouse turned out to be the workshop at the rear of a butcher's shop. How freakin' apt, Rink had thought. He didn't linger on the connotation of his discovery, but considered the best way in. Full-frontal attack was out of the question. Too many frog-giggin' punks were between him and his friends to take them on, though it hurt to admit as much. Face on, guns blazing, numbers'd simply overwhelm him. So he had but a single recourse. Cut the freakin' numbers.

And so it had begun.

This was the third man to fall beneath his blade since arriving in Agua Prieta, and still he hadn't made enough of an impact on those blocking his route inside. So get the hell on with your job, he admonished himself.

He was collecting weapons as he progressed, but there were

only so many handguns he could shove into his pants before they became an encumbrance. He left the latest gun lying beside the dead man and moved off, heading for an alleyway that ran the length of the warehouse. Parked cars and vans offered some cover, but there were gaps between each. Across these spaces he'd to time his runs, but he made it to the corner of the building undetected. The sun had come up, but in the alley, the second wall of which was formed from a furniture storage unit, day was yet to arrive. Rink still wore the black garb in which he'd first assaulted Molina's compound at Hermosillo, having discarded the more colourful clothing stolen from the rooftop laundry. He was practically invisible as he cat-footed down the alley and checked for the fire exit door he'd expected to find. But it was obvious that people who tortured and murdered had no care for rules, let alone fire safety regulations: the door was locked and barred with chains. It offered no ingress. Above him was a row of narrow windows, but they looked as if they hadn't been opened in decades. In any case, even if they did open, he'd need to lose fifty pounds in weight and many inches off his shoulders. He searched higher; saw that the roof overhung the supporting walls by about a handspan. There was no guttering, only the bare edges of tin sheets that formed the roof. If he could find a way up there then he could possibly force a sheet from the joists and climb inside the attic space, then downward to where his friends were held. But there were no downspouts or ladders that he could see.

Pointless groaning; you had to make your own luck in this business. He continued along the alley, pausing at the front corner. Listening. He counted three voices, but there could easily be more men guarding the front; more obtuse guys who had nothing good to say. Holding a gun in his right hand, his knife in the left, he moved out from the wall far enough that neither would make contact with the hard surface and betray his position. Then he slowly leaned out, checking numbers and positions of sentries.

There were four guys and one woman.

Ordinarily women were off Rink's killing radar, but this bitch was heavily armed and looked as cold-hearted as the men she stood guard alongside. He'd prefer not to kill her but if the choice was between her and his friends, then to hell with her. Females weren't known as the deadliest of the species for nothing.

As he considered his best course of action another man emerged. Unlike the rest, who were all Mexicans, this man was Caucasian, and probably one of Marshall's mercenaries. The guy had a machine-gun across his chest, his hands clutching his webbing vest as he stood near to the others. They didn't invite him into their conversation or to share a cigarette, but eyed him with open belligerence. They were allies, but only loosely, Rink recalled.

The white man was obviously ex-forces, maybe even an armed cop; from the way he stood he'd been on sentry duty more than a few times during his career. He'd be dangerous. Then again, so could any of the others. Many cartel fighters were soldiers or police who'd switched sides. He had to treat each as a potential danger, including the woman. He had decided against a full-frontal attack earlier, but now, armed with a pistol in each hand, he fancied his chances. Fuckers wouldn't know what had hit them until he'd dropped at least four of them; then he'd do the others while they were still trying to aim their weapons at him. He put away his knife, replacing it with a gun he'd taken from an earlier victim. He took a calming breath, centring himself, finding that Zen tranquillity necessary for cold-blooded slaughter.

A shout rang out from the far end of the alley.

Through the gloom he was happy he couldn't be seen, but he could make out the forms of two figures moving beyond the back wall, near to the row of vehicles. Apparently the last man he'd knifed to death had been discovered. He didn't concern himself with that. He had to ignore what was going on back there, concentrate on what was ahead. He straightened, his chest swelling as he prepared to go into action. But something stayed him, a subtle instinct for caution.

He'd seen the white man place a hand to the side of his head.

He was receiving a message over an earpiece, and Rink recognised the change in the man's demeanour. This wasn't good. The man was receiving a warning, most likely that an enemy was nearby, and that worsened the odds. The guy stiffened, and his gaze flicked towards the group of cartel foot-soldiers. Rink cursed under his breath, losing the recent calm in a wash of adrenalin that set him on fire.

Shoot now or abort, those were his only options.

He began to move, swinging out from the corner of the building, both guns coming up.

But he was a second too late.

The soldier was already sighting his machine-gun and he let rip with a burst of rounds that tore through flesh and bone.

Stunned by the impacts, Rink staggered.

His brain was edged in scarlet, the flash of gunfire causing mini-explosions in his vision.

The five cartel footsoldiers, grouped so closely together, were torn to shreds by the soldier's bullets. Three men went down, and another, knocked backwards by the impact, caromed off a parked car before sinking to his knees and butt as though praying for mercy. A burst of bullets tore his chest to ribbons. The woman had also been hit, and she was holding up the palm of an empty hand, as if it were enough to halt the jacketed rounds. The next burst of gunfire picked her up, made her dance a maniac-jig and then she slapped the ground as a wet tangle of shredded limbs and clothing. The soldier strode forward. One of the first three to fall writhed on the floor. He was dying, but still attempting to bring up a gun. The soldier calmly executed him with a short volley of bullets that smeared his cranium across the dirt.

Rink was confused by this sudden turn of events, but he was committed now to forward movement. His enemy's enemy was not necessarily his friend. He levelled both guns at the soldier, who was still not aware of his presence. Yet still he held fire.

A sixth sense warned the soldier of impending death and he spun quickly, sighting along the barrel of his rifle.

He didn't fire.

'What the fuck just happened?' Rink didn't relax a mote. His index fingers were flexed on the triggers of both guns, a hair's breadth from shooting.

The soldier checked him out, eyelids pinching.

'You're the one that was with Hunter,' the man said. 'We thought you'd be dead by now.'

'Do I look dead?'

'Do you want to be?' asked the soldier. His finger was also tight on the trigger.

'Do you?'

The soldier relaxed almost imperceptibly, and the gun lowered a touch. 'I'm not your enemy, pal.'

'I take it you ain't buddies with Molina no more?' Rink nodded briefly towards the steaming corpses piled nearby.

'Never was friends with the bastard,' said the soldier. 'Glad I finally got the order to take these fuckers out.'

Rink had no idea what was going on. There was some sort of double-cross in play, and he wondered if Marshall's team had been preparing for this moment all along. It didn't matter. Just because the man had turned on the cartel fighters didn't mean he'd become Rink's ally.

'The fuck you gonna do now?'

'I'm going to go inside,' the soldier said, 'and help get your friends free. You're welcome to join me, I could do with someone watching my back in there.'

Using the gun in his left hand, Rink waved the man towards the door. 'Right behind you, buddy.'

42

James Lee Marshall drove in with the commando dagger a second time. His first cut had parted the rope and dropped me to my knees, but it required some sawing to free the loops from round my wrists.

'What's going on?' I managed, my brain swimming as I clawed back from unconsciousness.

'What have you been told about looking a gift horse in the mouth?'

'Believe me, I'm grateful, but I wouldn't mind an explanation.'

'Shut it.' Marshall held me in place while he cut through the final strands of rope. My wrists popped wide as the stress went off them. The rush of blood to my previously constricted muscles brought new levels of stinging agony. But the pain was something I'd endure without complaint, because it was a good sign that my bindings hadn't cut off the blood completely. Worst-case scenario was that my hands had necrotised while bound. I brought my arms to the front, my hands forming claws close to my chest. The returning circulation made my fingers numb, then sore, but the sensations wouldn't last.

'Can you stand?' Marshall toed me with his boots.

'I'm not dead yet.'

'That's not what I asked. Molina gave you a severe beating; has he broken anything?'

'Only the record for being the world's biggest arsehole.'

'Knocked you off your perch then?'

'Ha! Funny, Marshall. Just give me a second or two. Can't feel my legs yet, and my hands are still asleep.'

'We don't have a second. If we're caught in here, we're fucked. Get up.'

Marshall gripped me under my right armpit, lifting me to my feet. I tried to help, but I was numb from the waist down, my feet skirting clouds instead of firm ground. Marshall steadied me, his left hand offering support. His right held the dagger, its needle point an inch from my liver should I try anything stupid.

'Relax. I'm in no shape to do you harm.'

'Why would you when I've just saved your arse?' Marshall allowed the knife to drop away, but I could feel the tension in him, knew that he was still evaluating his decision to free me.

'If you'd cut me loose the first time you paid a visit you'd have saved me a fuckin' beating.'

'Thing was, back then I had no idea that we'd be joining forces.'

'We are?'

'Yeah.' Marshall twiddled the blade around in his fingers. 'Unless you have other ideas.'

'What's the deal?'

'Hold on. I've something to do first.' Without waiting for an answer, Marshall released me and I swayed in place, stumbling to find my footing. Marshall tapped an ear/throat mike. 'Code Red.'

It had to be a prearranged signal. Muffled by intervening walls came the rattle of a machine-gun.

From nearer still a double pop of a handgun.

'Who the fuck are you?' I asked.

'You know who I am.'

'Don't be a dick. You know what I mean.'

'Military Intelligence.'

'Six?'

'Who else?'

'You've been playing both sides? Molina and the CIA?'

'Not *the* CIA; only a rogue faction within it.'

'You were sent here to derail Regis's plot to set Molina on the cartel throne?' The tingling in my extremities was growing to a buzz that had me twitching, but the signs were good that I'd be able to move within seconds. 'Or was there more to it than that?'

Having learned that Regis – under orders from someone higher up in the Agency – had been guiding Molina like a puppet, ensuring the CIA gained influence with any fledgling government should the impending takeover occur, it wouldn't surprise me if MI6 had similar designs.

'Does it matter why I was originally here? Things've changed, Hunter, that's all you need to know. Now if you want to free Kirstie and the others, I suggest you get your act together. The fighting's started and will be here any second.'

'Back on the road . . . first time you saw me when you launched that ambush . . .'

'Yes. I recognised you and backed down. I've been protecting you ever since.'

'What about McAdam? He seemed determined enough to kill Rink and me. Is that what you call protecting me?'

'I couldn't control him the way I wanted to. McAdam went ahead of the rest of us, and, yeah, don't forget he had a boner for you, Hunter.'

'Over knocking his teeth out all those years ago?'

'No, it was for fucking him up in that alley in Hermosillo. He didn't know I was Six, or what the real mission was. He was a merc, and he was in it for the money. Far as he knew he was going to earn a large bonus from Regis if he managed to kill you guys. He wanted to shoot you that time on the hill above Molina's place, but I stopped him. Couldn't do much with him when he got ahead of the pack. It was unfortunate.'

'For him, yeah.'

'When I knocked you out in the mountains? Believe it or not I was trying to save your life. Regis was going to blow you away so I had to act quickly. Hope you don't hold that egg on your skull against me.'

'It's small payment for letting me go now.' I touched the raw swelling on the back of my head, surprised to find sensation in my fingertips. My feet too could feel the floor beneath them. The downside was that I could also feel every other inch of my frame and there weren't many places where it didn't scream in pain.

'I'd have released you last time I was in here, but we weren't ready. I had to wait for the right opportunity.'

'So . . . like I asked earlier . . . what's going on? Why turn on Molina and Regis now?'

'Regis received word that his boss – Thomas Caspar – has been found dead. Someone almost took his head off his shoulders with a wire garrotte. Regis's line to the CIA has been severed as effectively as his boss's throat. He's fucked, Molina knows it, and it's only a matter of time before that mad wetback fucker turns on us all.'

'Hold on. You're not telling me that Regis *ordered* you to free me?'

'Regis doesn't give a damn for anyone but himself. He doesn't even know I'm here. Right now he's trying to distract Molina from killing him by urging him to take out his frustration on Kirstie and your mates.'

'I understand why you might want to help an old friend. Your team could have walked away though. Why help us now when they could all get killed?'

'Regis was their direct line to Thomas Caspar's wallet, but Caspar's dead. Now that none of them is going to get paid, they owe Regis nothing. The lads took a vote and agreed that getting you all out might just hold some sort of reward.' Marshall winked at the cleverness of his ploy.

'Fucking mercenaries, eh?'

'Some of them are actually decent guys, trying to make a living during a difficult time.'

'If any of them do help I'll see that they get compensated,' I promised. I was certain that Walter would find some cash from one of the shell company accounts that financed his Arrowsake endeavours.

There was another burp of distant gunfire.

'They've already got started. I suggest we do too. You good to walk yet?'

'Wait up.' I staggered to the sink and hose and turned on the tap. Gratefully I slurped cool water direct from the nozzle. I threw some of it over my face and hair, scrubbing the accumulated crap from my nostrils and mouth. 'Now I'm good.'

From inside his jacket, Marshall tugged out my SIG. 'Thought you might want this. I picked it up off the road after you were captured. Before you check, I already cleaned and reloaded it.'

Accepting the gun from him, I nodded in gratitude. It was good to feel the familiar weight of my gun in hand. Ordinarily I'd have fed it into my waistband, but I was wearing only my undershorts.

'Hope you're not going to shoot me in the back with it,' Marshall said.

'I'd do it looking you in the eye,' I reassured him.

His glass eye twinkled. 'That supposed to be funny?'

'No. Being totally frank.'

'So what we waiting for?'

'Don't have a spare pair of trousers, do you?'

'Bashful these days, are we?' he asked, moving for the door.

In boxer shorts and a grubby sheath of dirt and blood I moved after him. He was right. My current state wasn't important. I'd free the others bare butt-naked if necessary.

43

How had she ever been taken in by this man? When she first met Jorge she had thought him charming, witty, handsome; how had she missed the monster lurking beneath the veneer of designer clothing, manicures and coiffed hair? She believed that she was a good judge of people – but she had not been able to read the psychotic tendencies of the man she would marry. Jorge had been playing a part with the skill of an accomplished character actor, and she'd been sucked in by the act. She understood now that he had been using her. As far as he was concerned she was a recipient for his sperm, a wet nurse for his heir, and that was where her importance ended. As he looked down at her now she could barely recognise the man who'd swept her off her feet, married her, gotten her pregnant. This was a different creature altogether. This was a *monster*.

He hadn't touched her. Not yet. But it was only a matter of time before she was beaten the way he'd beaten Harvey, McTeer and Velasquez. Those three men had been dragged away by some of Jorge's lackeys, and Kirstie feared for their lives. She had not heard their death cries, or the bullets of their executions, but she knew that there were silent ways of killing. Some of those who'd dragged them from the room had been carrying machetes.

He hadn't touched her, no. But that wasn't the worst torture she could be subjected to. He had taken Benjamin, and she'd no idea where her boy was, and that was more hurtful than being kicked, punched, or even hacked limb from limb with a heavy blade. Kirstie wanted to scream, beg, plead, do whatever it took to get Benjamin back, but she couldn't. She was gagged, a tennis ball shoved into her open mouth, then a leather strap tied tightly round her head to stop her spitting it out. She could barely breathe for the constriction, and the mucus pouring from her nose hardly helped. Her hands were bound behind her back, so she couldn't even form a supplication to him. Her ankles were also bound. The only thing she could do was kneel, peer up at him, begging with her eyes, making pitiful sounds as if he'd already cut out her tongue. Jorge was unmoved.

If anything, he had grown more detached.

When first he'd visited her he'd ranted and raged. He'd accused, threatened, and verbally abused her. He'd shown her what it meant to try to take away what was *rightfully his*. He'd made her watch as he beat the three men to within an inch of their lives. Then he'd come at her, wielding the heavy length of rope that still dripped his victims' blood. But then he'd threatened again: this time taking lurid delight in describing how he'd ruin her for having sexual relations with anyone else, and his emphasis had switched to Joe Hunter. It was as if the thought of her with another man was the greatest of insults, and he swore that Hunter would die more horribly than any of them. When he'd rushed from the room, carrying the rope, Kirstie had been terrified for Joe.

Now her ex-husband had come back – without his torture implement – and the fresh specks of blood on his forearms made her fear grow tenfold. The thought that he'd murdered Joe twisted a cold blade through her heart, and placed her on the verge of total collapse. Only because Benjamin needed her to remain strong did she fight the urge to succumb to the creeping despair that attempted to dominate her thoughts and sink her into the miasma of shock-induced coma.

Jorge was weirdly silent, and the more frightening for it. He looked down at her with an expression she could only describe as disdain. Her punishment was not important to him the way it had been before. She did not believe he was showing pity for her: mercy had no place in his heart. Something had happened to alter his focus, and there was no hope that it would change her fate. If anything, his coldness, his detachment, told her he was capable of the most despicable and inhuman act imaginable.

'Do you wish to see Benny one last time?'

His question was totally unexpected, and for a moment she was unable to make sense of it. Was this akin to offering a starving child a morsel of chocolate before popping it into his own mouth and delighting at the taste and satin texture on his tongue? Was his new strategy to tease, before denying her final wish?

'Well? I will take you to him if that's what you want. But understand this, Kirstie, it will be the last time you see him. Believe me, I don't make this offer because I feel I owe you anything. You're a whore, a thief, a kidnapper, with no rights. I do this because Benny asked to see his mom and I would not deny *my* child.' He stared down at her, curling his lips back from his brilliant white teeth. 'Your choice, bitch. Agree or I'll make the decision for you. You can stand and walk, or I will drag you there by your hair. What will it be?'

There was only one answer. She mewled behind her gag, nodding her head emphatically.

Jorge took from his pocket a folding knife and snapped it open. He stooped and roughly cut away the ropes from her ankles. The gag and the bindings on her wrists stayed in place. With no care for her comfort, he caught her by an elbow and dragged her up.

'Time to say goodbye,' he said, pushing her before him.

They had barely reached the door when the rattle of gunfire sounded.

44

James Lee Marshall shot a kid in cold blood. The guy was a young Mexican, barely out of his teens, and he was terrified. Granted, he was a footsoldier of the cartel, but I still felt pity for him. He had backed into the large and echoing space of the warehouse to escape an assault from another direction, and on seeing Marshall he recognised an ally he felt he could rely on to get him out of there alive. He had no idea that Marshall wasn't the same man who'd travelled with him from the mountain pass, guarding their prisoner, and the betrayal was almost as painful as the bullets Marshall fired into his chest.

'What's up, Hunter: lost your taste for a fight?'

'That kid could have been disarmed,' I said. 'He had no fight left in him.'

'If we'd disarmed him he'd have found another weapon and then come on us from behind. Forget about it, forget about him, and concentrate on freeing your mates.'

Ignoring his words, I approached the young man who lay against some shelving units on which were stacked dusty plastic drums and cardboard boxes sealed with duct tape. Remnants left over from when this was still a thriving storage depot, I guessed. I checked on the kid, and he was gone to whatever afterlife cartel thugs made it to.

'What are you up to?' Marshall demanded. 'Grab his gun and get over here.'

'Wait up,' I said.

The kid was wearing chinos and a baggy 'Ramones' T-shirt and sneakers. The shirt was holed and slick with blood, the sneakers about two sizes too small for my feet. He no longer required his trousers, and they looked to be about my size.

'Are you a fucking grave robber? Leave him be, Hunter, for Christ's sake!'

'You're not running around in your underpants . . .'

I crouched down, apologised under my breath for looting the dead, and then stripped the chinos off the kid. I quickly pulled them on. They were a few inches too short in the leg, snug at the waist, but they beat the Tarzan the Apeman look I'd been stuck with before. Moving after Marshall I already felt better, so that I could ignore the stabbing of grit through my bare soles. More comforting was the addition of another handgun: by the sounds of gunfire coming from a number of positions inside and outside the building, I was going to need the extra firepower.

'OK,' Marshall said as I moved alongside him, 'are you good now?'

'Better.' My voice echoed from the high walls and ceiling. The place was cavernous; behind us I could see where Marshall's SUV had been driven inside via a roller shutter that was now firmly closed. It was far enough away to look like a toy car.

'So let's do this?'

'I'm with you. Marshall, what the fuck is this place? I thought I was in the back room of a butcher's shop. This place is massive.'

'Who gives a fuck what it used to be. If we don't get out fast it's going to become a death trap.'

Marshall was right. We had moved from the room in which I'd been tortured and down a short corridor that allowed access to the huge warehouse we now strode through. Judging by the layer of grit underfoot, it hadn't been used for some months, not for its original purpose. I could only assume that the cartel had seized the building and kicked out the original tenants. Whatever. It wasn't important; navigating a way through it was. Marshall wasn't familiar with the place; he'd been here only as long as I had, and hadn't traversed the building beyond the first room where I'd been strung up and the corridor and rooms next to it. He was simply following his nose and he'd no idea what waited for us on the other side.

'How many men are with you, Marshall?'

'Five. Would have been eight if you and that Jap hadn't been so trigger-happy.'

'How good are they?'

'Not as good as me.'

'What about Molina's men?'

'Some of them are ex-military, the rest are punks.'

'How many?'

'Dozens.'

'Shit,' I said.

'Yeah,' he replied.

He pulled the door open a sliver, and leaned close so he could peer out into the space beyond.

'Who was that kid running from?' he wondered aloud.

'One of yours? Has to be.'

Marshall shook his head, indicating his earpiece. 'My lads are all under fire at the front of the building. Haven't heard from Freeman for a minute or two; I guess he's dead.'

'So you only have four men left. If your boys are at the front, who was the kid fleeing?'

'Maybe it was Regis. I don't know where that piece of shit has got to, but you can bet your life he's trying to find a bolt-hole.'

'Yeah, that's the nature of rats.'

Marshall held up a fist, demanding silence.

The slap of running feet reverberated along the corridor. I readied my gun, as did Marshall. Then the footsteps faded, but there followed a rattle of machine-gun fire from some distant corner of the building.

'Clear,' Marshall said, and he went into the corridor ahead of me. Covering his back, I moved after him, watching back the way we'd come. The corridor made a sharp bend to the left. We went around it carefully.

Gunshots rang out closer by.

The stench of cordite hung in the air, and in the dull overhead lights there was a ribbon of blue smoke writhing in the space before us. Marshall brought up his gun, edging forward now. The corridor was long, narrow, and there was a sequence of four doors, two to each side marking entrances to other rooms. The second door on the left was open, the others closed. Someone had gone through that door recently: the lock had been smashed from the frame by a shoulder charge. Boots had scuffed the dust on the floor, more than one pair.

'Easy,' Marshall whispered. He approached the door.

A yell made him pause.

The shout had come from the room, but sounded quite distant.

A gun fired on automatic. To my ear the shooting sounded uncontrolled. There followed a solid thud and the gun fell silent. Marshall glanced my way, his right eyebrow steepling.

'Sounds like someone's hunting Molina's lot down . . .'

Experiencing a tiny leap of the heart, I checked the boot prints once more hoping that I could identify the wearer from their size and imprint. There was nothing to confirm that it had been Rink, yet I felt that my friend was out there, and it gave me the strength to push on. We entered the room and found ourselves in another storage area. In there the racks were empty. The shelves lined the two parallel walls on either side, another freestanding set running down the centre of the room. Some footprints went to the right, and a single set to the left. They would, I assumed, converge at the far end.

I was right. The single trail joined the others, following their passage through another door at the far right corner. Marshall continued to lead the way, totally at ease as I followed close by with a gun in each hand. He was taking much on faith that we were now allies, but he'd nothing to worry about. We entered an office. A large teak desk dominated the space. The Sheetrock walls were pockmarked with bullet holes. A couple of orange plastic chairs were stacked in one corner, a yellowing newspaper folded casually on the uppermost seat. A corpse lay in the other corner, in front of another open door. There was a single wound in the man's chest, and it appeared to be from a knife as opposed to a bullet. That would explain the thud we'd heard just before the shooting stopped: a heavy blade had been driven deep into his heart and the man fell dead without a cry.

Gunfire shook the office walls. A stray round actually punched into the room, trailing a cloud of plaster dust from the wall. Instinctively we both crouched to avoid the ricochets. Marshall went forward, placing the heavy desk between him and the wall, and I took the opportunity to rush by him and approach the next door.

'Slow down, Hunter,' Marshall rasped.

Ignoring him, I checked outside the room. The space beyond was open plan, filled with work cubicles and old touch-button telephones. Gunfire had torn a swathe through the room. Another body lay sprawled across a cheap desk in one of the cubicles. His blood dripped freely so he couldn't have died long ago. Although his heart had stopped pumping, his wounds were large enough to be leaking blood from his exposed innards. I was glad to see that the corpse was that of a small, dark-skinned guy and not a big Asian-American.

The gunfire had ceased in the adjacent room, but two hand-guns contested further on. Without waiting for Marshall, I slipped quickly through the office, swerving past cubicles. Behind me the soldier followed, and I could hear him mutter-ing. At first I thought he was cursing my impulsive ways, but he was demanding a status report from his mercenaries. By the harsh expletive that followed, the news wasn't good.

He caught up to me as I braced myself against the wall next to a doorframe. He leaned in close to my ear, whispering. 'Three down. Freeman, Albertson and Garretty are all dead. Mitchell and Paulson are the only ones left. They've had to retreat from the fight, but are in position to offer cover if we make it outside.'

The names meant nothing to me. They should have been branded in my psyche, because all five of them had given their lives – or were about to – for me. Not that any of them knew it. As far as they were concerned they were fighting for Marshall alone, and for the money they'd earn from him.

'Before he died, Freeman told the others to avoid firing on your pal. Seems I underestimated your mate Rink. He made it here after all.'

'Yeah.' That was already apparent to me.

The gunfire had stopped again. I placed a silent bet that it wasn't Rink who'd fallen, though I couldn't be sure how long that would last. Rink was a terrific soldier, but he was wholly outnumbered, outgunned and in unfamiliar surroundings. The odds were stacked against him surviving much longer.

'Come on,' I said, and went through the door.

Give Marshall his due, he didn't question the sudden switch of command.

45

'You must get him out of here, Jorge. For God's sake, he's only a baby!'

'You do not tell me what to do!'

Molina backhanded Kirstie across the face and knocked her to the floor. She landed heavily, unable to check her fall because her wrists were still bound behind her back. The collision with the floor made her head ring, but over the pounding in her skull she heard the terrified scream of her child as he watched her being beaten. Kirstie ignored Molina's next threat. She blinked away tears so she could check on Benjamin. The woman who'd taken him from her when they were captured was struggling to hold on to the boy, who squirmed violently in her grasp.

Kirstie craned up to meet the volcanic gaze of her ex-husband. 'Please, Jorge! This place is a war zone. You have to get him away from here. Please . . . if you love him . . . get him safely away.'

'He is a *Molina*. He must learn what it means to be a *Molina*. He must be brave and fearless, or he is no good to me or to his name.'

'He's only a child, a baby! Please, Jorge . . .'

Molina kicked her, sending her sprawling on the ground. He scowled down at her, perhaps considering retying the gag he'd pulled off her minutes ago. But it seemed he was happier to hear her complaints, as if it gave him more power to deny her most plaintive arguments. In the next instant he lunged down and grasped her by the hair, so she had to scramble up to avoid having her scalp torn off. Molina was holding the knife he'd cut her bonds with. For a second she thought he was going to slash her throat, but he used the knife as a pointer, aiming it at Benjamin.

'He is my son and his place is by my side,' he said. 'He must learn this valuable lesson. As must you.'

Benjamin squealed in response.

'For God's sake, you're frightening him. Can't you see . . . ?'

Molina forced her down, pushing the back of her head towards her knees. His next words addressed Benjamin directly. 'Do you see, son? She is weak. You must forget her now.'

'I want my mommy!' Benjamin howled.

'This . . . this *whore* is nothing to you. She is *nothing*.' He placed the knife tip against the prominent cervical vertebrae exposed by her bent neck. 'Forget all about her because you will never see her again. Believe me, son, you should not care.'

'Jorge,' Kirstie pleaded. 'He can't possibly understand you. Please, I don't care what you do to me, but not in front of Benjamin. You will scar him for life.'

'The only one scarred will be you.'

'How can you expect your son to love you if he sees you murder his mom?'

'It's not his love I want,' Molina snarled. 'He must grow up to be a great and ruthless leader of men, the only way he will survive in this damned country. He will understand this lesson when he comes of age. He'll know what it means to be the son of Jorge Molina, and he will act accordingly. It is the only way!'

'Please.' Kirstie now addressed the shrew-faced woman who held her child. 'Take him away. If you've pity in your heart, take Benjamin out of here.'

'Do that,' Molina snapped at the woman, 'and yours will be the next head I cut off.'

Kirstie could see nothing of the woman but her shoes, and they barely scuffled in place. Kirstie understood how terrified the woman was of Jorge's threat, but she hoped that her instincts to nurture and protect a child might outweigh the fear. 'Please take him away,' she cried.

The woman didn't move. Benjamin must have been struggling because Kirstie heard a harsh command spoken in Spanish.

'Benjamin.' Kirstie tried to offer a soothing tone, but her voice cracked on the final syllable. 'Close your eyes, baby. Don't watch. Turn your head away and close your eyes.'

'No, Benny! You will watch.' To the woman, Molina said in Spanish, 'Bring him to me. Now. I will not tell you again.'

Kirstie struggled against the inevitable, but there was nothing she could do. Molina commanded the woman to hold her and she felt hands pressing down on her skull. She could feel the trembling in the woman's fingers against her scalp. She thought that she might be able to pull loose of her handler, but Molina stood over her, using his knees to hold her in position. He had taken Benjamin into his arms so the boy had no option but bear witness. But there was worse to come, and Molina's words brought back the terrifying conclusion of the nightmarish dream she'd suffered two nights ago.

'Here, boy, take hold of the knife. You can help me.'

46

Harvey was sitting in the back corner of the room in which he'd been beaten. His hands and ankles were bound. Blood glistened on his chin from where he'd taken a blow to the mouth. Vivid welts decorated his chest, shoulders and thighs, purple against his dark skin. His silk designer shorts now looked like rags, stained and rumpled by his ordeal. Thankfully he was still alive, and appeared to be the least injured of my friends. McTeer was in the opposite corner, his face so bruised he was barely recognisable, nose crushed, eyelids swollen to the size of baseballs. Velasquez lay on the floor between the two, and he was unconscious, breathing raggedly through split lips. Bound as he was at wrists and ankles, he was collapsed in a tortuous position that didn't help his ability to breathe: if he wasn't moved soon, he could expire through lack of oxygen. Harvey and McTeer would have gone to his assistance if they could, but a trio of thugs with rifles threatened them. One of Molina's men also carried a stave, and its width corresponded to some of the wounds on my friends' naked bodies. The stave was dark with blood. I'd no regret whatsoever about killing that piece of shit, only that his death came too quick.

I stepped up behind him, placed the muzzle of my SIG to the nape of his neck and blasted a hole in his spinal column.

As the first dropped to the floor, I shot one of the rifle-wielders in the face and turned for number three. Marshall beat me to the punch and placed a round through the man's heart before his mouth could fully form an elongated look of shock as his allies fell. I was so enraged at the state of my friends, I put another round in his head as he went down: waste of a bullet, but it brought me some satisfaction.

'Thank the Lord,' Harvey said weakly as I bolted for Velasquez. Harvey tried to straighten, a show of strength that simply wasn't there. He sank down once more, even as Marshall brought out his dagger and approached him.

I pulled Velasquez round so he was in a more comfortable pose, and watched as his mouth opened and blood-thick saliva pooled on the floor. He gasped a couple of times, spat weakly, and his breathing grew less ragged. He didn't wake up, but his eyelids fluttered like beetles' wings. By then, Marshall was done cutting Harvey free and moved to assist McTeer. I touched Velasquez on the forehead; my fingertips found it cold and clammy with sweat. He was in a bad way.

Harvey clawed his way up, palms flat against the corner angle of the walls, barely capable of standing. His thigh muscles cramped visibly, jumping and bunching painfully. Yet he persevered and staggered towards me. I stood to meet him and supported him against me.

'Molina took Kirstie . . .' His voice was thick with shame, as if it was his personal failure that had put Kirstie into Molina's hands.

'Don't worry about that for now. We have to get you guys out of here first. If Val doesn't get help, he's going to die.'

'I can get the others out,' Harvey said, and he placed his cupped palms over his face. I thought that he was weeping, but didn't comment. In situations of stress, particularly during torture, even the toughest of people can't hold back the emotions. Soldiers who'd face an army single-handed were prone to weeping, and it was no less a measure of the man, or maybe it only made them more admirable.

'You're in no state to help yourself, Harve. Marshall?'

Marshall was helping McTeer to his feet, the older man having similar problems to mine when the circulation returned to my extremities. The notion that Marshall had once been our enemy was lost on him, as it was to the others, and it showed in the way he thanked Marshall profusely. Marshall glanced my way.

'That vehicle back in the warehouse: it's yours, right?'

He slapped a pocket on his jacket. 'Got the keys right here.'

'I'm going to need you to get the guys to it, they can't make it on their own.'

'Hold on, who died and made you the fucking boss?'

'Don't start with the bullshit. This is what you came to help me do, get the guys out safely. But Molina has taken Kirstie and her boy. I'm not leaving without them.'

Marshall shrugged. 'Your choice, your funeral. Go for it, Hunter.'

'You said you had two men left alive. That still the case?'

'Yeah.'

'Get them to go round the back and cover you as you leave. I'm assuming that more of Molina's men will be out there. Velasquez needs medical attention, and you can't afford to be penned inside.'

'How are you planning on getting out?'

'Don't know. But it won't be without Kirstie and Benjamin. Plus, Rink's still in here someplace and I'm not leaving him behind either.'

'Rink's here too?' Harvey visibly relaxed with relief. 'We heard from those assholes–' he aimed a bare foot at the three dead guards – 'that he'd been killed in the mountains when you were captured.'

'From what I've learned in the meantime, Rink's a long way from dead. He cleared the way here for us, and I'm guessing it's still safe to go back to the warehouse. Will you and Mac be strong enough to carry Velasquez between you? Marshall will need his hands free just in case I'm wrong.'

Harvey and McTeer shared a nod.

'We'll manage,' McTeer said. 'He ain't heavy . . .'

The strains of that old Hollies song played in my head, but only briefly. I moved to help them pick up Velasquez, the guys taking an arm each over their shoulders. Velasquez's head lolled briefly, but then it lifted and he spat more bloody muck from his throat. He grinned through broken teeth. 'Still beats patrolling a fucking mall for a living,' he wheezed.

Marshall shook his head, disbelief. He checked me out. 'Shit, you look like something out of *Die Hard*. But even Bruce Willis had a vest.'

'Is that your way of telling me to look after myself?'

He raised an eyebrow, but his lips twitched momentarily, almost a smile.

'Once I get these lads out of here, I'll see about making it back for you and the others,' he said.

'No. Don't do that. Make sure Velasquez gets to a doctor. The others too,' I said against Harvey and McTeer's objections. 'If Kirstie and Benjamin are still alive, I'll find a way. If they're not . . . well, the fight won't end here.'

'Like I said, it's your funeral. My job's done here as far as Molina and Six is concerned.' His singular gaze fell on the tattoo on my bare shoulder. 'I'll defer to Arrowsake if it's all right by you.'

'I'm not here on Arrowsake's behalf.'

'Think again, Hunter. Maybe you aren't, but they were there for you. Who do you think hit Thomas Caspar and derailed Regis's mission here?'

When I'd learned of Thomas Caspar's assassination, I'd immediately spotted the connection to Stephen Vincent, in the persona of Vince Everett, whose favourite method of killing happened to be a guitar-wire garrotte. I couldn't figure out how he'd become involved, or why, but the answer was staring me in the face. Whereas Rink and I had all but severed our ties to the assassination bureau that was Arrowsake, and Walter had sworn to distance himself, it was apparent that the old man had called in a favour. What did that mean for the future? Nothing good, I bet. Yet Marshall had warned me about looking too keenly at gift horses and he was right. I should be thankful that they'd helped turn the tide in my favour, and not worry about future implications. Hell, maybe I wouldn't have a future. I still had to survive a nest of armed killers and get Kirstie, Benjamin and Rink out alive. Bruce Willis had his lucky vest. Me? All I had was a pair of dead man's trousers, two guns and enough rage to burn Agua Prieta to cinders. I hoped that would prove enough.

I watched the others leave. The gunfire, more random now, was in the opposite direction, beyond a second door that the three guards had been watching. It was the only reason we'd been able to sneak up on them; they'd thought all the fighting was at the front of the building and had missed our stealthy approach. I wondered who was shooting. Marshall's two friends – Mitchell and Paulson – were outside as far as I knew, but the gunfire was inside the building. It had to be Rink continuing his running battle, unless Regis was also forced to fight his way out after losing favour with Molina. Caspar, his boss, had died. I hoped that Regis would earn a similar fate, but not on the receiving end of a guitar-string noose. Given the opportunity, I'd gladly slay him as coldly as he had the coyote back when all this began. Then again, that was too good for the bastard: if I could find a container to lock him inside, then park him in some hidden corner of the desert then I'd do that too.

Focusing my rage on him might sound wrong, because it was likely I'd have come into Mexico on Kirstie's behalf without Regis having any part in the outcome, but it was because of him that we'd been tracked in – obviously he'd been the one to have our van fitted with a homing device – making it necessary to ditch the van and find alternative passage from Hermosillo. If that hadn't happened, Rink and I wouldn't have been separated from the others, and none of them would have been in this fix now. Regis had earned my enmity, almost as much as Molina had.

No.

Molina deserved to die more brutally than Regis, and it had nothing to do with the fact he'd beaten the hide off me with a wet rope. It was that he intended murdering his ex-wife, and perhaps already had.

Following the sounds of gunfire, I raced on, desperately hoping that I'd be in time to save Kirstie.

47

Benjamin was sobbing, and the boy's distress was more heart-breaking to Kirstie than her own imminent death.

'Just hold the knife the way I showed you,' Molina yelled at the child. Out of her line of sight, Molina was losing patience with their son. Kirstie saw shadows writhe across the floor below her, knew that a struggle was happening between the two. A meaty slap followed, and Benjamin howled in pain.

'Do not touch him!' Kirstie's scream was strident, yet held power itself. 'You have no right to strike him like that. Leave him alone, you bastard.'

More jostling ensued, with Molina's body thumping against Kirstie's lower back and thighs. 'Take the knife. Like *that*! Yes, that's it. Now press down.'

'I don't want to . . .'

Kirstie screamed again.

Molina kicked her over and she went down on her side, her back to him. Shouting and crying competed in volume. Kirstie struggled to roll over, to see what was happening. The woman who had been controlling her, holding her down while Molina attempted to coax Benjamin into stabbing her in the spine, stood back with a look of relief. She had no desire to be there, or to help in Kirstie's murder, and she'd just been offered some respite. For the first time, Kirstie recognised from the woman's uniform that she was a Border Control official. When the woman had first accepted bribes to turn a blind eye against cartel activities, she couldn't have envisioned anything like this.

'You have to do something,' Kirstie yelled at her.

The woman continued to edge away, shaking her head, her gaze switching from Kirstie to Molina, then back again.

'Yeah. You can get the hell outta my way.'

The new voice struck silence into the room.

Kirstie turned to see a large figure silhouetted in the doorway. Bewildered, she watched as a hand plucked the border official off the floor by the collar of her shirt, and flung her bodily out of the room. 'You know what's good for you, get the hell outta here,' said the new arrival. The woman staggered as she was propelled into the corridor, then she jerked upright, took one last wide-eyed glance into the room, and fled. Her footsteps echoed down the corridor, staccato sounds against the sudden hush.

Jared Rington moved inside.

He barely glanced at Kirstie, his full attention on Molina and Benjamin.

'It would do you good to set the boy aside and face me like a man,' Rink said.

'You're supposed to be dead.' Molina stared at Rink with a look to curdle cream, as if Rink's survival was a personal slight.

'I was hoping the same about you. Now set the boy aside.'

'So you can shoot me?'

'Yup. That's the idea.'

'No, no, no,' Kirstie cried. 'You'll hit Benjamin.'

Rink gave her a warning glance, immediately returning his attention to Molina. 'Let the boy go, it serves no purpose for you to endanger him.'

Kirstie finally got her backside beneath her, and struggled up to stand and face her ex-husband. She saw now why Rink had chosen the words he had. Molina was shielding himself behind the boy, and the knife he'd recently threatened her with was now angled towards Benjamin's throat.

'The boy is useless to me. My whore of a wife must have conceived him with another man, because I doubt this coward came from my loins.' Molina's wrist twitched, and he appeared to be on the cusp of sinking the knife through Benjamin's tender throat. 'So . . . go on. Shoot me if you want, but I'll kill him first.'

'Jorge! How could you?' Kirstie wailed. She made to move forward, a last-ditch effort at wresting her son free.

'Get back!' Molina adjusted the blade tip so that it was nestled in the soft spot beneath Benjamin's right ear. 'I'm warning you both, another move and I will stab him.'

'No you won't. You're a punk coward, Molina, and you won't give up your hostage like that. If you stab him, I swear I won't shoot you; I'll tear you to pieces with my bare hands. I'll make you suffer in ways you can't imagine.'

'I don't fear you, big man. I'm afraid of no man.'

'You should be,' Rink said, and he slid out a large knife.

He didn't lower his gun; it was aimed directly at Molina's face and the cartel boss juggled Benjamin around to offer further cover. The boy kicked and squirmed. He reared backwards so that he could see his mom, wailing for her to help.

'Here's what's going to happen,' Molina said. 'I'm leaving, and I'm taking the boy with me. Now stand aside or I will cut the little brat's throat.'

Rink's face hardened, the blood draining from his features. His mouth was so tight, it was as if someone had pressed a thumb to his top lip and left its indelible mark there. A scar on his chin was bone white. He didn't give any ground.

'You're going nowhere,' he said.

'Then you're going to have to shoot me,' Molina challenged.

'Pick a knee,' Rink said and lowered his aim.

'Shoot me and I swear . . .'

'Yeah, yeah, so you said.'

Rink didn't squeeze the trigger. Shooting Molina in the leg would most assuredly cause him to stab the boy in anger. Molina understood the reason for his reluctance and hoped to capitalise on it.

'Get out of my way.' He wrapped an arm round Benjamin, holding the boy tightly to his chest.

'Don't let him take my boy!'

'Quiet, Kirstie,' Rink hissed.

'You. Bitch. Come over here.'

Kirstie would have gone to her ex-husband, offering herself as a human shield in place of her son, but Rink shook his head savagely. 'No, Kirstie. Don't give him a way out of here.'

'But if I go to him then maybe . . .'

'Maybe nothing. He'll kill you both. Get here, behind me, out of the way. Now, Kirstie, goddamnit.'

She moaned at her inability to help, but she obeyed Rink's instruction. Rink made her turn away and used the blade of his knife to snick through the cords binding her. She crouched behind him, rubbing the circulation back into her fingers, all the while never taking her gaze off her son. Molina began edging his way round them. Rink followed, the gun barrel never wavering from its target.

Molina gained the door, and now their positions were reversed in the room. He grinned at his small victory. He mimed cutting Benjamin's throat. 'Don't try to follow me. You know what will happen.'

What happened next stunned Kirstie by its speed and violence.

Rink barked a command, and lurched forward.

A bare arm snaked out from beside Molina and grabbed his

knife-wielding hand, yanking it away from Benjamin's neck, while another encircled his throat and pulled him backwards and off balance. Startled, Molina shouted out, his grip on the boy loosening as he fought to gain balance, grabbing at the doorframe for support. Rink swooped in low and snatched the boy out of the air, cradling him in his big arms, his gun and knife held clear of Benjamin's body. Without pause, he turned and offered her son to Kirstie. With a croak of relief Kirstie clutched at the boy, hefting him up against her chest. By the time she blinked over the crown of his head, Molina was gone from sight, but she could hear the scuffle of a short and brutal fight in the hallway. She pulled Benjamin to her shoulder, covering his ears so that he couldn't hear what became of his father.

48

'Brother, you look like crap.'

Those were Rink's words of welcome when I'd finally caught up to him as he stalked the corridors of the office wing attached to the large warehouse. But they were said with affection, and he enfolded me in a hug that threatened to finish the job that Jorge Molina had started on my ribs.

'It's good to see you alive, Hunter. Barely alive, I should say.'

'It looks worse than it is,' I lied.

'You look like you've been whupped by an ugly stick, and they didn't spare the rod.'

'Trust me, Molina got his licks in.'

'Where's the frog-gigger now?'

I shrugged, and even an innocuous move like that hurt.

'How the hell did you manage to escape?' Rink asked.

I told him about Marshall, and his change of heart.

'I still don't trust him, brother.'

'I hope you're wrong, Rink. Harve and the boys are with him.'

I didn't leaven the details about the beaten condition I'd found our friends in. It pained Rink to hear of their suffering. For such an adept killer he's a sensitive guy. 'Marshall took them to the SUV I was brought here in. I don't expect him to double-cross the guys, not now there's nothing left in it for him.' I explained that he was an MI6 plant, and that his mission was counter to that of Howell Regis. It actually suited

Marshall that Rink and me were about to complete the task he'd set out to do.

'I knew there was more to this than met the eye. Wouldn't put it past Walter to have known about Marshall all along.'

I shook my head. 'Walter doesn't have his fingers in every government plot . . . just most of them.'

We continued to move through the corridors, alert to ambush, but most of the fighting had died down. Either the cartel fighters had fled before the impending arrival of the police, or Rink had been more successful than any ninja assassin. As we progressed, I related Marshall's tale of how Regis's boss, Thomas Caspar, had been throttled to death by a garrotte, and how that had broken the alliance between Regis and Molina.

'Like I said: it stinks of Walter and his conniving.'

'Well, on this occasion, I'm happy that he's a sneaky old bastard,' I said.

That was when we'd heard the screaming and crying and knew that we'd found Kirstie and Benjamin. Moving very slowly, gaining distance on the room where the prisoners were held, we formulated our plan. From Molina's threats, we understood that he was controlling mother and child by brandishing a knife. If the two of us went inside, then he'd be cornered and desperate enough to follow through on his promise to stab them to death. So I hid, waiting my time, while Rink played dumb and allowed the bastard to back out of the door. Thankfully when Rink had tossed a female Border Control official out, she'd been too intent on escape to notice me lurking. I shoved both my guns away, freeing my hands. On pins, I waited until Molina appeared in the doorway, then I struck, my intention of freeing Benjamin uppermost. Killing Molina would have to wait a minute.

Tearing the knife away from Benjamin's throat, I looped my

other elbow round Molina's throat. Rink grabbed the boy as Molina reacted to my attack, and I bucked backwards, to take him clear of the doorway. I'd got his chin wedged in the crook of my elbow, and ordinarily by bracing my muscles on his carotid arteries he'd have been rendered unconscious in seconds. Molina proved quick and greasy, though. While I struggled to contain his knife hand, he slipped his chin to one side and dug under my forearm with it, negating the strangling effect. Then he pushed backwards, knocking me off balance, and we both crashed against the corridor wall.

The fatigue, the hunger and thirst, the prolonged chase, and finally the recent beating all conspired against me. It felt as if my strength had failed, and my limbs were perished rubber. Molina twisted in my grip and turned a shoulder to me, using it to force me against the wall a second time. He snatched his knife hand free, and tried to jab the blade into my abdomen. Luckily his angle was off and the sharp edge only raked my skin. I kneed him in the groin, turned and used the arm round his neck to toss him over my hip. It was no fancy judo move, more desperation than anything. Molina didn't go down on his back as I hoped; he managed to keep one foot on the floor and pivoted on it. The result was that he was off balance, and I'd made some clearance between my body and his knife, but I'd also lost my hold on him. Plus I was now between him and Rink, who – handing over Benjamin to his mom – came out of the doorway to help. Molina took a stab at my throat, forcing me to jerk back, and I further encumbered Rink. Then Molina took off along the corridor, disappearing round the first corner before either of us could get a steady footing.

Rink tried to get past me, but I held him with a bent elbow against his chest.

'Get Kirstie and Ben out of here,' I told him. 'Leave this bastard to me.'

'You're in no condition for a fight,' Rink argued.

I drew both guns. 'Don't worry, I don't intend playing around with him.'

Before Rink could object, I sprinted after Molina, my bare feet slapping heavily on the floor. Going after Molina was a stupid move, but I was incensed and the red haze of anger was on me. It's a fault that I'm aware of, being far too reckless for my own good. The trait was somewhat tempered by military indoctrination back in the day, but it had returned to me over the past few years. Back then a team relied on me and there wasn't room for maverick action. But right then, right there, it was Molina and me, and the rules no longer applied. Molina was a dead man; he just didn't know it yet.

Molina didn't get far before he switched knife for gun.

As Rink had progressed on his mission to thin out the opposition, he'd left their weapons to lie where they'd fallen. Molina had found one such weapon. I almost ran on to a burst of jacketed rounds from a machine-gun, and if Molina hadn't been so impatient he'd have killed me. He fired too soon, responding to my footsteps before I'd cleared the corner of the passage. Chunks of Sheetrock and plaster almost blinded me, as the corner of the wall was cut to pieces. I went to my knees, then my belly, and slithered across the floor. As the gunfire stopped, I leaned out, but had no target for the dust cloud hanging in the air. I fired a couple of rounds simply to provoke a reaction, but Molina didn't oblige. His retreat was marked by the snap of his leather soles on linoleum.

I went after him, running more smoothly now that my body had warmed to the chase.

The warehouse was somewhere to my left, the corridors and office spaces an annexe to the original construction. There were likely escape routes from this addition to the building, but I sensed that Molina was retracing the route he'd followed earlier when visiting me in the cold room.

I chased after him, listening for his footsteps to slow. He couldn't run full-tilt and shoot with any accuracy. Within thirty seconds, I was back at the room with the work cubicles. Molina chose to make a stand there. His machine-gun flashed yellow, spent brass shells dancing from the breech and tinkling on the desktops. I went to ground behind a solid desk, which was actually poor defence against his bullets. But I chose it more for concealment than protection, and while out of his line of sight I crawled rapidly for a different position, using the separating walls to block him. Once I was safe, I came up, targeting the racket of his gun and fired a close grouping of four shots – two from each handgun. Molina barked, a sound of agony. His subsequent curses meant he wasn't dead, but I'd winged him sorely. His gun fell quiet as he fled the room, and I went after him.

A seasoned warrior wouldn't have run away like that, he'd have returned fire, and torn the cubicles and me to pieces. A warrior might also have waited just outside the room and cut me down as I came after him. Molina was a killer, a murderer, but he wasn't skilled in this kind of battle. He continued to run along the passageway I'd earlier traversed with Marshall. Taking a stance, I aimed and fired and Molina went down, screaming.

As I approached, he made it to his knees and began crawling to where his machine-gun had fallen, leaking blood from his backside. I shot him in the opposite buttock, making it two for two. I'd always been loath to shoot a man in the back, but for this murderous piece of shit I was happy to make the exception. I lined up a shot on his skull.

That was when Howell Regis stepped up behind me and placed the muzzle of his gun to my head.

49

Howell Regis had already proven his willingness to shoot a man cold-bloodedly in the head. Why he chose to come to Molina's defence I could only guess, but he was possibly of the opinion that his only way out of this mess was to gain the cartel boss's favour once more. His CIA command structure was severed, and he likely understood that a return to the US might see him at the mercy of a garrotte one dark night. Perhaps he was looking for new employment, or protection, or maybe even reward. Whatever his motivation, I wasn't going to wait around for him to collect.

Immediately the gun nudged my skull, I spun counter-clockwise, batting his pistol aside with the barrel of mine, so that his round was redirected and cracked into the wall instead of my brain. My other hand came round, and the muzzle of my SIG jammed against his ribs. I was already squeezing the trigger, and three bullets tore his lungs to pulp. I swore savagely as he fell away from me, and in my anger I kicked at his body, thrusting him clear. Following the trajectory of his fall, I fired two more bullets into him: one into the heart, and one in the head for good measure. He died without a word, but that suited me fine. Sprawled in the corridor, he no longer reminded me of the Grim Reaper; for a start he'd lost his malicious grin.

With no time to spare on him, I returned to the job in hand. Good that I did, because Molina had laid hands on the machine-gun and was trying to find his target. Dodging into the room from which Regis had just come, I avoided the bullets. Molina's uncontrolled shooting stitched holes in the ceiling and walls, shattered a striplight, took some bloody lumps from Regis's carcass, but all missed me. Staying out of sight, I could hear Molina struggling to back his way along the corridor. I didn't chase him, but charged across the small anteroom, heading for a connecting door. The door was flimsy, cheap wood and Perspex. I booted my way through it and into a room adjacent to Molina's last known position. The walls were thin enough that I could detect his painful progress beyond. Letting loose with both guns, punching holes in the dividing wall, I yelled at him to die.

He didn't comply.

He fired back.

That was the result I'd been aiming for.

Now with a true target I aimed more accurately and this time was rewarded with a strangled curse.

There came a wet slapping noise of his palm against the wall. The bumping of the rifle stock against the floor followed as he used it to propel himself away. I glanced right to where I'd come in the room, and left to where another door presented access to the next room. I went left. Unfortunately I found myself in a short vestibule that led to an outer door, with no access to Molina. Cursing my bad luck, I ran back the way I'd come, through the two anterooms and into the corridor. By then Molina had made it into the space that gave access to the warehouse. A bright ribbon of blood showed where he'd clawed his way out of the firing zone. Handprints decorated the wall at the corner, vivid crimson against the dull grey paintwork.

Give Molina his due; he had proved himself resilient, or a reluctant corpse. I moved after him, my bare feet sliding through blood. At the corner I paused, recalling that a doorway stood only a few short yards away, and beyond it the open expanse of the warehouse. Ducking low, I took a quick look. Molina was waiting for me, wedged in the doorframe, his trousers dark with gore, the gun held tight to his side. He saw me, and his mouth came open in challenge. He was ready to shoot, and I wasn't. I ducked away, backpedalling a few steps to avoid the bullets blasting through the wall.

He had a better shooting position than me, and until his ammunition ran out, there was no way to meet him head on. I prepared myself, waiting with both guns extended, should he decide to follow me into the corridor. When he did come it wasn't in the fashion I'd expected.

Over the racket his gun was making, I didn't hear the engine, and I guess Molina didn't either. Marshall's SUV slammed into him at speed, catapulted him through space and he crashed face first into the angle made by the ninety-degree turn in the corridor. The impact itself would have been enough to kill him, but the SUV came on, crashing through shelving, wall and doorframe alike. It tore out the wall and debris was thrown into the corridor where I was, making me stagger back in surprise. The SUV still didn't halt: it struck Molina, scooped him up on to the hood and drove him through the next wall and into the vestibule I'd recently been in. I could no longer see Molina, but the SUV had become wedged in the collapsing walls, and peering at me from the back seat were Harvey Lucas and Jim McTeer. They were grinning in victory. If Velasquez was in any fit state, I believed he would have been grinning too, but I took it he was slumped on the back seat between my friends.

Kicking my way through shattered drywall, broken beams and collapsed ceiling tiles, I forged my way to the

SUV. Making it to the driver's door, I caught a glint of Marshall's glass eye and knew I was on his blind side. But he knew I was there.

'If you can find a way round, get in,' he said.

I checked beyond the blood-smeared hood, and could see where Molina's pulverised corpse lay among the rubble in front of the exit doors. Jorge Molina would never trouble his ex-wife or son again, that was certain.

Throwing Sheetrock and beams aside, I ploughed a way round the back of the SUV. Harvey and McTeer followed my progress. On their way through the warehouse and annexe buildings, they'd scavenged clothing from the dead. I remembered that I was barefoot and bare-chested, but it was no major concern – I often went that way while at home in Florida. Making it to the passenger door, I tugged it open and slipped inside.

'Couldn't get the damn roller shutter to open,' Marshall said by way of explanation, 'so I had to look for another way out. These walls aren't as flimsy as they look though.'

'Not as flimsy as that fucker,' I said, indicating the half-buried corpse.

In the back the guys were laughing, but truth be told it was more like hysteria. I looked round to check on them, saw that Velasquez was out, but breathing naturally now. Harvey reached over and gripped my shoulder.

'Did you see Rink?' he asked.

'Yeah. He's as ugly as ever.'

'He's OK though?'

'More than OK, he has Kirstie and Benjamin.'

'Thank God,' Harvey said, and sank back in his seat.

McTeer was lost for words, just sat giving me that half-insane grin. I gave him a gentle nudge with my fist. 'You OK, buddy?'

'Could do with a cold beer,' he said, and laughed as if it was the funniest quip ever.

'Come on,' I said to Marshall. 'Let's get out of here, shall we?'

He took it slowly, the SUV in four-wheel drive, and ploughed a route through the collapsing corridor. None of us bothered to move Molina out of the way. He was churned beneath the heavy tyres, but there was enough junk on him that his body fluids didn't cause any loss of traction. Marshall crashed the doors open and we were outside the building at last.

If any of Molina's footsoldiers remained alive, they'd had the sense to make off. Some police were bought and paid for, but not all. The Federales would be arriving in force before long and we couldn't be found at the scene. Marshall drove round the office building towards the front of the structure, watching keenly for his men. As far as I recalled Paulson and Mitchell had survived the battle and were out here some-where. So, I hoped, were Rink, Kirstie and Benjamin. Arriving at the front, I heard a horn beep.

'There!' I pointed towards where Rink had commandeered an abandoned vehicle. Kirstie and her boy were in the back.

Another vehicle approached, and though I didn't know Mitchell or Paulson from Adam, Marshall sighed in relief. He looked at me. 'Are you up to driving? Those lads are still my responsibility . . . I should go with them.'

I clapped him on the shoulder.

'I owe you one, pal,' I said.

'You owe me more than one. I saved all your arses.'

'You did, and I'm grateful.'

Marshall stopped the SUV and climbed out. I slid across into the driving position, as the other car pulled up and Marshall waved to the two men inside. He bent down, looked in at my three friends. 'I knew Joe way back when he was still young and reckless. Now he's just reckless. Keep an eye on him for me, will you?'

After receiving affirmations, he returned his gaze to me. His fake orb was still, his real one jiggling. He extended a hand. 'It was good serving with you again, Hunter.'

'You too, Marshall.' I accepted his hand.

'Don't know how they're going to clear up this mess,' he said. 'But that's not for us to worry about, I'm sure between them our sponsors will come up with enough bullshit to confuse the issue. But they won't get started for a while yet. I don't suggest you try to leave by the border crossing here. It'll be shut down tighter than Howell Regis's arse.'

'Maybe I can find one of those coyote gangs willing to smuggle us across the border,' I joked.

'No need. The fences are high here, but it's all for show. The North American Alliance is gaining impetus; the border's not so heavily patrolled now that the Yanks, Canadians and Mexicans are all becoming buddies. Go west a few miles and you'll find the fence is non-existent. That's the way I brought my guys in-country.'

'You going out that way?'

'No. We should head east. If there is any pursuit, I'm hoping they go after you guys.' He winked. Then he slapped the roof of the SUV. 'Go on. I'd best get going too.'

'Regis,' I said.

'What about him?'

'You don't have to worry about him causing any more trouble. He's back in there under all that rubble.'

'Best place for him, in the dirt,' Marshall said. 'Buried alongside his pal Molina.'

'Hopefully when the cops arrive, they'll think Molina and Regis were shooting at each other. It'll let us off the hook, unless someone spills the beans.'

'Who's going to admit that they were part of that mess?'

He shrugged at his own question.

Then he got in the car with his friends and they drove away. He didn't look back. Or if he did I didn't notice. I was too busy smiling at Kirstie as she peered at me from inside Rink's commandeered vehicle.

50

'Come in, Joe. I'm glad you're here. For a few days there I thought I'd seen the last of you.'

The doorway of her first-floor apartment framed Kirstie Long. The soft light spilling from within added an amber halo to her hair where it hung loose around her shoulders. Her face was partly in shadow, but her eyes and lips glistened, reflecting the streetlamps outside. Her apartment was in a nice neighbourhood of Washington DC, and must have cost a huge amount of money. The house, Kirstie had told me, had been his parting gift when Jorge Molina returned to Mexico. He owed her more than a decent home for the trouble he'd caused her and Benjamin, yet, compared to the poor hovels of those that Molina had used and abused in Mexico, Kirstie had done all right out of the deal. However, I'd noted the realtor's sign before mounting the wooden stairs to her front door. She was selling up.

'Thinking of moving house?' I asked, hitching a thumb towards the FOR SALE sign.

'Too many bad memories here, Joe,' she said as she stood aside and beckoned me in. 'For me and for Benjamin.'

'A fresh start might help. How is the boy?'

'Taking time to adjust, but that's to be expected, I guess.'

'He's young enough to forget what he went through, it's you that will have nightmares for months to come.'

'I've put it behind me. What have I to fear now that Jorge can't harm us any more?'

Truth was, trouble could come at her from any number of directions, but it wouldn't serve any purpose to tell her so. I offered a consolatory nod. I moved from the vestibule into the living space while Kirstie closed the door.

Her sitting room was spacious, stylishly furnished, with overflowing bookshelves that lined the walls. Recalling that Kirstie worked as a PR manager for a number of best-selling authors, sports stars and celebrities, I assumed many of the books were gifts from her clients. 'How many books are here? Thousands? I don't envy you having to pack all these when you move.'

'I thought that you might be around to lend a hand . . .'

Her words held more meaning than their face value. I hid my smile as I sat down on the settee. Kirstie sat opposite, in a recliner. She was wearing a cream-coloured sweater over blue jeans that adhered to her slim thighs. She was barefoot. A paperback thriller lay open on the floor, where she'd placed it on hearing the doorbell. She was relaxed and at ease, believing that the threat to her and her son had ended when Marshall's SUV smashed Molina to death.

'Do those kind of books still excite you after everything you experienced?' I asked.

'I read them to escape the real world,' she explained, 'and to force out the memories of what happened in Mexico. They work for me.' She toed the open book. 'Those fictional characters suffer much more than I did. Though I haven't read about anyone who endured your pain. I'm surprised you're up and walking around.'

'You should see me when no one's looking. I'm like an old man of ninety.'

It was almost a month since we'd escaped the warehouse at Agua Prieta. When driving the SUV across country and into the USA I'd existed on adrenalin and the need to find medical assistance for Velasquez. His injuries were more concerning than mine, and I'd barely given my wounds a second thought until we got him to a hospital at Sierra Vista. To be honest, other than the bullet wounds to my forearm and leg that I'd practically forgotten about, most of the cuts were minor and didn't need stitching. The gunshot wounds I cleaned and dressed myself later, because – if I'd announced I'd been shot – the surgeons were duty bound to report all shooting incidents to the police. They didn't believe our story that we'd been in a traffic collision, but the doctors there were discreet enough to give us a break. After Velasquez was cleaned up and medicated, he discharged himself, and we continued to a rendezvous with Walter Conrad at a private airstrip near Fort Huachuca.

My goodbye with Kirstie had been brief, before her grandfather whisked her and Benjamin away in his private jet. He made room for Velasquez and McTeer, but Rink and Harvey stayed behind with me. It was important that I didn't tag along, because Kirstie and Walter had a lot of talking to do, and many lost years for Walter to explain. The rest of us had taken rooms at a tiny motel on the fringe of the Coronado National Forest, where we crashed out and, having eaten and drunk my fill, I'd slept for a full eighteen hours. When I woke up, and made myself presentable, we headed to the airport at Tucson and took the first plane out to Florida. I slept all the way back, and on waking felt like I'd been strapped to one of the wings the entire flight home. I felt even worse over the next couple of days, before the agony began to subside. I could move OK now, but anything vigorous had to be considered first, and attempted gingerly.

'Where's Benjamin?' I asked.

'Bed.' She indicated a baby monitor on a table next to her chair. 'He's sleeping soundly.'

Jorge Molina had doped the boy with medication to help him sleep, I recalled. 'How're those teeth of his? Still troubling him?'

'He already has all his teeth, he is almost five, remember.' Her eyes flashed. 'I think the reason he had a sore mouth was because he'd been slapped, and the medication was to stop him crying. Jorge didn't want a weakling for a son. You've heard what Jorge wanted him to do to me . . . I dread to imagine what else he had tried to force Benjamin into.'

To think I'd entertained thoughts that Jorge might be a good father, and didn't blame him for chasing us so diligently to get his boy back: how wrong could I be? 'He was sick in the head, Kirstie.'

'Did you hear that he'd been poisoning his own father?'

'That doesn't surprise me. He was on a power trip, and the only way he could secure his position with the cartels was to kill off his old man and step into his shoes.'

'What has happened in Hermosillo?'

'I haven't heard much. Only that one of the other cartels has moved in, seeing as Old Man Molina is on his last legs. But that was always on the cards. Without his CIA connections Jorge was a bit player; the other cartels would have eaten him alive. As far as the fighting's concerned, the general consensus is that two cartel factions were competing for control, and our presence there has never come to light. Same thing at Agua Prieta. As luck would have it, the Federales were already engaged in fighting with some of Molina's crew at Moctezuma. It's believed that the battle spilled over to Agua Prieta, where Molina's men had a falling out. It actually helped our case that Regis and some of Marshall's men were found in the warehouse, because it gave validity to the story. They've been identified as mercenaries, and to all intents and purposes they didn't get on too well with their employers. People are swearing that the two sides broke into a gun battle when they couldn't agree on their share of profits. Anyone who knows the truth is happy to play along.'

'What about the Border Control officials that were involved?' Kirstie asked.

'Some of them have disappeared, others have been arrested and face charges of corruption. Who knows how that will pan out.'

'One of them was there in the room when Jorge tried to force Benjamin to stab me: what if she tells?'

Yes, I remembered her: the woman who Rink tossed out of the room. I also recalled how quickly she ran away. I was willing to bet that she'd kept on running. There was nothing to gain by staying in the area until the police arrived. Even if she hadn't, was she likely to admit that she had held down a foreign national while a maniac coaxed a child to cut her throat?

'To be honest, Kirstie, the trouble we were involved in was only one of dozens of violent confrontations throughout the country that week. Things are in turmoil, and the Federales are hard put to keep up, let alone spare any time to investigate ancient history. They'll be happy that another of the major gangs has been broken, rather than start looking for motives why.'

'So you think we're safe from prosecution?'

Shrugging, I said, 'Pointless worrying about something unlikely to happen.'

'Only unlikely?'

'There are always crusaders for the truth. We can only hope that there are juicier lies for them to concern themselves with. The impending North American Alliance already has the conspiracy theorists jumping up and down; our story will be lost among thousands of other tales soon enough.

When they can go after the politicians and make loads of noise, who's going to trouble a woman who simply retrieved her abducted baby?'

'It makes a good story, you have to admit.'

'Hope it doesn't end up in another of those mystery books you're so fond of,' I joked. 'Please don't tell any of your author friends what happened.'

'My lips are sealed.' She mimed zipping them together. When she caught me staring she relaxed her mouth, her bottom lip protruding. I watched as blood flooded her lips and would swear they were riper than before. There was nothing I wished for more than to touch her.

Three days earlier, Rink had warned me about this moment. I'd limped into his office at Rington Investigations, grunting as I sat down opposite him. I stretched out my leg, rubbing at the muscles in my thigh.

'You're getting old, brother,' Rink said.

'Tell me about it,' I said. 'It's been weeks since I exercised. I'm going to do some running soon. I'll be good once I've put the miles in again.'

'Your knee still giving you trouble?'

Actually it was. Of all the minor injuries I'd picked up in Mexico, the twisted knee I'd acquired while avoiding being crushed by the SUV in Hermosillo had stayed with me longest. But it was on the mend, and I was confident of a full recovery. All my other injuries had faded, even the horrendous welts from Jorge Molina's rope. The bullet nicks on my leg and forearm were pink scars now, the myriad scrapes and scratches from flying glass a network of fine scars that would disappear now I was back in the sunshine.

'It's fine,' I lied.

'I'll come with you,' he offered. 'A nice easy ten miles to get us started.'

'Maybe tomorrow, eh? Or the next day.'

Rink winked. 'Knew that knee was giving you hell.'

I offered him a sheepish grin. 'Just don't tell anyone, eh?'

'You seeing Kirstie this weekend?' Rink asked.

'Yeah.'

'You should take it easy, brother.'

'We're taking everything one step at a time, Rink. The same as my fitness regime.'

He held me under his gaze. I knew something was troubling him: our association with Walter had grown to be a burden he wasn't happy carrying these days.

'You still think it's wrong for me to date Walter's grand-daughter?' I asked.

'No. Not in that sense, brother. What I said back then, I was just trying to make you see where a relationship with Kirstie might lead you.'

'Don't worry, you won't be hearing any wedding bells if that's what's bothering you.'

He grunted out a laugh, but it was hollow and humourless. 'You know what I'm worried about.'

He was intimating that if I was close to Kirstie then I'd be too close to Walter, and by virtue to Arrowsake. And, because he'd never turn his back on me, so would he.

'You don't find it strange that, after what went down in Mexico, we haven't been hauled in by the feds yet?'

'I know where you're heading with this,' I said.

'Good. You need to heed my warning. Walter had another CIA agent murdered, for Christ's sake, and it's like Thomas Caspar never existed. How could he get away with that?'

'We don't know for sure that Walt had anything to do with it.'

'Bullshit! You know exactly who was on the other end of that garrotte. And you know who sent Vincent after Caspar.'

'Stephen Vincent doesn't work for Walter,' I reminded him.

'No. Agent Vincent is Arrowsake through and through. But doesn't it make you think . . .'

'It does,' I admitted. 'How or why did Arrowsake get involved? I know what you're thinking, Rink: you believe Walter asked them for help and now he owes them, and it's most likely us who'll end up repaying his debt.'

Rink shook his head. 'What I'm saying is that we don't know Walter the way we think we know him.'

'Shit,' I said.

'Shit doesn't begin to describe it if I'm right,' Rink said.

'You mean Walter hasn't cut ties with Arrowsake? For a hit on someone as important as Caspar, it would take someone with a lot of juice in the organisation to give it the green light. Caspar's death has been covered by a smokescreen, the same way as the trouble down in Mexico has. We've been allowed to get away with everything because to name us would also name Walter. Arrowsake aren't going to let that happen, are they?'

'You've got it,' Rink said, though he didn't seem happy with my epiphany. 'Walter hasn't moved away from Arrowsake at all. He's moved *up* in rank. He's where he always intended to be, Joe, and you know where that leaves us.'

'He can't make us work for him again.'

'Can't he? I'm not saying he'd force us, but if he can play on your loyalties . . . Shit, Joe, if you're canoodling with his grand-daughter you're as good as hooked in.' He mimed snicking a dog leash to a collar round his neck. 'We're fucked, brother.'

'No. I won't let it happen again. No more Walter Hayes Conrad. No more using us as his personal assets.'

'You think so, brother?' Rink asked with a slow exhalation. 'Then you're stupider than you look.'

Simply by being here in Kirstie's apartment, I'd kind of proved Rink's point for him. Didn't stop me from coming to a decision. Getting up from the settee without showing discomfort was a struggle, but I pulled it off. Kirstie stood also.

'You're going so soon?' she asked, her disappointment obvious.

'No.' I held out a hand to her. 'Just wanted to finish something we started back in Mexico. You asked me if I'd kiss you again, and I said we'd talk about it once you were safely home. You ready for that talk?'

'My grandfather warned me about you.'

'He did?'

'He said you're too impulsive for your own good.'

'Maybe he's right. But I won't know for sure until you order me to get out.'

Kirstie flushed, but she didn't give me my marching orders. She began kissing me in the living room, and didn't stop until much later in the bedroom, as we slept naked in each other's arms.

THANKS AND ACKNOWLEDGEMENTS

My thanks and gratitude goes to Denise Hilton, Luigi Bonomi, Alison Bonomi, Sue Fletcher, Swati Gamble, Eleni Lawrence, Jim Hilton, my family and friends, and to all the readers who choose to pick up a Joe Hunter book.

Special mentions of thanks this time go to Lee Marshall, Ian McAdam, Graham Smith, and Kirstie Long, for allowing me the use of your names. Hope you don't mind the Joe Hunter treatment your fictional equivalents went through?

JOE HUNTER

BRITAIN'S BEST VIGILANTE V AMERICA'S WORST CRIMINALS

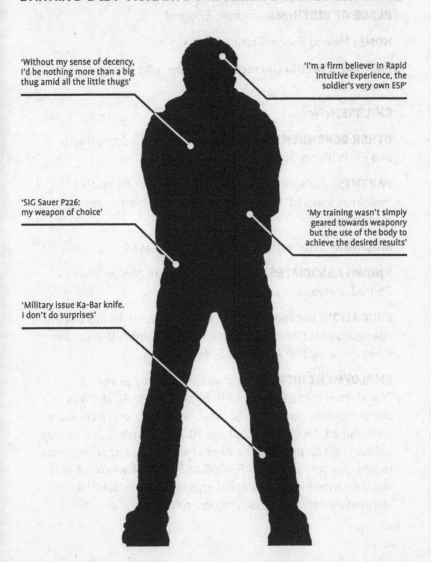

'Without my sense of decency, I'd be nothing more than a big thug amid all the little thugs'

'I'm a firm believer in Rapid Intuitive Experience, the soldier's very own ESP'

'SIG Sauer P226: my weapon of choice'

'My training wasn't simply geared towards weaponry but the use of the body to achieve the desired results'

'Military issue Ka-Bar knife. I don't do surprises'

CURRICULUM VITAE – JOE HUNTER

NAME: Joe Hunter.

DATE OF BIRTH: 8th August.

PLACE OF BIRTH: Manchester, England.

HOME: Mexico Beach, Florida, USA.

MARITAL STATUS: Divorced from Diane, who has now remarried.

CHILDREN: None.

OTHER DEPENDENTS: Two German shepherd dogs, Hector and Paris (currently residing with Diane).

PARENTS: Joe's father died when he was a child and his mother remarried. Both his mother and stepfather reside in Manchester.

SIBLINGS: Half-brother, John Telfer. Deceased.

KNOWN ASSOCIATES: Jared 'Rink' Rington, Walter Hayes Conrad, Harvey Lucas.

EDUCATION: Secondary school education to 'O' level standard. Joe received further education and underwent self-teaching while in the British Army and Special Forces.

EMPLOYMENT HISTORY: Joined British Army at age 16. Transferred to the Parachute Regiment at age 19 and was drafted into an experimental coalition counterterrorism team code named 'ARROWSAKE' at age 20. As a sergeant, Joe headed his own unit comprising members from various Special Forces teams. Joe retired from 'ARROWSAKE' in 2004 when the unit was disbanded and has since then supported himself by working as a freelance security consultant.

HEIGHT: 5' 11".

WEIGHT: 13 stone.

BUILD: Athletic.

HAIR COLOUR/STYLE: Short brown hair with slight greying.

EYE COLOUR: Blue/brown.

APPEARANCE: Muscular but more lean than bulky, he has the appearance of a competitive athlete. His demeanour is generally calm and unhurried. Due to his background, Joe has the ability to blend with the general public when necessary, but when relaxed he tends to dress casually. He doesn't consider himself handsome, but women find him attractive. His eyes are his most striking feature and the colour appears to change dependent on his mood.

BLOOD TYPE: AB.

MEDICAL HISTORY: Childhood complaints include measles and chicken pox. As an adult Joe has had no major medical conditions, but has been wounded on several occasions. Joe carries numerous scars including a bullet wound in his chest and various scars from knife and shrapnel wounds on his arms and legs. He has had various bone breakages, but none that have proven a continued disability.

RELIGION: Joe was raised in a Church of England environment, but is currently non-practising.

POLITICS: Joe has no political preferences and prefers morals and ethics.

CHARACTER: Joe can come over as a little aloof at times. He is a deep thinker who prefers only to speak when he has something important to say. He is very loyal to his family and friends. He dislikes injustice, hates bullies and will stand up to defend others in need of help.

MUSIC: Wide choice of music, but particularly enjoys vintage rhythm and blues.

MOVIES: Joe's favourite movie is 'It's a Wonderful Life'. It is a morality tale that resonates with his belief that a person's actions – good or bad – continually affect those around them.

BOOKS: When he was younger he enjoyed classic fiction by HP Lovecraft, RE Howard and Edgar Allan Poe, but currently reads a wide range of crime and suspense novels.

CIGARETTES: Smoked various brands but gave up.

ALCOHOL: Drinks only moderately and infrequently. Prefers beer to liquor.

DRUGS: Has been subjected to drugs during his military career, but has never personally taken any illegal drugs. Joe hates the influence that drugs have on the world and stands against those producing and supplying them.

HOBBIES: Fitness. Joe works out whenever he can with a combination of running, circuit training and martial arts.

SPECIAL SKILLS: As a soldier Joe gained many skills pertinent to his job, but also specialised in CQB (Close Quarter Battle), Point Shooting, Defensive Driving and in Urban Warfare Tactics. He is particularly adept with the handgun (usually a SIG Sauer P226) and with the knife (usually a military issue Ka-Bar).

CURRENT OCCUPATION: Joe describes himself as a security consultant and sometimes PI, but some people call him a vigilante.

CURRENT WHEREABOUTS: USA.

In the best books, the ending often comes as a shock.
Not just because of that one last twist in the tale,
but because you have been so absorbed in their world,
that coming back to the harsh light of reality is a jolt.

If that describes you now, then perhaps you should track down
some new leads, and find new suspense in other worlds.

Join us at www.hodder.co.uk, or follow us on
Twitter @hodderbooks, and you can tap in to a
community of fellow thrill-seekers.

Whether you want to find out more about this book,
or a particular author, watch trailers and interviews, have
the chance to win early limited editions, or simply browse
our expert readers' selection of the very best books,
we think you'll find what you're looking for.

And if you don't, that's the place to tell us what's missing.

We love what we do, and we'd love you to be part of it.

www.hodder.co.uk

@hodderbooks

HodderBooks

HodderBooks